The Son of a Nobody

D1482399

Kathleen O'Connor was born Kathleen Sheehan in Waterford, Ireland, in the 1930s. In 1969 she launched her successful freelance writing career, contributing in the ensuing years to all the major Irish newspapers, especially the *Evening Press*. She also wrote for RTE's popular radio programme *3-Oh-1*. She currently lives in Glenageary. She is the author of the highly successful novels *Silver Harvest* and *Hold Back the Tide*.

The Son of a Nobody

Kathleen Sheehan O'Connor

Basement Press
DUBLIN

First published in Ireland in 1995 by
Basement Press
a imprint of Attic Press
29 Upper Mount Street
Dublin 2

A catalogue record for this title is available from the British Library

ISBN 1 85594 156 2

Cover Illustration: Sheila Kern
Cover Design: Verbatim Typesetting & Design
Origination: Verbatim Typesetting & Design
Printing: The Guernsey Press Co. Ltd

This book is published with the financial assistance of The Arts Council/An Chomhairle Ealaíon, Ireland.

To Pat, remembering all the good times

Acknowledgement

A special word of thanks to Declan and to Connie, for helping me untangle the mysteries of computers and discs and printers.

Prologue

Ciara glanced up and saw that the light was still on in the sitting room. It must be earlier than she thought, she told herself, pushing the key into the lock and opening the hall door. She decided she wouldn't disturb her parents – few enough hours they had, she thought, to sit and talk over the events of the day. She closed the door softly and tiptoed up the stairs, passing the murmur of their voices in the sitting room. She would wait a while before she went into them. She picked up the old copper kettle and filled it from the tap. She sat down, glad of the respite before it boiled; it gave her a chance to recall the last few hours spent with Peter.

The knowledge, wonder, even puzzlement, that he wanted her never failed to amaze Ciara. She supposed that he could have anyone. It was generally accepted that Peter Murray, the tall handsome son of T.J. Murray, could have had any girl in the town. The Murrays had carried on a successful legal business in Dungarvan for generations. Tim Murray had taken over from his father and, now that his son Peter was qualified, he in turn would undoubtedly take over when the time came. The two younger brothers were attending university in Dublin and came home most weekends, stamped with the same aura of money and assurance that Peter had.

Ciara glanced in the mirror as she waited for the kettle to boil. She saw her dishevelled dark hair, the pallor of her face and the glow of excitement in her dark eyes. How had he put it? He hadn't said, 'Will you marry me?' He certainly hadn't, like the heroes of old, said, 'Will you do me the honour of becoming my wife?' He had run his hand through the tangled mass of dark hair and had held her by the arms and smiled.

'Hey, you little blow-in you, do know what I want?'

'No,' she had said.

'Well, I'll tell you. I want you to be buried with my people.'

'What do you mean by that?'

'Oh, the years in London have stamped you when you can't recognise an Irish proposal of marriage.'

7

'You want to get married? You want to marry me?'

He had looked around the car, made a pretence of glancing under the seat. 'I don't see anyone else, so it must be you.' He had smiled and had taken her in his arms again. 'Well, what do you say – yea or nay?'

'I'll say yea, because I think it means yes.'

He had kissed her again and afterwards they had excitedly made their plans. They would get engaged at Christmas and married the following September. They would keep their engagement a secret until Christmas and then surprise their families with the good news.

The kettle started to hum as Ciara sat there enjoying the memory of the evening.

She rinsed out her mother's favourite blue teapot. She spooned in the tea and noticed the slight shake in her hands. Aware of the cause of the tremor, she decided there and then that she would pull herself together and not allow Peter to have such an effect on her. It seemed to her that she had been trembling with excitement since the moment she had met him. That very first evening, he had walked into her father's shop and asked for twenty cigarettes. She had handed them to him, and he had thanked her warmly, and it had all started there.

That was over a year ago now. She had returned from her secretarial course in Dublin and had begged her father to let her work in the shop, just for a spell. He had put his foot down, telling her she hadn't gone to an expensive boarding school in Waterford and a more expensive secretarial course in Dublin to work in a glorified huckster's shop. She had told him it wasn't a glorified huckster's shop, and that if she got a free hand there'd be no end to where they could go.

'It's so big, Dad,' she had said. 'So much wasted space. You should introduce all sorts of new stock – crafts and gifts for the summer crowd, and toys and books for the kids – and make it wide and spacious, the sort of place tourists would come and browse in. Come on, Dad – let me stay.'

Her mother Peggy had seen the pleading look in her eyes and, knowing how much Ciara loved being at home, had gone along with her.

'Sure, Bob, let her try it for a bit – give her a bit of leeway now that you know Paul and William aren't interested in the place.'

Now, over a year later, Ciara had introduced all sorts of

new innovations and fresh ideas to the shop, and business had improved considerably.

The kettle boiled and as Ciara poured the water into the teapot she was surprised to be able to hear her parents talking so clearly. Sipping her tea, she realised that the radio was turned off, an unusual thing in the Fitzpatrick household, where the radio was a constant thing: someone switched it on in the morning and it usually provided background noise all during the day. She noticed the sagging plug from the socket, which explained the situation. She was about to go over to shove it in when she heard her mother say her name.

So they were talking about her. She idly wondered why she was the subject of discussion. She knew she was a bit wild – a bit impetuous, very restless – but she wasn't the worst. She could clearly hear her mother and the realisation came that her mother seemed upset – agitated.

'We should have told her, Bob. We shouldn't have kept it from her all these years. She had a right to know.'

'Look, you're upsetting yourself. She's a down-to-earth girl – when we tell her it won't knock a feather out of her.'

Ciara wondered what they were talking about. What would upset her? Was anything something wrong with them? Maybe something had happened to upset them. Her curiosity was aroused, and she listened intently. There was no point in barging in at this stage.

'Anyway,' her father was saying, 'you and Aileen became so close, it was almost like having your own child. You wanted a little girl desperately and you couldn't have one. It all worked out perfectly, didn't it? What's the use in telling her now? There's no point.'

'But that's where you're wrong,' Ciara heard her mother say. 'She has to know. I was a fool to keep putting it off. She's going steady with Peter Murray for nearly a year now, and a line like that could lead to marriage. Then she'll have to get a birth certificate and she'll know then, won't she? Most adopted children know that they are adopted these days. This is the seventies, after all. I heard a big discussion about it on the *Liam Nolan Hour* only the other day. About how you should tell your adopted children when they come to the age of reason. We'll have to tell her, Bob, that she's not our child – that we adopted her when we were in England. I'll have to explain to her that her mother was my cousin's daughter. Maybe if we're lucky she won't want to know much about her father – but knowing her, I suppose she'll ask a thousand questions.'

Even though the kitchen was warm from the heat of the range, a strange, alien chill caught hold of Ciara. This is a dream – no, a nightmare, she thought. Any minute I'm going to wake up and hear Paul and William arguing about football or politics, and Dad running down the stairs saying he's late, and Mam already starting to clean and hoover.

But she didn't wake up from the unwanted dream. She was still sitting on the edge of the large scrubbed wooden table, her tea unsipped as her whole world lay crumbled around her. So if she wasn't theirs – they weren't hers. Bob and Peggy Fitzpatrick, the two people who had always been there for her. Her beloved father, who spoiled her a lot and put his foot down a bit. Her mum, who had begrudged her nothing. She remembered when she was a little girl living in the red-bricked house in Islington, north London, about how her mum brought her to school every day, then waited patiently at the gate when school was over. How she allowed her to have friends in to play, and quite often to stay. In the evenings, when they'd sit in the parlour in front of the gas fire, how her mum would tell her about Ireland and Dungarvan and the lovely sweeping bay, the blue misted Comeragh mountains and the old monastery of Mount Mellery. She used to promise Ciara that some day they would all go back.

They had, eventually. Her father bought a shop in Dungarvan from his carefully hoarded savings, and soon they had all settled in. London and the suburb of Islington had become a memory. Ciara had loved her school, and her brothers were soon leading lights on the hurling team. She had shed tears unashamedly when she went to boarding school, but her mother wrote to her every single week, long rambling letters about everything and anything that might interest her, including the antics of her kitten, Joey.

But if this wasn't a nightmare, she thought, her brothers weren't her brothers and Peggy wasn't her mother and Bob wasn't her father.

Dear Jesus, she prayed, let this really be a dream, let me wake up, so that I can run down the stairs to Mam and tell her all about this. Tell her about a cousin of hers called Aileen and how I dreamt that I wasn't theirs. And we'd laugh and she'd tell me I had a nightmare because I stuffed myself with too much chocolate when I was at the pictures with Peter.

PART ONE

Chapter One

Aileen MacMahon saw Stephen Rodgers on the very first day she went to school. She was standing with her mother waiting to go into First Babies. He passed her by with his schoolbag and an unfriendly expression on his dark face. He was obviously a lot older than she was, because he was unaccompanied and on familiar territory.

The small two-teacher school in Glenlee, Co. Kilkenny had only forty-six pupils, and Stephen and Aileen came across each other often over the years. Aileen often remembered the first time Stephen ever spoke to her. She was chasing Maggie Power across the playground and she stumbled and fell, cutting her knee badly. The pain was excruciating and she bit her lip, trying desperately not to cry. She was sitting there, looking at the blood welling out of the deep cut, when a rough hand on her shoulder helped her to her feet. She stared at the brown hand and looked into the darkest, blackest eyes she had ever seen.

''Tis always bad first, but if you put a hanky on it it'll soon stop hurtin'.'

'Thanks,' she had sniffled before walking away with as much dignity as an eight-year-old could muster.

After that she seemed to see him everywhere. Places like Mass on Sundays and Confessions on Saturdays. Sometimes in the village shops. Once she saw him at the creamery when she had gone with her dad and the milk-filled churns. Her friends, Maggie Power and Ann Murphy, told her he had no mother or father. His grandfather was rearing him and, according to Maggie, 'He is the oldest and crankiest oul man in the whole place, or so my mammy said.'

'But why hasn't he a father or mother?' Aileen wanted to know. 'Did they die or somethin'?'

'Well, I heard so I did, but I'm not saying.' Maggie's voice dropped to a whisper.

'If it's a secret we'll keep it. Won't we, Ann?' Aileen turned to Ann, a beseeching look in her eyes.

Ann nodded her head eagerly in agreement.

'All right,' Maggie whispered. 'Cross yere hearts and hope to die if ye tell a soul.'

Aileen and Ann did as they were told and stood there, two twelve-year-old girls who had grown up in a rural community with rural values and the knowledge that a cross-your-heart was a secret that you really tried to keep – at least until it was prised and probed from you by entreatments and promises you couldn't resist. Maggie enjoyed her moment of power when she had their total attention.

'Stephen Rodgers's mother, Teresa, ran off with a gypsy and Stephen was born and his mammy died, and old Johnnie Sheridan brought him back to his grandfather in a cardboard box because they didn't want him – because they felt he wasn't really one of them, so there. Ye know now and ye're not to tell a livin', breathin' soul.'

They stood in the sunlit dusty road, their lips tight, their arms folded like they had seen their mothers' folded dozens of times. As the news slowly seeped in, Aileen was the first to break the silence.

'He looks different all right – his hair is as black as a crow. I wonder was he born in a camp?'

'I wonder does he know that his father was a gypsy?' Ann asked.

'Maybe he does,' Maggie answered. 'Maybe that's why he's so cranky-lookin'.'

'Do you think they were madly in love?' said Ann.

'Sure they must have been to run off like that.' Maggie had just finished reading *Little Women* and had got all caught up with what she hoped would be the budding romance between Jo and the lovely boy Laurie.

The cross-your-heart secret concerning the raven-haired Stephen Rodgers added to the girls' interest over the years. He had left their school a few years before and was going to the secondary school in Ross. Aileen and her friends were to start secondary school in the autumn. They were to go to the Mercy nuns in Ross, like most of the girls in the area.

During the long summer holidays, Aileen's mother made her mind Eddie and six-year-old Maeve. Often, when she had her jobs done, Aileen spent the long, hot days down in the field near the road where Denis, their father, had slung a rope over a huge elm tree to make a swing.

'I'm sick of that oul swing. Why can't we go fishin' down to the river?' Eddie complained.

'Because Mam said we're to stay here. And if you're bored, think of me,' Aileen shouted heatedly. 'I'm almost a grown woman and I'm stuck here with two sticky kids driving me mad when I should be doing somethin' excitin' and different.'

'Like I said,' Eddie insisted, 'let's go fishin'. That's excitin'.'

Aileen sniffed disdainfully and leaned over the wall. Someone was cycling down the narrow dusty road. For a brief second the cyclist disappeared behind the high ditch and then reappeared, coming at them swiftly. Her heart missed a beat as she recognised Stephen Rodgers. He was shirt-sleeved and wore long trousers, and looked very grown-up and as remote as ever.

As he drew nearer Eddie joined her at the wall and young Maeve shouted, 'Come back, come back, I need someone to push me.' Stephen braked and slowed down, and his dark eyes swept over the trio. To Aileen's amazement he smiled. The white teeth in his dark face made him so nice, far, far nicer than any boy she had ever seen.

'Where are you goin'?' Eddie asked.

'Fishing – I'm going to the weir to try and catch a couple of trout.'

'Can I go with you, can I?' Eddie begged.

'If your sister says yes, I'll take you on the bar of the bike – if she says no, I can't.'

'Oh come on, Aileen – say I can come.'

Aileen glanced at Stephen. His black eyes were looking straight into hers. From somewhere the most peculiar uncomfortable sensation she had ever experienced seemed to envelop her. She found herself blushing.

'He can't go, not today.' Then, realising that she herself, only a few minutes before, had been bored with the interminable length of the long hot summer, she added, 'Maybe tomorrow. If you're goin' fishin' tomorrow we might see you there.'

'All right. Tomorrow so,' he grinned at Eddie. Then his expression sobered swiftly as he briefly saluted Aileen.

*

13

The next morning Aileen got up early, the plans for the day already tripping through her head. I'll help Mam with the chicken and the turkeys. I'll tidy out the henhouse and maybe she'll give me a day off from minding Maeve. I'll mention how much Eddie wants to go fishing and that it would be a danger to take her over with us near the weir.

She went into Eddie's room. He was awake already, reading his *Beano*, his small freckled face registering intense interest in the antics of Dennis the Menace.

'I'll ask Mam can we go fishing over at the weir,' she whispered. 'Don't mention anything about Stephen Rodgers, because if you do she won't let us – all right?'

'All right,' he answered, his interest already straying from the comic to the exciting possibilities of a day at the weir in the company of his sister and the comparatively unknown Stephen Rodgers.

After she had done her tasks, Aileen approached her mother. 'Mam, could Eddie and I take a little picnic and go fishin' at the river? I'm sick minding Maeve and there's nothing else to do. Please?'

Mary MacMahon saw the pleading look in the blue, blue eyes of her twelve-year-old daughter. She's starting to grow up, she thought to herself, she's gone tall and leggy. Already Mary could see the small outline of her daughter's young budding breasts. Aileen had inherited the blonde, silvery looks of the MacMahons. Lord, Mary thought, I should be telling her about things like periods and where babies come from and preparing her to be a young woman and to be aware of talking to strangers. And I will, soon. But not yet – not yet.

Looking at the anticipation in Aileen's hopeful eyes, Mary softened. Sure, there was little to do for a young one after the chores were finished, and now that the school was closed Aileen rarely saw her friends Maggie Power and Ann Murphy.

'Oh, all right. Sure 'twill do you a power of good not to have Maeve tagging along with you always. And poor Eddie, God love him, would like the day at the river. But for God's sake be careful and keep an eye on the rascal in case he falls in. I'll fix you a bit of a picnic and fob young Maeve off with some story. I might give her a treat in town next Saturday.'

Aileen couldn't believe her success. The thought of the cool rushing river, away from the hot meadows and yards of the farm, was a treat in itself. The thought of meeting Stephen Rodgers, and maybe getting to know him more, was so exciting that it caused her heart to hammer in a strange, unfamiliar way. Wouldn't she have something to tell Ann and Maggie when she met them again? In fact it was a miracle that she had been down at the wall pushing Maeve at the swing when he had passed by. Maybe it wouldn't be the most boring summer she had ever ever experienced after all.

He was sitting on the bank waiting for them. He was so still and quiet that he almost merged in with the bracken and the tall reeds. Aileen could see his unsmiling face, and suddenly she felt shy and embarrassed and wondered what she could say to him. Eddie had driven her mad with his prattle since they left the farm with their rods and sandwiches. She could see that Stephen had his lunch; there was a brown-paper parcel beside his fishing rod. He looked over and waved as they emerged from under the willows, watching as they jumped over the flat stones to where they sat.

Eddie was off, rattling ten to the dozen. 'Well, Stephen, will we catch anythin'? Is it too hot for them to be risin'? What bait have you? Will any oul maggots do?'

'Hey, one at a time. We could be lucky, 'tisn't too hot and they might be rising.' Stephen looked at Aileen and asked, 'Do you fish often?'

'No, I don't fish at all. I just brought my Dad's rod just in case – like.'

'That's all right. Sure I'll teach you.'

Suddenly everything was fine. The three sat on the warm stones and chatted as if they were old friends. Eddie told Stephen about the time he and his friend Jimmy Dolan planned to make a raft and go sailing down the river, shooting down the weir and maybe going away forever, or as far as the river would take them. 'We had it just finished and we were carryin' it along the road when Jimmy's father caught us, and when he saw the raft he gave out stink and took it off us and we never went sailin' anywhere. But we'll try again,' he vowed, his young freckled face set in determined lines as he recalled the first aborted plan.

Stephen asked Aileen how she felt about starting

secondary school in September, and she told him she was glad.

'I want to get old as fast as I can and get a job in Dublin or maybe London. I'm not goin' to live in the country. I don't like livin' on a farm.' She looked at him, her electric-blue eyes curious. 'And what would you be doing when you leave school? You're nearly finished school in Ross now, aren't you?'

'I am. If I had my way I'd be gone. But my grandfather insists I stay and do the Leaving Certificate, and I suppose 'tis better I go along with him. When I'm finished I'll be leaving this place.'

Aileen wanted to know every single thing about this black-haired boy. Was it true what they were saying? Did his mother run off with the gypsies? Did she die when he was born? Was he brought back to his grandfather in a cardboard box because the gypsies didn't want him, because he wasn't one of them? She looked at Stephen's dark face and his almost black eyes, but she couldn't bring herself to ask any of the questions that stormed through her mind. But maybe some day. Before she had the chance to ask him anything he suddenly jumped up and shouted to Eddie.

'Come on, Eddie – let's get going. Something is stirring.'

Eddie, only too eager to get going, ran after Stephen, jumping over the flat rocks with the agility of a mountain goat. Stephen helped both of them bait their hooks, and with an ease born of long practice lifted his rod and cast it expertly into the middle of the peat-coloured water. Eddie did a fair imitation, his bait nearer the water's edge but sufficiently in to give him some chance of a bite. Aileen failed miserably. Her effort to imitate Stephen ended when the hook soared a few feet then landed in the mud beside the riverbank. Eddie jeered at her futile effort, and Stephen smiled and winked at him, as if to imply that girls weren't much good at anything.

'Anyway,' she muttered, her young face flushed and embarrassed, 'I never liked fishing. I only came to please Eddie. And I hate fish – rotten mullet and trout and stuff.'

'All right – all right,' Stephen answered. 'Just come over here and hold my line. I'll cast that for you and if you feel a tug just call. You see, I like rotten mullet and trout and stuff.'

They laughed, and with the sun warm and hot on their backs, they were filled with contentment for this lovely, stolen, summer's day and the knowledge of getting to know each other better and maybe becoming friends.

Later, as they sat happily eating their sandwiches, Aileen shared her mother's home-made lemonade with Stephen, who gratefully accepted. Once again, she was filled with the urge to question him and find out more about him. But she had warmed to this strange brooding boy, and thought it wouldn't be fair to question him with ten-year-old Eddie all ears.

After lunch they fished for two more hours. At least Stephen and Eddie did. Aileen lay down on the warm rock, hoping that her pale skin might get a faint tan. She couldn't believe that anyone could look as dark and as tanned as Stephen Rodgers did. She'd even bet he was darker than Heathcliff in *Wuthering Heights*. She had just started reading it. Her mother thought it was much too grown-up for her, but was secretly pleased that her daughter was capable of reading such an advanced-looking book.

By the time they packed up and went, Eddie had caught a small mullet and a strange-looking squiggly creature that looked like a young eel.

'You should put that back,' Aileen advised. 'I can't see Mam frying that yoke.'

But Eddie was adamant that the eel was coming home. 'Anyway, the cat will eat it and I want them to see what I caught.'

Stephen had three trout to show for his patience and effort. He offered one to Aileen. 'Maybe you might like it and not think it rotten,' he said. His dark eyes were serious but she thought he was grinning somewhere inside him.

'No, I don't want it, and anyway you should take it home and show your grandfather that you weren't idling.' She thought he looked even more serious than normal at the mention of his grandfather. She'd have to find out more about him. She'd *have* to find out more, or she'd burst with curiosity.

As she walked ahead of the two boys, she took the initiative. The flat stones were in shadow now as the sun had dipped behind the trees.

'Maybe we'll come again sometime,' she said, trying to sound very casual. 'Maybe I might get the knack next time?'

He nodded but didn't speak. Eddie was prattling non-stop about a character in his *Beano* who had found secret treasure in a tunnel near the railway line beside his house, and Stephen

17

seemed to be giving him his complete attention. Aileen supposed that if you lived with an old grandfather and had no parents, brothers or sisters, you would give your ear to a ten-year-old bore. She'd airily mention the possibility of seeing him again when they'd got to the fork of the road before going their separate ways.

Aileen never got the chance. Just as they were climbing over the fence to drop to the road they were confronted with a scowling angry man. It was obvious it was Stephen's grand-father, old Tom Rodgers.

'Where in the name of God were you, you good-for-nothin' –' He glared at Stephen, totally ignoring the other two. 'Wastin' yer time at the river when you should be helping me with the turf. Get home quickly – or you won't be the bether of it.'

Stephen's face was suffused with anger. 'I'm going now,' he muttered.

Aileen looked at the cranky old man and any thought she had had that Stephen Rodgers was living with a kind old grandfather dissipated. She put out her hand and touched Stephen's arm. 'I'm sorry you're in trouble because of us.'

'He's never any different,' Stephen told her as he watched his grandfather striding away to the van, parked across the way.

'Maybe we'll see you again?' she asked. He looked at her, taking in the sunburnt young face, the very blue eyes, the tossed blonde hair, the now slightly grubby summer dress.

'I hope so,' he replied, and he followed his grandfather to the waiting van.

Chapter Two

Stephen Rodgers had grown up in a household where there was neither love, companionship, nor the easy laughter that lightens the tedium in most families from time to time. From an early age he knew he was different. He had no parents, no brothers or sisters, only a grandfather who resented him, who seemed to bear him some sort of grudge for the very fact that he was there at all. Stephen had never spent a night away from the eighty-acre farm. He had never gone on holidays, had never seen the sea, had little or no conversation with anyone outside school. Of course there was Máire, who came to do the cleaning and washing a couple of times a week, or Joe, the farm hand, who cycled up the boreen every morning at eight-thirty and cycled down the boreen every evening at seven. When he was very young, Máire would sometimes come when his grandfather was working on the farm, bringing him a small sticky paper bag of sweets. She would pick him up and give him a hug and they would play a little game: she would put her arms behind her back and he would have to guess which hand held the sweets. When he got it right she would pick him up again and give him a little hug, saying, 'Sure God love you, almost no one cares about you at all, at all.' It didn't warm Stephen's heart to know that no one cared about him, but the sweets were some compensation. He would sometimes eat them sitting on a stool in the cowshed or over in the far corner of the meadow, lying low in the grass listening to the buzz of a thousand insects. Afterwards, when Máire had gone, a great loneliness would descend on him and he'd count the hours until she'd be back again.

Joe Power, the farm hand, liked to have him around and though he replied only in monosyllables to Stephen's childish questions when he was very young, there was a kindness in the gruff replies.

As Stephen got older, his grandfather exacted the same amount of work from him during the school holidays as he did from his paid hand. It was Joe Power who asked Tom Rodgers to give the lad a break. They were sitting after the evening meal in the silent kitchen. Stephen had gone out to finish off his chores, lock up the hens safe from the marauding fox, and secure the pigshed to keep the new litter of bonhams safe.

Joe cleared his throat and spat into the open fireplace. 'Tom, you're too hard on the lad. Sure a young lad like that would want a break. A day with young people. 'Tis his summer holidays and he shouldn't be doin' the work of a man.'

The older man cleared his own throat noisily and growled, 'Hard work never killed anyone. Anyway, he has the body of a man and the strength of an ox, and 'tis only right that he earn his keep like the rest of us.'

'I know, I know,' Joe told him. 'But sure we all know you can't put an oul man's head on a young man's shoulders. Let him have a bit of time to do the things a young fella might want to do – like a bit of swimmin', a bit of fishin'.'

And so it was that Stephen got a few hours off once a week to go fishing down at the river in the quiet pool before the weir. He usually spent two hours there, and made it a habit to be back in time to help with the milking and the other chores on the farm. But the day he'd met Aileen and Eddie MacMahon there, he'd lost all track of time. Being with the young girl and her chatty, friendly little brother had been like a sort of healing day – a day which filled him with hope that things wouldn't always be the same, that someday he'd break away from the tyrannical old man and be free and even happy. When his grandfather had come along with his bellicose shouting and his ferocious temper, he must have looked a fool in the eyes of the young girl and her brother. Was it sympathy or pity he had seen in the blue depths of her eyes? He hoped it wasn't pity. He had seen enough pity in Joe Power's eyes. Sometimes even in the eyes of the women who chatted after Mass. He didn't want it. He didn't want any of their pity.

Someday he'd show them – he'd come back to this place where twopence looked down on a penny, where there were nudges and winks, where things happened behind closed doors and not a word about it.

Stephen knew that his mother had been the only daughter of Tom Rodgers. Over the years he had heard the broken outline of the happenings of the time before he was born. His mother had been old Tom's only child. At eighteen she had run away with a tinker, he had heard it whispered. Over the years more whispers filtered through. He'd heard that the tinkers had come back and camped near the woods the following year, and had left the child with his grandfather. They said it was Tom Rodgers's grandchild, and that the baby's mother Teresa had died at its birth. The people in the know held their breath, wondering what the embittered man would do. He had taken one long look at the baby and then had taken it in.

Sometimes Stephen was curious and wanted to know more – much more, so that the dislike that he felt for his grandfather might lessen with understanding. This evening he felt swamped with restlessness and a peculiar loneliness. Whether it was because of his grandfather's anger at his dawdling at the river or being in the company of Aileen MacMahon, he wasn't sure. He remembered the day she had fallen in the school yard years before. She had grown so much since then. The outline of her young vibrant body flashed to his mind and he felt a rising hunger in his groin and a desperate longing somewhere inside him. He decided he'd go and look for Joe and talk to him – if he didn't talk to someone he would burst.

Joe Power was leaning on the wall of the cowhouse, sucking his pipe and looking at the antics of a playful marmalade kitten. He looked up as Stephen joined him, and saw the restless discontent in the boy's dark eyes. God above, Stephen was a handsome young devil, he thought, so dark, the hair like a raven's wing, and the black eyes. He almost looked like one of them foreign fellows. But so often he looked troubled and unhappy. A fine young lad like him should have a different life.

Joe remembered her – the cloud of hair, the mischievous dark eyes, the dimples. She used to swing in and out for hours on the gate waiting for him to finish his chores. 'Come on Joe, you promised you'd make me a swing in the meadow.' 'Ah Joe, you said we could go fishing.' 'Joe, did you hear the gypsies were camped near the woods?' 'Joe, I can see the smoke at night and I can even hear them talking sometimes. Come, on Joe – let's go and have a look at them. Sure it'll be something to do.' Jesus above, wasn't he glad he hadn't taken her to see them? At least he was grateful for that. Now he looked at her son: the same determination in his chin, the same shape to his face – and shades of her smile, the odd time the boy smiled. He looked at him now – and tried to damp down the sympathy he felt.

'Ah look, boy, you shouldn't mind the old man. Sure we all know his bark is worse than his bite. There's a kind of anger underneath him all the time but it's nothin' to do with you. You must know that.'

Stephen leaned beside him on the whitewashed wall, his eyes following the antics of the marmalade kitten. 'Joe, do me a favour, will you?'

'If I can I will, boy. Tell me.'

'Joe, you might think this strange, but I want to know more about my mother. Anything you know about my father. I'm old now – I need to know, don't I?'

Joe slowly removed his pipe, cleared his throat and spat, missing the kitten by a hair's breadth. 'Sure, maybe now isn't the place and time. Anyway, 'tisn't my place to tell you.'

'It is, Joe – 'tis you or Máire I'll be asking eventually. I've no one else, you know that. So you might as well tell me what you know.'

Joe saw the pleading look and something inside him softened. 'Tell him we're going for a bit of a walk down the boreen. He'll be wonderin' where you are if you don't.'

Stephen went to the half-door of the kitchen. His grandfather was sitting on the stool near the fireplace. The day was so hot he had let the fire die down and now there were only a few dying embers beneath the soft grey cushion of ash.

'I'm going along the way with Joe – I'll be back in a while,' Stephen told him.

His grandfather glanced up from his beloved *Irish Press* and said, 'All right, but don't be wanderin' the roads like a bloody –'

Whatever he was going to say remained unsaid, but Stephen guessed it might be 'tinker' or 'gypsy' or some such thing.

'I'll be back soon.'

The weariness in the boy's voice caused the grandfather to glance at him. 'All right – all right so,' he muttered before burying his head in the farm section and the market price of sheep.

*

22

When they were a bit from the farmhouse, Joe suggested that they sit on the ditch, and when they had settled he asked Stephen what it was he wanted to know.

'Everything. What was my mother really like? How did she get on with grandfather? Did you ever see my father? Jesus, Joe, tell me, because it all keeps going around in my head and I want to get it right.'

'There's not all that much to tell, boy. Your mother Teresa was the light of the oul man's eye. He doted on her. She was all he had after his wife Ciss went. Ciss, your grandmother, died of something' inwardly, and they lived in terror the child'd get it. He used buy her all kinds of things – big jars of malt. You should hear the row she'd kick up when they'd be spoonin' the muck into her.' Joe stopped for a bit. He could already see he had the lad's total attention.

'She was a beautiful little thing – all dark blue eyes like the night and a mass of dark hair. When Máire brushed it she'd yell and scream and tell her to cut it off. When she went to school one of us used to have to meet her to take her home. Her prattle went on all the time. She'd follow your grandfather around all the time, asking questions or demanding things, and he'd refuse her nothin'. Sure we were all cracked about her. When she got older Father O'Connor suggested that she should go to boarding school, that 'twould be good for her. I thought your grandfather would blow up. The Father pointed out that she would be with other young people, and that livin' the way she was wouldn't be the best trainin' for her.

'Anyway she went and the place was like a tomb after. Máire decided there was no point in coming every day, and then she stayed at home with her family and only came a couple of times a week.'

Joe stopped and took a few deep sucks from his old pipe, watching the red glow with satisfaction. 'Your grandfather got her a pony the first Christmas she was home from school. She was wild with excitement. She called the pony Laddie. She was a right little madam on that pony. There wasn't a fence in the place they couldn't clear.

'She left the school when she was seventeen. God above, he was so excited when the time came for her to come home. He got her room all painted and papered for Easter. Sure 'tis your room now – you can see the paper, all those little roses and ribbons and things.'

The boy nodded. ''Tis faded now but I can see what you mean.'

'It was the summer of '40,' Joe went on. 'It started late, but when the sun came out in early July it didn't go in till late October. That was the year she met your father, God help us.'

Joe stopped and, sucking at his pipe, stared ahead at the gentle rolling countryside, his gaze wandering as far as the woods which sloped to the river. Stephen followed his gaze and didn't break the silence. If I let him go on, he thought, I'll hear the whole story – I'll be able to pierce the fog. I might even understand why my grandfather hates me so.

'She had a young wan stayin' with her for a while that summer. A grand lively girl, and Teresa and herself were up to all kinds of high jinks. They used cycle away on picnics, taking themselves everywhere. The Barrons and the Ryans had girls that age at the time, and you'd often see them down at the river swimmin', and once I saw them and they must have got the notion without thinkin', because they hadn't a screed on.'

Stephen listened, enthralled. The thought that his mother would do something so outrageous amused him. From somewhere in the depths inside he was swamped with gratitude to Joe, who was shedding a light on so many things he would never know. His heart lifted as he pictured a group of young girls planning and plotting how to spend the summer days in the second year of the war – a year when, according to Joe, the sun came out late and didn't go in till October. Afraid that something unwarranted might break the spell, Stephen nudged him on gently.

'Well, maybe it was for a dare or somethin' they got into the river without a screed, but 'twas after that she met one of the gypsies.

'Sure we only heard most of it. But she was seen again and again with this young dark fella.' Joe stopped his story and looked at Stephen. His pale blue faded eyes roamed over the boy's face. 'A bit like yourself, lad – a handsome devil with hair as black as yours is and eyes the same.

'But I never saw a madder man than your grandfather was when he found out that she was seen out with a gypsy. Jasus, Stephen, the devil himself would be like an angel compared to Tom Rodgers that night. Actually, he hit her and knocked her to the ground. Jasus, who could believe it? A man that had never, ever laid a finger on her, she was so precious to him. He went wild. Told her if she ever was seen with the likes of that fella again he'd shoot them both. I believed he would too. Anyway he never got a chance. On the following Saturday she was gone. How she got away I'll never know. He had her locked in her room with Máire bringin' her in her food and emptyin' her chamberpot. How she got out was peculiar. 'Twas as if she was spirited away. He was crazy with grief. He was a changed man after that. I don't think I ever saw him smile from that day to this.

'When old Sheridan brought you back I thought he'd kill him, but he didn't. He asked him in and heard that his only daughter Teresa was dead. Your father had died too in an accident. As you weren't wan of them 'twould be bether he took back his own.' Joe stopped. He lit a match and it flared for a second and then went out. He tried again and was successful the third time. When his pipe was going nicely Stephen broke the silence.

'Thanks, Joe – I feel good that I know things now. Maybe I even know now why he hates me.'

'No, lad, he doesn't hate you. When he sees you he remembers the way he lost her, and sure it drives him mad. Anyway, Stephen, he's not gettin' younger and if you stay put and let the hare sit you'll end up with the farm when he goes. Sure you have to – there's no one else.'

'One thing, Joe – did old Sheridan say they were married?'

'He did. He said they were married and that you were six weeks old.'

Stephen smiled briefly, the smile not reaching his eyes. Joe, watching, thought, He's a man already. Sure he was never a boy, happy, mischievous and full of fun. From inside Joe a sorrow welled up that a young lad could live out his young days without knowing a normal childhood, playin' and sometimes fightin' with the brothers and sisters, waitin' for his turn for a wash in the tin tub on Saturday nights, fightin' for a place in the trap to go to Mass, boastin' about his success on the football team. Joe cleared his throat and spat with total accuracy, hitting a bee who hovered over a cowslip on the far ditch.

'Anyway, boy, at least you weren't a bastard.'

Stephen threw back his head. The black hair fell across his

forehead, and his laugh rang out warm and genuine. 'Thanks, Joe. 'Tis something to know I wasn't a bastard.'

*

Aileen MacMahon didn't see Stephen Rodgers again that summer.

Her mother showed surprise at her eagerness to take young fractious Maeve out so often. She seemed to spend hours at the swing down in the field overlooking the road. Eddie, bored out of his mind, nagged her to go fishing again.

'And maybe we'll see Stephen – he was great at the castin'. C'mon, ask Mammy can we go?'

Her mother wanted to know, 'And what's down at the river? Sure ye'll see no one exciting at the river, no more than down at the swing. And why all this longing for company all of a sudden? Ye don't know how well off ye are. When I was a child I only had my brothers and sisters to play with. Who else would ye want?'

'She wants Stephen Rodgers,' Eddie blurted out without thinking.

Aileen, looking at her mother, expected some reaction, but not the rampant disapproval that followed. Mary glared at Aileen.

'Stephen Rodgers! You mean ye've been out with Stephen Rodgers – old Tom Rodgers's grandson? Are you mad, girl? That's one lad I don't want you next, nigh or near. He's been dragged up without a mother or anyone to give a thought to him. His poor grandfather is a decent hard-working man but – but –'

She glanced at Eddie, who was demolished by Aileen's furious glance. 'Get out, will you, and play with Maeve in the yard.'

Eddie slunk out without a backward glance.

'I don't want the child to hear me – he's too young. But you, Miss, are growing up and you have to know what's right and wrong. Stephen Rodgers's mother was a lovely decent young girl – but she had wilful blood in her. And his father was a travelling nobody. Well, you might as well know – they say that he was one of the tinkers that camp near the woods every summer. He must have mesmerised the child, because she ran off with him and broke her poor father's heart. And then they came back and just dumped the child on his doorstep. But I don't want you or Eddie next or near him.

26

There's gypsy blood in that young fellow. Sure you need only look at him.'

Aileen glared at her mother, and her words came out tumbled and heated. 'I'm not next or near him as you put it. Eddie and I went fishin' with him once – once. And wasn't he at school every single day and weren't we all with him? There's nothing wrong with him – in fact he's very, very nice. He taught Eddie and me how to cast the bloody line so he did.'

'Don't you dare use language like that to your mother, Miss – I'll tell your father who you're knocking around with. Maybe 'tis from the likes of him you're learning language like that.'

'No, it's not – he's better than anyone I know. So there.'

Her mother leaned over and gave her a sharp wallop on the cheek. Shocked, Aileen stared at her and burst out crying before running out of the kitchen, shouting, 'I hate this place – I wish I was dead.'

Eddie, hearing the raised voices and his sister's sobs, gathered she had got a wallop for answering back.

'C'mon,' he muttered to his young sister Maeve, 'we better get away before Aileen comes and kills me stone mortal dead.'

Aileen, lying on her bed, the sobs now reduced to an occasional hiccup, wondered what was wrong with her – wondered why she cared whether she ever saw Stephen Rodgers again. She tried to grapple with the thoughts that filled her head. When had she first noticed him? At school, of course. Was she always aware of him standing at the wall during lunch hour? Alone. Mostly alone, eating his lunch and almost defiantly looking around at the other children playing or chasing in gangs. She remembered the day he put a hanky on her knee. Maggie and Ann were a bit jealous he had spoken to her. In fact they thought he was lovely – completely different from the red-headed, freckled, rough-looking boys that were the best St Joseph's National School had to offer.

She lay on her bed and remembered the wonderful unforgettable day by the river. How he had stood beside her and put his brown hand over hers on the rod and had raised it up and cast it out over all the reeds, right on the centre of the quiet part of the river.

It had been the most beautiful day of her life – better than first Holy Communion or her Confirmation, better than all the Christmases and Easters and holy days. Her sobs subsiding now, Aileen wondered why a day spent with Stephen Rodgers could be the best day she had ever spent in her whole life.

The yearning to have even a glimpse of him was like a sickness. She had promised her mother she would never talk to him again. Even when she had made the promise she had asked God to forgive her lie. She knew that if ever she saw him away from all the eyes that searched and seared and glanced, trying to find out things to talk about, she would talk to him.

August slipped by – hot and airless days that seemed to drain energy from everyone. Even Denis did his work apathetically, looking to the blue, cloud-free skies to try to catch a glimpse of a break.

Her mother said no more about Stephen. She was obviously lulled into thinking her young daughter had put the whole episode from her.

One particularly hot day Aileen went with Eddie and Maeve to the stream that flowed below the meadow.

'At least we'll stick our feet in and cool ourselves,' she told her mother.

'Mind yereselves,' her mother warned. 'Don't fall in.'

'Sure there's not enough water to drown a cat,' Aileen told her. 'Unless it rains the stream will dry up.'

Aileen felt a peculiar restlessness on her. She also felt dizzy, and she had strange stomach cramps at the pit of her stomach. She wondered had she an appendix. She remembered Maggie had to go into the hospital with an appendix and there was great excitement about the whole business. She'd had heaps of visitors and had got heaps of sweets, comics and books. Aileen hoped the pain would worsen. It would be great if she had an appendix and if it burst, maybe half-killing her. Everyone would be stopping her parents after Mass, asking about her. For a while she'd nearly be famous with all the attention she'd get.

When they reached the stream Maeve wanted to take off her clothes and lie down in the water.

'C'mon Aileen, I'll just keep my knickers on – c'mon, let me, I'm roastin' so I am.'

'Oh all right, but don't any of ye get me into trouble.'

Eddie stripped off his shirt and, removing his shoes and socks, walked into the shallow stream, kicking up the water as he jumped from rock to rock.

'This is boring – there's nothin' to do. I wonder is Stephen Rodgers down at the river?'

'Don't talk to me about him,' his sister told him heatedly. 'Didn't you get me into right trouble telling Mam we met him? Now, you little idiot, we can never talk to him again.'

'That's stupid,' Eddie said. 'What's wrong with him? You'd think he was a crook or somethin'.' Eddie was very hung up on crooks or baddies, and when they played games he always had to be the bad guy.

'He's not a crook – something about his father being a tinker.'

'Oh, is that all? Sure that's nothin'. I wish I was a tinker living in camps. Lightin' fires all the time, travellin' around, not being bored on an oul farm all the time.'

Aileen looked at Eddie, standing freckled and fair-haired in the shallow stream. His toes had found the soft mud and they were busy churning it up and squelching it back. 'Yes, maybe you're right – maybe it would be great to be a tinker.'

Eddie wandered off to join Maeve who was blissfully happy in six inches of water, her silvery-blonde head resting on a moss-covered stone. ''Tis great, Aileen, 'tis like a swimmin' pool. Why don't you take off your clothes and leave on your knickers too?'

'I'd look just great,' Aileen muttered, already conscious of her budding breasts and still feeling queasy from these unfamiliar cramps that wracked her.

That evening, when she was preparing for bed, she saw the bright-red blood. Maggie and Ann had told her about periods. Ann had already got them, and little skinny Maggie was waiting anxiously for something to happen. 'When we get them we'll be sort of women,' she had told them. 'We can even have babies.' Aileen, looking at the blood, wondered if she should go down and tell her mother, who was still in the kitchen. Her mother had not told her anything much beyond a vague mutter that girls get a little monthly trouble or visitor. She had ended the little discourse with, 'When it happens you'll know.'

So this was it. Maybe this was the reason she felt so restless and strange. This was probably the reason she had the cramps and pains. She wouldn't be going into the hospital after all with a burst appendix and getting all the comics and sweets and attention. Aileen decided she'd go down and tell her mother. If she didn't she might ruin the bed and maybe get into trouble again, like she had when she'd spent the day at the river with Stephen.

Her mother had finished her chores and was sitting near the open fireplace. There was turf and some withered gorse bushes placed in readiness for when the weather would break and fires would be needed again. Mary was knitting a navy sock for Eddie. The heel was already turned. Her mother obviously had school on her mind.

'Mam.'

Her mother glanced up and saw her daughter standing there in her nightdress, a look of apprehension on her young face. 'What is it?' she asked quietly.

'It's – you know, the time of the month, the thing that happens, the visitor, it has happened to me.'

'Oh, I know. I should have told you more. It's all right. It's natural, it even happened to Our Lady. It means you're growing up now and your body is going to change. Look, I'll get you a packet of towels and a belt I have put away for you. Read the instructions and put it on, and everything will be over in a few days. It's part of being a woman. Just accept it and don't talk about it – not to anybody. It's better that way.'

Aileen nodded as she watched her mother bustle out of the kitchen to get the accoutrements. Aileen could see that Mary was embarrassed and uncomfortable, so she would take what she was offered, read the instructions and do what was obviously necessary. Of course she would talk to Ann and Maggie about it. She saw no reason why not. She already knew that her mother was a very old-fashioned woman. She had no interest in anything outside the farm, her husband Denis, and her children.

When Mary returned with a brown paper bag, she handed it over furtively, as if what it contained was something not quite right, something just a little bit shameful, something that should hurriedly be borne away to a secret place. 'For God's sake, don't let Eddie or Maeve see you, and for the next few days you're not to wet your feet, or under any condition, wash your hair.'

Aileen reached out her hand, and nodded, somehow already aware that this was an old-fashioned view and if she felt like bathing she would, and if she felt like washing her hair she would also. Her mother need never know. She would keep these things from her mother who was so busy she hardly knew what was happening.

Stephen Rodgers spent most nights, before dropping off to sleep, making plans. He would stay with his grandfather for two years after finishing school. He owed him that much. His grandfather had gruffly promised him a wage when he was labouring full-time on the farm. He'd save most of it and then he'd leave quietly – no one would know, not Máire, or Joe or anybody. He'd go to London and get a job in a factory or on the building sites. He was big and strong and looked so much older than his years that he could see no problem there. Then, when he had enough money, he would go to Australia and stay there forever. There was nothing to keep him here.

He borrowed books from the master, Mr O'Rourke, at school, and read so much about this wonderful land where the sun shone almost forever, and where there was work and money to be made. But what attracted him most was the newness of the place. He could walk there with his head held high. No one would know or care who he was, or where he came from. He would be accepted for his strength and worth and work. No one would ever know that his mother – how had Joe described her? A lovely girl, wilful – had run away at seventeen and had married someone undesirable. Or maybe she hadn't married him. Maybe Joe only said that to console him. And if so, what was what was so terribly wrong with that? Weren't tinkers a group of people who travelled and moved on, who preferred to live out in open places and earn a living from scrap-dealing, horse-trading and tinkering, making cans and mugs and things? But Stephen was only too aware that some of them drank too much and fought like wild things and stole.

Then, God above, did it matter? Why had his mother's reckless deed destroyed him in this Godforsaken place, where everyone knew everything? Stephen knew he didn't really hate his grandfather. He could understand his bitterness. And as the time went by, was there a sort of healing? Was he less abrupt? After the row over the long time he had spent with Aileen MacMahon and her brother by the river, Stephen thought he had noticed a subtle change. Maybe the old man was ashamed of his outburst in front of the girl and her brother.

He often lay in his bed at night and thought of Aileen MacMahon, and was filled with a longing he couldn't fathom. With the exception of Máire, who displayed a gruff kindness to him, he had never known any female. He clearly remembered the first day he had seen Aileen at school. Her silvery blonde hair was in two thick plaits tied with red ribbons and she had stood at the wall in the playground, looking around a bit fearfully at the other children, who had been charging wildly all over the place. He could remember her clearly, her pleated skirt and knitted jumper, her socks right up to her knees, not rumpled or hanging down. She had been standing on one leg, the other back against the wall as if to steady herself in case the charging brigade would knock her to the ground. He recalled the day she had fallen and how he had wanted to run over and pick her up and get down on his knees and wipe away the blood.

Like moving pictures, she flashed through his mind, getting older, taller and prettier. He was sometimes filled with such a longing for this girl. He knew it was wrong. She was only a child, or little more than a child. He had gone over every single second of the wonderful day at the river until he was weary recalling it. The shy way she had walked around the willow trees, carrying the rod and the lunches. The way she had hauled Eddie into view as if to say, 'Look, I'm only here because of him.' The way she had tried to cast the line, too independent to ask him to help. The way he had helped her. The feel of her cool hands when he held them to show her how to cast. Her blonde hair, no longer in thick plaits but hanging down like a curtain. Her long brown legs and small waist, and her budding breasts, already showing early womanhood.

He tossed and turned, knowing that he might never see her again. After all, she was the daughter of Denis MacMahon, who had a sizable farm and a strict wife who would see that her daughter didn't talk to a fellow who was considered a nobody because his father had been a nobody. That sort of thing would never be forgotten in a place where every wrong-doing was remembered.

No, he would go away and start a new fulfilling life, and put all this behind him.

Before he fell asleep Stephen fantasised that he was standing on the deck of a big ship crowded with people. They were friendly and excited, as if they were travelling somewhere in high hopes. He was with them and accepted, and they were calling him Stephen, and talking and laughing with him without constraint and with ease. Even in the dream he wondered why he was so happy, so lighthearted and then he knew. Aileen MacMahon was over across the deck, smiling that shy little smile and looking at him as if she had eyes for nobody else. He had never known contentment like it.

When he woke up and saw the sloping ceiling above him, the tall chest of drawers with the statue of the Infant of Prague, his school books, and the old brass oil lamp, reality came crashing down. Stephen looked at the faded wallpaper with the roses and ribbon, and through the emptiness of knowing that this, his newfound happiness, was merely a dream, he found himself thinking of his mother, a lively, dark, impulsive girl who had broken with all convention to run away with someone she loved.

Chapter Three

In the middle of August the weather broke, with a night full of such torrential rain and wind that it woke Aileen up. She lay in bed and, pulling the clothes around her chin, was glad of the storm. No more boring hot dry days, wandering like a lost soul to the stream with Eddie and Maeve. She glanced over at the bed and saw that her little sister was awake too. Maeve seemed to be listening to the howling wind, her eyes like saucers staring at her sister. 'Oh Aileen, listen will you? The house will blow away. 'Tis like the banshee too.'

Aileen could hear the wind shrieking and moaning outside. ''Tisn't the banshee Dad will be worrying about, but the corn. It'll be flattened.'

Suddenly the dark room was lit up by a flash of lightning so brilliant that everything was illuminated.

'Oh God, Aileen, get the holy water, will you? We'll be killed.'

Aileen knew that her mother was terrified of thunder and and lightning, and that whenever a storm came she drenched them all with holy water.

'Don't be daft,' she began but her words were lost in the crash of thunder overhead.

'Oh God Almighty, Aileen, get the holy water,' Maeve sobbed.

In the silence that followed Aileen thought she heard a loud banging on the front door.

'Do you hear something?' she whispered to her little sister. 'A banging? Listen.'

Maeve poked her head outside the covers of her bed. 'Yeah, there's someone banging at the door. Who could be out in weather like that? Oh Aileen, maybe 'tis the devil. Oh God above, save us from all harm.' Maeve had picked up all the sayings of the people her mother met after Mass and evening devotions, and they were a source of amusement to everyone. But right now Aileen hardly heard them.

Her heart thudded as she heard the continuous hammering at the door. Who was it? Should she get up and see? Suddenly her mother appeared at the door of their bedroom in her pink nightdress, carrying a large bottle of holy water which she shakily flung around, drenching the girls in their beds.

'Mam,' Aileen told her, 'there's someone down there. Listen to the knocking at the front door. There's someone out in the storm who's in trouble.'

Her mother stopped the holy-water ritual and listened. 'You're right, there's someone there. I'd better get your father.'

Aileen jumped out of the bed and ran to the landing. Just as her father came out of his room, pulling an old tweed overcoat on over his striped pyjamas, another flash of lightning lit up the room.

'Aileen, come back, come back, I'm terrified – 'tis the devil,' Maeve screamed.

'Go to her, will you,' her father said. 'I'll see who it is.'

Aileen ran back in to the room and whispered, 'Shut up, will you, I want to see who's there. If it is the devil I'll tell you all about him.' She ran back to the landing and followed her parents down the narrow stairs. As her father opened the door a loud crash of deafening thunder blocked out Maeve's whimpering.

A young bedraggled couple stood in the doorway. They were drenched to the skin. The rain had flattened their hair and was running in rivulets down their bodies. They were very young and the woman held a child in her arms. 'Mister MacMahon, will you help us, for God's sake? We're camping near the woods and the child got terrible sick, fierce bad – rollin' in agony she is. We need to take her to the hospital in Ross. We have no way. Could you drive us in the van and God will reward you, sir?'

The dark-haired young man looked pleadingly at Denis MacMahon. 'Please sir, help us, will ye? If you don't she'll die.'

Aileen watched as her mother brought in the wet, shivering couple, and removed the small child from the young woman's arms. 'She's burning with the heat. She's running a high temperature.' Mary placed the child on the settle near the fire. 'Denis, get the van out and drive them in to the hospital in Ross.'

Her husband had already gone upstairs and in seconds

appeared, pulling up his trousers as he walked. 'We'll go,' he told them. 'We'd want to go quick.'

Aileen watched as they walked out the door, carrying the small child with the blazing-red cheeks.

She crept down and stood beside her mother, listening to the sound of the engine spluttering into life.

'God help them. Isn't it a hard life they have?' her mother said.

'Will she be all right?' Aileen asked.

'I don't know. She's a very sick baby. Sure how could they be anything else out in the weather? With God's help your father will be in time. Go back to bed. Maeve is up there, terrified.'

Aileen walked slowly up the stairs, her thoughts in a turmoil. Wouldn't it be terrible to be married and so poor that you had only a canvas covering for protection? How could you be happy living like that, watching the skies for signs of rain and snow and wind? She lay in bed and listened to the storm that was now burning itself out, the thunder rolling away and becoming fainter and fainter. She couldn't sleep, and she wondered whether Stephen Rodgers was lying awake listening to the sounds of the dying storm. Had he, as a tiny, newborn baby, lived under canvas just like that little sick child? Had his mother lain awake at night remembering all she had left behind? Her father and a fine farm with cows and horses, warmth, comfort and money? Or maybe she had been so happy living with someone she loved that these things hadn't mattered.

Aileen tossed and turned and Stephen Rodgers's face swam before her eyes, just as she had last seen him – dark and angry, his mouth set in grim lines as his grandfather shouted at him.

Sometime before dawn broke Aileen heard her father come back into the yard. She heard him come up the stairs and listened to the muffled conversation between him and her mother. For some unknown reason she couldn't resist finding out about the drenched, bedraggled couple and their little baby girl. She crept out of the bed and in the grey light of a rain-drenched dawn she went into her parents' room.

'Well, Dad? Tell me, was she all right?'

Her father was sitting tiredly at the side of the bed, the old tweed coat still on him, and she could see that he still wore his pyjama top.

'No, alannah – I'm afraid she's not all right. The little soul died shortly after we got to the hospital.'

'Sure you did your best, Denis,' his wife whispered. 'The little child is better off – she's warm and in Heaven now.'

Aileen walked back to her room. She crept into bed and, pulling the blankets over her head, she cried as if her heart would break. She didn't know if her tears were for the young mother and father who made a valiant effort to save their little child, if they were for the little girl who wasn't in pain and burning up any more and who, according to her mother was now warm and in Heaven, or if they were for Stephen Rodgers, who could have died just like that if his young mother hadn't died instead.

The birds were in high chorus before sleep came.

The next day Mary took Aileen aside and told her that they had made plans for her to go to boarding school in September. They hadn't told her until all their plans were final. Her school was to be the Loretto nuns in County Dublin, where Mary MacMahon had a cousin who was teaching.

'You'll be mixing with the nicest girls in the country,' her mother said.

Aileen apathetically accepted their decision, but in her heart didn't agree. She wandered about all day, even more desolate than she had been before.

Chapter Four

Tom Rodgers sat on the old oak settle smoking his pipe and listening to the howling wind and rain slashing off the small glass-paned windows. Huge drops spattered now and then into the open fireplace. The sound made old Shep twitch his nose, maybe breaking dreams of his sheep-chasing youth as a hard-working collie.

The wind rose and fell, creaking the old smoke-darkened rafters and rustling the thatch. Emptiness and loneliness were nothing new to Tom Rodgers, but somehow the storm brought an added desolation. He sucked his pipe, but the comfort he normally experienced eluded him this evening. Unwanted thoughts crowded in. Maybe I'm too hard on him, he thought. Maybe I should just let him be. Maybe Joe is right – you can't put an old head on young shoulders. Maybe that's what I'm trying to do.

He spat into the fire and watched the spit settle on red turf and sizzle briefly before it disappeared. Despite the heat he shivered. He was getting old, and more and more he found himself looking back instead of looking forward. Then again, why wouldn't he? Most of his living was done and he hadn't that much more to do.

He'd have to think of the farm and making it over to the lad. 'Twould be only right – the boy was all he had.

Sometimes in the gloom of the evening, when he sat alone, the place seemed filled with ghosts. Ciss, his wife, was there, smiling that crooked, begrudging, little smile, as if she didn't want to laugh when he told her something that amused her, or brought her home a funny yarn from the creamery or the market. They had been married all of five years when she'd got the news that she was expecting. Sure she'd nearly died with the happiness of it. When she'd had the baby girl she'd insisted on calling her Teresa, because the child had been born on her favourite saint's feast day. She had adored the child, although she had tried to be strict and disapproving at times, and had five years' happiness with her little girl before the sickness came.

A blockage. That's what the doctors had called it. The big-shot specialist up in Dublin had called it a large growth. Why couldn't they say what it was? Hadn't he seen cancer in animals and known they were finished? But because they hadn't said it, he had hoped, just like Ciss had hoped. Sure she hadn't even lived to see the little one make her first Holy Communion.

Teresa had been a beautiful child, with her dark blue eyes and a cloud of dark hair. Sure, she could charm the birds out of the bushes. At least she could wind him around her little finger.

The place had always been full of life when Teresa was around. 'Daddy, what's this?' and 'What's that?' and 'Where are you going?' and 'Can I come?' He thought his heart had been broken when Ciss died, but he knew it was broken when Teresa went.

Tom had often railed to high heaven about the cruelty of it all, but he had never got any answers.

He recalled that Teresa had had a young friend staying with her that summer, and they had been full of high jinks and up to all sorts of things. When they had been in the kitchen in the evenings he'd ask them what they had done all the long day and she'd say, 'Everything, Daddy – everything.' She would laugh at him and sometimes poke him in the ribs, and he would be happy that his little girl was so content. God above, when she went he knew why she had been so happy.

And now her son was up in bed, maybe lying there wide awake listening to the storm. He'd known at first glance that child was his grandson. Old Johnnie Sheridan had brought him, and he knew and trusted the old man. He was the head of the clan who came, summer after summer, and camped near the woods. Tom had been was too proud to talk to him and ask him any questions at the time. Had his daughter been happy that last year of her life? Had she laughed and joked with that vagabond of a tinker who'd charmed her away from him? Had she been so happy lying with him under the tent or under the stars that she'd never missed her father or the farm or her friends or Joe or Máire or any of them? Could she have been so mesmerised that her old life had stood for nothing?

When they were lifting the hay on to the cart the next day, Tom decided he'd talk to Joe. 'Does he say anything to you, Joe?'

'About what?' Joe wanted to know.

'About the place and what he wants when he leaves school. The place will be his some day. Does he realise that?'

Joe Power looked at Tom Rodgers and realised, not for the first time, that he was a sort of go-between. The young fellow spoke to him and the oul fellow spoke to him and he was stuck in the middle. He scratched his head, lifting his cap with his knuckles.

'I don't think he wants the place – I don't think he feels 'tis for him. Sure Tom, you never gave him any notion you'd leave it to him.'

'And what else would I do with it? Isn't he all I have? There's quare blood in him, I know, but still he's all I have.'

'Why don't you talk to him? Why don't you see what might be going through his head? 'Tis only last week he came to me and asked me all about things.' Joe stopped and gave an embarrassed cough. Maybe he shouldn't have said that. Maybe 'twould be stirrin' up old flames.

'What did he want to know?'

'About things – the way they were, and about his mother. 'Tis only natural that the lad would want to know.'

Tom Rodgers looked at Joe. The pain and the hurt of his loss still showed in his eyes, and in the lines etched so deeply in his face. 'Sure 'tis all in the past. What good will it do knowing all them old stories? Maybe it would only make him worry some more.'

'No, you're wrong there. He seemed glad to know things – glad to hear things about his mother.'

Tom nodded. A silence settled between the two men as they worked, each of them thinking how things could have been so different. Tom was thinking that Teresa could have met some hard-working lad who could have worked the place and maybe improved it and modernised it, and he could have grown old with his grandchildren around him. Children he'd be proud of, because more than likely he'd have known their seed, breed and generation.

Stephen can't wait until his schoolin' is over; then he'll go away, Joe thought. He had seen the restlessness in Stephen's eyes and knew that the lad couldn't wait to shake the dust of this place from him and go away and start a whole new life out in the world.

Chapter Five

The last few weeks of the summer were all caught up in preparations for the boarding school. Mary MacMahon pored over the required school lists; because her cousin was a nun at the convent, she wanted everything to be just right. She and Aileen went to Dublin for the bulk of the uniform, rising at the crack of dawn for Denis MacMahon to drive them to the train station in Kilkenny.

Aileen hadn't seen her mother in such good humour for a long time. She had her good suit on her, the one she had bought two years before for her cousin's wedding. Mary MacMahon was very close to her cousin – they were like sisters and young Peggy had spent all her school holidays on the farm helping Mary when Aileen was only a toddler and when Eddie was a new baby.

Peggy had married a young man, Bob Fitzpatrick, whom she had met at a dance in Ross when she was staying with the MacMahons, and because of that Mary had an extra interest in the relationship. The young couple had gone to live in England, but now Peggy was in Dublin for a few days, and after the shopping they were going to meet her for lunch in the Capitol restaurant.

'After we get your uniform we'll have heaps of time to have a nice chat with Peggy. You know how quiet your father is, so it was great to have her stay when I was married first and when you were a baby. She met a grand lad and they're doing great in England and I hope to hear news soon – she'd make a wonderful mother, so she would.'

Aileen was still reading *Wuthering Heights* and her interest in the book was all-absorbing because she thought that Heathcliff in all probability had looked like Stephen Rodgers when he was young. She stuck her finger in the book to keep her place and tried to concentrate on her mother's chatter.

'Yes, Mam, it will be great to meet Peggy – she was very funny and always in good humour, when we were young.'

Her mother looked at her fondly. 'Honestly – when you were young. Sure what are you but an innocent child?'

Aileen smiled back at her mother because she knew Mary wanted her to – she wanted everything to be right on this day – and then went back to her book, thinking there were times she didn't feel very young. She already had the developing body of a young woman. And yet at times she felt such a child, playing and chasing with Eddie and Maeve. Yet there was one emerging clear-cut thought in her mind – and it was Stephen Rodgers. She wondered why she couldn't forget him. She pooh-poohed the idea that she could be in love. She was much too young for that. Still, it was puzzling that she couldn't stop thinking about him.

Her mother's happy anticipation and excitement as the train arrived at Kingsbridge station were contagious. She jumped down off the train like a young girl, urging Aileen to hurry.

'We don't want to be standing on the bus. If we don't get a seat we'll be swinging and swaying all over the place. Come on.'

Aileen eagerly followed. She had never been in Dublin before. She wanted to take everything in – the shops she had heard so much about, the historic buildings, the cinemas and restaurants that obviously abounded. She had heard that inside the GPO there was a bronze statue of Cuchulainn with the raven on his shoulder. Ann had been up on an excursion the summer before and had had her picture taken beside it. Aileen was very interested in Irish folklore, and the legend of Cuchulainn particularly intrigued her. She certainly would insist that they pay a visit to the GPO.

As the bus trundled up the long quay her mother pointed out various things of interest. 'That's Guinness – you know, where they make the stout. I believe it's a great place to work. The employees even get a pint of Guinness for free every day if they want it. Imagine!'

Aileen wondered how that worked. Did they get it eating their lunch, or maybe at the end of their working day? It was interesting thinking of all the hundreds of workers getting free stout as a sort of bonus.

'Say if they don't want it?' she asked her mother. 'I don't think I'd like it if I was working there.'

42

'I don't think you need worry about that. I don't think you ever will.'

Dublin was thronged with people. They were the strangest people to Aileen's eyes. They weren't standing or gossiping like country folk, just rushing around, heads bent, as if they all had the most urgent appointments. No one even glanced at her mother or herself. That surprised her, because there was no doubt if two strangers went to their part of the country everyone would look at them, even if it was only sort of sideways or under their eyes, and everyone would want to know all about them.

'We'll get your uniform first and when we have that I'll feel happier in my mind. After our lunch we can do a bit of shopping for Daddy and Eddie and Maeve. And sure I might see something I'd like myself. Your father told me to buy myself a new dress.'

They walked up through the one of the busiest streets imaginable with shops full of beautiful clothes and bedspreads and the most delicate china.

'This is Grafton Street,' her mother told her. 'They say it's the nicest street in Ireland.' Aileen could well believe it was.

They bought the uniform in another busy street off Grafton Street. The gymslip and the blouses were oversized so that she'd have room to grow, her mother told her. She got a blazer with an unfamiliar crest, and a gaberdine coat which seemed much too big for her. The shop assistant was very friendly, and to Aileen's young eyes very old. She had grey hair and teeth which Aileen knew were false, because they kept coming down when she spoke, giving her smile a sort of wolfish look.

'A lovely girl – lovely, so tall and developed for her age. And her beautiful blonde hair – sure you wouldn't see that on the screen.'

Aileen felt the familiar blush which always came when people praised anything about her. She wondered did 'fine and developed' mean she had a bosom already. Maggie had told her she was quite jealous of her bosom – she herself was praying for one but here was nothing doing yet. Aileen had blushed then, too, telling Maggie she hadn't particularly wanted one but she reckoned every girl got one some time or another.

Aileen and Mary carried their bags down Grafton Street

and her mother led the way to the Capitol cinema, where they were to meet Peggy. Peggy, with her bright welcoming smile and her brown hair all tied back, was already waiting outside, her eyes scanning the passing crowd. When she saw them she waved, and Aileen stood aside as her mother hugged her cousin and gushed over her.

'Oh Peggy, you look marvellous, so smart. You'd know, honest to God, that you were living in England.'

'Yerra, go away with yourself – aren't you looking right smart yourself? And who is this gorgeous girl? Don't tell me it's little Aileen? It is – it is. Now isn't she sprouting up fierce?'

Peggy held Aileen by the arms and stood back and looked at her, a big wide smile on her face, her dancing eyes taking in the embarrassed look on the young girl's face. 'God almighty, Mary – you'd better keep the young fellows away from her.'

Aileen saw a brief cloud cross her mother's face. 'Oh, sure we know that – isn't she going to a boarding school soon? Sure, that's why we're up, buying all the uniform and books.'

They walked up the wide stairs to the Capitol restaurant, the two cousins all chat. They were great friends, though Peggy was years younger than her mother. Peggy was all smiles when Aileen's mother squeezed her arm, telling her it was wonderful – wonderful news altogether. Aileen wondered what the wonderful news was, and then she guessed it must be that Peggy was having a baby. Her mother was terribly interested in people having babies, and always told them it was the most wonderful news.

As she walked behind them, carrying the bags, the handsome smiling face of Stephen Rodgers came into Aileen's mind. Peggy's joke about keeping fellows away from her had been only a friendly sort of teasing. Yet, going into the crowded dining room, Aileen wondered whether the brief cloud she had seen crossing her mother's face, and indeed the decision to send her to boarding school, had anything to do with Stephen.

A lot of the other diners in the crowded restaurant were young men in navy suits and white collars, with pens stuck in their pockets. She supposed they must have very good jobs to be able to eat in a posh restaurant like the Capitol. There were quite a few that looked as if they were up from the country like she was. She noticed a girl about her own age with a woman

44

who was obviously her mother. She was staring at Aileen as if she had two heads. The girl had very spotty skin and as she looked at Aileen, she ran her finger through the eruptions on her chin and at the side of her mouth. As if her gesture were contagious, Aileen surreptitiously searched for spots on her own face, but could find none. She didn't particularly want them, and idly wondered whether she would get them. She also wondered if she'd like the boarding school. Would she make new friends or would the posh Dublin girls be bothered with a culchie like her? As she ate her tart, which was covered with the brightest yellow custard she had ever seen, she wondered if she would ever see Stephen Rodgers before she went away – in fact, would she ever see him again? By the time she'd be finished with the boarding school he'd be grown up and maybe gone away – maybe, if it was true that he was the son of a gypsy, maybe he'd be gone to wherever he was supposed to have come from.

Peggy's question scattered her thoughts.

'And tell me, Aileen, are you thrilled to bits you'll be going to a fine boarding school with all the nobs? I know I was mad to go to a boarding school when I was a kid but my parents never sent me. I used to read the *Girl's Crystal*; I could see myself having all these pillow fights and midnight feasts, but sure it never happened. Anyway, love, when you're a bit older you'll have to come over to us for a holiday. We could go in to London for a day.'

Aileen looked at her flushed, happy face. 'Yes, I'd love that, I really would. I like towns. I don't think you get bored in town. I was right bored during the summer.' Then she remembered the wonderful day fishing near the weir, and, with a touch of defiance, added, 'Except for one day we went fishing. I wasn't bored then.'

Chapter Six

September came in blustery and cold. After Mass everyone complained the winter was upon them, that there wouldn't be an Indian summer this year. But God was good and the summer had been right fine and the storm hadn't ruined the harvest after all, so there was no use complaining.

Stephen Rodgers daily cycled the ten miles to school in Ross. He liked school, liked to get away from the oppressive house and spin down the long winding road that went past MacMahons' place before joining up to the main road to Ross. Up to a few weeks ago he'd been constantly hoping that he'd see Aileen MacMahon. Now he knew he wouldn't. He had heard on the grapevine that she had gone to boarding school up in Dublin. Somehow the knowledge had filled him with a sort of inexplicable loneliness. He had foolishly hoped that she too would go to school in Ross, and maybe she'd cycle, and maybe they'd meet up and get to know each other better. Sometimes he saw Eddie and little Maeve going to the national school. Eddie always waved and shouted, 'Hello, Stephen.' It wasn't much, but Stephen found it gratifying that the young lad remembered his name and maybe the pleasant day they had spent at the river.

At school Stephen was considered bright and hard-working. He was popular with the other fellows and with the teachers. They didn't seem to care or know that his father had been a travelling nobody, or that his mother had run away with him when she was a young girl. They were interested only in his ability to hit a ball with an alacrity that was at times uncanny. He was already on the school senior hurling team, and Brother Halley told him that if he attended all the training sessions and kept up the progress that he had made so far, he would play for the Kilkenny minors team the following year.

Just when he was turning in the school gate, Stephen saw his friend Richie Casey pedalling beside him.

'Howya, Stephen. Did you do your ekker last night? There was a bit of a hooley on over in Kearney's near Graigue and I did nothing. One of them was off to the States. Good crack and not too many of them bawling. They had porter too – and though the mother had her eye on me I got a few mugs. Don't feel great today though. Jasus, he'll whip me for not doing the sums.'

'We're early – maybe you can copy mine,' Stephen said, grinning. He liked Richie Casey – although they had never known each other before, they had become good friends at school.

'God, that'd be great, Stephen. Although when I get them all right that shagger will smell a rat.'

'He might think you're improving a bit.'

They cycled over to the bike shed and then rushed to the classroom. Richie grabbed the proffered copy and went to work like a fiend, copying down the sums, his red curly head bent in concentration while Stephen kept a wary eye on the door. When he had finished he flashed his friend a grateful smile.

'Thanks, Stephen – sure I'll do you an oul favour one of the days.'

That lunch hour Richie filled him in all about the American wake over at Graigue.

'The Kearneys have heaps of young ones, so the place was full of birds. God, Stephen you should have seen 'em. Smashing. If you had been there they have gone down like ninepins for you. I'm glad you weren't, though. I laid my hands on a right little smasher. She was Sheila Kearney's friend and she was grand. At least you could get a word out of her, and I'm telling you, me boy, she had it all in the right places. We even had a grand little court. We made a date for the ceilidh in a fortnight's time. Tell us, Stephen, did you ever kiss a girl?'

'No – no girls in my part of the world.'

'Jasus, boy, you'll have to change that. Are there any young ones at all, at all?'

'Well, there was one girl not far from where I lived. She's very young – only a kid. But we had a grand day in the summer together. But there's no hope of anything else – she's gone to a boarding school up in Dublin.'

47

'Sure she'll have to come back. There's holidays and breaks and things. Sure she can't stay in a boarding school for ever. Snap-apple Night isn't too long away – bet she'll be home for that.'

Richie noticed a sort of weariness in his friend's face. He often wondered what sort of life Stephen Rodgers had, living with his grandfather on that remote farm. Richie had come to the conclusion that Stephen was a very lonely fellow – he never talked about his home or his activities outside school. Richie was gratified that he had mentioned the fact that he even knew a girl.

The school bell rang and both of them stubbed out their cigarettes, knowing if they were caught all hell would break out. The next class was Latin and both of them loathed the language; in fact, they were in total agreement that it was the greatest waste of time imaginable.

'Imagine spouting Latin when you're out saving the turf. If I did the grandfather would have me certified,' Stephen laughed.

'Imagine spouting Latin in the throes of a court,' Richie hooted.

'Ah God, lay off – the boasting is fierce since you went to the American wake.'

Aileen thought the boarding school in Dalkey, in County Dublin, was situated in what must have been the nicest place in all of Ireland. The building was so near the sea that sometimes, if you looked out the window, you could almost imagine you were on a ship surrounded by water. Most of the girls in first year were, surprisingly enough, from the periphery of Dublin. A few, like herself, were what they called 'up from the country', and when they called her a culchie, it was usually accompanied with a smile and she didn't take offence. She had become very friendly with most of the girls in her class, but her best friend was Niamh Turley, from Skerries in north County Dublin. Niamh's bed was next to hers in the dormitory and often, after lights out and before falling asleep, they whispered to each other, confiding little secrets about the happenings of the day.

It had soon become apparent to the nuns and teachers that Aileen was a very bright pupil who took her new subjects in her stride.

48

'Now, tell me,' Niamh complained, 'have you a notion what algebra and geometry are about? How? And you're even good at rotten old French and as well as that, you're blonde. 'Tisn't fair.'

Aileen grinned and told her she'd help her, and that blonde hair was very colourless and she'd much prefer brown hair. Niamh told her not to be stupid, but she was pleased as punch with her new friend. She seemed so grown up, and certainly was as nice as she looked.

'Look, the next Saturday we get off maybe you can get permission to come out to our house in Skerries. I have three brothers and they're all right, and we have a boat and you might like it. Now I think you'd have to get permission from your mother but we'll find out.'

Aileen wrote to her mother and her friends Ann and Maggie two weeks after she started in the boarding school.

Dear Mam,
I hope you and Daddy and Maeve and Eddie are well.

The school is fine and I have made plenty of friends. My best friend is a girl named Niamh Turley and she comes from a place called Skerries somewhere in North Dublin. She's very friendly and we get along fine. She asked me to ask you, could I go with her to her house when we get some Saturday off. Her father would collect us and bring us home. Maybe when you reply to this you can let me know and I'll show it to the Reverend Mother.

How is Maeve getting along at school? Does Eddie still drive you and Daddy mad? What is he up to now? Do you ever see Maggie or Ann after Mass? I will write to them after I finish this letter. Have you heard from Peggy since? It was nice meeting her in Dublin the day we bought the uniform. I enjoyed that day a lot. Please write, Mam, and let me know everything. The school is lovely, and honestly I'm happy here. It's wonderful to have the sea so near. On the sunny days it's all blue and dazzling, and on the grey days it's very dark and swollen-looking with white tossing waves bashing off the rocks below the classrooms. Sometimes at night if you look out the window you can see the ships leaving Dun Laoghaire and going over to

England. All the lights are lit on the ships and it's like something in a film.

Please write soon, Mam, and tell Eddie and Maeve to scrawl a few lines. Tell Daddy I was asking for him.

All the best,
Love, Aileen.

PS. By the way, I finished *Wuthering Heights* and it was great.

She didn't tell her mother that *Wuthering Heights* made her think of Stephen Rodgers. It made her think of him so much that sometimes, when the foghorns were sounding at Lambay Island and over at Howth and the Kish Lighthouse, she lay awake thinking of him, going over in her mind every single minute of the lovely day she had spent fishing with him near the weir.

Dear Ann,

It's about time I put pen to paper to write to you. I'm also writing to Maggie now, so if I forget to tell one of you something I'll surely remember it for the other one.

The school is situated near the sea – in fact, not near but right on it. Sometimes I play games and persuade myself I'm on a big boat, because if you look out the dorm windows you'd honestly think you were.

Anyway I persuade myself I'm going away to foreign places with all my bags packed and I'm going to have a great time. I have made lots of friends, but my best friend here is a girl called Niamh Turley from Skerries, North Dublin. She's small and funny and has asked me to visit her house when we get Saturday off. I hope I'll get permission, because she has three brothers and a boat and lives near the sea.

Tell me, Ann, how are you getting on in the secondary in Ross? Do you like it? What do you think of all the different teachers for the different subjects? It's a change not to be looking at the same old face. Remember how sick we got of old Master Casey in St Joseph's National? Most of my teachers are nuns, except for two lay teachers. One of them has a daughter in the school – a day pupil and she's a right brainbox and everyone says her mother is ramming her with education all night long. By the way, some of them call me a culchie but I don't think they mean it in any bad way – it's just slagging.

Tell me, has anything exciting happened in the parish of Coola since I left? Have you seen Stephen Rodgers? Have you heard any more gossip about him? It's not that I'm that interested, it's because of what we know.

At that stage Aileen crossed her fingers and asked God to forgive her lie, because she was very interested. Sometimes she wondered if there was anyone in Tulla that really interested her except Stephen.

Maggie, this letter will be the same as the one to Ann. The school is a fine building situated almost in the sea. It's marvellous to see the boats go by, so different from Coola where we never saw anything. Every Thursday evening all the little yachts go out in sailing races. They look like white butterflies on the water, particularly when there's no wind. Dun Laoghaire is only a a short distance away. On Saturday evenings we're allowed out for the afternoon. It's a sort of holiday town with small cafés with windows full of lovely cakes, and a lot of people bustling around shopping. An awful lot of people go there to get the boat to England. You'd always know them, they look sort of sad and have shabby suitcases with them.

I have made a few friends but my very best friend is Niamh Turley, who is from North Dublin. But Dublin is so big that the place she's from, Skerries, is so far away she might as well be from a different town. She's asked me to visit her some Saturday soon. She has three brothers and they live by the sea and it should be interesting.

I'll tell you all about it in my next letter. Write soon and tell me all about school and anything else interesting you might hear. I'll be home for Snap-apple Night – they call it Hallowe'en here – anyway I'll be home and I'm looking forward to seeing everybody.

Your fond friend, Aileen.

Chapter Seven

There was no noise except the binging sound of the milk as it hit the side of the well-scoured aluminium bucket. Denis MacMahon, well used to this daily exercise, moved with dexterity from one swollen udder to the next. He liked the peace and quiet of the milking shed, particularly when he was alone with the docile, accepting animals standing patiently during the twice-daily ritual. With his fair head resting on the shiny flank of the two-year-old Clover, christened by his daughter Aileen way back, his thoughts went away and memories came flooding in from nowhere. Normally a hard-working unimaginative man who went about his day content and at peace with himself, he was happy with his wife Mary and his three fine children, and the way things were going on the farm. In a year or two he wouldn't have to do the milking – he hoped to invest in one of the milking machines and maybe sometime in the future he'd have an up-to-the-minute milking parlour, which to his mind was one of the great advantages of rural electrification.

Maybe it was because his fortieth birthday was coming up that he felt restless – or maybe it was because it was the end of September, and it had been the end of September when his dream had crashed all those years ago.

He had loved her – he probably had loved her more than he had ever loved anything or anybody in his life. Before going to meet her he used to try to think up nice flowery words to say to her, so that she might listen and be impressed and not be so restless and gay and funny, like a dancing sunbeam that he couldn't hold, couldn't pin down, couldn't own. She was so beautiful, with thick, dark, blue-black hair and big eyes. Once, when he had kissed her after the dance on a bright June night, he had told her that her eyes were navy, the colour of his Sunday suit. She had thrown back her head and laughed and then kissed him whispering, 'God, Denis MacMahon, I do love you – honestly I do. But not the way you want me to love you.

You're too good for me – solid, dependable. I want someone like myself, not someone good like you. I want someone to sort of – fascinate me.'

'You're cracked,' he had said, taking her in his arms again. She had lain there, her dark head against his thumping heart, allowing him to kiss the top of her head again and again.

Really he had known that he could never satisfy her and could never hope to win her as his wife and the mother of his children. Teresa Rodgers ran away with a man the following September, and rumour had it that he was a traveller, a roaming gypsy. Maybe this young man had captured the beautiful, restless creature and maybe he had given her everything her peculiar nature clamoured for. Maybe he had even – what was it she had said? ah – fascinated her. Denis MacMahon would never know if he had or hadn't – he knew only what he had heard, that she had died giving birth to a son somewhere in the west of Ireland. And all dreams of a match between Denis MacMahon, eldest son of Dick MacMahon, and Teresa, only daughter of Tom Rodgers, were over – dried, arid dreams in the dust.

'Denis.' Mary's voice woke him from his daydreams – dreams he hadn't entertained for a long time.

'We got a letter from Aileen. From the school. I left it inside on the table for you so you can read it with your cup of tea. She seems very happy, and the school is a grand novelty for her. Anyway, I know we did the right thing sending her there – she'll meet the right people. I know she will.'

'I don't know about that, Mary. She's a sensible girl, and sure there wasn't much wrong with the girls she knew up to now.'

Mary sighed. She loved her man with a possessive love; she wanted to protect him and keep at bay from anything that might hurt or upset him in any way. But he had no imagination – she knew that he just lived down the days, solidly working and going about his business providing a good living for herself and their children. She was still grateful to God and His blessed mother that she had caught the eye of the fair-haired young man at the dance on Saint Stephen's night in Ross. Denis MacMahon had been a catch – a great catch – and they had done a steady line after that and married three years later. Mary O'Regan from the Glen of Aherlow in County

Tipperary had been no beauty. She had been staying with her aunt for a few days over the Christmas because her aunt had been ill with pneumonia and she had gone to give her a hand. She'd never have known, the day she had reluctantly agreed to spend Christmas away from home, that her reward would be everything she had wanted: a handsome young farmer with a sizable farm. She had heard some rumour during their courtship that he had a hankering for someone else. It was after they were married in Nenagh, with a fine wedding breakfast in O'Meara's Hotel, that she had learned it had been Teresa Rodgers from over the way in Tulla.

Dismissing her thoughts, she came back to the letter from Aileen. 'Sure I know there was nothing wrong with her friends – sure you couldn't meet nicer than young Ann or Maggie. But she's thirteen now, and if you have eyes in your head you can see she's very attractive. All the young fellows around would be eyeing her any day now. And if Eddie hadn't told me, I'd never have known she had spent a whole day at the river with that Stephen Rodgers. I wouldn't want him for her now, would I? And he's as big as a grown man.' She looked at her husband, her eyes narrowed. She wondered what he'd say. But she couldn't read a single thing in his open, honest face.

'I don't know what gets into the mind of women. She's only a child, and what was so wrong with her going fishing for a day with her brother and another young lad? And Stephen Rodgers is hard-working, according to Joe, and there's good stock in him – sure we know that.'

'*Some* good stock, Denis, but there's bad blood in him too – sure the birds in the bushes know that.'

Their conversation was interrupted by the spiky head of Eddie sticking around the shed door.

'I can't find me coat, Mam – and 'tis goin' to piss rain.'

His mother flung around and ran to wallop him. 'Where in the name of all that's holy did you hear language like that, you tipper, you?' she shouted. She must have got him a sharp clip, because Denis could hear his son yelping as he ran off to find the missing coat. He smiled as he went back to his milking.

The young ragamuffin Eddie was always in trouble. There was never a bit of peace with him, but then again where would they be without him? At least the incident and the episode with Eddie had brought him back to earth. Teresa Rodgers receded to the back of his mind. But he knew she'd come back again. He was never sure when, he was never prepared, but as sure as God made little apples she'd be back, dancing through his dreams. And if a miracle happened and she didn't, wouldn't a glimpse of her young handsome son bring her back? The turn of the head, the shape of the eyes, the look of the mouth were the very same. But the sparkle, the gaiety, the laughter were missing. There was a serious, grave look about the lad. Sure then again, why wouldn't there be, living with old Tom and only Joe Power and Máire Ryan to bring a bit of relief?

Mary busied herself tidying up around the kitchen, relieved that Eddie and Maeve had left for school. She sighed, thinking of the run-in with Eddie. She wondered where the young rascal had got that guttersnipe language from. She supposed it was the school. Yes, it had to be. For the umpteenth time she was so glad that her eldest daughter was going to that fine school situated at the edge of the sea in the posh area of Dalkey. In years to come the expenditure would be justified, when Aileen turned out to be a refined young lady, maybe superior to the girls around. Mary filled the black kettle, her heart lifting at the thought, and put it on the blackened hook over the fire. As she sat and turned the wheel, she watched the flames leap and knew it would be mere minutes before the kettle would sing. She smiled, reminding herself again that her beloved unimaginative husband didn't understand the importance of their daughter going to the right school, mixing with the right people. Sure, poor Denis didn't see beyond his nose or the task of the hour.

The kettle started to hum and Mary smiled with content-ment as she made the tea. She was happy in her ignorance concerning her unimaginative husband. She had no idea that Denis at times looked inwardly to a desire-filled time when the solid foundation of his life was shaken by a lovely girl whom he could never possess.

The Leaving Certificate, their position on the hurling team, their rural upbringing and the easy rapport between Stephen Rodgers and Richie Casey bonded them together during their last year at school. They were always together during lunch time, before school, and after school before they went their separate ways.

One glorious late September day, as they cycled away from the school, Richie asked, 'Would the oul lad, your grandfather, let you come and stay with us for a weekend? We have a bit of a hardware shop in the village and I might have to give a hand on Saturday morning. But then we'd be free and we'd go to Waterford and look at the birds outside Woolworths. My brother might get the van and sure we could go to the hop in the Olympia. I believe 'tis mighty. What do you say?'

'I don't know,' Stephen answered. 'Although I can't see why he'd refuse. Most of the work is done on the farm, 'tis only the milking and there's Joe for that. I'll tell you what, I'll ask him – and I'll let you know tomorrow.'

'Grand.'

'And thanks, Richie – it's nice to be asked.'

That evening, when the tea things were cleared up and Richie had begrudgingly decided that he'd better do battle next with Shakespeare's rotten *Hamlet,* he approached his mother.

'Ma, would you mind if I asked a fella here for the weekend? Stephen Rodgers – you know, the fella I hang around with at school.'

His mother looked up from her browse of the *Far East* magazine her daughter Noreen brought home from school.

'Stephen Rodgers? That's the lad living with his grandfather over in Tulla?'

'That's right.'

'Is that the gorgeous black-haired fellow I saw in Ross?' said Noreen. 'Julia McEvoy pointed him out – her mother was a great friend of his mother, and there's a fierce story there altogether.'

Her own mother glared at her. 'I hope you have more to do than listen to gossip from a busybody like Julia McEvoy.' She looked at Richie. 'And tell me, son, why do you want to bring him here?'

'Because I like him and because I think he has a terrible life with that oul crank of a grandfather. That's why, Ma – not another reason in the world.'

'Well, I don't see why not. I'll mention it to your father, although I know what he'll say.'

Later that evening Richie's mother told him that Stephen was welcome to come and stay for the weekend.

'We'd better give your room a good scouring, get all those dirty hurling socks from under the bed – you can't have the fellow fumed out coming from a fine farm to a place over a shop.'

'Thanks, Ma,' Richie said. 'Sure he'll think he's on 42nd Street New York. A shop in the main street will be high life for him – coming from the back of beyond.'

'God, I'll have to do something with the pimples,' Noreen said, 'I look like a leper in Molokai.'

She was reading about Father Damien, the Belgian priest who had given his life to the lepers in Molokai, and secretly wondered if her pimples could possibly be the onset of leprosy. She had examined them in the mirror and thought the current bunch were very suspicious-looking. She had come to the part where Father Damien had put his feet into boiling water and, feeling no sensation, had known then he had fallen victim to the disease.

The evening before, in front of the mirror on her dressing table, Noreen had pinched her chin so viciously that she had yelped with pain. He mother had shouted up, 'What's wrong? Another mouse, I suppose.' The field mice were coming into the house now, and one or two had been seen scooting across the kitchen. Noreen was terrified of them, and when her mother had shouted her question she had answered, 'Yeah, I think so.' But it wasn't a field mouse this time, it was her leprous chin, and now Stephen Rodgers was coming. She'd absolutely love to look beautiful when he was there. Maybe he'd even notice her. After all, she was fifteen going on sixteen, only a year younger than Richie, or Stephen for that matter. Say if he did notice her, wouldn't she have a right boast for Julia McEvoy, who thought she was the bee's knees, and who actually had had the audacity on one occasion to ask her did she think she looked a bit like Debbie Reynolds?

Stephen broached the subject of the weekend after tea. Máire Ryan was still there, tidying up, and Joe was sitting on the settle, sucking his pipe before going home. Stephen looked at his grandfather, who was reading last Sunday's paper.

'Do you think I could go away for a bit this weekend? My friend Richie Casey asked me to stay in his place till Sunday.'

He looked at his grandfather, who had lifted his head and was looking at him, his face expressionless.

'What would you be wantin' to do that for? Stay away from your own bed?'

'Because he asked me, and because most of the work is done and it's easy here now. And then again, I'd like to go.' Stephen looked at his grandfather and the thought came that he rarely addressed him as 'Grandfather' or 'Granda'. It seemed like years since he had called him anything.

'I can't stop you if you want to go, can I?'

Joe removed the pipe from his mouth and spat into the fire. 'Ah sure, Tom, sure we were all young wance.'

Máire was quiet as she tidied away the washing, folding the sheets into a pile in readiness for ironing when she'd come on Friday. She was standing behind Tom and, looking at Stephen, she gave him a big wink.

'Ah, sure go, if you want. Go if you want,' his grandfather said.

'Thanks, Grandfather.' The word slipped out but Stephen wasn't sorry. The old man was getting old now, and even if he lived another decade or more, Stephen wouldn't be there to see it. As soon as he finished school he planned to work on the farm for a few more years and then off with him to Dublin or London to earn the fare to Australia. But for now he was content enough. He knew he'd have to get his Leaving Certificate at least; it would be something to prove he had finished secondary school.

He was looking forward to a weekend at Richie's. He was surprised at his feeling of anticipation. He rarely experienced a feeling like it – a childish joy that something pleasant was going to happen. In fact, he hadn't felt anything like that since the hot summer morning he had made himself some bacon sandwiches in preparation for the day's fishing with Aileen and young Eddie MacMahon. It was strange how every single second of that day, even the ignominy with which it had ended, was etched forever on his mind.

Later that evening, as he locked up the hens and the ducks away from the prowling fox, Stephen wondered if he'd see her again. He wondered if she would be all changed, not as childish and shy as she had been before she went to the boarding school in Dublin.

*

58

On the first Saturday in October, the Reverend Mother gave permission for Aileen to spend the weekend with Niamh Turley and her family. Niamh's father collected them in his Ford car shortly after breakfast. Aileen was excited about every aspect of the day that lay ahead. Putting aside the now all-too familiar uniform, she put on her new blue jumper and pleated skirt. Niamh had told her so much about her three brothers – Aidan, who was nineteen and a great sailor and a member of the Skerries off-shore lifeboat, David, the middle one, who was seventeen and doing his Leaving Cert, and the baby of the family, eleven-year-old Jimmy, who was the same age as her brother Eddie.

Driving away from Dalkey, Niamh coaxed her father to go through Dun Laoghaire, 'So that we can see something – anything.'

He indulged her, but Georges Street, the main street, was quiet due to the early hour, and the few shoppers that were about had their heads bent against the gusting wind.

They drove along the coast road to the city Niamh's father commenting on the forecast. 'Would you believe we're in for a right storm tonight, force ten to twelve? You didn't pick the best weekend to visit.' He grinned, looking at the the young, fair-haired pretty girl that was Niamh's 'brand-new best friend', according to her letters. 'I hope you won't be blown away.'

Aileen smiled. 'I doubt it, I'm not that frail. We had a fierce wind down our way in August. Do you remember? It was the end of some hurricane that started in America.' Aileen found herself telling them about the terrible night of wind and rain, and the knocking on the door, and the two tinkers from the campsite with their little girl. 'It was terrible. She was all burning up with a sickness. My dad got out the van and drove them to the nearest hospital, but he was too late. The little child died. It was terrible.'

'Aye,' Mr Turley commented, 'I don't know how they live out there in all weathers under canvas. How can they survive? How can small children survive?'

As they left the city behind and went out the Malahide road to Skerries, Niamh was prattling away, all excited now at the prospect of seeing her mother and her brothers, her very own dog, Lucky, and her stray cat, Bubbles. Aileen half-listened, the other half of her mind remembering the terrible night the little child had died. She recalled how she had lain in bed thinking of Stephen Rodgers and wondering if his mother had lived on a campsite, wondering if he, as a tiny baby, had spent the first few weeks of his life under canvas.

If his mother, who had been young and beautiful, hadn't died, Stephen would never have been brought to his grand-father's to live. It was well she had, because if she hadn't, I would never have got to know him. I'm committing a terrible sin, she thought, glad that she had asked Jesus to forgive her for the confusion of her thoughts. She usen't be confused. Maybe she was confused because of her age – she had read something about the effect of hormones in her mother's *Woman's Weekly*. About how hormones affected you in your teenage years and in your middle years. Yes, that was what was wrong with her. A sort of hormonal trouble.

'Will you stop daydreaming – we're here. We're free, we're free of school for a whole weekend – wake up,' Niamh said.

Mrs Turley was a lovely woman – she looked little more than a girl. She had short bouncy hair close to her head, and she actually wore a trousers, with a leather belt around her slim waist, and a skinny, polo-necked jumper.

'Hello, Aileen – Niamh told us so much about you. She said you were the prettiest girl in the school, and now I know she's right.'

Aileen felt the familiar blush rise up from somewhere. It always happened when people said nice things about her. She wished they wouldn't; she hated compliments. She smiled shyly and shook her head in an effort to dispel such notions.

Helen Turley, guessing she had embarrassed the girl, said, 'Come on up and leave your bag in your room.' She put her arm through Aileen's, chatting non-stop. 'You're sharing with this messer and the room is topsy-turvy– but I know you won't mind.'

Aileen marvelled at her lovely easy manner. Her own mother was so different – so earnest, fussy and – and – was it old-fashioned? Yes, that was it. Her mother was a farmer's daughter and very old-fashioned in her ways, whereas Niamh's mother looked great – a bit like a model.

As she went upstairs she wondered what her brothers would be like. She hoped they liked her and wouldn't think her a little culchie kid, and her coming more of a nuisance than anything else.

Niamh was mad anxious to show Aileen the sights and to take her down to the small harbour and the sailing boats.

'Most of them are out of the water for the winter – ours is called *The Survivor* and it's in the boathouse. Come on down and we'll have a look.'

Mrs Turley insisted on them having tea and scones before leaving the house. When they were finished she told them that dinner was at one-thirty and to be back on time. As they ran down the road to the sea, the wind, already rising, made their eyes water and lifted Aileen's hair, now free from the plaits which she wore at school.

'Hey,' Aileen shouted, 'where are your brothers?'

'Oh, them,' Niamh answered. 'They could be anywhere. Aidan is probably down with the boats – he's working in town now but is a lifeboat member. David is probably playing a match, and Jimmy the nightmare is out doing no good – he's always in trouble.'

Aileen smiled. 'So is our Eddie. When you come to stay with us you'll meet him. He's a terror – he even curses.'

Niamh nodded in conspiratorial agreement. The pair had so much in common in ways, even though they came from totally different backgrounds – Aileen from a farming community, and she from a seafaring family.

'There's something I want to tell you,' Aileen said. 'You won't laugh or anything? You won't call me a culchie?'

'No, I won't, you dope – what is it?'

'I've never been near a boat and I've rarely seen the sea except a few days when we went to Tramore, and of course from the school window. So don't expect me to jump in and out of boats and to be all seafaring and stuff.'

Niamh laughed.

'No, I won't. Anyway, if you want to know, I've never been near a cow – I don't think I've ever seen a bull, and I know nothing about chickens, ducks, geese and things.'

'Okay,' Aileen laughed, her words nearly taken away by the wind. 'You don't laugh at me today because I'm thick about boats, and when you come to me I won't laugh about you.'

*

Aileen was starting to enjoy herself now more than she could have imagined. Down at the slip near the water's edge she met Aidan, Niamh's oldest brother, and he was so nice and easy that she felt her shyness slip away.

'Look, you two,' he grinned. 'I'd love to take you out for a run in *The Survivor*, but the wind is rising and ye'd both be sick as dogs, and neither of you would forgive me for spoiling your weekend.'

'Ah Aidan, come on,' Niamh begged. 'We won't be sick, I promise, and Aileen was never out in a boat. She lives on a farm with cows, bulls, ducks and things?'

'I could think of worse things,' Aidan smiled. 'But I'll tell you what – I'll give you both a run tomorrow if the wind drops.'

They wandered off, Aileen more than happy to forgo the run in the boat. She was nervous of the grey, heaving sea and didn't fancy being sick all over her new jacket with Niamh's big brother looking on.

Walking along the coast road, Niamh linked arms with her and Aileen felt a glow and thought how lucky she was to have made such a great friend, particularly when she was so dull herself, and from the country where so little happened. The girls talked non-stop about the school and the nuns and the other girls, Niamh giving out about snobby Liz O'Brien from Kildare.

'She thinks she's a great one, just because her father is a horse breeder and rich. Did you ever hear anything like the way she goes on and on about her father going to America all the time? God, she's a bloody pain. And did you ever see the way the other dopes all kowtow to her because of who she is?'

'Well, one thing is for sure. They won't be kowtowing to me because of my father,' Aileen told her.

'Tell me what it's like living on a farm.'

'Ah, it's all right. There's heaps of space and fresh air and stuff. And you have to work like a slave – at least my dad and mam have. They're up early for the milking and all the chores and things. Sometimes Dad is up all night when a cow is calving, often Mam too. Then they just stay up and go on just as if they had a night's sleep.'

Niamh was fascinated. 'Is it true you see all the animals – you know, *doing* things? All that mating and stuff, then all the little animals being born, and it doesn't take a feather out of you?'

Aileen, puzzled at first, burst out laughing. 'Sure you see nothing else since you were a baby but the cows brought to the bull and the mare to the stallion, and 'tis all part of farming.'

'Then,' Niamh asked in wonder, 'do you all know about babies and men and things since you were young? Do you all talk about it as if it were nothing unusual? Do you?'

'Oh Lord no – it stops at the animals. There's never a whisper about anything like that. My mother would die before she'd tell you anything like that. She didn't even tell me about periods, and got all flustered when it happened.'

'Imagine,' Niamh said, almost relieved that she wasn't missing out on a lifestyle where everyone talked openly and loudly about all the things that were taboo for most families.

They walked along through the gusting wind, both silent, thinking their own thoughts, when a shout disturbed them. Niamh glanced up.

'Here's our David – like I said, he was playing a match.'

Aileen saw a brown tousle-haired boy cycling towards them, his head bent, pedalling against the wind. There was a basket in front of his bike and she could plainly see a pair of football boots sticking out. When he came near he alighted and grinned at them both.

'Well, look what the wind blew in,' he said.

'I know you knew I was coming home with my friend,' Niamh told him haughtily. 'This is Aileen MacMahon, and you'd better be polite.'

David gave a mocking bow to his sister and, looking at Aileen, gave a little appreciative whistle. 'Hello. Don't know how you put up with her – but it's great to meet you.'

His brown eyes met hers and then seemed to roam all over her. Aileen felt the old familiar blush, but somehow managed to mutter 'Hello,' and then added what was customary down in her part of the world: 'I'm very pleased to meet you.'

He gave a mock salute and then mounted his bike and cycled off. 'I'll see you at home,' he shouted over his shoulder.

Aileen thought how nice and easy and relaxed he was, not gauche and shy like the country fellows were. But all the Turleys were like that, easy, relaxed and talkative – maybe it was something to do with the sea air; maybe it made them all so breezy and bright. Maybe it blew away all the shadows and inhibitions and things that rural people had locked inside them. She found herself smiling at the thought.

'What are you grinning at? You're like a Cheshire cat,' Niamh said.

'Nothing – honestly, nothing at all.'

Niamh glanced at the black clouds piling in from the east. 'We'd better go home,' she decided, 'it's going to be a fierce night. We'd better fly before the rain.'

On Saturdays the Turleys ate the main meal of the day at six o'clock. Everyone was seated in the big kitchen around a big wooden table, waiting for the giant casserole to be served. Aileen had never seen such a big dish, or such a variety of things in what looked like a stew. The taste was as good as the appetising aroma and she found herself trying to remember what was in it so that she could tell her mother, who made the most unimaginative stew. As well as the meat, cut in small brown chunky pieces, there were carrots, mushrooms, green spring onions, little bits of celery and green things she didn't recognise. She was ravenous and ate every bit, and afterwards there was tart and cream followed by mugs of tea.

When the meal was over, Mrs Turley asked about Aileen's family and how old her brother and sister were.

Niamh's father joked with her, saying, 'Sure I can understand why your father sent you to boarding school. He wanted to keep you away from all the young bloods down in that part of the world.'

Aileen blushed again and shook her head, and suddenly the peaceful scene was shattered by a loud terrifying bang. She jumped up, startled, and noticed they were all still sitting, waiting. The second loud bang came and Aileen, terrified, wanted to know if it was a bomb. They were all standing now and Aidan was running to the door with David at his heels, yelling, 'They might be shorthanded – they might need me –'

'What is it?' Aileen asked, her eyes dilated in fear.

'It's the maroons, love – someone is in trouble out there. They sent up signals for a lifeboat.'

'Can we go down and see it going out?' Niamh asked. 'Come on, Dad– let us go.'

'Oh, all right – all right, but for God's sake be careful.'

Outside there were voices on the wind as people ran down towards the slip. The two girls rushed down there themselves to see Aidan Turley there in his yellow storm gear. Two other men were there also, stamping and impatient, their eyes raking the road, obviously waiting for more crewmen. Aileen could see that David was already geared up.

'Oh God, will he go out in a boat in the storm?' she whispered.

'He will, if no one else turns up.'

Suddenly there was the sound of the throbbing engines of the lifeboat. Standing in the small crowd which had gathered, their voices almost drowning out the throb of the lifeboat, the girls watched as the boat pulled away from the pier and was instantly hit by a huge wave that washed over all of them.

'Oh, my God, Niamh,' Aileen whispered, 'they'll be drenched – they'll die of the cold.'

'No, you goose – they're used to it, although it's only David's second time.'

They shivered in the wind and the rain – darkness was already down – and through the fitful gusts there was the occasional throb of the departing lifeboat.

'Who's in trouble? Have ye heard?' a woman asked a man standing beside her.

'A young couple pulled out this afternoon with a few pots. Absolute madness on a day like this.'

Aileen, shivering with fear for the safety of Niamh's brothers, whispered, 'What kind of pots would they have, and why would you bring pots out in a boat?'

Niamh laughed. Aileen could see her white teeth in the darkness. 'Oh, you culchie, you – not pots like saucepans. Lobster pots – sort of traps.'

'Oh.' Aileen nodded, thinking to herself that it was a strange world where people lived such different lives doing such different things. She thought of David and Aidan and the other men looking for a young couple who were out looking for – was it lobsters Niamh had called them? She found herself trembling. 'Will they be all right?'

'Oh, they will – I've seen them go out in worse than this. Come on, we'll wait at home.'

For what seemed like an age, they waited by the lighted range, Niamh's mother calmly knitting a heavy jumper for

Aidan, her father smoking his pipe and reading the paper. Jimmy had insisted on staying up to wait for his brothers' homecoming. Aileen was amazed at their calm – once again she found herself wondering whether people who lived by the unpredictable sea developed these traits, knew how to handle this patient, stoic waiting.

'Are they worried?' she asked Niamh in a whisper.

'They're pretty worried but they won't pretend. They're like that. They've always been like that.'

It was after midnight that the word broke that the lifeboat was seen coming ashore. To Aileen's astonishment everyone in the house stood up and wordlessly searched for coats, jackets and hats, as if preparing to go somewhere.

'Where are you all going?' Aileen asked.

'Down to the harbour – we always do, love,' Niamh's mother explained. 'We go to see was the rescue successful.'

Aileen joined the rushed preparations and soon they were outside in the howling wind, almost running down the hill to the harbour. Other people had gathered in the dark, and they could hear their muffled voices discussing the young foolhardy couple who had put to sea in such appalling conditions. Through the gloom the throb of the lifeboat came fitfully, and Aileen saw the green and red lights way out in the mist, heaving and dipping and sometimes disappearing altogether.

'God, Niamh, they'll never get in safe.' She nudged her friend, her voice shaky and tremulous as she stared into the blackness.

'Don't you worry – it's a duck pond in here in comparison with what it was like out there.'

Soon the lifeboat was running alongside the harbour wall, and men walked over and helped the crew tie up and alight. Aidan Turley was shouting something, and someone leaned down and helped out a blanket-clad figure. More helping hands followed and soon David Turley was there with them in his yellow oilskins. Others surged forth, and the girl with the blanket around her shoulders was gently placed on the ground.

'Is she dead?' Aileen was aghast.

But before Niamh could give any opinion on the girl's condition, they heard the shrill alarm of an ambulance. The ambulance attendants alighted and it seemed mere seconds before the half-dead girl was placed on the stretcher and whisked away. Aileen watched it all in a daze: the slashing rain, the oil-skinned yellow-clad crew members, Aidan grim-faced and silent as he tied up the boat… Even young David looked older, and little Jimmy had lost all his jauntiness.

As they sat over steaming cups of hot cocoa back in the house, Aidan told how terrible it had been, how visibility had been down to nothing, how they had come across the wreck of the small boat way up on the rocky coastline, with the young girl clinging on and no sign of her companion.

'We'll search tomorrow but there's no hope we'll get him – no one could live in conditions like that.'

'Oh God, Niamh, will we ever forget it?' Aileen asked. 'Will we?'

They were back in school, lying in the now-dark dormitory, whispering in undertones as they went over the events of the day before. A bright windswept Sunday, with the sun shining brightly on a blue heaving sea, with the white horses whipped high and frothy.

The lifeboat had gone out at first light and three hours later they had found the body of a young man in his early twenties washed up near Downey Cove. The place was abuzz with the tragedy. How the couple, who had taken up lobster fishing and who regularly went out at weekends, had misjudged the weather conditions on that day was a mystery to everyone.

'I wonder will she even live without him. Will she?'

'Oh God, wasn't it fierce, Niamh –?' Aileen almost sobbed.

Niamh started to sob quietly too, and suddenly she jumped out of her bed and crept in beside Aileen. The two young girls lay close together, the heat from their bodies somehow helping to remove the chill and the sadness from the terrible tragedy they had witnessed on their brief weekend away.

'We'll never forget it, that I know,' Aileen sobbed. 'And everyone said they were so much in love – always holding hands and stuff.'

'I know,' Niamh whispered. 'When we're old and grey we'll remember it and talk about it. No matter where we'll be, you'll always be my best friend – promise?'

'I promise.'

'And if you're in trouble ever, I'll help you,' Niamh

promised. 'And if I'm in trouble, you'll help me. Promise.'

'I promise,' Aileen said softly.

Niamh crept back to her own bed.

Aileen lay awake in the dark. From somewhere the tears came again. They came like a great well, flowing and unstoppable. They ran down her face and across her cheek and into her blonde tousled hair. She remembered the bedraggled couple who had come in from the night with the dying child. She remembered her thoughts on that occasion when she had lain in another bed in the peaceful farmhouse almost in a different world. How she had thought of Stephen Rodgers, and wondered had he too been neglected as a tiny baby before finding refuge with a bad-tempered, begrudging grandfather. She thought of him now and then, and was filled with the strangest sensation. She didn't know what it was – was it longing? Could someone as young as she was want someone like Stephen Rodgers to hold her, to kiss her, to – to –? Oh God, it surely was a sin to even think of him like that. She would go to Confession and confess her bad thoughts and desires.

In her half-awake half-asleep state, his dark unsmiling face came, and the memory brought more tears. She found herself crying for him, he who was so handsome but so unloved. For his young mother who had run away with a traveller who had come on a summer's night. She found herself crying for the young woman who had been carted away half-dead, not knowing that her husband had already drowned, his body bashed against the rocks. She cried until there were no more tears left. Her last thought before she fell into an exhausted sleep was the promise she and Niamh had made to each other. That they'd be very best friends for life, and if they were ever in trouble they would help each other. Somehow the thought was consoling and she fell into some measure of a peaceful sleep.

Chapter Eight

Stephen put two clean shirts and his pyjamas, razor and a toothbrush into a shabby zipped bag Máire had found for him. The simple little exercise highlighted the fact that he had never done anything like this before. He had never been away anywhere before.

The plan was that he and Richie would cycle to Brennanstown on Friday afternoon, and when the weekend was over, Richie would accompany him halfway home.

Stephen was looking forward to the visit; he knew Richie had a sister, Noreen, who, according to Richie, was a scourge and a misery. He knew they had a hardware shop in the main street of the village, and that their family had run the shop for generations. Richie had often complained that his life wouldn't be a bag of laughs when he left school. Running a hardware shop in Brennanstown, the highlight of his life would be selling a pot of paraffin to old Mrs Barron for her Tilley lamp.

After school they cycled all the way, Richie all chat about what they'd do and who they might see.

'And maybe we'll pick up an oul court after the dance in Graigue-na-Manna.'

'Are we going to a dance in Graigue-na-Manna?'

'Oh, we are, so we are. The youth club there runs a dance every Saturday night and the band isn't bad and the place is usually jammed.'

Stephen was silent. He didn't want Richie to know he had never been to a dance before, had never danced with a girl, had never kissed a girl. Well, he had never kissed a girl voluntarily and with desire.

He remembered what he considered a peculiar experience last spring. He and Joe and his grandfather had been to a fair in Waterford, and afterwards they had gone into a pub on Ballybricken Hill. The place had been packed and his grandfather had treated him to a glass of stout. There was some wheeling and dealing going on between his grandfather and another farmer about a young mare, so the hours had slipped away and Joe had surreptitiously bought Stephen another two glasses of stout. He remembered that, just before they were away, a small door had opened up at the far end of the pub and three women had come out. One of them, maybe in her late twenties, had a satin blouse that strained over her full breasts. She'd worn bright orange lipstick and had given off a distinct smell of whiskey. The women had spent half of the day in the snug and were well on the way as they made their way out of the crowded pub. Stephen had been standing at the door waiting for his grandfather and Joe when this woman had bumped off him. Her slightly bloodshot eyes had taken him in. 'Beggin' your pardon,' she had muttered. Then, without the slightest warning, she had flung her arms around him and pressed herself up against him in the dark hallway, and kissed him sloppily on the mouth. She had then looked at him and whispered, 'Jasus boy, you're some looker,' before staggering away after her noisy companions.

He had been shaken and surprised and even now, cycling along the October sunlit road with Richie, he could smell the cheap perfume and recall the bright orange lipstick that had been still visible on his hand when he had come home later that night.

Mrs Casey couldn't do enough for Stephen. She fussed over him and told him she'd love to have given him a room for himself, but unfortunately he'd have to share with that raga-muffin Richie. But she had given him the good bed and Richie would have to put up with a bed-chair they used when they had guests.

'Don't worry, Missus Casey,' Stephen told her. 'Everything will be great – I'm not used to gracious living where I come from.'

He completely disarmed her. As she fussed getting a high tea with cold meat, tomatoes, crusty homemade bread and a rich fruit cake, she wondered what all the veiled gossip had been about. A fine handsome fellow like Stephen Rodgers had the distinct look of breeding on him. All that faraway gossip about his mother – the only daughter of Tom Rodgers, a well-to-do farmer, who, by all accounts, had run away with a tinker and had a child for him – seemed remote and unreal now. As she looked at the broad-shouldered young man doing justice to her meal she thought how stupid all the prejudice was.

*

The following day they woke up to the wind and rain. Richie, listening to the downpour clattering down the gutters into the street outside, said, 'That puts paid to the Casey outdoor display, Stephen.'

Stephen made exaggerated purring sounds and stretched himself to his full length in his comfortable bed, grinning at his friend on the bed-chair.

'And what might the Casey outdoor display be?'

'Buckets, shovels, spades, tools, paints and anything and everything that an unsuspecting farmer might need goes out on path every Saturday so that the Caseys can eat. But the rain put the kibosh on that, so I'd stay in bed if I had a bed to stay in.'

He jumped out of the narrow bed-chair and stretched out his hand for his clothes, but like a flash turned around and tore the eiderdown and sheet from Stephen's bed. Stephen jumped out and they fell on each other, rolling around the floor in good-humoured horse-play.

Suddenly the door opened and Noreen's head appeared. 'For God's sake will ye stop the racket,' she shouted.

Stephen had Richie pinned to the wall and, hearing her voice, he dropped his arms and was suddenly swamped with embarrassment with her nearness. He had never seen a girl at such close quarters in a bedroom, and he nearly half-naked too, with his pyjama top torn off by Richie.

Her eyes seemed to roam over him, taking in the broad shoulders and the dark hair already spouting on his chest.

'Out,' Richie ordered. 'No women allowed in here. Not for the next thirty hours anyway.'

'I wouldn't be next or near ye if ye hadn't made a racket,' she sniffed as she banged the door.

Stephen sank down on the bed, still discomfited. 'I'm not used to girls – you know, in the same house. It must be strange.'

'It isn't a bit strange. I grew up with three of them. One is married, one works in Dublin, and Noreen's the youngest. It's not strange, it's a complete pain in the arse having girls wandering around all over the place.' Richie mournfully looked out of the window at the torrential rain. The main street in Brennanstown was narrow and he could see that the Post Office across the road had lost some slates off the roof. They were lying broken on the footpath, and an old woman, head bent and protected by a shawl, was picking her way through them into the Post Office.

'There's old Missus White in for her old-age pension. When

71

she gets it she'll spend half the day in Barry's snug.'

Stephen joined him. 'You wouldn't see a thing in Tulla except on Sundays and Mass days.'

'Well, I'll tell you what, we'd better see something tonight at the dance. If this weather doesn't ease up it could be cancelled, and even if it isn't there'll be no chance of a court with the rain pelting down on top of us.' Richie's gloom evaporated slightly with the delicious smell of bacon and eggs that came wafting up the stairs from the kitchen below.

During the morning Stephen helped Richie tidy out the storage sheds, and when his father asked them to deliver paraffin to three elderly customers outside the village, they went gladly. Richie's blue eyes raked the heavens hopefully.

'I hope the dance will be on. And if it is, I hope she'll be there.'

'Who's she?' Stephen asked.

'She's the nicest-looking bird in the place. She's the guard's daughter and her name is Breda Kelly, and I'm hopeful, so I am.'

After they had delivered the oil, they walked to the edge of the village and went down to the bridge. The Barrow was in full spate, running and swirling past the ramparts, the water dark and frothy as it flowed swiftly by.

'Funny thing about rivers,' Stephen said. 'When they're low and dry they're sad but friendlier.'

'Rivers? What are you on about rivers for? I never think of blooming rivers.'

'Ah, that's what comes when you live with old people. You go a bit daft,' Stephen laughed.

They were silent then, Richie wondering would the red-headed Breda Kelly be at the dance and if she was, would she have that blue dress on her with the little square neck where, the last time he danced with her, he had got a glorious, delightful, heart-thumping glimpse of the top of her breasts. He had had only two old-time waltzes with her, but he hadn't been able to get her out of his head for the whole following week.

Stephen was thinking of Aileen MacMahon and the summer's day at the river. He presumed he thought of her so often because he never met any other girls. He was half-hoping he wouldn't think of her this weekend. At least it would be a distraction to go to the dance and see Richie's friends. He wondered would Noreen be there, and her friend Julie.

'Come on.' Richie's voice broke into his thoughts. 'Come on, we'd better get back to Ma – she'll have the dinner ready and she gets mad if we're late.'

Even though the storm hadn't lessened, they heard the dance was still on. Mrs Casey thought they were mad to go out in such weather.

'We'll put on every oilskin in the shop,' Richie consoled her. 'We'll be fine. What would a drop of rain do to two fine fellows like us?'

'I don't know what Stephen's grandfather would think of us letting him out on a night like this,' she fretted.

'Don't worry,' Stephen told her. 'I don't think he'd mind too much.'

Her eyes met Stephen's dark ones for a minute and she felt that maybe it was true – maybe the old man resented him, even hated him, holding him some way responsible for the trouble all the years ago. Her expression softened. 'Go so, and have a great time – sure you're only young once.'

Despite the terrible weather the place was packed. The band was in full swing and in the throes of murdering 'Your Eyes Are the Eyes of a Woman in Love'. The girls, some bright, eager and laughing hysterically, others feigning total indifference, stood at one side of the hall, and the fellows in best suits stood at the other. The floor was wet from their rain-sodden shoes, but few seemed to care or be even notice.

Richie nudged Stephen. 'She's here, and she has the blue dress on her. Look, over near the exit door.'

Stephen saw a slim, red-headed girl with shoulder-length hair talking to a small, plump, dark-haired girl who was obviously her friend. He thought it was nice for Richie to have a girl that interested him. Before his thoughts went down familiar roads, he switched off and saw Richie's sister Noreen and her friend Julie talking to a group of girls not too far away.

The next dance was an old-time waltz and Richie whispered, 'Here goes,' before making a beeline for Breda Kelly.

Stephen, standing alone and uncomfortable, felt all eyes were on him. He walked purposefully towards Noreen Casey and asked her to dance. As he tried to waltz around the floor he stumbled once or twice on the wet patches. Shyly he apologised. She said she didn't care, and chatted brightly about school before spying Richie across the floor. 'He's cracked about her, so he is,' she told Stephen.

Stephen told her he knew that.

'Oh, so he's that cracked about her that he told you already? Are you doing a line with anyone?' Her question was asked lightly.

'No – sure who'd have me?'

His dark eyes held hers and she guessed he wasn't even teasing. He meant it. Was it possible that the tall, broad-shouldered Stephen Rodgers had little or no idea of his impact on girls?

'Sure they'd all have you, so they would.' Her grin was impish – so friendly, so open.

He danced with Noreen twice more, and then with her friend Julia, and when the band tuned up 'Save the Last Dance for Me', he once again took Noreen on to the floor, realising he was enjoying himself more than he had done for a long time.

Stephen and Richie walked home most of the way; the wind was so high it was impossible to cycle. Richie was in high mood because Breda Kelly had told him she would see him the following week at the dance. He had picked up courage and had asked her would she go to the pictures in Ross sometime. She had promised she would.

That night, lying in the comfortable bed and listening to the wind, Stephen couldn't sleep. His mind went back over the evening and he thought of the girls he had danced with. He recalled Noreen and the way the top of her curly head had just come to his chest. Julia was smaller, if anything. His thoughts drifted and he found himself wondering what it would be like to hold Aileen MacMahon in his arms. The top of her blonde head would surely reach to his chin or even above it. As he listened to the howling wind he made up his mind there and then that he'd have to do something about this girl – this girl that was no more than a child. He'd bide his time and wait for her. Wait until she got older and then see if he'd have a chance with her.

He had no idea that she too was lying wide-eyed and awake in storm-lashed Skerries in County Dublin, her young mind saturated with thoughts of him. Had he known, he would have slept easily and peacefully like Richie, and the restless yearning hunger that assailed him from time to time would have been no more.

Chapter Nine

When Mary O'Regan had gone to give her ailing Aunt Lizzy a hand over the Christmas in the early forties, she'd had no idea her good turn would land her the prize of a lifetime – Denis MacMahon. She wasn't particularly pretty. Her hair was more mousy than fair, her blue eyes watered almost non-stop due to a variety of allergies, and she was far too thin. When Aunt Lizzie had insisted that she go to the dance, telling her, 'You must, everyone will be there, sure you wouldn't know who you'd meet. Paddy will see you there and back, and 'tis only a mile down the road,' she had reluctantly agreed.

The place was fairly crowded and she didn't know a single soul. Paddy was hailed heartily by his friends – country lads who stood in their Sunday suits smoking and guffawing, sometimes eyeing the girls, sometimes grinning behind them, making the odd snide remark she could barely hear. She stood near them and when they tossed an odd word at her, she tried to toss one back. She shivered in a pool of terrible isolation and loneliness for three whole dances.

Eventually, whether it was through pity or some other motive, one of Paddy's friends asked her to dance. Light on her feet and with a good ear for music, she allowed herself to be pivoted heavily around the floor to the strains of 'The Rose of Mooncoin'. When it was over, her new navy suede shoes were crushed and her feet sore from the many times the reluctant dancer had stumbled over them in his big brown boots.

After what seemed like a lifetime standing alone again someone from behind tapped her on the shoulder and asked her to dance. Suffused with relief, she nodded and followed a broad-shouldered young man with the fairest hair she ever saw on to the floor. They danced, her feet light like thistledown, never stumbling once because this fellow at least knew the motions of pivoting a girl around the floor to the strains of an old-time waltz.

Not wanting to study him openly, Mary looked shyly between her lashes and decided he was nice-looking and, more importantly, he had a kind sort of face. They went through the usual ritual, telling each other that the place was too crowded and the floor was terrible and the band was too loud, and then he asked her was she a stranger and she told him she was. After three dances in a row, she knew he was a farmer, and that his name was Denis MacMahon, and that he lived six miles away. He knew she was from the Glen of Aherloe in County Tipperary, and her name was Mary O'Regan, and that she was a farmer's daughter, one of six, and that she was staying with an aunt over the Christmas holidays, helping her with the chores while the said aunt was recovering from a gall-bladder operation.

When the dance ended and they stood up for the National Anthem, he asked her would she like to go to the pictures the following Saturday evening. She readily agreed.

Sitting in the shabby cinema she realised her seat was broken. But she never complained, but instead suffered the discomfort of trying to wedge it upright with her thigh. He gave her a box of chocolates and they watched the film *Rebecca*. Her nervous heart was singing and she was afraid to think of her extraordinary luck in case it would all evaporate and end.

Three years later Mary and Denis were married in the church in Portroe, and the wedding reception was in O'Meara's in Nenagh, and they went to Dublin on their honeymoon, and her love and pride of possession for Denis MacMahon was the prime factor in her life. He was a man of few words, yet in a myriad ways he showed her that he liked and respected her as they worked side by side on the farm over the years. If she were to stop in her tracks and ask herself had he ever told her he loved her, she wasn't sure if she could remember.

After the three children were born, and as she watched her eldest daughter Aileen grow lovelier over the years, some of the possessive pride she had for Denis transferred itself to her daughter.

The first small gathering cloud on her horizon, in the first year of married life, was born of a few carelessly tossed words from Betty Ryan, young Maggie's mother, at the ICA meeting. They had a demonstration in smocking. They sat, heads bent, grappling with the intricacies of the chain stitch, when the talk got to Tom Rodgers's threshing day.

'Johnnie will be there and I'm sure Denis will be there, and sure you might go over yourself if 'tis only for curiosity.'

'Why would I be curious?' Mary asked.

Betty got a bit flustered and hesitated before she answered. 'Ah, sure 'tis nothing – nothing. Sure you know that Denis was doing a bit of a line with Tom's only daughter Teresa. But nothing came of it. She ran off with one of the tinkers – I'm sure you know all that yourself. Her baby son was brought back and Tom is rearing him. Sure you know that too. I just thought you might be interested in it.' Her voice trailed away and she concentrated on her smocking.

Sometimes, after that, Mary wondered had Denis MacMahon married her on the rebound. Was that why he never openly told her he loved her? He was honest, so maybe he couldn't because he loved someone else. Now and then she asked innocent little questions about Teresa Rodgers. Astute and intelligent, she always managed to slot them in when she had steered the conversation in the right direction. Maybe, one day, a bit of a word about Máire Ryan. old Tom Rodgers's housekeeper. Maybe, another about Joe Power, his helping man – and even talk of Tom himself. She got her answers: yes, yes, Teresa Rodgers was the light of his eye; aye, a lovely little thing, all dark and blue-eyed. Ran off she did, and sure you know that yourself – wasn't your own fellow taking her out for a bit? Aye, it was sad for poor Tom and the baby loaded on him by the tinkers so that he could never forget. Ah, sure God's ways were hard to understand, so they were.

Once she asked Denis about Teresa. They were in bed and it was a summer's night and the room was flooded with moonlight. They had been talking about sinking a new well in the yard and what a help it would be; they had been discussing the fact that Tom Rodgers had just completed the same job, when the question came, unbidden and rushed.

'Denis, do you love Teresa Rodgers?'

He had lain there and in his characteristic way had shown no shock. 'Mary, sure all that was a long time ago.'

'But did you love her?' she repeated.

'Sure we were fierce young, and what's love? At that age do you know the difference between love and just wanting?'

He took her in his arms then and kissed her, and as she ran her work-scarred hand through his fair hair, now slightly sprinkled with silver, she had felt content, content that a dark-haired, blue-eyed girl who had died all those years before could hold no threat now.

But strangely, as the years went by, any resentment she felt that she wasn't the first love of her husband's was turned into a deep dislike towards Teresa's son Stephen Rodgers. She couldn't abide the lad. She couldn't abide his looks – the black hair, the dark eyes, the swarthy alien look that made him stand out. Now and then, when she saw him, sometimes after Mass, once at a fair day, a few times in the Saturday crowd in Ross, she had sensed his brooding look, and wondered if he felt the resentment she had felt towards him.

When she had discovered that her daughter Aileen had spent a whole day in his company down at the river she had panicked, filled with an inexplicable fear. She had tried to tell Denis about it and he had merely shrugged and said, 'He's a fine lad, goes his own way and not a bother to anyone.' So she had secretly planned to remove her daughter, and had written to her cousin Sister Philomena, requesting all the information about the school in Dalkey. She had worked hard at it, persuading Denis that it was the very best thing for his daughter.

When Aileen had gone and when she was sorely missing her, Mary wondered had she overreacted. Had she been imagining things? Still, it was done and no doubt it would be all worth while in the end. Her daughter would stand out head and shoulders above the other girls because of her education in a fine school in County Dublin.

Chapter Ten

H e was standing at the gate with a red-headed fellow and was in the act of striking a match to light their cigarettes. Aileen felt her heart pound as she studied him. He was so old and grown-up looking that he undoubtedly would look on her as a young gauche child. She nudged Niamh Turley, whispering, 'See the black-haired fellow over at the gate? That's Stephen Rodgers – you know, I told you a little about him. I don't know who the other fellow is – never saw him in my life.'

It was Hallowe'en, and Niamh had come to stay with Aileen for the mid-term break. Aileen had asked her mother could she invite Niamh to Coola for the few days to return the hospitality she had been shown in Turleys? Her mother was only too happy to have young Niamh.

'Denis,' she'd said, 'she wants to bring one of her school friends home for the weekend. Isn't that great? Getting to know the city girls and their – well, you know, sophisticated ways. These things are good for her. So we'll tell her she can have her friend to stay – is that all right?'

Denis had sighed. 'Sure of course it is – sure 'twill be grand to have the girl stay. I hope Eddie behaves himself.'

It was Mary's turn to sigh. Eddie was the bane of her life, up to all sorts of devilment – and his language left a lot to be desired. She warned him if he let them down in front of Aileen's school friend he'd get the back of her hand for a year.

When the girls came home Mary had made a great fuss over Niamh. Little Maeve was putting on her baby act and simpering at the young visitor, and Niamh was enchanted with little girl – she would have loved a baby sister of her own. Even Eddie gave her a pleasant if gruff greeting, his eyes raking her small hold-all, wondering if in there somewhere there might be a bag of sweets for him.

Now they were coming out of second Mass and Aileen had seen Stephen with the red-headed stranger.

Just then Stephen looked up, and his dark eyes met hers.

Even though she felt the familiar blush creeping over her fair skin, she decided she'd put on the sophisticated act and walk over to him to introduce Niamh. After all, she was just fourteen and going to a school in Dublin, and she should be able to do a simple thing like introducing a friend without dying a thousand deaths. She was glad her mother had gone to the Mass before – it gave her some chance to be normal.

'Come on, Niamh, I'll introduce you if it kills me.' They strolled over as if talking to two fellows hardly caused them a thought.

Stephen's look had an element of surprise, but there was a small smile playing around his mouth, as if he was pleased at the turn of events. She wasn't to know that his heart too was thumping painfully. He was swamped with desire, and had to shift his position so that his sudden erection would go unnoticed.

'Hello, how are things?' Her voice was unrecognisable to her own ears, but she hoped it sounded woman-of-the-world and right casual.

'I'm okay. How is school in Dublin?'

'It's okay.' Her young mind tried to grapple with the look in his dark eyes. It was so disturbing that it made her heart thump more, and made her feel weak and shaky. 'This is Niamh Turley – she's a friend from school and she's staying for a few days.'

'That's a coincidence,' he said. 'This is Richie Casey and he's not from Dublin, but he's staying a few days also.'

They all laughed and the tension evaporated. They chatted and Niamh made them all laugh more, telling them she had never seen a cow before and she was amazed at the business of milking. She had had a vague idea where milk came from, but she had never thought she'd experience the whole business at first hand. Richie, recovering from the fact that Breda had jilted him, told her he wasn't much of a hand at the milking either; he was better at selling paraffin, but it took all types to make a world and what have you.

Richie himself was aware of the extraordinary interest between his friend Stephen and the tall fair girl. 'He tells me,' he grinned, 'that even in this neck of the woods there's diversion in the shape of a ceilidh on Snap-apple Night in the parish hall – are ye going?'

'We might,' Aileen said. 'That's if Mam lets us and if Dad can bring us there and back.'

'Well, if ye're there we'll see ye – although, Stephen, we'll be accused of cradle-snatching. Will we?'

'That we will,' Stephen answered, the same small smile playing around his mouth, 'but I'm used to being accused of all kinds of things so it won't matter.'

'We'd better go,' Aileen said. 'My mother is so strict – I'd better keep in her good books so that we can go to the dance.'

They said their farewells and moved away. Aileen and Niamh had a mile's walk back to the farm, and Stephen and Richie had a three-mile cycle in the other direction.

'God, Aileen, isn't he the most pencilled fellow you ever saw?'

'Who?' Aileen asked innocently. 'Richie?'

'No, you idiot – Stephen. You know it, and he couldn't take his eyes off you. Although I liked Richie – he's funnier.'

'Hmm – I know what you mean. But Stephen Rodgers hasn't an awful lot of reasons to be funny. And God, don't breathe a word to anyone at home that we met them … My mother hates him.'

'What? Why would she hate him? He's gorgeous.'

'Look, 'tis a long story, but today my friends Ann and Maggie will be over and they'll tell you. The country is so different from the city – you won't believe the things they hold against people.'

'Things like what?' Niamh's brown eyes were flooded with curiosity.

'Ah, all sorts of things – we'll tell you today.'

'Oh, all right – and you're a right mystery, so you are, Aileen MacMahon. Knowing a guy like Stephen Rodgers and knowing all kinds of mysterious things, and you doing the innocent culchie at school and you wouldn't think butter would melt in your mouth.'

That evening, Maggie and Ann cycled over. They were burning with curiosity to see Aileen's school friend from the posh boarding school in Dublin. A fine autumn drizzle had started to fall, so after the initial greetings they reluctantly agreed they'd have to stay indoors. Mary MacMahon made them tea and buttered a fresh batch of scones, and afterwards Aileen invited them up to her bedroom.

'For a chat, Mam – is that all right?'

'Of course it is. Ann and Maggie would like to get to know Niamh better and to hear all about the boarding school.'

Aileen found herself sighing. Her mother emphasised the Dublin boarding school to such an extent that Aileen found it someway boastful, as if going to a boarding school gave her an edge on her old school friends.

'Mam, we don't want Maeve. We'd like a chat without her.'

Maeve looked at Aileen, aghast. 'I promise I won't be a bit bold – I won't listen to a single thing. I'll just sit there readin' my *Dandy* – honest.'

'Huh,' Eddie, also housebound by the rain, put in as he sat gloomily staring into the fire. 'If she heard anything it would be all over the school by lunchtime tomorrow.'

Maeve rushed to him, bashing him with her comic. 'Shut up, 'tis you that told Mam about Aileen and you fishin' with Stephen Rodgers.'

'Enough,' shouted Aileen's mother, 'or I'll get your dad to get out the belt when he comes in.' She looked at Niamh. 'What must you think of us? They're like tinkers, so they are.'

Aileen thought her mother looked pale and strained as they turned to troop up the stairs to sit on the big double bed that Aileen shared with Maeve. In seconds flat they were chattering away like magpies, as if they had known each other all their lives. Ann and Maggie told Niamh that she wasn't a bit like what they expected.

'Sure we thought you'd be all notions and stuff,' she added.

Niamh grinned at them. 'It's great to meet the two of you. Aileen wouldn't tell me all that much about you, so she wouldn't. In school they call her the blonde culchie, hoping she'd open up and joke back. But talk about the secretive type. Anyway, who is this Stephen Rodgers, and what's all the mystery? You better tell me all about it.'

'Okay,' Maggie told her. 'We're not as secretive as your woman there. We'll tell you if we can call you a Dublin jackeen.'

'Honestly, Niamh,' Aileen said when they'd stopped laughing, 'there's nothing much – he's just a fellow who lives down three miles beyond the church.'

'No, he's not – don't mind her. He's not just a fellow who lives a few miles down beyond the church – he's different.'

'Okay, tell me,' Niamh asked low, her brown eyes filled with curiosity.

'Well, first and foremost,' Ann said, 'most of the oul gossip about him is only what we heard from our mothers when they spoke about it and thought we weren't listening. Anyway, Maggie will tell you – she's the story-teller.'

'Stephen Rodgers's mother was, according to everyone, beautiful-looking and a bit wild and had everything. Her father, old Tom Rodgers, doted on her and when his wife died, he had only her. She had ponies and lovely clothes and, like Aileen there, went to a boarding school, and when she came home she had all the fellows after her. But when she was only seventeen or so she ran off with one of the gypsies and they say she got married and Stephen is her son. They brought him home when he was a little baby because she had died having him. Her father never got over what happened. Anyway, that's it. Because of that, Stephen Rodgers is sort of taboo for a lot of girls. All the people around here like to know who you are, seed, breed and generation. Farmers are like that – good stock and what have you. And because his father was a gypsy, mothers won't let their daughters talk to him or have anything to do with him. Anyway, he doesn't want anyone – he only has eyes for our Aileen.'

Niamh looked at her friend in wonder. 'And you knew all that and told me nothing? All those nights we lay there in the dormitory talking, you knew all that and you kept it all a secret?'

Aileen had gone quite red. 'Don't mind them at all. They're just showing off because you're here. I hardly know him – me and Eddie went fishing with him for a day, and other than bumping in to him now and then I never see him.' She glared at her old friend Maggie. 'Ye should be seanachies, so ye should – talk about storytelling.'

Niamh was hardly listening. 'He's absolutely gorgeous – in fact the most interesting fella. I wish he was living in Skerries. I don't think my mother would give a hoot who his father was. That's because things are different in cities?'

Ann agreed. 'Sure, we'll just marry old farmers and it'll nearly be a match-making job – honestly, you couldn't understand the country if you lived here a hundred years.'

The conversation drifted to other things, like would they get to the dance in the parish hall on the Monday night, and if they did would they get one single little dance from a fellow, and if they did would he be a pimply horror or would he be anyway nice? But Niamh kept coming back to Stephen Rodgers and how awful it was to be living under a cloud because his mother fell in love with the wrong person.

'And what do you think of the other fellow, Richie Casey?' she asked.

'Who is Richie Casey?' they asked in unison.

It was Niamh who told them they had met him with Stephen that very morning after Mass. 'He's a school friend there for a visit. '

It was Ann and Maggie's turn to be interested. 'Maybe old Tom Rodgers is getting soft in his old age, allowing him to have friends staying. Is he nice?'

They were told he was very nice, and sort of funny too. Maggie and Ann asked Niamh all about living in Dublin near the sea. They heard about the couple who went out lobster fishing and how the husband was drowned and the young wife was brought ashore in the lifeboat. Niamh told them that her father and older brother had found drowned people before.

'We were demented,' Aileen told them. 'We couldn't get to sleep thinking of the wife living in the little cottage and he dead and gone.' But she didn't tell them that she had lain in bed that night and remembered the evening the little tinker child had died, or that her thoughts had all been for Stephen Rodgers and how awful life would be if he wasn't around. She didn't tell them how, on the night the baby had died, she had lain awake, wondering if he had been out under the weather, in danger of his life, before he'd been brought to the safe if loveless existence he had with his grandfather.

It looked as if everyone over ten had come to the parish Hallowe'en party in the creamery co-op hall. Niamh's excitement was contagious as she looked around at the crowded scene.

'I've never seen anything like it. Look at all the fellows at one side and all the girls at another. Will anyone ever move? Will we stay like this all the time?'

The voice of the microphone roared over the damp throng. 'Welcome to this Snap-apple Night dance. Father Dwan, the parish priest, and Father Farrell hope that everyone will enjoy themselves, and they thank you for coming. Now, boys and girls, to liven things up, the first dance will be a haymakers' jig.'

'Any sign of your Stephen Rodgers here?' Niamh whispered to Aileen.

'Yes, they've just come in. Don't attempt to look or I'll die.'

'But they're just coming in over at the door. Of course I'll look. I'm not like you, see – I'll look.' Niamh glanced over and saw the two lads standing at the door. 'See, I've looked and I haven't been struck by lightning, and they haven't seen us.'

She made them laugh. 'You're a mad jackeen so you are,' Maggie told her.

The takers for the haymakers' jig were few, and the floor was only thinly covered as the musicians sprang into life. Unused to socials and dances, the girls were restless and uneasy, and they moved to stand behind a group of older girls who smelled of face powder and perfume, and who seemed altogether too old for such a social.

When they eventually heard the chorus of the old-time waltz, Maggie complained, 'I knew no one would ask us to dance – but in case a miracle happens, they mightn't find us here. 'Tis too dark. Come on, we'll move on to the front.'

'Come on, let's,' Niamh agreed.

Aileen, with thumping heart, reluctantly followed them. Had she really seen him, or had it been a mirage or what? Anyway, if the miracle Maggie was talking about did happen, and if someone did ask her to dance and if that someone was Stephen Rodgers, she'd get into fierce trouble. There was bound to be someone spying who couldn't wait to talk about anything or everything that might happen here tonight.

'Will we try it?'

Oh God, it was him and he seemed to be towering over her.

She wiped her sweaty hands on the sides of her skirt. 'Okay – I hope I can make a fist of it.'

'It doesn't matter if you can't.'

In the emotional panic of being near him, she automatically walked ahead of him, her thoughts churning so much that she only half-saw Richie Casey asking Niamh, and two other boys converging on Ann and Maggie. At least they wouldn't be standing all night long. Maybe Maggie's little miracle was taking place, and maybe if God was good no one would notice her with Stephen and salt away the incident to tell her mother as soon as possible.

It was the night for miracles, because she found it easy to keep in step with Stephen.

'Who taught you how to dance?' he asked.

'Some things come naturally,' she said. She looked at him. This is the very first time I've been this close to anyone for a long time, she thought. Her mother rarely hugged her now;

maybe it would be embarrassing, because she was growing up so fast. Her father had given up his little hugs too. She studied Stephen thinking, I'll remember later on what he's like. Why does he always look so serious, so unsmiling? 'Honestly, Stephen Rodgers, you'd think you were at a funeral.'

He smiled, and his eyes caught hers, and they were the darkest eyes she had ever seen. She wondered had he his father's eyes or his mother's. She even wondered how his mother could have been so beautiful, because she thought Old Tom Rodgers was a very ordinary cranky sort of man.

'I missed seeing you around.' She wondered had she heard right, and then realised she must have, because he went on, 'I used to like seeing you going to school or coming home, or at Mass sometimes in Ross.'

She knew she was blushing again and she wondered if she could think of something witty or bright – something Niamh or Maggie would come up with. She merely said, 'You know I'm in school in Dublin now.'

'I do. And I know where the school is and I know you like it and I even feel I know why you went there.'

'Because my mother has a cousin there who is a nun, that's why.'

He shook his head and then pulled her closer. She felt embarrassed that someone might see, so she pulled away confused and asked, 'Okay, why do you think they sent me?'

'To keep you away from me.'

'Now, that's stupid, so it is – how do you know such a thing?'

'Because I do – don't forget, there's gypsy blood in me somewhere.'

She could see there was suppressed laughter in his eyes, but there was a grim look around his mouth. She wondered in her childish way if he was telling her or testing her, to try to find out if she knew all the gossip about his mother, his birth – everything.

Suddenly the dance ended and he walked her back to her friends. He asked her to keep the next old-time waltz and the last one for him. Her eyes shone with excitement as she nervously nodded in agreement, crossing her fingers and hoping that there were no spies looking at her.

'Gosh, Richie Casey is gas – gas. I nearly died in stitches laughing at him. Is Stephen gas?' Niamh asked Aileen.

'No, I don't think he's gas. Maybe he could be funny, but I wouldn't call it gas.'

After Niamh had finally exhausted every single aspect of the social and finally succumbed to sleep, Aileen lay wide awake, thinking about the dance, thinking about his nearness, thinking about the hurt on his face when she had pulled away from him. She recalled the feel of his hands, big and brown, holding hers, and the tingle that had coursed right through her body. Torn between childhood and early womanhood, she wondered why his touch could have had such an effect on her.

During the last dance he had put his hand under her chin, lifted her head and said, 'You must have the bluest eyes in the whole world. Do you put blue rinse in to them like Máire puts in our sheets?'

She had got a fit of giggles then, and he had pulled her close again and whispered, 'Your father will be here any minute to take you home. We'd better finish this dance now.'

They had walked off the floor before the National Anthem, and before he'd moved away, he had said, 'I suppose it will be Christmas now before I see you.'

'I suppose it will.'

'Don't let anyone run away with you up in Dublin now.'

'I won't.'

She had watched him walk away, and thought that the grey tweed jacket made his shoulders look broader and his hair blacker. With dry mouth and thumping heart, she realised that he was becoming the most important person in her whole life.

'I'll tell you what, me lad, that little Niamh Turley will be ripe for pickin' in about two years' time. And I wouldn't mind being around then, so I wouldn't.'

'Well, sure you know where she is – she's only up in Dublin. She won't run away.' Stephen leaned over and extinguished his cigarette on a saucer on the floor. The house had been silent and dark when they came from the dance. They had stealthily come into the kitchen and quietened Shep, who had been barking frenziedly. The fire had still been glowing and Stephen had just put on the kettle and added a fresh sod of turf. Turning the fan belt and watching the flames lick around the black kettle, he had warned, 'We don't want to wake my grandfather – he can be as sour as hell if he doesn't get his sleep.'

'I think you're too hard on him – he's not the worst. Have you ever tried to talk to him – get closer or something?'

'No. Not lately, anyway. When I was young, maybe – but not now.'

They had drunk their tea and walked up the stairs to the raftered bedroom.

Lying in bed, Richie talked non-stop, whispering so as not to wake old Tom Rodgers.

'Aren't you the cute hoor? Not a word about the gorgeous blonde, and not an eye in her head for anyone only you. I tried to excite her when I was dancing with her but nothing doing. She had eyes, as the song says, "Only for You".'

Stephen put his hands behind his head. Richie was aware that his friend wanted to talk, confide, maybe reach out. He realised now what a lonely, terrible life Stephen had, living with the dour old man who resented him for things that happened a lifetime ago. He decided to encourage him. 'Well, aren't you going to tell me more about the delectable Aileen?'

He heard Stephen chuckle. 'Where do you get the words? Maybe you should be a writer. You have a great flow, so you have.'

'Stop changing the subject. Amn't I about to get inside the head of the mysterious Stephen Rodgers?'

'There is no mystery.' Richie thought he heard a sigh. 'Everyone in the place knows that my mother, his only daughter, ran off with a tinker, and I'm all he has and I'll inherit the place, but he can keep it. I don't want it – I'll hang around for a couple of years after the Leaving. He tells me he'll pay me then to work the place, and when I have enough money I'll off to America – then Australia. Somewhere out of this gossip-ridden hole.'

'Maybe you'll change your mind. Maybe when the old man goes, the resentment will go too. These are the late fifties, boy. The country is moving. Things are changing.'

'The country could be moving and things could be changing, but you'd need an earthquake to change people here. In this neck of the woods people never ever forget. As for Aileen –?' Stephen got up on his elbow and leaned over, looking at his friend. He could see the bare outline of his face. The moon had broken from behind the clouds and its beam had lightened the darkness in the room – the bedroom that had belonged to his mother and which still had a girlish look with its pink wallpaper and the deep pink curtains and matching

88

eiderdown, all dulled, shabby and darkened now with the passage of time. 'I feel I've known her forever. I remember the first day she came to school. You won't believe this, but I could even tell you what she wore.'

Richie made no comment. He thought it better. Maybe if he didn't interrupt the flow of low, whispered confidences, it might do a power of good to his friend.

'I saw her when she made her First Communion, again when she made her Confirmation. I always tried to go to second Mass, because I knew I'd see her there. It wasn't easy – I used to have to lie to get there because of the chores. But it was worthwhile. I'd do anything to get a glimpse of her. Sometimes she'd be down at their lower meadow wall where there was a swing. She'd be there with her small sister and Eddie, her brother. One day I was in luck – Eddie put his talk on me and we made an arrangement to go fishing the following day. We did, and it was the greatest, grandest day of my whole life. The old man came along and made a fool out of me in front of her, but even that didn't take all the pleasure away.

'I have a dream and I have it always – that I'll marry her and take her away. Maybe I haven't a snowball's hope in hell of it ever happening, but what's wrong with dreaming?'

'Honest to God – honest to God,' was all Richie managed. 'Isn't it amazing the things that go on in a fellow you consider your best friend and you wouldn't hear a twitter of them? But tell me more. It gets better.'

'The reason I wouldn't have a hope is her mother. She's a bleak sort of woman, and the odd time I see her she looks me up and down with cold calculating eyes. I know she hates me. And now you know it all, so don't talk about the mystery man any more. Okay?'

'Okay,' Richie promised. 'And you know what, Stephen Rodgers?'

'What?'

'My grandmother has an old saying – there's a long road that has no turning. Who knows what'll happen?'

After that he fell quiet, and when Stephen heard his deep breathing he knew that Richie had fallen asleep. He lay on his uncomfortable narrow bed and let the dreams and the desires swamp his mind. He fell asleep eventually, but woke up cold and uncomfortable, with the unwanted knowledge that he had had a wet dream.

Chapter Eleven

After second Mass a few weeks before Christmas, Mary MacMahon lingered a little longer than usual to talk to Betty Power. The friendship between the two women had flourished over the years, and was cemented by the fact that their two daughters, Aileen and Maggie, were great pals. The two women stood relaxing in the winter sunshine as their menfolk gathered at the wall opposite the church gates, no doubt talking about the local football team and their chances against the Graigue team in the winter league final to be played the following Sunday. They spoke about their daughters and their hopes for them after they left school. Betty wanted to know how Aileen was getting on in the school in Dublin.

'Very well,' Mary told her. 'She settled in more than I thought she would. She made a great friend with that Niamh Turley – you know, the little one that was here at Hallowe'en.'

'Oh, indeed I do, Maggie was on non-stop about the weekend. They had a great time and no end to the excitement over the social. Maggie was terrified she'd be a wallflower, but sure you remember yourself – doesn't it all bring it back to you? Anyway, sure they're only children. Little more.'

'Aileen didn't talk too much about it. She was up in her room, all chat with the girls. Who asked her to dance, I wonder?'

'Sure she danced all night with young Stephen Rodgers. They must have been a right pair – she's so fair and he's so dark.'

Betty Power wasn't at all like Mary. She didn't pay any heed to the stories that abounded in the area – all the gossip about Teresa Rodgers running away with one of the tinkers. If she ever did think about it, she thought it was very romantic – a bit like the Mills & Boon books she devoured when she had time to spare. Secretly she thought Stephen Rodgers was the handsomest young man she had ever seen. She couldn't guess for one minute how her casual throwaway words would upset

Mary MacMahon. Looking at her friend now she saw the compressed lips, the pallor, the look of shock in her eyes.

'I had no idea she was in sight or sound of that fellow. If I thought he laid a hand on her I'd kill her. Wouldn't you think she'd have a bit of sense? If her father knew she was dancing and flying her kite with him he wouldn't be too pleased.'

'Ah sure Mary, what's wrong with you? A harmless dance, their first dance, and they enjoyed the bit of excitement.'

Betty went on to talk about the ICA meeting the following Tuesday and the prospect of getting a prize for the rug-making. Mary answered only desultorily. She knew that saying Denis wouldn't be too pleased if he knew was almost wishful thinking on her part. Her husband thought Stephen Rodgers a good lad, hard-working and studious. Hadn't she said to him how upset she had been way back last summer when she discovered that Aileen had spent the day with him down at the river? When he had made light of it she had been secretly furious. She wondered if he had a certain feeling for that boy because he had been in love with his mother.

Just then the subject of her fearful thoughts came round the side of the church, accompanied by another young man. He glanced up and for the first time their eyes met.

The expression in his dark eyes was unreadable, inscrutable. Mary looked at the black hair, the handsome face, the broad shoulders and the easy walk. She felt her heart lurch painfully as a strange weakness washed over her. She wasn't well, that what it was – maybe it was her age. She had heard all sorts of things about the change of life. Maybe she was getting the change early. Maybe that would explain the fear and hatred she felt for this young man, who was only a young lad really, a lad who couldn't be held responsible for the actions of people a whole generation ago. She dropped her eyes from his and shivered.

'Are you all right, Mary?' Betty asked.

'Yes. Maybe I'm getting a cold or maybe 'twas someone walking over my grave. Come on, we better get these menfolk home for their dinner.'

Sitting beside her husband driving over the long narrow twisted road, Mary was silent. All sorts of unwanted thoughts came to mind. Aileen dancing with that fellow! Would it be possible that the child thought she was in love or something?

91

Of course it could not be so – she was too young. She wouldn't know what love or attraction to the opposite sex meant.

Would she ever again bring up the buried, dead subject of that boy's mother with her husband? Maybe it was true. Maybe Denis MacMahon only married her on the rebound, married her because he was in love with Teresa Rodgers. When that thought had touched the fringes of her mind before, Mary had put it away, buried it beneath her contentment with having a nice hard-working husband and three lovely children. Why was she resurrecting all this stuff now? Was it because she was getting on for the forties and the change? Was it because she knew that a young fanciful girl would be attracted to a fellow as handsome as Stephen Rodgers? Was it because she was jealous of his dead mother who, according to rumour, could have had her Denis before she herself had come on the scene?

Denis was driving at his usual easy pace, his strong hands steady on the wheel. Mary looked at them and noticed the blonde hairs on their backs glinting in the sun. Why was she such an idiot, worrying about all those things that should be buried in the past? She'd go and see the doctor and get a good tonic. Her mother swore by a tonic containing phosphorous – 'Keeps your nerves strong, so it does,' she'd tell her. Yes, that's what she'd do the very next week – go to the doctor's and get a tonic.

"Twon't be long now till Christmas,' Denis said.

'No, sure 'tis nearly on top of us.'

'You'll be glad when Aileen is home again. Sure you miss her, I know.'

'Aye – I miss her. It'll be great to have her here to help with the Christmas. By the way, Denis,' she blurted out, unable to keep it to herself, 'I just heard from Betty that she was dancing with that Stephen Rodgers at the Hallowe'en social. I wouldn't like that, I wouldn't like that at all.'

'Ah, sure they're only children. What's wrong with a dance? You make worries for yourself. It's nothing – youth will have its fling. She'll be dancing with many more fellows – he may be the first but he won't be the last. Sure you know that yourself.'

"Tis true, and I hope you're right.'

And it was true she was ridiculous, sick with stupid fears. She supposed all mothers were like that when their girls were growing up. She tried to think of other things now. She tried to think of the coming festive season – the new clothes she'd get for the children, the toys for Maeve and Eddie and something nice for Aileen. She'd send a present to Peggy in Islington too. She always did, and Peggy always sent her one back. She loved getting something in the post with the English stamps on it. Mary's thoughts ran along happy lines for a bit. But even the thought of the approaching festive season couldn't fill her thoughts entirely.

Stephen Rodgers's dark eyes and the expression in them came back to her. His gaze had been steady, unflinching, yet there had been an interest, even a curiosity, in their depths. Why? Why would a young fellow look at her like that? Why such a summing-up expression? Mary shivered again. She'd have to be more vigilant in the future about the boys her daughter danced with.

As the van turned into the muddy lane that led to the farmhouse, a row broke out between Eddie and Maeve in the back. Maeve was screaming and had buried her hands in Eddie's fair thatch. Mary was glad of the rumpus – it got her mind off the things that were torturing her.

*

Dear Niamh,

I was delighted to meet you with your friend Aileen at Hallowe'en. I think it's so important that we girls make new friends all the time. Girls usually go around in whispering twos, and I don't like that. So I hope you will continue to be my friend for a long time, and that we will do lots of things together. Tell Aileen that my friend Stephanie enjoyed meeting her and hopes to see her over the Christmas.

We won the camogie winter league and we drank a few lemonades in celebration. Perhaps you will be invited to the MacMahons over the Christmas. If you are perhaps you'll let me know, just a little scrawl on the back of a Christmas card, and I'll get around Stephanie to ask me. I'll sign off now and I must wash my hair. Please drop me a line soon. I wish you and your family a very happy Christmas.

Your fond friend, Rita Casey.

*

On the long journey home on the train to Waterford Aileen had thought of the letter. She smiled to herself again and again as she memorised the line 'Tell Aileen that my friend Stephanie enjoyed meeting her and hopes to meet her again over Christmas'. She got regular letters from her mother, even one from Eddie, and even a childish, hand-printed, well-spaced one from Maeve. She had read Eddie's letter out to Niamh and their two other friends, Pauline O'Rourke and Cathy Morrissey, and Niamh had read the letter from 'Rita'. They had collapsed laughing, envious of the intrigue that made a boy like Richie write to Niamh and pretend he was a girl.

Aileen's heart lifted as the train swallowed up the winter landscape. She was looking forward to going home. She laughed and then, from nowhere, tears came as she remembered Eddie's one and only letter.

Dear Aileen,
I hope you are well. Mammy told me to write to you so I will. There is no news and not much to tell. Maeve is getting worse every day and is a scourge. I had a lovely pet and she told Mammy and I had to get rid of him. He was a little rat I found in a nest behind the big barn. I brought him in and washed him in Jeyes fluid and kept him in the cage I had for the white mouse that ran away. Anyway I used play with him every night and old Maeve saw and told. I called him Neddy but he's gone now. I saw Stephen Rodgers the other day and I was so fed up I was going to ask him to help me build the raft so as I could go sailing away. But he only waved and I waved back. I hope we can go fishing again next summer and I won't tell if we do.
    Your fond brother, Eddie.

Yes, it was great to be going home to see everyone. Aileen hoped she'd get something really nice to wear for Christmas. There was sure to be a parish social or a GAA ceilidh, and she hoped she could go. She wondered if this constant thinking of Stephen was wrong. Was the peculiar glow and sensation she got, the way her heart jerked and thumped when he was near, wrong? Was all that a sort of loving? It must be, wasn't she thinking of him nearly all her life? She hardly remembered a time she didn't think of him.

Rain started to beat against the windows of the train, becoming quite heavy. It lashed in a quivering little stream. Somehow it reminded her of the stolen day at the river when a strong brown hand had held hers and patiently taught her how to cast and in doing changed her, so that things were never quite the same since.

Her family were at the station in Waterford to meet her, and there were smiles and sheepish hugs. Eddie frowned as she greeted him, yet somehow she knew that he was glad to have her home.

'Tell me everything about the school,' her mother asked when they were settled in the car. 'Did you do well in your Christmas test? Were the nuns asking for me? Did you make more friends as time went by? I'm sure that school must have girls whose parents are very rich – doctors and judges and what have you.'

Aileen answered, 'I'm not sure, Mam, what their fathers do, but the girls are nice, and after all that's what matters.'

Her father told her, 'That's what matters, love.'

During the drive home Aileen listened to Maeve's chatter and Eddie's grumpy answers, and realised for the first time that her mother was a snob. All that talk about doctors' daughters and possible judges' daughters was so stupid. Momentarily Aileen felt sorry for her mother. Looking at her, she thought she didn't look that well. She had got thinner and her hair was straggly, and she seemed to fidget more than she used to. Then the old boreen appeared in view, muddy and rutted as ever, and suddenly they were home in the farmyard and Aileen felt a lump in her throat as she saw all the familiar things that she had nearly forgotten.

The following Saturday they went shopping in Ross. Her father gave her money to buy presents. She bought Christmas cards too, and in a wild impulse she decided to send one to Stephen Rodgers. She picked one with a river and snow-laden trees and a big fat robin on a snow-covered branch. Her hand was unsteady as she wrote, 'With best wishes, Aileen'. Before she changed her mind she bought the stamp and stuck it on, and dropped the envelope into the box outside the post office.

She met Maggie and Ann outside the café and asked her mother could she stay with them for a lemonade or a cup of tea.

'All right – just for a half an hour and I'll meet you here then.'

'Well, tell us all the news,' Maggie asked, all excited, once they were sitting down.

'There's no news, not really – sure 'tis you that has all the news.'

'Okay, we know what you want to know. I saw him once lately and he was outside Woolworths in Waterford. He was with Richie Casey and a girl, and they were chatting there and that's it. I saluted him and so did Ann, and he saluted back and that's it.'

Aileen smiled. 'Well, that's not earth-shattering stuff – any more. Don't tell me I've come all the way from Dublin to hear nothing.' She hoped they thought that she was indifferent to the little snippet of information. But her heart had started the old familiar rumpus at the very mention of Stephen's name. She felt a right idiot now, sending a fellow who was years and years older than her a Christmas card with a big fat stupid robin. And who was the girl outside Woolworths in Waterford? More than likely Stephen had entirely forgotten Aileen at this stage. After all, she hadn't spoken more than ten times to him in her entire life.

She changed the subject and heard all about their school and the girls in the class and how terrible the teachers were – old cranky women or sanctimonious nuns who were always on about how they should behave with decorum and never ever be involved in a situation that would be considered an occasion of sin with a member of the opposite sex, and about how boys would have no respect for you if you were brash or forward or over-chatty.

By the time Aileen met her mother the stars were out and the sky was clear and frosty. She said goodbye to her friends and promised that they would get together over the Christmas.

He wasn't at the ceilidh on Saint Stephen's night. She stood near the door with Ann and Maggie, expecting him in any minute. Her heart was pounding so much at the thought of seeing him that she felt almost sick. She thought it quite extra-ordinary that she should feel ill at the thought of seeing someone you liked. No, loved. Face it, Aileen, she told herself, you're in love – you must be, because your thoughts are full of him. 'I wish Niamh was here,' she whispered to Ann. 'At least she'd have the neck to look at the door and let us know who's coming in. Isn't it awful the games we play, pretending that we don't care about things?'

'I know, I know,' Ann consoled. 'But Aileen, I promise if I ever get a glimpse of him you'll be the first to know.' Ann choked off her nervous little laugh when she was asked out for the haymakers' jig.

Aileen and Maggie were both going to bolt for the ladies' when they saw two fellows they knew bearing down on them. Aileen's partner was Mick White, a young lad who had gone to the same national school as she had. He had an impish grin and was sort of funny, a bit like Richie Casey. She had made up her mind to enjoy herself, telling herself she was a right idiot to be straining her eyes looking for someone who wasn't there.

When young Mick asked her for the next dance, an old-time waltz, she was happy to go with him. To the strain of 'Tipperary So Far Away' she turned and twirled, at times giving herself a twist in the neck trying to keep her eye on the door.

'Are you expecting someone?' Mick asked.

'No, no, I'm not expecting a single soul,' she answered with an embarrassed grin.

They danced in silence but just before the end he casually said, 'Wasn't hospital a terrible place to spend Christmas?'

'Who was in hospital? Anyone I know?'

'Yes – I think you do. Stephen Rodgers is in hospital since the day before Christmas Eve.'

Her heart started to hammer so much she was full sure he'd hear it. She moved away in case he would. She hoped he wouldn't notice how pale she had gone –she felt she must look like a ghost with the shock.

'What happened to him?' Her voice was a mere croak, and yet she tossed her hair, as if that chap – what was his name? Oh yes, Stephen Rodgers – being in hospital mattered very little.

'There was a bit of an accident at home. Seemingly he was up in the loft and his grandfather didn't know, and took away the ladder to do something or other. Stephen just stepped down, assuming it was there. He fell and strained his back and broke his leg.'

'Where is he?' she asked lightly.

'Ardkeen Hospital in Waterford. He'll be there for a couple of weeks.'

'I wonder did his grandfather take the ladder away deliberately?' Aileen asked. 'They say that he doesn't get on with Stephen – in fact, some people say that he hates him.'

'Ah God no, Aileen. My da heard that old Tom was very upset.'

'He's upset because there's no one to do the bulk of the work.' Aileen's voice was curt.

Mick White looked at her in surprise. 'Since when did you take up the cudgels for Stephen Rodgers? I didn't think you even knew him that well.'

Oh, I know him all right, she thought. If you only knew, Mick White. I feel I know him all my life. And another thing – if I have my way I'll get to know him a lot better because if I don't I might go mad or something. 'Thanks, Mick,' she said casually, and walked away to join Ann as the last strain of 'Tipperary So Far Away' ended.

In seconds a red-faced perspiring Maggie arrived and told them that every single joint in her ten toes was broken because she had been trampled by that big oaf Joe O'Brien. Had it been one of her father's heifers she would have escaped easier.

'He's in hospital,' Aileen blurted out when she got a chance. 'He fell down from the loft and broke his leg and maybe his back. At least I don't have to stare at the door any more. He won't be here.'

'That's terrible,' Maggie and Ann spoke in unison, 'terrible.'

'Look,' Aileen implored, 'I wonder could we go to see him. Could we get the bus from Ross to Waterford the day after tomorrow? I could lie to my mam, tell her that one of the girls from the school will be there and that we had a sort of arrangement to meet her. She might let me go – she is sort of impressed by things like that. I wonder would your mothers let you go?'

Maggie and Ann saw the desperate pleading and the worry in Aileen's blue eyes. Maggie tried to lighten the moment. 'You have it bad, so you have.'

Aileen, embarrassed, felt the giveaway blush starting. 'No, I haven't. I just thought it would be sort of interesting.'

'Tell that to the Marines.' Ann was grinning too.

The following morning Jack the Post became an unwitting accomplice to Aileen's plan. She didn't recognise the handwriting, but, when she opened her letter her mother saw the obvious confusion on her face. The letter was from Rita Casey.

Dear Aileen,
I hope you are enjoying your holidays. I hope that Christmas was good and that Santa brought you a nicely filled stocking and the things you wanted. Isn't it nice to be away from the school and back home with our families? I had a great Christmas but for one thing. You remember Stephanie Rodgers, the best in the class at languages, particularly Latin? Well, she had a bad crash off her bike at home in Woodstown, Co. Waterford, and broke her leg badly and strained her back. She wrote to me and asked me would I visit her. She also asked me to let you know and maybe you could visit her soon. Undoubtedly she will get the best of attention because her father is a doctor, but even so you need friends at a time like this. I know she'd love to see you. I know you'll do your best. Looking forward to seeing you when the holidays are over.
    A very happy New Year,
    Your fond friend, Rita.

'Who's the letter from?' Eddie asked. 'Is it Niamh? Will she be coming? If she is, tell her to bring heaps of money. I want her to play cards with me.'

'Oh, shut up, you little Shylock,' Aileen told him, her face flushed at the letter and the open deception she was planning.

'Who is the letter from?' her mother asked, looking up from a mail-order catalogue that had come in the post.

Aileen crossed her feet under the long wooden scrubbed table. She hoped it would be as good as crossing your fingers when you were telling a jet-black lie. 'It's from a girl at school. She wrote to tell me that another girl in the class is in Ardkeen Hospital. She fell off her bike and broke her ribs and her collar bone and something else. Her father is a doctor so she'll be all right, I suppose. Could I get a bus from Ross and go in and see her? Maybe Ann and Maggie would be allowed to come with me. It would be something to do, I suppose.' She had her finger almost twisted with the easy lies that seemed to roll off her tongue.

'Oh, I don't know if your father would like you to go to Waterford on your own. Maybe we could all go for a spin.'

Aileen's heart thumped in sheer terror at the possibility of such a plan. Her beloved father, who was sitting by the blazing fire enjoying his cup of strong tea after the milking, saved things.

'Oh, I couldn't go to tomorrow, Mary. Ned Ryan is coming over about the new bull. Sure what harm would they come to? It's only a half-hour in the bus.' He smiled at his daughter and she was so grateful that he always seemed to say and do the right thing that a lump came to her throat.

'See, Mam – Dad says it's all right.'

'A doctor's daughter, did you say? Well, maybe you and the girls would enjoy a day in Waterford. She'll get the best of attention no doubt – a doctor's daughter.'

Ardkeen Hospital didn't look like a hospital at all. It was a collection of long low buildings which had been built as a TB sanatorium.

'It's a bit like the new polish factory they've built in Kilkenny,' Maggie muttered.

Aileen was so nervous she couldn't say anything funny or witty; in fact she felt the old familiar nausea and the heart-thumping excitement she always felt when she felt she was going to see Stephen.

'Stephen Rodgers.' The man at the information desk looked at the three young girls. 'Any relations?'

'No,' the tall blonde girl whispered. They looked so young and nervous his heart softened. He had two daughters around the same age – all courage, brash and loud at times, and other times floods of tears and recriminations. He felt he knew a lot about young teenage girls. These looked nice kids and were from the country, as far as he could gather from their accents. The tall blonde one was a beauty – her blue eyes were the bluest he had ever seen. They were filled with worry now – worry that he might turn them away. 'Stephen Rodgers – now, let me see.' He was smiling, and he could see the relief in their young faces. 'He's in the surgical. That's Saint Gabriel's – just down the corridor and take the second turn to the left and there you are.'

They walked away, thanking him with a smile.

'Oh God,' Aileen whispered, 'I'm shaking like a leaf. I've lost my nerve – I don't think I can face him. And my God,' she almost sobbed, 'say if my mother ever found out all about the lies? I'm dead.'

'Come on, me girl,' Maggie ordered. 'We're gone as far as this, so we're not turning back.'

Ann linked Aileen's arm in hers and the contact brought a measure of comfort.

The other four occupants of the ward had visitors. Stephen was alone. He had his back slightly turned away from the door, as if he knew he wouldn't have anyone in to see him. He was reading a book, and his leg was in plaster and raised on a sort of pulley affair.

Looking at his black hair, in stark contrast to the snow-white pillow, and the strong brown hand holding the book somehow disturbed Aileen and brought a blurring mist to her eyes. When they approached the bed, Maggie bent down and almost shouted 'Hello.' The book nearly fell from his hands. He looked at them and his eyes slowly filled with pleasure at their visit.

'Hello.' He took in all three of them, but then his eyes went straight to Aileen and he repeated, 'Hello,' his tone obviously softer.

Aileen was tongue-tied but Maggie came to her rescue. 'God, you look a right crock, Stephen Rodgers – were you in the wars or what?'

'No, I just didn't look, and like a fool I fell out of the loft. Nothing warlike or romantic about my injuries. How did you know where the poor crock was?'

'I got a letter from your friend Rita, so I did.' Aileen suddenly broke out laughing. 'Isn't it well Stephanie's father is a doctor? She'll get great care.' Her heart was still pounding, but he was obviously so happy to see her that some measure of calm was seeping in from somewhere.

'Look, Stephen, we'll go for a little walk around the place, and sure you can talk to Aileen for a bit.'

He glanced up at Maggie, thanking her with his eyes.

When they left he looked at Aileen, slowly taking in every single inch of her.

'Don't do that please –' she whispered. 'It makes me feel embarrassed.'

'All right. But you know what, Aileen MacMahon – you're a sight for sore eyes. Here, sit down.' He patted the bed, but she sat on the cubicle chair that was nearby.

'I missed you at the dance. In fact, it was at the dance that I heard about your fall. Does it hurt?' She nodded at the leg in plaster, and it was then she noticed that his pyjama top was open and there was another plaster on his chest.

'No, other things hurt but not these sort of things.'

'Why did you ask Richie to write?'

'Because I wanted to see you.'

'Why?'

'For a million reasons. Do you want me to outline them all?'

'If my mother ever finds out she'll kill me.'

'I know. Tell me, what'll we do about it?'

'What do you mean?'

'Aileen MacMahon, sure you're only a child but I think you know what I mean.'

She felt the telltale blush and, because there was no escape, she tried to be flippant. 'Well, there's not a lot you can do and you a right old crock.'

'Why are you blushing then?'

'Because I always bloody blush – that's why. Now I'm cursing like Eddie.'

He reached out and took her hand in his. The pressure of his strong fingers nearly hurt, but his touch flooded her with the extraordinary unfamiliar tingle that she experienced only when she thought of him or when he touched her like he had the day at the river or the night of the dance. 'Don't panic now, or anything, when I tell you what I must tell you.'

'What's wrong with you? Sure the accident must have affected your brain.'

'Aileen, I love you. I really do. I even feel I've loved you since I was born. If I haven't, I've certainly loved you since the day you fell and hurt your knee in the playground.'

She stared at him, her blue eyes never straying for one second from his dark, almost black ones. This is a dream, she thought. I'm not here, he hasn't broken his leg and his chest or whatever. I'm in bed with Maeve, dreaming like I often dream – but this time it's so real. I wonder will I cry with disappointment when I hear Maeve stirring or Mam calling or Dad clinking with the buckets in the yard?

'I hope you won't be frightened because I'm telling you this. I want you to know how I feel. See, I've had time to think lying here. So I had to tell you.'

She shivered and withdrew her hand. Like the time she had pulled away from him at the dance, she saw the hurt in his eyes.

'I'm too young for all this, you know I am. And I'm a bit afraid when you look at me like that.'

'You're afraid because of all the old talk?'

'No, I don't care about all those old biddies – and anyway, when I grow up I'm leaving the country. I'd much prefer to live in the city. I sometimes dream about it.'

'So do I. And I dream about much more?' He glanced towards the door and she guessed that the girls must be coming, because his words came rushed and clipped. 'Do you even like me –?'

She reached out and brushed the black hair off his forehead. She noticed how hot it was. The words tumbled out in a rush. 'I must, Stephen Rodgers, so I must, because I never, ever seem to think of anything or anybody but you.'

Once again he reached out and took her hand.

'You know what, Aileen MacMahon? Because of your boarding school and because of the way things are with me, I mightn't see you four times in the next few years. But remember now, I'll be there and I'll be waiting. All right?'

'All right,' she answered. Once more she felt unreal, as if any minute someone would shake her and say, 'Get up – it's tomorrow.'

Chapter Twelve

Máire washed and dried the ware, and put it into the dresser. She had had a word that day with Joe, and they were both of the opinion that Tom Rodgers was even more silent and more taciturn than ever.

'Do you think he's worrying about young Stephen, Joe?' she asked.

'He might be. Maybe he feels guilty or what. He feels he should have checked before he took the ladder away.'

'Do you think he'll go to see him? After all, he is his grandson.'

'I don't know. He phoned from the pub and knows that the lad will be all right. But 'tis terrible to have him there on his own. I'll get in to see him on Sunday, so I will. God knows 'tis a lonely life for him.'

'Sometimes I wonder would it have been better if he'd never been brought back.'

'Ah Máire, sure have sense. Would you want such a fine lad to be brought up with the tinkers and be roaming the country and camping out and no respect from anyone?'

'Ah, Joe, but there's such a thing as love and being wanted. Maybe things like that are more important than a full stomach and a warm bed and being in out of the weather.'

'Aye, maybe you're right. But travellin' the country, livin' at the side of the road out in all weather? I don't think there'd be much lovin' or carin' with a life like that.'

Tom Rodgers walked into the kitchen, scraping the mud of his shoes on the old mat near the kitchen half-door. A brave pullet ran in out of the cold, maybe hoping for a few crumbs off the table, but it was quickly shushed out the door with the back of old Tom's boot.

''Tis turning frosty,' he said to no one in particular.

'Aye, it is,' Joe answered. 'Anyway, Tom, I fixed the roof on the sow's shed and the fence at the far side of the meadow, so there's no more to be done except the milkin'.'

104

'Aye, sure there's no more to be done,' Tom agreed.

Joe cleared his throat. 'We were wonderin', me and Máire – would you be going to see Stephen? We were just wonderin'.'

'Maybe he doesn't want me.'

'Of course he wants you – aren't you his kin? Aren't you his grandfather? Sure 'twould only be right you went in and saw him.'

'Maybe I will so. I'll drive in after Mass tomorrow. Maybe you'd like the spin, Joe.'

Tom didn't talk much on the journey to Waterford. When the tyres of his van hit the potholes on the narrow roads he muttered that the country was going to wrack and ruin. That crowd in the Dáil should have their eye to fixing up the country and not be so interested in the savages out in black Africa.

'What do we know about the blacks in the Congo? What do we know about their wars? Sure Joe, we only know about hardship in the land and the poor price we get for out produce.'

'True, Tom, true,' Joe muttered in response. He's talking his head off, he thought, because he doesn't want to think about Stephen and what he'll say when he gets to the hospital. He never had to say much to the lad before, only growl at him, and now he's afraid he'll have to be different.

Joe was surprised when they stopped the van in Waterford and parked at the river side of the quay. The wind was from the east and the few stragglers on the quay had their heads bent against the fitful gusts. Because it was Sunday most of the shops were closed, but a few sweet shops were hopefully open.

'I'd better get something – sure I can't go in with my hands hangin',' Tom muttered as he clambered out of the driving seat.

Joe watched him as he pulled his hat down further over his eyes and, with head bent and hands thrust into his pockets, walked over to the shop. Some minutes later he emerged with a brown paper bag, but Joe had to nurse his curiosity all the way to the hospital, because the old man didn't volunteer any information about his purchases.

Stephen was lying on his back, his face paler than Joe remembered. He seemed surprised to see them, as if he had accepted that he would have no visitors, although the patients in the adjoining beds were surrounded by callers. His eyes moved over their faces, but a slight wariness returned to their dark depths as he held out his hands to greet his grandfather. They shook hands like strangers who had been briefly introduced.

'Well, how are you?' his grandfather asked. 'Did they patch you up?'

'They did – it won't be too long until I'm back helping on the farm.'

'Take your time, take your time. 'Tisn't the work I had on my mind, 'twas yourself.'

'I'm fine – I'll be fit as a fiddle when the plaster goes off my leg. They've removed the bandages and stuff from my chest, so 'tis only the leg that's keeping me here.' Stephen looked at Joe and consciously tried not to show his pleasure at seeing his confidant and friend. 'Well, Joe, how are things? Anything exciting happening at home?'

'No, lad, no – the oul fox is on the prowl, there's a fierce flu goin'. The priest is hopping mad because the attendance at Mass is down, and two of the cows have dried up.'

Stephen laughed and Joe's heart lightened. The tension between Tom and Stephen eased. Old Tom rummaged in his pocket and his red, roughened hand drew out a packet of cigarettes and the brown paper bag, which he hastily thrust at his grandson. 'A few things I got on the way,' he muttered.

Stephen reached out and took the proffered gifts, his face momentarily showing pleasure at this rare moment of intimacy between himself and the man who had reluctantly reared him. He looked into the bag and drew out a box of iced caramels. He placed them on the locker with the cigarettes on top. 'Thanks, Grandfather – these are great.'

The two men then sat on the chair and the three of them spoke about the farm, the possible rotation of crops for the following year, and the poor prices cattle were making at the market. With the farming in common they were at ease. After a half-hour the men got up to go.

Tom Rodgers's farewell was gruff. 'Well, I suppose I'll be hearing when you'll be let out.'

'I suppose you will,' Stephen told him.

Joe shook hands with Stephen and, with a big wink, told

him, 'We'll be lookin' forward to seein' you home, lad – 'tisn't the same.'

Stephen returned the wink and said, 'Thanks Joe. Any day now.'

Stephen Rodgers left hospital two weeks later with a limp and a stick and an exercise programme that, he was told, would soon see him right as rain if he adhered to it. Early spring saw him working on the farm after school again.

He tried to study for the Leaving Certificate when he could. His grandfather had little or no interest in his studies. Quite often, when he saw Stephen's head buried in his books, he muttered, ''Tis hard work and not books that put the bread on the table.'

Stephen usually ignored these remarks. But there were times when he would lie in bed, listening to the wind in the thatch and looking at the pink wallpaper put there to please someone who had been beautiful, wild and impulsive, a girl who, according to Joe, could turn the hardest heart to butter with her whimsical ways and charm and wonder, was this taciturn man who now only gruffly spat out a few words the same one who had sent his daughter to school far away so that she would get a good finish? Wasn't that what Máire had said? He thought of the girl who, despite the finish, had come back for the summer and romped naked in the river. The girl who had walked away, leaving it all behind to lie down with a travelling tinker and make love with him and have his child – in fact, to die having it.

Sometimes he felt that something didn't quite fit. There was some little piece missing. Despite her impulsiveness and her fun-loving nature, his mother had been educated. Would an educated young girl, the sole heir to a sizeable farm, lie down with a tinker? And hadn't he heard a word from Joe that there was a hint of a match between his mother and Denis MacMahon? Maybe some day I'll find out all about it, he thought. I'll know who my father was. Maybe I won't always wallow in this mysterious void. Then he'd think of Aileen and a terrible fear would clutch him that he had terrified her in the hospital with his serious demands, telling her he would wait for her. She was little more than a child, as far as he could see. To have him plunging at her with talk of a lasting love, and tying her with such talk, was stupid. Worse, Richie Casey was in the throes of correspondence with young Niamh Turley. Only that day, when they were coming home from school, he had said, 'I think I've ensnared that young one. The letters are coming down from Dublin like manna. Have you heard from the beautiful Aileen I sent to your arms in the hospital?'

'No – I think I frightened her away.'

'Sure, if you have, I can get you a strong line up to replace her. My sister and her friend can talk of little else but yourself since they met you.'

''Tis nice to know I'm a bit of a hit with someone.'

They cycled down the drive of the school and got off their bikes at the turn of the road. Richie slowed for a bit.

'I suppose, Stephen, we should study hard for the Leaving. My old man will go mad if I don't get it. He waffles on all the time about how important it is and how we'll be nothing without it. If he tells me once more again that education will hold for a lifetime, I'll hit him with a milking bucket.'

Stephen smiled. 'It's good to have his interest. I don't think anyone gives a damn whether I get it or not.'

Richie looked at his friend and ruefully understood his sister's and her friends' obsession with Stephen Rodgers. He had so much to offer that Richie felt it was down right unfair. He wondered how the Maker could dish out so much to one fellow and give another a red head of spiky uncontrollable hair, a face full of freckles and a shortage in inches. Still, he thought so much of Stephen he sincerely hoped they wouldn't lose touch when they'd leave school.

When Stephen was about to get up on his bike he impulsively grabbed him and asked, 'Tell me, are you still burning the candle for her?'

'Yeah, you could say that,' Stephen said, his eyes unreadable.

'Would you like me to tell Niamh to tell her to drop you a line?'

'God, no. She knows how I feel.'

''Tis as serious as that?'

'Yeah, and from now on it's a waiting game.'

'Waiting for what?' Richie asked.

'For the right time, because I feel there will be a right time for both of us. I sort of know these things. Don't ask me how.'

Richie suddenly laughed, 'Jasus, boy, you sound like a fortune-teller.' And then he could have kicked himself when he remembered the old gossip about his friend's origin. But Stephen was laughing too.

'Sure, maybe I am – if I fail the exam I can always buy myself a crystal ball and go to the carnivals.'

He saw her only once at Easter. It was at the Stations of the Cross on Good Friday. She was kneeling in the church, accompanied by her mother, Eddie and her small sister Maeve. He sat three seats behind her and lost all interest in the ceremony. He stood up and down and automatically gave the responses when the priest intoned the familiar prayers. Everyone in the church had to turn and face each Station when the priest and the altar boy stood in front. The station directly behind him was 'Jesus Meets his Mother'. The crowd stood up and genuflected and turned towards the picture, but Stephen stayed looking ahead.

She saw him and her blue eyes met his. Her face was almost instantly suffused with deep red. He never turned to the Station although Máire gave him a little nudge. His eyes burned into Aileen's until she looked away. He knew he had embarrassed her but he didn't care. He had been starved for one look at her, one glance, one word to reassure him that he hadn't frightened her away. He glanced away to please Máire, and as he did he found himself saying a rare prayer.

'Jesus Christ, I know you died on the Cross and I know you suffered for sinners in this life. So have I, and all I ask you now is that I'll see her somewhere soon. I know little about love – I've never had any – but I do know I love her. Please help me if You will.'

In the intensity of his prayer he lost interest in the proceedings and suddenly realised that Máire was kneeling and nudging him again and that he was the only one standing. He knelt down and tried to keep his mind on the rest of the service, hoping wildly that he would get a glimpse of her outside the church if her mother's eagle eye strayed, and if luck or God was on his side.

God was on his side. Her mother was in serious conversation with her friend, unaware that Aileen had strolled to the gate and was leaning with her back against the pillar, listening to Maggie, who was talking away nineteen to the dozen. Even as he walked over to her, he could see she was startled and uneasy.

To lighten the moment he smiled and addressed both of them. 'Great that we've all decided to do penance for our sins.' He was looking at Aileen, his glance hungry to take in every single detail of her lovely face, her arresting blue eyes, the silver-blonde hair thrust inside the collar of her grey gaberdine school coat.

'How is the leg, the chest? How are you after the accident?' She was blushing furiously, as if the allusion to his injuries seemed intimate or too personal.

'I'm fine – everything works again.'

'Good. I'm glad.'

'Will I see you over the Easter?'

'I don't know. Honestly, I don't. There's only next week and then we're back at school.'

'You will,' Maggie said. 'She's cycling down to see me on Monday, and if you're in the right place why can't she see you?'

He smiled warmly at Maggie. 'You're a brick, so you are.' Looking at Aileen once again, he said, 'What about the cross-roads near the woods? At four o'clock?'

'All right. I'll be there, but if my mother finds out I'm dead.'

'She won't. The bushes won't tell. They haven't eyes.'

'Hey, come on. I see your ma is looking around. Come on, bend down and we'll keep under the wall and she'll think we went ahead,' Maggie interrupted.

'Goodbye, Stephen Rodgers,' she whispered. 'Amn't I great now?'

'You are. I won't forget.'

Easter was early and the lamb season was late, and it looked as if every ewe in the place decided to have her lamb on Easter Sunday and in the early hours of Easter Monday. Stephen, Joe and Old Tom were up most of the night easing lambs into the chilly air. One young ewe bleated consistently as they tried to help the lamb out of her.

''Tis a breech and there's two, and we're going to lose her,' Tom told Stephen as Joe held the ewe and Stephen knelt beside her.

Stephen saw her eyes rolling in terror and he rubbed her head telling her. ''Twill be all right. Just keep at it, keep at it.' Suddenly the ewe staggered to her legs, and gave a mighty bleat. In the wavering light of the lamp they could see the two tiny hooves appearing.

'God, boy, you have a way with you.' Joe glanced at Stephen. 'They've turned around.'

The little lamb came with the next contraction, and twenty minutes later the second appeared. But the young ewe had used up all her strength over the long weary night. She could only feebly lick them before lying down and rolling. She gave a few pants and then her breathing stopped.

'She's gone,' Tom said as he turned to Stephen. 'Will you stop gawking at her as if she was a woman? Take the lambs into the shed and feed them and keep them warm. We don't want to lose the lot.'

Stephen got up off his knees and wordlessly collected the two tiny woolly creatures into his arms. Their tiny cries indicated that they were already looking for warmth and food. He hurried through the dark to the farmhouse.

Dawn had broken and the sky was light before they got a few hour's rest.

When he awoke he heard Máire bustling around below. He could hear the sharp snap of her breaking the small dried furze bush to burn and bring the fire back to life. He remembered that Aileen had promised to meet him that day near Barrons Wood. Thinking of her, his raw desire for her flowed through him, taking away all the tiredness and the exhaustion of the night before.

'Don't delay too long in Maggie's. It gets dark early enough – I don't want you meeting some old tramp or some undesirable on the way home. Things aren't what they used to be – people aren't safe out any more.'

'Oh, Mam, have sense – nothing ever happens in a place like this. Who would I be meeting, for the Lord's sake?'

'Do you know what, Miss? I think you're getting too sharp with your answers and too cocky for words since you went up to Dublin to that school.'

'It was your idea, not mine.'

'See what I mean? You're getting right smart with your answers.'

'Will you let the child go, Mary?' Denis MacMahon intervened. 'Sure what's coming over you, worrying about her cycling down the road to Maggie's – a trip she's done a hundred times before? Sure, have a bit of sense, girl.'

Mary bit her lip and tried to swallow a lump in her throat. The lump came a lot lately, and tears and tiredness were never far away.

She wondered yet again if she needed a good tonic. After all, it was the spring and everyone knew how run down you were after the long grey winter. Yes, she might go and see the doctor and get something to help her perk up. She had avoided it for long enough. Mary watched Aileen pull on her navy duffle coat, shoving her hair hurriedly inside the collar. She saw her glance into the mirror near the old pine scrub-up table at the wall. Denis used to shave there before the water was piped in. Today the table looked so different. Aileen had flung out the old oilcloth and she filled an old blue jug with daffodils. They were there now, a flaunting touch of spring, almost obliterating Eddie's two goldfish who, for two years now, had been desultorily swimming around and around in their glass prison.

What's wrong with me? she wondered once again. I have everything, so I have. Why do I feel such foreboding, as if something queer is going to happen?

'I'm off,' Aileen shouted as she mounted her bike outside the door.

'Mind yourself,' Mary called.

'Bye, love,' Aileen's father shouted, heaving himself out of the chair before returning to the job of repairing fences to keep the young lambs in.

Chapter Thirteen

Aileen cycled down the narrow sunlit road. Her long, slim, stockinged legs went round like her churning thoughts. What would she say to him? Why did all the words stick in her throat when she was with him? Why was she so afraid to really look straight into his eyes? Why couldn't she be all chatty and friendly, as if talking to a boy was the same as talking to a girl? Niamh had the gift. She hadn't a bother on her when she was talking to boys. Even when she met some of her brothers' friends she chatted and blathered away without ever stumbling or blushing.

Maybe he wouldn't be there. Yes, that was it – maybe he wouldn't be there. Everyone were so busy on the farm now, what with the lambing and the sowing. Ignoring her pounding heart, Aileen tried to pray. She couldn't make up her mind whether she was praying that he would or wouldn't be there.

Her whirring tyres swallowed up the long road and, way down at the bottom of the road, she could glimpse the dark solid trees at the beginning of Barrons Wood.

He was there. She could see him quite clearly, standing at the bridge wall, looking down into the river. His bike was beside him and he was smoking a cigarette. God almighty, she thought, he looks so grown-up, a man already. What kind of talk can I put on him? What does he want me for?

He glanced up when he heard her approaching. She drew up beside him and put her foot on the road, but remained sitting on the bike. Aileen was glad that the sound of the weir was so noisy – if God was good it might drown out the sound of her thumping heart.

'Hello.' His voice was low.

She glanced up. 'Hello yourself.'

'I thought you wouldn't come.'

'I thought you wouldn't come either. The lambs and things.'

'You don't think small things like lambs would keep me away, do you?'

113

'I don't know. Sometimes I feel I don't know anything.' She thought her voice sounded abnormal. Kind of high and shaky. Maybe it was her imagination. Would she dare look at him now, really have a good hard look, so that tonight, lying beside Maeve, she could try to recall him?

He helped her off the bike and for a while they stood side by side, leaning on the wall and looking into the fast-flowing river.

'I won't offer you a cigarette. You're too young.'

Will I be flippant and say something like 'Try me', or will I agree like a young idiot that I am too young? 'I've never smoked – but I might some day.'

'Would you like today to be the day?'

'No.' She watched as he flung his cigarette into the river and the red glow of the ash for a disappeared into the frothy foam. They were silent.

As if he could read her thoughts of some minutes before, he straightened up and put his hand under her face. Looking straight into her eyes, he said, 'Why are you afraid to look at me?'

'Who told you that?' Her heart started to thump again and she wondered how he had guessed what was going through her mind. She tried to relax and look straight into his eyes. They weren't black – not really. It was the thick jet-black lashes that made them appear so. She had never realised that he had such a firm, beautifully shaped mouth. She wildly wondered what it would be like if he kissed her and then hoped he never would, not for years anyway, because if he did she'd die.

'Well, what do you see?'

'I thought your eyes were black, but they're not. They're brown.'

'I have no idea what colour they are. I can see without glasses so they do me.'

He was smiling. She grinned too and found the knot inside her easing a little.

'Look,' Stephen said, 'why don't we put the bikes into the woods and go down to the river?'

'Good idea. I don't want anyone to see us.'

'I know you don't. And if they did, I'd be accused of baby-snatching.'

She leaned against the wall as he wheeled both their bikes

into the woods. I'm glad he didn't suggest a walk in the woods, she thought. They're too dark and shadowy and cold. And maybe something terrible would happen. Oh God, what could happen? I'm getting right fanciful.

They clambered over the low stile and he held her hand in a warm grip as she jumped down beside him. Still holding his hand, she walked down the steep muddy track to the water's edge. She noticed that the gorse was still in little tight buds, the tiny yellow slits peeping out here and there offering an early promise of the explosion of colour that would soon happen.

He turned round before they made their way to the gap. He reached out and wordlessly slid his hand under her hair and lifted it from the confines of her collar. It blew into her mouth over his hand and he held it briefly. 'It's like silk, ivory silk. Did you know that?'

'No, I didn't. I only know that it's there and I'm not bald.'

He threw back his head and she was glad she had made him laugh. They ran the rest of the way and he held her hand again as they leaped over the moss-covered stones scattered near the water's edge. There was no sound except the gurgle of the water as it tumbled down the weir. In the middle of the wide river they could see the undercurrents and tiny whirlpools as water tore by.

'You know,' she told him, 'that our Eddie has a dream that he'll go off on a wide raft and sail away to the river's end? He still talks about it.'

'I know. He told me,' Stephen said. 'Maybe he just loves the river. Did you know that some people are river people? They feel for it. They love to watch it in all its moods. In full spate in winter, low in summer tides, and struggling for life in a drought.'

'I didn't. Tell me, Stephen Rodgers, how do you know all that stuff?'

'I know. Come on over and we'll sit down by the willows. We'll be sheltered there.' He saw her hesitate and glance around, as if she was afraid of being seen or what might happen. He could see the fear and apprehension in her blue eyes. 'You'll be all right. You'll be all right with me.' He could see the beginnings of the blush that was becoming so familiar to him.

She shook her thick blonde hair. 'Sure I know I will.'

They sat in the shelter of the willows. She sat a little away from him with her arms around her knees, her blue eyes unwaveringly looking at the river, her thoughts in a tailspin again. She wondered if he would try anything like – Oh God, she wouldn't think of what might happen. She remembered the religious teaching and how wrong it was to put yourself in a situation that might lead to sin. But even the little sweet nun would agree that sitting at the side of the river on Easter Monday without a single living soul in sight would have to be an occasion of sin. And sitting with the best-looking fellow in the whole of Ireland too. She shivered for no reason. He reached out and put his arms around her and pulled her near him.

'Don't panic – I'm only keeping you warm.' She moved nearer, and suddenly they both had their arms around each other and he was kissing her lips, eyes, neck. She felt inside her the strange peculiar sensations she had become so used to when ever she thought of him. Now they swept over her and she felt herself returning his kisses, running her hand through his black hair as she pressed his head nearer to her. As he kissed her again and again, their hearts hammered so loudly she felt they would explode.

She was the first to gain some control. She looked at him in wonder, taking in every line of his face. She reached out and brushed back a black lock that had fallen across his forehead. 'How did I know what to do? I've never ever kissed anyone before. But God, we must stop now, I know we must. I know in here.' She tapped her breast. He reached out and tried to kiss her again. She stopped him, turning her head away.

'No. We can't do that again. I'm only fourteen, Stephen – I'd be afraid.'

'I adore you. You know that,' he told her.

He was looking straight into her eyes and the thought came: I won't have any bother remembering him now. No matter what happens, I'll always remember him.

'I know if thinking of someone forever is adoring that I adore you too. Look, Stephen, we'll make a sort of pact.' She could see he was still breathing heavily, and in her young way she knew that this was the way it would be every time they'd meet. She had read that boys were more easily aroused, that girls were more careful, more watchful. With her own heart still beating erratically and her young body swamped with desire, she knew she wouldn't be careful and watchful when she was in Stephen Rodgers's arms. 'We'll make a promise that we won't see all that much of each other until I'm sixteen. Oh sure, we'll meet at times outside Mass – maybe devotions and retreats and things. Maybe in Ross or in Waterford or places.'

He was about to object, but she leaned over and put her finger on his lips. ''Tis for the best, you know that.' She stopped, but continued to look at him as if she couldn't get enough of him. Then she said, 'If we feel a change or feel differently as time goes by – we'll let each other know.'

'You have a body and a face like an angel, and a mind like a wise old woman,' he whispered again, taking her in his arms. 'I couldn't live without seeing you.'

'Oh, you'll see me so you will, and you can write to me and call yourself somebody else, a girl's name. What about Richie Casey's Stephanie? Will you promise?'

'I'll try. I'll do that, but you need never worry that I'll change. I can't, I know that. I know these things.'

'Now who's the wise old man?'

They kissed each other long and tenderly, but while they still had some measure of control she jumped to her feet and pulled him up.

'Wait, will you? It's easier for you than me.'

She blushed as she got his meaning, and waited until he was beside her. Walking back over the stones, she knew she would never love anyone else. She didn't care about his father or his mother or all the old gossips.

'Well,' she said when she reached the edge of Barrons Wood, 'when I'm sixteen?'

'Yes, my love, when you're sweet sixteen. And may God help me till then.'

Denis MacMahon had noticed over the months that his wife wasn't looking too well. He knew she wasn't one to complain, even when she was sick. He was happy and content with her as a wife. He was an unimaginative man and went down through the days without too much comment. He wasn't sure if he loved her, in the sense that couples loved each other in books and films and things. He wasn't even sure if he really knew what love was.

What he had felt for Teresa Rodgers had been completely different than what he felt for his wife Mary. Way back, nearly twenty years ago now, he had briefly clutched at something that sent fire through his veins. If that dark, smiling, impish girl had asked him to throw himself under a bus, he would have done it. Sometimes, lying beside his wife at night, when sleep eluded him, she came back to him. In his dreams she hadn't changed. She was young and slim, quick-moving and always smiling – her black hair blowing across her face, her hand constantly brushing it away. She'd be older if she had lived – sure she'd be in her late thirties now. Would she have gotten old, with lines around her mouth? Would the white of her teeth be yellow now – maybe full of gold fillings, like the two Mary had? He hated the gold fillings but Mary had had them when he'd met her and, if anything, she was proud of them. Strange, he thought, getting gold in your teeth. He gave himself the luxury of these thoughts only when he was in bed in that half-dreamworld between sleeping and waking. He often thought of Teresa's son, living only six miles away. A fine tall handsome lad – but not like her. Except for the black hair and a certain glance – a fleeting sort of expression – there wasn't much of a look of her.

Mary turned towards him and he put his arms around her. She murmured something in her sleep and he thought he heard the word 'afraid'. *Afraid.* He tightened his grip and told her to hush now. Instead she opened her eyes and stared at him.

He asked, 'What woke you?'

'Oh Denis, I don't know. I'm just tired all the time. I was thinking of going to Doctor O'Neill for a tonic. Maybe 'tis the change of life or something.'

'Well, if it is, then don't be bothering yourself about it.'

'But I hope it isn't. Lately I got a notion that you might like another son before I'm too old. One son isn't great, is it?'

'One son, particularly one like our Eddie, is more than I can cope with. Sure aren't you just saying you're feeling tired? Imagine how tired you'd be if we had another child. Hush now and go to sleep, and see that you go to the doctor.'

'I will, Denis, I will.'

She put her arm around him and put her head under his chin. His pyjama top was unbuttoned and she could see the fair hair on his chest. Lately she had noticed that it was more grey than fair. The same with the hair on his head.

She soon heard his deep breathing and she knew that he had fallen asleep. She recalled that it had been ages since they had made love. He wasn't a very demanding man. She had insisted on the safe periods for a few years after Maeve was born, but then, when she hadn't bothered and no other baby was conceived, she felt she was getting past it. She loved Denis with a fierce protective love, a bit like she loved her three children. He was hers, just like they were hers. The thought that she'd ever have to let them go was so abhorrent to her that she always shut it out of her head. She had read about women who made demands on their husbands, who actually initiated intercourse and made the first move. God above, she couldn't imagine ever doing that. She'd die of shame. Denis had never seen her naked. She always undressed in the dark. For that matter she had never seen Denis naked either; he always sat on the other side of the bed and put on the pyjamas bottoms before the top. No – no, she couldn't ever imagine herself ever doing these awful peculiar things that the article in the magazine had hinted at.

She thought of Aileen, growing more beautiful by the day, and shuddered, thinking that some day some man would lay his hands on her beautiful girl. He had better be the right sort of young man. Someone up in Dublin – a man from the college or with a big job in Dublin Castle. She'd have to watch Aileen and be vigilant when she was home on holidays. There were so few suitable young men around. She felt afraid sometimes when she saw Stephen Rodgers. There was something in those eyes. He didn't look at her like he'd look at other women. There was something in his eyes, as if he knew something that she didn't. She'd have to be on guard and be more watchful – ah, with the help of the Blessed Mother, it was all her imagination and when she get the tonic all the fear would go away.

Aileen MacMahon's pact stood the test of time. She saw Stephen Rodgers only ten more times before her sixteenth birthday.

Lying in bed next to Niamh in the dormitory, or studying in the evening, or kneeling at Mass in the early mornings, she could recall every one of the ten times, every nuance, word, glance or movement he made.

On three occasions during the holidays she had danced with him at the Ross Carnival dance in the marquee.

They danced together in perfect tune, in perfect motion. Neither of them wanted to converse and whisper the silly trite prattle that was usual under the circumstances. They didn't discuss the heat inside the marquee, the band, the floor. She knew he had left school after finishing the Leaving Certificate, and was working full-time on the farm. At the end of the last dance in the stifling marquee, where the smell of hair oil mingled with that of sweat and the beer imbibed by young men who needed the courage to request a dance, he asked, 'Our pact still stands?'

'Of course,' she told him.

'So you haven't changed?' he asked quietly.

'No.' She looked at him in blue-eyed alarm. 'Why – have you?'

'No – I'll never do that. I told you that.' He pulled her close and dropped a kiss on top of her fair head. She could feel his heart starting to thump. It pounded so much against her breast she thought it would tear out of his chest. She pulled away. 'A year more,' she whispered.

'Yes, but why sixteen?'

'Because at sixteen I'll be a woman.'

He laughed. 'You think so?'

'I know so,' she told him.

During the following week someone told Aileen's mother that she had been seen dancing at the carnival dance.

Mary hadn't been well for a whole year before. She was suffering from what Aileen's father described as 'nervous trouble'. Aileen had been quite shocked when she had come home from school for the summer holidays.

Her mother looked pale and older. Aileen could see thin lines at the side of her mouth and under her eyes. There was a large bottle of greenish-yellow mixture on the dresser, her mother's tonic. She saw her taking two dessert spoonfuls of the liquid after every meal, and though the daily ritual went on and on, her mother didn't get much better. Once Aileen asked her what it was, and before Mary could answer Eddie piped up, 'Phosphorous from fish bellies.' They all laughed and Eddie was glad he had caused some merriment. There hadn't been that much laughter around the house lately.

Eddie was thirteen now and had grown long and lanky. Every other morning there was a row over his short pants. He wanted long trousers to hide his 'long stupid sticks of legs', he told them over breakfast on Saturday morning. His mother wearily told him when he was back at school he'd have long trousers.

'I don't want those clerical grey trousers like old-age pensioners, I want pants like the fellow staying in Powers has. He's home from America and he has trousers like overalls but there's no top, and they're called jeans. That's what I want – shaggin' jeans.'

His father reached out and gave him a cuff on the cheek.

'Stop annoying your mother, she's worked herself to the bone taking care of you all.'

Aileen saw her mother flash a grateful yet sad little look at her father. Eddie slunk away.

Maeve, nine now, had a little friend to stay. The pair recognised that they'd be better off out in the sunshine and wandered away, arm in arm, already immersed in plans for the lovely free day ahead.

Aileen stood up, about to clear the dishes.

'Sit down, Aileen,' her father told her. 'Your mother has something to say to you.'

Aileen glanced at them and wondered if something had happened. Maybe her mother was seriously ill and her father was about to tell her something awful.

Her mother cleared her throat and then the words came, hurried and tumbled. 'Aileen, I was told by someone – I won't say who now – that you were seen with that Stephen Rodgers at last Thursday's carnival dance. You were dancing with him all night, and it was the sort of dancing that was too, too – oh, I don't want to say it.'

'Well, I'll say it. Too intimate and close.' Her father looked at her. This is the first time in his whole life he has sat united with Mam about something, Aileen thought.

'There's nothing wrong with Stephen Rodgers,' she muttered through her fast-drying lips.

'Aileen, your mother isn't well, so I want you to listen and promise her that you'll do what she says. I want that now.'

She looked at her mother and could see that Mary had

121

thought that her friendship with Stephen would pass and die down as if nothing had happened.

'Listen, Aileen, I don't ever, ever want you to see Stephen Rodgers again. Maybe 'tis only a fancy, a childish crush, you have on him, but I know you like him. I've seen you talking to him after Mass and when you meet him in Ross on Saturdays. I was demented when you spent the day fishing with him a few summers back. But you were only a child then. You're a young woman now. I heard – don't ask me how, but I did – I heard you went to visit him in hospital when he had that accident. I can't have it, Aileen – your father agrees with me. Stephen Rodgers isn't suitable for you. I don't have to repeat that. We don't know anything about him. We don't know who he really is, or what blood is in him. These things are important in the farming community, where people know what good stock is.'

'Mam – stop, will you please? Let me tell you that Stephen Rodgers is very nice. You have never spoke to him in your entire life, you know nothing about him. He's gentle, educated, well-read – and he's above all the other fellows around here. He's better, so he is.'

'Mother of God, so I was right. You are interested in this nobody. He's the son of a travelling tinker, you know that. Do I have to keep telling you?' Mary's voice trailed away and ended in a sob. 'Please, Aileen,' she cried, 'promise me you'll keep away from that boy. Promise me.'

Aileen looked at her parents. Her father was the picture of discomfort, his work-scarred hand rumbling his hair, pushing it back and forth on his forehead. It was obvious that this whole conversation was distasteful to him. Aileen could see that his mind was already gone to the work that lay ahead out on his increasing acres.

They don't know, she thought, they don't really know what love is. She realised that her father had never really loved her mother – not in the wild, wonderful, mad, heady, physical sense, when love and need and desire were emotions that accompanied you through all the mundane tasks every single day. I will promise, she thought, looking at her mother's thin, lined face and the brown hair already greying so noticeably at the sides. I will promise because it's the best thing now.

She muttered a quick prayer to the Sacred Heart whose painted eyes were looking steadily into hers. The picture, with the small red globed paraffin lamp underneath, had been there as long as she could remember.

'All right, Mam, I promise – I promise.' She had her hands behind her back, and she crossed her fingers and muttered a lightning prayer that God would forgive her for her terrible lies.

'Thanks, Aileen. I know you'll keep your word.' Her mother stood up and gave her a quick, sheepish hug. If anything, her unfamiliar gesture highlighted how seriously Mary looked on Aileen's association with Stephen.

Almost in a dream, Aileen collected the rest of the dishes from the breakfast table. She walked towards the sink, thinking, I must be more vigilant. I must write and explain that we must not be seen together again. At least not until next year, when her suspicions will be lulled, because I'll be older and maybe expected to have more sense.

'Well, that's it then,' her father said, awkwardly patting her shoulder as he passed on his way out. His clumsy touch made her realise how little physical contact they had as a family.

She didn't feel bad about telling a lie, making a false promise. She remembered the dance and the way Stephen held her. She remembered his soft-spoken question, 'Why sixteen?' It had been a childish pact on her part. But now her mother's dislike and animosity towards Stephen made it feasible. They would bide their time because, as sure as night followed day, she knew she would spend most of her life with him.

PART TWO

Chapter Fourteen

O ld Sheridan came on a bright spring day. Tom Rodgers and Joe were at the cattle mart in Waterford. Stephen had spent all the morning working at the drainage in the low field. Máire Ryan had just finished hanging out the washing, content that the lively breeze and the April sunshine would do the job of drying in a few hours, and was drinking a mug of strong tea – he always felt that a mug of what she called foxy tea would set her up for the day – when she heard Shep barking excitedly in the yard. Looking out of the window she saw old Sheridan coming in, carrying a brown-paper parcel and shouting something to the dog, who backed off, growling. She wondered what brought him so early in the year; the tinkers didn't come to the place until late June or early July. Shouting, 'Down boy, down,' to the barking dog, she arose from the table, reaching the half-door at the same time as old Sheridan. Máire had never seen him at close quarters and the thought came to her that she had never seen a face so lined, so pitted, and as brown as a nut, yet with such kindness in the bright brown eyes.

'Well, ma'am, good day to ye – and a nice fresh day it is, thank God.'

'Good day to you, Mr Sheridan.'

'Is the young lad in, would you be thinkin'?'

'No, he's draining the low field. Can I be of help?'

'No, Ma'am, no, thanks all the same, Ma'am. But what I have here,' he tapped the soiled paper parcel, 'is somethin' I'd like to hand over meself. I've waited till now – 'tis the time now.'

Máire could see that this was an errand that was important to him. There was a serious look in his still-bright, shrewd eyes, and she realised that it hadn't been easy for him to come to Tom Rodgers's place after all these years. Her curiosity rose. What could he want after so long? Had he some conniving and shrewd plan to upset them and cause trouble? As if his type hadn't caused enough trouble to Tom and Stephen, who had to live with the slur of being the son of a travelling man all his young life.

'Well, I'm afraid if you want Stephen Rodgers, sure you'll have to go down to the field yourself. You can't miss him – he's a big fellow with hair as black as a raven.'

'Sure Ma'am, I know well what he looks like,' old Sheridan muttered as he walked away.

Blessed Virgin, she wondered as she watched him going out the gate, have I done right in sending that man to poor Stephen? What does he want from him? As far as Máire knew, old Sheridan had never set foot in the yard since he had brought the child back. Bad cess to him and all his ilk, she thought, remembering the terrible heartbreak and sorrow that he had brought to the household.

Stephen, digging his drain, saw old Sheridan coming from a good way off. He had seen the old man from time to time over the years but had never spoken to him. He knew the story of how he had come to his grandfather's house. He bore no ill will towards the man; in fact, he often thought he should have been grateful to him he hadn't been brought up with a tinker's tribe at the side of the road.

Stephen watched him as he made his way down to the drain. He appeared old and beaten now, and seemed to have shrunk in inches. When he was younger he had instilled fear in all the children in the parts. There had been rumours that if you met him on a dark lonely road he would snatch you and put you in a bag and take you away to his lair. Yet, over all the years, there was no tangible evidence that he had ever harmed anyone.

'May God bless the work and keep your strength with you,' he greeted Stephen as he approached.

Stephen stood up to his full height, towering over the old man. 'Good day to you. What brings you to the parts as early as this?'

'I have something to give you, and it should be in your keepin'. I have it with me many a long day, and the time has come – aye, the time has come.'

Stephen looked at the proffered brown-papered and

twined parcel. It was small and insignificant, and he idly wondered what it could possibly contain to interest him. In silence he took the parcel. It was light and very dirty, as if it had been wrapped and tied and carried around for years and years.

'Thank you – I appreciate it,' he said quietly.

'I thought you'd like to have it – you're a man now and might want to know things. I came with it because I won't be here this summer. My son Ned is takin' over. Things are changin' – not like the old times. There's no livin' for tinkers any more. All that plastic and stuff ruined us. I'll go now, lad, and 'tis a relief to my mind that I've put it in your hands. May the road always rise with you.'

A strange sadness came to Stephen as he watched the old man make his way to the gap, around the bend and out of sight. He knew somehow he'd never see old Sheridan again. But sitting on the ditch, with the April sun warm on his back, he felt his heart racing at the thought of what he might discover when he finally had the tightly bound knots undone.

Inside there were two leather-covered black books. Their gold lettering was fading, yet he could clearly make out the word 'Diary' and the year at the top of each: 1940 and 1941. Oblivious of the cheeky robin who had come to perch on the handle of his shovel and the crows who cawed noisily in the nearby trees, Stephen noticed that his hands were shaking as he opened the first book.

Her name was written in a firm slanting hand – *Teresa Rodgers, Tulla, Co. Kilkenny. 1940.* He noticed that the pages were charred at the edges, as if they had been near a fire. Flicking through them, he saw that the first little book was almost full. Although the ink was fading in patches, most of the words were clearly legible. He saw that his hands, still shaking, were putting fresh earth marks on the pages, and wiped each one in turn on the front of his shirt. His heart was still racing. Was it possible that these little books would answer his questions, tell him all the things he so desperately wanted to know?

The house was silent as he lay in bed that night. The silence had a waiting urgency about it, as if the April night was as eager to know what was between the pages as he was. The decision to put off reading the diaries until night time hadn't been easy. But he knew he would have to read them from start to finish to get a feel for them – to understand why his mother had left everything she had known for a man she must truly have loved.

*

January 1st. Today is brand new, sunny and freezing. The frost is everywhere, twinkling and gleaming, and is very beautiful, yet the blooming thing means I can't ride out Laddie. He'll be bored, snorting, stamping and sniffling, but I'll soon go down to him and make it up to him. Sometimes I think he's the only thing that really understands me. He just stands there shivering, and quiet, when I'm sad and licks my hair, snorts and stamps when I'm happy. I know that Daddy loves me in his way. But sometimes I think that it's out of duty, because I'm all he has and maybe he feels he should make up to me because Mammy is dead. I hear Máire banging and clattering below so I suppose I'd better go down. If anything interesting happens today I won't forget to write it down in you, my brand-new diary, before I go to bed tonight.

It's after midnight – well after midnight. Today wasn't as boring as I thought it might be. I went to Ross and met Kate Barron. She told me there was a bit of a hooley on in her house. She asked me to come and told me it could be all right, her brother had asked a few friends. So I said yes and I went. Daddy insisted on me going in the pony and trap which was so stupid. I wanted to cycle. It meant poor old Joe had to hang around in Ross waiting for the do to be over. Still, I don't think he minded. I also think he had his bit of New Year celebration. Denis MacMahon was at the hooley and I know he's interested in me. He asked me to go to the pictures with him in Waterford. I told him I might, so I might. He asked me not to tease him – would I or wouldn't I? I told him I would so. And I will. I think he's nice and solid like a dependable rock. I love his fair hair and those blue eyes. I think his eyes are the colour of cornflowers – imagine telling a fellow like that that his eyes are the colour of a wild flower! I don't think he'd know what I meant. So before I left I promised I'd see him on Saturday at seven o'clock. Dear diary, I'll let you know how it goes.

*

The next few entries were short and simple, but soon there was something more.

127

Helped Máire around the house today. She reminded me that I was going back to school next Monday, and she asked me to help her sew on some tapes on my clothes. I don't like going back to school but, joy of joy, this is my last few months. Daddy wanted me just to come home after school and stay here and help Máire. A sort of waiting game until he marries me off to a nice prosperous farmer. I think he would approve of me going to the pictures with Denis MacMahon. After all, he is the eldest son and will get a sizeable farm.

Got the curse today and the cramps were appalling. Still, the worst will be over before I go out on Saturday night. I'm glad. I don't think that a fellow likes a pale, cramp-ridden girl crawling along beside him...

I met him standing outside O'Connors sweetshop. He was dressed up in his new suit and had a lovely new overcoat as well. He was holding a small bag and I could see him before he could see me. I thought he looked sweet, even nervous, looking up and down the road. The picture was a bit soppy, Jeannette MacDonald and Nelson Eddie in *Maytime*. The singing was lovely, though, and Denis went groping for my hand when Nelson Eddie was singing 'Sweetheart'. His hands were strong and a little rough. I let him hold my hand, and he seemed very content intertwining his fingers in mine. Admittedly, holding hands made it impossible to eat the chocolates he bought.

After the pictures we walked back to his small van. He said very little driving home the three miles. I kept sneakily looking at his profile and decided he was very nice. Very nice – doesn't that sound awful? No one anywhere should be called very nice. When he arrived at the end of our lane I told him I would like to walk the rest – to clear my head and appreciate the night. I told him I loved the night when it was all dark and velvety and the stars a million miles away. He told me I was mad and then he put his arms around me and kissed me. Then he kissed me again and asked me would I do a line with him when I was home for good. I told him I wasn't the type to do lines, and that he could have any girl in the whole parish. He kissed me again and told me he didn't want any other girl in the parish or anywhere else; he wanted me. I felt good that someone really wanted me for me – not out of duty bit like Daddy, not because they're paid for it, a bit like Máire. No, no – that's not fair. Máire is great and has been so good to me. So I asked him why he wanted me and he told me because I was lovely and because I was crazy. I liked his answers and I'm not a bit beautiful – my hair is too black and my eyes are neither black or brown or grey, more a dirty navy like my school uniform. But I kissed him on the nose and told him I'd let him know about the steady line at Easter, or maybe I'd write. I then ducked from under his arm and he tried to catch me, but I ran up the lane. I was well at the farmhouse door before I heard him drive away.

Nothing much happened today. We just got my cases ready for school. Daddy drove me to the station in the pony and trap. I got up early because it was a mild day. I rode out Laddie and we had a great gallop. The last one until Easter. I kissed him goodbye a dozen times and he kept looking at me with his big mournful brown eyes. He knew I was going away. I think he is the most intelligent friend I have and he knows absolutely everything.

*

Stephen could see that the next few entries were short, all about returning to school and meeting her friends, and them all telling each other everything about their Christmas and their holidays. Teresa's best friend was Anna, and she referred to her again and again, describing how they went down to Waterford on their day off, and how Anna met this boy from Waterpark and blushed so much she cried down the rain afterwards. She mentioned studying for her Leaving Certificate, and how she hoped she'd get a good result for her father's sake. She mentioned what she called the curse and the cramps; she had had to stay in bed on one occasion, and the matron had given her a warm drink and a hot water bottle to ease the pain. She seemed impatient with it – 'Imagine, if I live to be fifty I'll have to put up with that every single month. Ridiculous – absolutely ridiculous.'

*

February 10th. I got a letter from Daddy today. It was in his beautiful copperplate writing. I often wondered how or who taught him to write so beautifully. I find it hard to visualise him sitting at he kitchen table with the oil lamp casting a long shadow and he, God love him, wracking his brain to write to me. He told me that everything is fine and that Laddie is good, that Joe is riding him out every day for a while. He said he has a touch of the flu and his sciatica is back, but I'm not to worry, that Máire has made him some red flannel belts for his back. He told me that they are all looking forward to Easter when I'd be home again. Then again, he sent his fondest regards and signed off, 'Your Daddy'. He has never, ever told me he loves me or anything like that. I wonder if I had a mother would she tell me these things or what? If I do decide to do the line with Denis MacMahon, will he tell me he loves me? I really like him, but I don't think I love him like I should. I don't lie in bed thinking of him like one should. My heart doesn't go racing wildly when I remember his kiss. Anna tells me that when she thinks of her boyfriend John she feels all sort of melty and peculiar. I don't feel like that, and yet I think that Denis is lovely and very handsome.

The letter from Denis MacMahon was short and to the point. I liked it; it was honest and direct like himself. He enjoyed going to the pictures with me, and he's counting the weeks until Easter. He hopes my answer will be yes.

Dear diary, will it be yes? I honestly don't know. If the word gets out that we are courting – isn't that a peculiar word, 'courting'? Peculiar or not, that's what they'll say. 'Teresa Rodgers and Denis MacMahon are courting.' Even Daddy will be happy. They say matchmaking is going out, but underneath it still goes on. I know that. A match between Teresa Rodgers, only daughter of Tom Rodgers, who has a sizeable farm, and Denis MacMahon, eldest son of John MacMahon, would be perfect. Blessed Virgin, I don't really want that. I don't. Though I think Denis MacMahon really is nice and the best around, I don't want to settle down on a farm just three miles from where I was born and bred. I want to travel, I want to experience life – real, throbbing life, not just a dull routine existence on a farm, having children and working like a black and having more children until I'm old and the crampy curse goes away. But of course if I tell Denis that, he'll tell me I'm mad and he'll kiss me and I'll like the pressure of his nice mouth on mine and I'll feel a glow that someone loves me. Is that enough? I don't know.

Stephen glanced at the clock over near the Infant of Prague, and reluctantly put the diary carefully away under his mattress. Already he felt he almost knew Teresa. It was what Joe had told him – she had been an impulsive, restless girl. And the most astonishing thing was that Denis MacMahon, Aileen's father, had been in love with her. The thought filled him momentarily with a strange, peculiar feeling that things were going full cycle, and a peculiar sense of loss that he would never see Teresa, never get to know her.

His last thought before falling asleep was he would have loved her. He might even have been able to tell her that he loved her. She seemed to want to know that people felt things like that.

I hope I do all right in the Easter exam. Sister Bernadette tells me that the Easter test will be marked like the Leaving. I hear her saying it in my dreams – 'If you fail that, dear girls, you'll fail your Leaving Certificate and all your efforts and your good parents' money will be wasted.' She's cheerful, is our Sister Bernadette.

The other day we had the end-of-school lecture about how we are young women now, and how our young bodies are temples pure and undefiled. She went on about purity, telling us it was one of the greatest virtues: 'And don't fool yourselves, dear children, purity is something not only you yourselves will value. The time will come when you are out in the big wide world, and the time will come when you will meet members of the opposite sex. That is the way of the world. But don't fool yourselves into thinking that men like girls of easy virtue. I can assure you that it is not so.' Anna winked at me then, and I couldn't suppress a giggle, and Sister Bernadette glared at me. Sure I know what Anna was thinking – maybe Bernadette joined the nuns because she found that out. Sister Bernadette went on after her glare at me: 'No man in this world wants spoilt goods. Oh yes, maybe for a short distraction, but not forever. So, girls, you must remain as pure as the driven snow until you marry. To do that might not be easy. The devil is always on the lookout for the moment of weakness, the wavering of standards. You must be constant in your daily vigil to keep your bodies pure and undefiled. Never be caught in a situation that might be considered an occasion of sin. A dark lonely road, outside a dance hall, in dark seats in unhealthy cinema houses. You must never forget to pray, every single day, to Our Lady the purest star in God's firmament.'

What a long spiel! She went on a bit more but my thoughts starting straying. I tried to think of all the occasions of sin where I might be in danger. The fumbling kisses of Mike Power the night after the crossroads dance. My own cousin grabbing me after the wedding in Waterford. I'm glad he had a black eye for days. Denis MacMahon's kisses after the pictures. They were nice – oh God, that horrible word again. Nice. They were lovely and I nearly love him – I really do – but is nearly enough? I think Anna is in love. I wonder will I ever really be? Will I ever meet someone who will sweep me off my feet? God, I sound like a lovelorn shit. Now that's a very terrible word, but very descriptive – and not suitable for a girl who goes to an expensive boarding school. Anyway I have Laddie. I really love Laddie.

April 2nd. The tests are over and I think I did all right. If I did I suppose I'll get the Leaving Certificate. But what then? Where will I go from there? What is out there for a girl if you don't want to be a teacher or a nurse? I don't want to be a teacher, trying to ram a modicum of education into some numbskull's head. I don't want to have my nostrils filled with chalk and ink and dusty floorboards. Neither do I want to mop up blood and heave old men and women on to bedpans. Honestly, I don't know what I want. I only know I want to be out there and feel the wind and the rain, and smell freedom. Am I cracked altogether, as Máire would say? One thing I hope is that I won't be a disappointment to Daddy. In his own way he has been so very good to me.

Tomorrow we're going home on holidays – yippee, yippee. Oh, maybe I shouldn't be yippee-ing, because I'll have to make up my mind about Denis MacMahon. What'll I do? I don't know.

April 3rd. I'm home, and a lovely surprise welcomed me. Daddy and Máire stood there in the kitchen smiling after Joe had collected me in the pony and trap. I wanted to just dump my case on the floor and hug Shep and see the new kittens and, more important still, run out and hug Laddie. But they insisted I take my bag upstairs and unpack first. I did and what a lovely surprise! My room was all done up. Lovely new pale pink wallpaper with little roses and ribbons and a little silvery thread running down through it. There was new varnish on the dark floorboards and a lovely new pale green rug. Máire had got old Mrs Duggan to make new curtains and they are short and full and they match the new cover on my eiderdown. I turned around and the two of them stood there, Daddy clearing his throat as if he was embarrassed that he was involved in such flibberty-jumpety things as fixing up a girl's room. I just flung up my arms around both of them and thanked them. He just patted me on the back saying, "Tis nothing, 'tis nothing.' I do love him really, and I worry sometimes, because I'm all he has. Wouldn't it have been wonderful if my mother hadn't died and if I had hordes of brothers and sisters like so many other girls?

I'm lying here in the bed in my lovely new decorated room and I'm writing in you, my dear diary, wondering what I'll do about Denis MacMahon. I do like him so. And he is so nice – no, not nice, I hate the word – so well-built, so attractive, with that lovely fair hair. I can hear all the women saying, if I do agree to the strong line, 'Aren't they lovely, she's so dark and he's so fair.' I probably won't see him until the dance on Easter, or maybe after devotions on Good Friday, or in Ross on Easter Saturday.

I suppose I'll get a few Easter eggs, although I heard they're positively inedible because of the war. Isn't it amazing that the war is raging in Europe and England is being bombed and things, while we're cocooned in our safe little world? I wouldn't mind being over there in the thick of it, maybe in the WRENS or the WAAFS or something like that. Imagine running around, saluting your superior officers and clicking your heels and being given orders to go overseas or something. Think of it. Wouldn't it be so exciting? Sometimes I get so restless and bored. Then I hate myself. Sometimes I feel so guilty because I'm like that. I should be grateful to God for all I have. And now I have my lovely newly decorated room. I must pray to Our Lady for a grain of sense. Goodnight.

April 4th. The weather is very cold, no sign of spring, although the early daffodils are peeping out from under the trees in the low field. I went for a lovely ride today on Laddie. I would normally go towards MacMahons', but today I didn't, just in case I would see Denis. I went in the opposite direction. Why I don't want to see him I can't say.

Even as I write, Daddy and Joe are out in the cold wind because some of the lambs are very late. It seems sinful lying here in luxury, knowing they're out there for hours and hours hauling some reluctant little lamb, probably a breech position, into the cold world. I'm wide awake and if they're not in soon I'll just dress myself and put on my tweed coat and go down and help them.

April 5th. I did go out last night to help with the lambing, but Daddy was annoyed and told me to go in, that it was too cold. Did I want to get something on my chest that would kill me? I told him to have sense, I was as strong as an ox. He muttered something about my mother thinking she was as strong as an ox and where did it get her? I ignored him and helped them with the late lambs. It was a bit of bedlam – just when one poor ewe had given birth, another across the way would do the same. It looked as if they had made a pact to drive us all mad by having their lambs at the same time. We lost three poor lambs and one ewe. It was so sad to see the limp little lambs, with all their woolly curls and their little hooves. After the ewe went, Daddy told me to take the lamb into the kitchen. I gave her a feed of beastings and she's fine now. So beautiful and trusting – her little eyes never leave my face when I'm feeding her. It made me think what it must be like to have a baby. A real live little wriggling baby suckling your breast. I'm sure it would be wonderful, so fulfilling. Then again, before you have a baby, you must have a man. And you must love that man – really love him – before you'd want a baby for him.

I really want to love someone like that – I want the heavens to explode when I'm making love with a man. If a tiny baby is the result then it would be a wonderful baby, a magnificent baby – not just a pallid little thing conceived out of duty and obligation. Will the heavens explode with Denis MacMahon? I honestly don't think so.

April 7th. I met him today. I was in Ross as I knew I would be. Daddy gave me five pounds to buy a new dress or whatever I wanted for Easter. I got a lovely one, red, with a wide belt and a bow at the neck and a full skirt. Red is a bit flamboyant, but I love it, so if Máire shakes her head and Daddy raises his eyes, I'll tell them it's my dress and I'll be wearing it. Anyway, dear diary, there he was, coming out of Corcoran's hardware shop, carrying a parcel. He stopped when he saw me and I declare to God he went bright red. He's lovely really. Sort of vulnerable – is that the right word? Anyway, I went over and he reached out with his free hand and held mine. He asked me how it was and did I like being home on holidays, and then his oh-so-blue eyes met mine. He cleared his throat and asked me would I go out with him, had I made up my mind? I told him I'd see him at the Easter Monday night dance and I'd tell him then. He seemed happy with that. We stood there in the sunshine and talked of this and that. I told him about my efforts at the lambing and about my little pet lamb who was now in a box near the fire. I told him I had christened her White Cloud and he laughed heartily. I could see all his white teeth and even one at the back that needed a filling. He told me that you only called Indians White Cloud and names like that. Then he held my hand again and said softly, 'I hope when we have kids you'll think up more suitable names.'

It was my turn to laugh. I said, 'Take it easy now, Denis MacMahon, I'm only going to marry a man who absolutely fascinates me. Will you be able to do that?'

He said, 'I don't know much about fascinating you, but I will take care of you because I think you need taking care of.'

Goodnight, sweet diary – goodnight.

April 8th. Today, Easter Sunday, was lovely. The son shone, and there was a feeling of resurrection and renewal. I went to Mass with Daddy in the pony and trap. He looked so distinguished in his grey suit and grey hat. It's sort of true – clothes do make the man, because you wouldn't look at him in a month of Sundays slouching around in his working clothes with his old battered cap. I know Denis goes to first Mass, so I wasn't expecting to see him at second Mass – and I didn't. I don't know if I was disappointed or glad. When we came home, Máire had the goose in the over and the smell was all over the kitchen. We broke up the Easter eggs and I thought they tasted a bit peculiar. Máire said she had read that the chocolate was cooking chocolate, and the sugar was saccharin because of the war. I went down to Laddie and he didn't care whether it was war-time chocolate because he gobbled the lot.

After dinner I cycled over to Kate Barron's and we walked down to the river and sat near the weir and just talked and talked. I asked her what I should do about Denis MacMahon, and she thought I'd be a right idiot if I let him slip through my hands. Afterwards we went back to the house and she put on a new record on their gramophone. 'You Made Me Love You, I didn't want to do it, you made me love you and all the time you knew it.'

The words are going through my head now, so I'll finish off and hope the lovely tune will lull me to sleep.

*

Stephen noticed that the writing was a bit fainter on the next page. Not wanting to miss anything, he put the book away reluctantly until he had more time. He was in her bed in her very room where, in all probability, Teresa had propped the diary on her knees as she had chronicled the events of her day and her life as she lived it in 1940.

Sometimes, before sleep and exhaustion overtook him, she was so vivid in his thoughts that he felt he could reach out and touch her, talk to her – talk to her like he had never been able to talk to anyone. He wanted to tell her about the way he felt, being brought up by a man who had given him the necessities of life, a man who had, in odd patches, shown a hint of kindness but who could never really care for him. He wanted to tell her about his love for Aileen MacMahon, the daughter of the man about whom Tereas had felt badly because he was only 'nice'. He could see himself talking to her and maybe laughing with her about the many facets of rural life that obviously linked both of them, like their love of animals. Her love for Laddie, her pony, was very obvious. Her restlessness and disregard of convention was obvious also. He would like to tell her about the pact with Aileen, and how he had agreed to wait until she was of an age where they could seriously consider their future together. He might tell of his own terrible restlessness, and maybe laugh at her and remind her that he had inherited it from her. He would tell her that when the time was right, he was leaving and taking Aileen with him to Australia, where there was land and few people and where, if he worked hard, he could maybe make a small fortune. Then again, he thought, if Teresa hadn't died giving birth to him, he wouldn't have gotten inside her heart – he

wouldn't have known her like he felt he knew her now. She would be –
what? Thirty-five, thirty-six now? Maybe with lines at the side of her
mouth and the edges of her dark eyes. There would be a heavy sprin-
kling of silver through that unmanageable mop of black hair.

Sometimes he fell asleep with the slanting fading handwriting
dancing before his eyes; other times sleep eluded him and he ached
with a hungry longing to be lying there with Aileen in his arms,
telling her all about the mother he had discovered through the pages
of an old diary written almost twenty years before. He knew she
would share his almost obsessional interest, because, he felt, she was
part of him already.

*

April 9th. The dance hall was packed – too packed. It had
rained heavily this afternoon and the smell of damp tweed and
serge suits mingled with the smell of smoke and sweat. Kate
Barron said my red dress was beautiful, and I honestly think
she meant it. Máire told me it was perfect with my hair and
eyes. Daddy looked at me for a long time before I left, his eyes
wandering all over my face. He said nothing and I was
wondering was he thinking that I was like my mother. He
never talks of her, but Máire tells me that he was a madman
after she died. I was only five but I remember her – little occasional pictures flash though my mind. She was tall and slim,
and most days she used to wear a crossover apron. I remember
her with clips in her mouth as she battled with a hairbrush and
my unyielding, tangled mop of hair. Anyway, before I left for
the dance he cleared his throat and muttered, 'Mind yourself –
don't let any of those fellows at the dance go to your head.' I
told him not to worry, and right now he has no need to worry
because I can't ever see myself letting anyone, even Denis
MacMahon, go to my head.

Anyway, dear diary, Denis was there and he looked great.
He had a lovely pale-grey sports coat and new grey flannels,
and his thick blonde hair was slicked back with hair cream,
which made it look darker. We danced every single dance
together – no one else asked me. I think maybe that the other
fellows think we're already doing a line. He told me I was
beautiful (God help him) and that my dress was lovely and
that I was the absolute belle of the ball. After the dance was
over and before I met poor old Joe, he kissed me and asked
had I made up my mind to go out with him. I said yes, yes,

and why not, and he kissed me sort of long and sort of tenderly and quietly told me I had made him very, very happy. He was lovely but very calm; I think he knew I'd say yes. Maybe he firmly believes we'll be a match. I told him I'll see him on Thursday and we'll go for a walk.

April 10th. Nothing much happened today. I went riding for quite a long time on Laddie. It was the sort of bright fresh day that made me just want to go out there and be free, with the wind in my hair and on my face, and not to have to think a thought about anything or anyone, like school or Denis MacMahon or my future and what might be in store for me or what mightn't. After helping Máire around the place, I went and visited all the lambs and their proud mothers. What beautiful little creatures they are, all those light little curls and the innocent little faces. To look at them so brand new, it's hard to accept the fact that they'll grow so old and shaggy, and full of lice, ticks, worms and mange. Why do things have to grow old? I don't think I'd like to grow old and gnarled and spent. Anyway, as I said, nothing exciting happened today.

April 12. It's so late that I'm tempted to put you away without writing a single word. But if I do that I'll fall down on the job completely and you'll end up like all my other diaries. I don't want to do that. We went for a walk. Denis was very happy. I think he must truly love me. He had on his good sports coat and grey flannels. His brown shoes were so shiny I could see my face in them. I was sorry that I didn't wear my tweed belted coat. I fancy myself in that. Anyway, he didn't seem to mind my old mauve rag.

We went down to the river and all along the bank until we came to the willows. We ducked in under and it was so lonely and quiet that it was undoubtedly a place Sister Bernadette would consider an occasion of sin. We walked over to the grassy place near the flat stones and sat there a while talking. Denis smoked a cigarette. He offered me one and I refused at first. Then I said, 'Why not? I'll try and puff the things.' I took it and I held it away from me. I said, 'Look – this is how Joan Crawford looks in all her films.' I puffed and tried to blow out, and at the same time I narrowed my eyes and tried to look smouldering. He laughed at my efforts and pulled me into his arms and kissed me. He wanted to take his good sports coat off and put it on the ground for me to sit on. I told him not to be daft. We sat down on the grass and he kept worrying that I would get a cold. He held his arm around me and didn't say much; he just seemed as content as a sandboy to be sitting there in the dusk. I thought the river never looked more beautiful – wide and smooth in parts and then, further on, dancing and rushing towards the rocks and the weir.

'Look, Denis,' I said, 'let's take off all our clothes and go straight in and swim to the weir and then cling on to the rocks and let all the water flow over us.'

He looked at me aghast. 'Jasus, but you're a cracked young one altogether,' he said, his blue eyes registering absolute shock.

'Wouldn't it be nice, though?' I taunted.

'I'm going to have to spend a lifetime tamin' you,' he answered, but he was laughing and he has the most beautiful white teeth. He kissed me several times; then he got very excited and his heart started to thump so loud I could hear it battering off my old mauve coat. I was so disappointed that there wasn't a thud in the world in my own chest. My heart was on strike or something. But I do think I love him. We're going to the pictures in Ross on Sunday – it's *Rebecca* and everyone says it's quite good. Then horrible school on Monday. But yippie, it's the last term.

April 15th. Rebecca was the best and most brilliant film I've ever seen. I sat entranced through it all. Laurence Olivier is so handsome. Wouldn't it be wonderful to meet someone like him who had a great big house with untold wealth and a terrible past? But here in County Kilkenny there are no Max De Winters and no Manderleys – just dull farmers and dull farmers' wives who work their hands to the bone.

Denis held my hand tightly all the way through the film, but he didn't try to do anything else. Anne in school said her boyfriend gets very excited at the cinema. She said he tried to put her hand between his legs and tries to put his own hand up under her clothes but she discourages him. She said she must or he'd go mad and the next time they were alone he'd jump on her and then God knows what would happen. She might end up in trouble and disgraced. I could never see Denis doing anything like that. He's strait-laced in a way.

After the pictures, when my head was swirling with Max De Winter and Mrs Danvers, he said, 'Well, Teresa, can I take it that you're my girl?'

'I said, 'Yes – yes for now.'

'No,' he said. 'For always.'

I kissed him then, right outside the cinema. He was utterly taken aback and looked around to see if anyone had seen us. You know what? I think, dear diary, he'll make a nice husband for someone, but I don't think it'll be me.

Oh God, I'm tired. I'd better try and get some sleep. I bet I'll dream of Max De Winter and instead of Joan Fontaine he holds in his arms it might be me.

School tomorrow – dreadful thought.

*

Stephen went about his work as always. If he was quieter than usual no one seemed to notice. Once Máire asked him what old Sheridan had wanted.

'Nothing,' Stephen told her. 'Nothing. I think he was in the parts and wanted to chat. He said 'twas unlikely that he'd be back here this year.'

She didn't question him further.

Though his workload was heavy, tiring and never-ending, he went about it with a lighter heart and a lighter step. He looked forward to nighttime when he could go to his bedroom and read the diaries. He entered Teresa's world, and already felt he knew her more than most sons might ever know their mothers. He could have sat up and read the diaries through with the fiery impatience of youth. But he resisted. He wanted to savour every single word. He wanted to lie there and think of her day with total recall. He was like a child who had been given a creamy chocolate treat and who was sparing it to savour the last tiny particle. Once he was tempted to tell Joe that old Sheridan had called with the diaries. But he stopped. Sometimes he found it strange – as if he, her only son, was now an intruder, almost like a peeping Tom, particularly when he read some of the more intimate aspects of her young life – like when she complained about her crampy pains before her monthly cycle or when she urged the reluctant but stolid Denis MacMahon to tear off his clothes and run into the river with her.

As his strong hands deftly milked the swollen udders of the cows, his head resting on a hairy flank, Stephen thought it a peculiar quirk of fate that he was so much in love with the daughter of the man his mother had gone out with.

Once, when he was loading turf on to the cart, he innocently asked Joe, 'What became of Laddie?'

Joe looked at him suspiciously with narrowed eyes. 'Who's Laddie, boy?'

Stephen realised he had put his foot in it, but he brazened it out. 'You remember, Joe, that you told me that my mother had a pony named Laddie. I was just curious. I get like that sometimes.'

''Tisn't good to be thinking of the past, so it isn't. Sure a fine fellow like you should be out chasin' women. But if you want to know, after she went your father kept him for about six months, hoping she'd be back. When she didn't come he sold him off. Somehow, after Laddie went I knew she was gone for good, too. Don't ask me how I knew – I just did.'

Stephen went back to the yellowing handwritten pages, making a conscious effort not to devour them. He spared and savoured every word so as not to miss a single nuance. During the following nights as the world slept outside, the stillness broken only by the sound of a lone dog barking or the snarling spitting of the cats mating outside, he read about Teresa's days at school: her irritation during the long confined hours of supervised study, her days off, her friends, particularly her best friend Anna McEvoy. She worried about her relationship with Denis MacMahon; she wrote that she hoped his feeling for her would have cooled by the summer. She wrote of her own high hopes for the coming summer.

She'd asked her daddy if Anna could come for a few weeks, and was always dreaming of the good times they'd have. After all, she wrote, 'The war is, according to everyone, a terrible war that could go on and on. I hear that the German bombs are blowing up the British cities and causing devastation. Maybe Ireland will be all caught up in this, and if so, maybe we'll all be blown up. So I'm going to have a wild and wonderful summer. Why, even as I write, do I feel Denis MacMahon will have no part to play in it?'

The final exams that had worried her for so long were comparatively easy, and her class attended a farewell Mass:

*

We all looked so scrubbed and immaculate in our navy gymslips and white blouses. We sang all the responses during the Mass and it was very beautiful but sad in a way. A lot of

141

the girls started to cry when the priest gave his little homily about one aspect of our lives ending and the whole world opening up for us as we walked across the threshold into adulthood. I had a lump in my throat and tears in my eyes also. Why at times do tears come so easily? I was envious of some of the girls. They are going home to hordes of brothers and sisters, and I go back to a farmhouse with a sad man who has lost his wife, and Máire, who has been good to me but who has her own family closer to her heart. I love Joe, of course, and I adore Laddie, and maybe all in all I'm not too badly off. And of course there are so many girls in rural Ireland who would give their right arm for Denis. Undoubtedly he would be presumed a great catch, the eldest son of a fairly prosperous farmer who married late in life. When his father passes on, he will rest in his grave easy because his son is carrying on the work. I wish I was normal. I wish I had a mother. I wish I had brothers and sisters. I wish I was home – I wished I loved Denis MacMahon the way he'd like me to love him or the way I think he'd like me to love him.

I wish – I wish – I wish.

June 21st. It was a lovely homecoming. Joe picked me up at the station in the pony and trap, and I could see he was as pleased as punch to see me. Daddy gave me a rough hug and Máire shook my hand. After I unpacked all my awful clothes away, I examined my summer dresses and decided there and then that summer dresses made in tovralco and seersucker are too young for me now. Crêpe-de-chine and a sort of frail voile is more in now. Anne got a new flowery skirt with a big waist band; it's called a dirndl skirt. I want one of those, and the new short-sleeved blouses with the collar and the three buttons. Tomorrow I'll ask Daddy for the money and I'll get the early bus to Waterford and I'll buy a few glad rags. I know he won't refuse me, because I feel in my heart he knows that Denis MacMahon is interested in me, and sadly I know he would be happy with the outcome.

June 22nd. As I guessed, I got the money for the new summer dresses no bother at all. Máire came with me on the bus and I bought two dresses in Robinson & Ledlies in Waterford. They hadn't the dirndl skirt, but I got one in the Bargain Shop in

Michael Street. The shop assistant was an old woman with silver hair, but when I tried on the dresses, particularly a salmon-pink one with tiny white and green sprigs, she told me – listen to this, dear diary – that I was a beautiful girl and that I should enter the Dawn Beauty competition. She said the first heat was being held in the Atlantic Ballroom in Tramore the following Saturday. Imagine me saying to Denis MacMahon, 'Come on to Tramore in Waterford, I want to be the Dawn Beauty'! God, I'd love to see his face.

June 23rd. I got a letter from Denis this morning. He was writing the letter because there's a dance on in Ross on Saturday night and a great new band is going to be there – someone called Mick Delahunty. As he won't see me until Mass on Sunday he asked me to forgive him for writing the letter. He hoped it wouldn't get me into trouble. Daddy had come in from the turf cutting, and so had Joe. I was back from a run on Laddie and I was having a mug of tea with them when Máire asked, 'Who was the letter from, Teresa?'

Daddy was lifting the mug to his mouth and he sort of stopped in mid-air, and Joe was coughing as he stopped too. So I decided I'd take the bull by the horns and tell them with truth and honesty. 'It's a letter from Denis MacMahon. He asked me to go to the dance with him on Saturday evening. He'll pick me up at the end of the lane in the van. There's a great new band in Clonmel. Can I go, Daddy?' I asked, as innocent as pie, but my thoughts were racing wildly. I said to myself that if he doesn't give that little growl and if he hasn't any objection, I'm right – he would like a match between me and Denis. He just looked at me over his white enamel mug and said, 'Aye, sure you're only young once. Young Denis MacMahon knows what side his bread is buttered on and he's a hard-working lad, so he is.'

I know that although it isn't an arranged match, Daddy is as pleased as punch about it. I also know that I'm not going to marry Denis MacMahon – but, dear diary, I won't tell him yet. I would just go along with him for a while, because I do really like him very much.

June 24. It was a fantastic dance. Everyone was there – Kate Barron and her friends from Ross, and Nell and Áine from the

Ruhr with two cousins they had staying with them from Kilkenny. Denis was so happy. He told me my dress was the loveliest one he had ever seen. His eyes lingered all over me, and they stopped for a long time at my breasts. I know I shouldn't write a word like that. None of the girls call their breasts, 'breasts', isn't that strange? They call them 'my top', 'my chest', 'my bosoms'. One girl in school was very funny, she called hers Dolly and Dora. Anyway, when his eyes lingered, I knew he was getting very serious somehow. I danced the first three dances with him and then I went to the ladies', and on the way back to him Frank Quinn asked me and I danced with him. It was an excuse-me and I got a new partner every single second. Once or twice Denis cut in, but he didn't last too long. He was a bit upset after that but he pretended he wasn't.

I danced the last dance with him. It was a long slow waltz and I could feel his heartbeat, and I was afraid he might feel something else, so I tried to keep away from him a bit. At the end of the lane near our house he kissed me so hard and so passionately that he got all excited, and I knew the only way I could handle him was to tease him. I broke away and ran behind the van. He followed me, and it looked so strange to see Denis, who is a bit on the sober side, chasing and laughing. When he caught me I kissed him, and then bit the end of his nose and told him if he was going to be all passionate and stuff I'd call it a day. He promised me he'd restrain himself in future, and we kissed goodnight. I so sort of love him and I hope he meets someone really nice. No, not nice again. Someone good. No, no, not good, I hate that word too. Someone suitable? No, that's worse. Oh, goodnight, dear diary – I'll see you tomorrow night.

June 26th. I asked Daddy today if I could invite Anne for a short stay. He was more than agreeable, so I wrote to her immediately, inviting her for two weeks. I hope she'll get the letter tomorrow, and I hope I'll hear from her by return. I notice that Daddy is in good humour lately. I sincerely hope it has nothing to do with Denis MacMahon, but I have a hunch it might have. I will introduce Anna to him next Saturday night at the dance – her reaction will be interesting. She will probably tell me he's lovely, or maybe she'll just think he's a fair-haired freckled country fellow. Next week we'll do great things – I'll plan a picnic down at the river. I notice that the gypsies are camping there again this year. Sometimes I see the glow of their fire at night, and when the river is still I hear their voices across the way, the children sometimes laughing and more often crying. it's a strange nomadic sort of life they lead. I wonder what it would be like to be one of them.

*

As Stephen read the lines he was tempted for the very first time to skip the next few pages. His heart thumped with excitement – or was it apprehension or fear? – as so very soon he would know exactly what had happened to his mother. The answer to all his questions was between the pages of the two small diaries. He was surprised to find himself whispering a broken prayer that no terrible tragedy had touched Teresa, that at the end of her brief short life she found the happiness and peace that had seemed to elude her. Stephen decided he'd no longer savour and spare every single word, and picked up the diary and lay on his bed. Or was it her bed? He wasn't sure any more. He no longer felt an intruder, somehow. He felt he was entitled to know Teresa in death, if not in life. After all, she had been his mother, and had carried him around for nine months. More important still, he was entitled to know who his father had been. Not really knowing had scarred him for almost as long as he could remember.

*

1st July. Anna came today and brought the most extraordinary atmosphere with her. She was so bubbly and open, and seemed to love everything and everybody. She asked Daddy all sorts of questions, and surprise, surprise – he was only too ready to answer her. Joe told her she was a quare character, so she was, and she thought that terribly funny. Any time she asked him a question he answered with another – she thought that terribly funny also. What makes her so different is the fact that she's a townie, and townies are so open. None of that secrecy and hush-hush stuff. She looks lovely now that she's out of that awful uniform. She has lovely dresses, and matching slip and pantie sets. She's had her hair cut short like those liberty cuts that are now fashionable. Because of Daddy's good humour, I asked him if I could have mine cut the same. He was dead against it, and told me to leave well enough alone, that my hair was grand. It's too long and too dark – too unruly. Some day when I'm free I'll do exactly what I like, so I will.

By the way, Anna was afraid of Laddie. When he lifted his head and snorted, she said, Jasus. It was rather funny. Eventually I got her to approach him inch by inch, and she gingerly rubbed him. But his ears were laid back flat and his eyes were rolling. He wasn't that happy – maybe horses don't like townies.

*

The next night Stephen went to bed, nodding goodnight to his grandfather and saying he was going that bit early as he wanted to put in a longer day tomorrow. He wanted to finish the turf as well as snag the turnips in the high field. His grandfather growled goodnight and nodded in agreement when Stephen mentioned the necessity of a longer day.

When he got to his room, Stephen didn't undress. He lay on the top of the faded rose-sprigged eiderdown and, turning up the oil lamp, settled down for what was the final read of his mother's diaries. He knew he was reading about the last year of her life and he wanted no interruptions, no distractions – nothing that would detract from her story. He decided he'd ignore the days and dates – that way it would be better. It would unfold like a conversation; it might even come across as if she was telling her only son the story of her life.

*

We went to the dance on the Saturday night in Ross. I wore my new crêpe-de-chine dress with the crossover bodice and the waisted inset. Anna told me it was the nicest dress she ever saw, and I told her hers was the nicest dress I ever saw – so we set off in good form. Denis was there and I introduced her to him and she said, 'Good evening, I've heard so much about you.' He got pink and embarrassed and I think he thought she was a grand city type. I put him at his ease, telling him she was like that with all the fellows. They both laughed then, and when the first dance was announced, she was asked out in seconds. Denis held me too close and I laughed at him, telling him that if he was like that at the first dance, I'd be smothered and dead by the last one. he laughed and said, 'All right, all right. I'll behave myself. 'Tis the feel of the silky dress – 'tisn't you that's exciting me.' I pretended that I was offended then, and he pulled me close and whispered in my ear that I was the craziest young wan he ever knew.

I introduced Anna to Kate Barron and Kitty White, and they liked her instantly. At least I think they did. Anyway, we decided we'd go on a picnic down by the river the following Tuesday. At the end of the dance Denis wanted to take both of us home, but I told him that Joe would be coming, so he asked me to go outside. I did, and I told him I can't see him again until after Anna goes home. I tried to explain that it wouldn't be fair to ask someone on holiday and then leave her with a mixum-gatherum lot like Daddy, Máire and Joe. He accepted my explanation and said he hoped that was my real reason. I told him he was a worry-bags and he told me he loved me.

We cycled into Ross today and had tea and pink cakes in Meagher's café. We met the others and we had a good time. We started to talk about the war, which seems so far away for us. We complained that it was a nuisance as we're rationed for foodstuff. And Anna argued that we're spoilt, with plenty to eat – it's in the cities that the rationing is felt. We wondered what it must be like living in London during the bombing and the blackouts, and we were all unanimous that it must be fierce exciting. Anna thought the British were very brave keeping up their spirits with all those funny programmes on the wireless, and she thought Joy Nicholls was a riot, laughing and telling jokes in the face of death and the threat of being blown to smithereens. Kate didn't agree. She said they were getting their just deserts when you considered they tried to conquer the world. Hitler was the boy for them, she almost shouted, 'When you think their greatest boast is or was that the sun never set on the British Empire.' She was getting so excited that we pushed another pink cake at her, telling her it would calm her. She laughed then and we settled down to plan our picnic.

Today we had the picnic. Even though we are in the throes of a heatwave, it seemed to be the hottest day of all. There wasn't even the tiniest fluffy cloud or breath of wind anywhere. Máire made us her rhubarb tarts and scones. Because of the war she had no fruit for the scones, but she cut up prunes real tiny and they were a perfect replacement. She cut the smoked bacon down from the beams in the kitchen, telling us we were real lucky as it was a lovely mild bacon and not too leathery. Anne and I cycled to the river to meet the others. We had planned to have our picnic at the trout pool up from the weir. Kitty, Mags and Nancy were there already. It was so hot that there wasn't a single breath of wind. The willow trees hung so still, they were like a green lacy wall. The girls were lying on the flat stones with their dresses hiked up above their knees 'so that we'll get a bit of a colour,' Mags said. We joined them and we too hiked up our dresses and lay there to recover from the cycle. After a bit we sat up, looking at the brown water of the gently flowing river. Restless, I wandered down to the edge of the river and stood where the reeds grew thick and luxurious. My dress was sticking to me and I could see the wet patches under my breasts and my arms. I bent down and touched the water. It was cool and welcoming.

'Look,' I shouted back. 'Let's go for a swim. We'll have our meal and rest a bit when we come out.'

'We can't,' Kate said in her explanatory tone, as if she was talking to a child. 'Teresa, we haven't any swimming togs, so we can't.'

I had rejoined them at this stage. 'Look, will ye? There isn't a single thing moving in our world. Look around, we're perfectly shielded by the trees and the reeds. Only the insects and the odd rabbit will see us.'

'You mean with no clothes?' Mags whispered, her eyes showing absolute horror.

'Yes,' I told her, 'with no clothes.'

They looked at each other, the idea starting to catch despite the sheer outrageousness of the plan.

'Jesus, Mary and Joseph,' Kate Barron whispered, 'if anyone saw us we'd be disgraced forever. Imagine my mother – she'd leather me so much I wouldn't be able to sit down for months. But it's a lovely idea. I'm melting, so I am.'

'Well, if we're going to go, we'll go,' Anna said, glancing around, her grey eyes scanning the beautiful but isolated countryside, the wide sluggishly moving river.

'No, I can't. I'm too big on top – I'm a disgrace.'

'No, no, you're every man's dream. Come on,' I told her.

We jumped up and four pairs of eyes scanned the scene. Then we stripped off our dresses, our slips and finally our knickers. We were sheepish at first, noting breasts, waistlines and private parts, and then something strange seemed to get hold of me. I started to dance on the wide stones – I felt wild and filled with abandon. I whirled my inoffensive knickers around and around, and then I flung them into the air where they landed on a branch of the weeping willow tree. As if my madness was contagious the other did exactly the same, jumping up and down in a wild Indian war dance before flinging their respective knickers up into the tree. Then we started to laugh hysterically, seeing the poor willow tree festooned with four pairs of pastel-coloured knickers.

'It's like a pagan ritual,' I yelled, 'we're offering up our drawers to the Willow God.'

Then, looking around and relieved that our madness had gone unnoticed, we crept stealthily across the moss-covered stones, careful not to slip on the green slime. Then we were at the water's edge – and we tiptoed in and suppressed our screams as the cold water inched up our naked bodies. Suddenly we were in and all swimming. I swam further out, allowing the cool peat-coloured water to flow over my breasts and between my legs, lapping at my shoulders. It was sheer heaven. I ducked down and opened my eyes. I could see a myriad tiny particles of mud and moss, maybe disturbed by my invasion. Up a bit of the way I could see my friends swimming and splashing. I felt an extraordinary freedom – something I've never experienced in my entire life – freedom from the restriction of clothes. I thought of darkest Africa where the natives go around naked, and I thought that it would be wonderful to be like them. I started to imagine all the people in the parish without their clothes – when I thought of twenty-stone Missus Murphy and poor skinny scrawny Joe, I laughed so much I choked and went under completely. My hair was saturated when I surfaced and almost completely covered me to the waist.

When we were satiated and satisfied with the wonderful pleasure the river had given us, we decided that enough was enough, and once again four pairs of eyes scanned the scene before we emerged from the water. Nothing stirred only the swarms of midgets that moved in darting lacy clouds. We ran up to our possessions and grabbed our dresses. Only Kate struggled with a brassière, and hissed, 'My mother insisted on this contraption.'

Then we looked at the festooned tree, and the others insisted I was the one who should do the needful. I climbed the tree and in seconds had flung down the knickers. In record time we had them on, telling ourselves that we'd dry out in minutes.

'Wasn't that a taste of heaven? I never thought that country culchies would be so outrageous,' Anna laughed.

'Shush,' Kate whispered. 'You don't know, Anna, but if this ever got around we'd have to emigrate. Wouldn't we, Teresa?'

'We would,' I said. 'We would.'

'Will you ever forget Teresa dancing like a lunatic whirling her knickers to high heaven?' Kate said, and then we started to laugh and we all got hysterical again. We were still laughing as we ate our picnic.

After our picnic we were as full as the proverbial egg. We lay in the hot sun, the heat seeping through our bones from the wide stepping stones. The drowsy day closed in and I think I dozed, because I dreamed I was back in the river, without my clothes. When I tried to hide my nakedness with my hair, I heard someone say, 'Jesus, Mary and Holy Joseph.' I awoke then and it was Kate, who was pointing down near the weir to a man who was near the bank, dressed in something green or brown. The perfect camouflage.

'We're finished,' Mags whispered. 'He's fishing, so he must have been there for hours.'

'Teresa, he has to have seen us,' Kate shakily whispered. 'You know how long it takes to catch a fish in this heat – hours and hours.'

'Maybe he fell asleep in the sun,' I consoled.

'Even if he did,' Mags almost wailed, 'wouldn't four naked lunatics dancing and flinging their drawers up in a tree wake him up? Oh, he had his eyeful all right – we're bunched so we are.'

'It's your fault, Teresa Rodgers, and you haven't even a mother who'll whip you.'

'Look,' I told them, 'we might as well be hung for a sheep as a lamb. Let's go down and talk to him, and we'll know by his eyes if he saw us. We've nothing to lose. Come on.'

We gathered up the remains of our picnic and tried to tidy our dishevelled hair. Our dresses were nearly dry, with just an odd damp patch where the sun hadn't pierced the pleats and folds. We walked, a bedraggled foursome, down to the river path where the tall bull rushes were motionless in the sun.

'What can we say to him?' Kate whispered. 'How can you talk to a black stranger? It's crazy. Everything about today is crazy.'

As we approached him, he glanced up from his job of holding a fishing rod with one hand and reading a book with the other. He must have been surprised at the four apparitions, but it didn't register.

'Good evening,' he said. 'A beautiful evening for a riverside stroll.'

I noted immediately that his accent was a little clipped, neither local, Irish nor countrified.

'Good evening,' we chorused, wary eyes searching his to see if there was a knowledgeable look, a jeering gleam, high-lighting the fact that he had seen us. I didn't worry for too long, because I was completely distracted by his eyes. I had never seen more beautiful eyes – dark as the night with long black ridiculous lashes. They were so long they cast shadows like spider's legs on his cheekbones. If in their depths there was a knowledge of four naked cavorting girls, it didn't show.

'How was the fishing?' I asked, my voice shaky and unsure.

'Not so good. To quote from the Bible, I've laboured all day and caught nothing.'

'Virgin Mary, if he was here all day he has seen us,' Kate whispered. 'All day?' she croaked.

'Yes, all day.' It was then I noticed a humorous flash which touched his eyes and played around his mouth briefly. I knew he had seen the four of us naked as the day we were born. I tried to quiet my mounting fear.

'Are you a stranger to these parts?' I asked.

'Yes and no. I live with the families camping near the woods.'

I tried not to show my amazement that someone like him lived with the gypsies.

'How come I've never seen you before? I know the families that come there every summer. The Sheridans and the Connors and the McDonaghs. Old Johnnie is bringing them for years and years.'

He seemed surprised at my curiosity or effrontery or whatever, because his glance held mine and any bravery I had just flowed away. I felt gauche, shy and at a decided disadvantage that he had seen too much. But I hid my feelings and brashly talked on. 'You're not one of them. I know that.'

'How are you so sure?' His eyes were still holding mine.

'Because you're too clean.' I pointed to his hands and nails. 'They're too clean. And you don't speak like one of them. You don't speak like one of us. You're different. Anyway, we must go home.' I glanced towards the fishing line hanging limp and dead. 'I hope you won't labour much longer in vain, wasting your day.'

'No, Teresa Rodgers, I haven't wasted my day.'

I swung around and it was my turn to stare straight into the depths of his unreadable dark eyes with the spider's-leg lashes. 'How do you know my name?' My voice was shaking and my heart had started to pound so much I felt they must all have heard it.

'I know it. I also know you live in Tulla with your father and a man called Joe Ryan. I know you have a pony called Laddie whom you adore. Shall I tell you more?'

I don't know if it was his knowledge, or his unblinking searing glance and the feeling that the others weren't there – but whatever it was, it was enough to make me almost lose my voice completely. 'We must go,' I croaked.

We almost ran to our bikes which were flung behind the ditch in Michael Kelly's meadow.

'How did he know you?'

'How did he even know about Laddie?'

'How?'

Their voices were filled with curiosity and excitement. They didn't know, dear diary, that I was trembling, my legs so weak they could scarcely go around on the pedals. They didn't know that my body and my shaking limbs were filled with an extraordinary sensation that was to me absolutely unfamiliar. Now, dear diary, I recognise it as a terrible longing and a terrible compulsion. I must – I absolutely must – see him again. The unbroken heatwave hasn't ended, with cloudless blue skies without one sighting of a single fluffy cloud. Daddy and Joe complain daily about the drought. The farmers' plight makes news on the wireless, that is, when any news filters through in a world which depends on the vagaries of an unreliable battery.

I begged Anna to come down to the river today. She said

she was weary of the place, and asked me impatiently why I wanted to go back. I told her I wanted to see him desperately. She looked at me and told me I was mad.

'Teresa,' she said, 'you don't know a thing about that fellow. He's with the gypsies – we always call them the tinkers. You can't possibly want to see him again. If your father heard he'd kill you. He dotes on you.'

I pleaded and begged and said, 'If you come with me I'll teach you how to ride Laddie.'

She hesitated. I know how her mind works. I know the prospect of going back to Waterford and telling her friends she was horse-riding on her holidays would take her fancy. She reluctantly promised she'd come with me the next day.

She kept her promise and as we cycled down we had little to say. I know she thinks I'm an idiot but I don't care. She continued to nag. 'We'll only stay a while, and if he doesn't turn up we'll go on to Ross, because I want to get a present for my mother. Anyway, I think you're crazy.'

She's right. Here I am, seventeen years of age, with a good life – only daughter of a wealthy farmer, and Denis MacMahon in the palm of my hand. Another girl would give her eye teeth to be in my position. But I'm not content. If I was, why would I be sitting on a rock waiting for someone I can never have or even be seen going out with, because in a way he really is one of them – one of the tinkers?

After about twenty minutes he came. One minute we were sitting there, my heart thumping with anticipation and Anna obviously bored, her mind already on her shopping trip in Ross. He slipped down beside her with a sort of graceful ease, but his eyes were for me.

'Hello,' we said in unison. I sat feeling a total fool, with my head spinning and my heart doing acrobatics for a stranger who probably looked on the whole thing as a bit of a novelty. I decided I'd make up for my presence by being haughty. 'I'm here because I like being here. I ride here a lot in winter when there isn't a single soul about. So you could say I'm the one who's always here.'

'I see,' he answered.

I lost my haughty air then.

'Look,' I said. 'How is it if you're living up there,' I nodded

153

towards the smoke in the woods, 'you look like you – well, clean and stuff?'

He smiled then and I could see his even white teeth, which were in startling contrast to his tanned face. 'You are most curious about my cleanliness. Well, if you want to know how I do it, I do exactly what you did the day before yesterday. I swim in the river. But, Teresa Rodgers, I don't do the preliminary dance, and neither do I fling my shirt on a tree, and I do bring a bar of soap.'

My face started to go blood red. I could feel the blooming blush starting down at my navel. He had seen us.

'Yes, I saw you.'

'Oh God. What must you think? You must think we're right terrible?'

'No, it was a beautiful display of girlish innocence. If your Catholic priests asked me if I took pleasure in the sight, I would say yes. But not in a lewd way.'

Anna, who had gone to the river's edge, strolled back. 'You're English, aren't you?' she asked.

'Yes and no,' he told her. 'My father was Spanish and my mother English.'

So that accounted for the black in his eyes.

'What are you doing with the gypsies?' she asked.

Oh God, I was so glad she was talking – it gave me and my poor thumping heart a chance to recover.

'I'm with them because I like their way of life. I like their freedom. I like their nomadic existence.'

'I see,' she said. 'I suppose it's not everyone's cup of tea, and you're hardly going to stay with them for ever.'

'No.' He was smiling at the impatience in her voice and at her line of questioning.

'Well then, why are you with them?' I blurted out. 'Sure they have a terrible life, out in all weather, under canvas or in old rickety horse-drawn caravans.' My voice was shaking slightly and I wondered why I was attacking him, almost.

'All right, I'll tell you why, where and when a man called Hugh Morena lives with the Sheridans, the Connors and the McDonaghs. I'm a writer. I'm writing a book on nomad tribes. I joined up with the Irish tinkers in Essex when I met them there. It was the year before the war and I'm with them still. Have I satisfied your curiosity?' he asked us.

Looking at him I felt we were like two little busybodies, questioning him almost as if he was trespassing or something.

'I'm sorry,' I said.

'About what?' He was smiling and I could see the smile had reached his dark eyes.

'About our Irish snoopy curiosity. We're terrible people, did you know that?'

So he was a writer, I thought. A writer! He was the first writer I had ever met. My English teacher in school had told me on a few occasions that I was good, even very good, at the 'written word', as she put it.

'We must go,' I said.

'How long will you stay?' Anna asked.

'Until spring. I must go back to England then. I feel I should be there now.'

'We must go,' I repeated. I made to scramble and get up. He held out his hand and I noticed it was strong and brown, with long fingers. I also noticed that when he held me, a current like an electric shock went through me. If he noticed the effect he had on me, he hid it, and helped Anne to her feet also.

'Maybe I'll see you both again?' he asked, his eyes holding mine.

'Not me,' Anna told him. 'I'm going home tomorrow, I'm just with Teresa on holidays.'

'Well, safe journey then,' he told her. 'And you, Teresa Rodgers?'

'Well, I'm going nowhere,' I said.

'That's nice to know. So I'll see you around then.'

'Maybe,' I said but I didn't meet his eyes this time. We walked away and I could see out of the corner of my eye that he had resumed his sitting position on the rock. I knew his eyes were following my every move. I felt so self-conscious and awkward, knowing he had seen us stark naked only a short time ago. How, I thought, could you be so easy and relaxed to someone who had seen so much? Even as Anna and I jumped across the stones through the clouds of midges I knew that I would see him again. I also knew that I wasn't in love and never would be in love with Denis MacMahon.

Today we went to Waterford. Ann bought presents for her

family. Small token presents, but she lingered over each purchase before she made it. I envied her. I thought it must be nice to have a mother and sisters and small brothers. I often told my friends that I envied them their mothers. They tell me I'm nearly as well off as I am. They tell me they find it difficult to talk to their mothers. I imagine if I had a mother I could talk to her. I might be able to tell her the way I feel about Denis MacMahon, and that I feel safe, nice and easy with him. I could never tell her or any other living soul about what I feel for the handsome stranger I met by the river. I know I'll see him again. I often think I'm psychic. I feel things and they happen. I often wonder, dear diary, if I was a mother, would my daughter or my son be able to talk to me to confide in me? Or would I be a cranky oul one in a crossover apron, my hair in a tight bun, my lips in a tight line, giving out to them about everything they do? God, I hope not. I think I'd love my children so much I'd let them know a certain freedom. I'd trust them and wouldn't interfere so much.

*

The words blurred and danced, making Stephen Rodgers clutch the little diary even tighter.

Suddenly he felt his throat restricted and the unfamiliar tears sprang to his eyes, blurring the writing. He closed his eyes, surprised that the slanting written words affected him so much. Yet inside a weight he had carried all his young life seemed to lighten as the faded yellow pages in the diary introduced him more and more to someone he had never known. He lay deep in shadow, his finger on the page so that he wouldn't lose a single word, looking around the room. Had she lain exactly like he was lying now? Lain there, maybe sometimes biting her pen, other times writing non-stop as her youthful emotions stormed on to the page?

A large moth flew into the golden circle of light and hit with a decided thump off the lampshade. Stephen brushed it away – he didn't even want a moth to die on the night that held all the answers.

*

Anna went today and I missed her. It was nice to have someone young around, someone that had an inkling of the way I felt. I went to the dance mostly to meet Denis and to tell him that I wanted whatever we had between us to end. He was there, and the dance-hall was crowded and the heat was terrible. The forecast was that the long heatwave was coming to an end and that storms thunder and lightening were imminent. If anything, the sultry sky made things even warmer. Denis seemed so happy to see me, and my heart felt like a stone when I saw his warm smile and his blue eyes. He asked me to dance the very first dance and I went with him smiling, and yet felt bad that I was such a cheating girl in a way.

'I really missed you, Teresa,' he said almost as soon as the dance began. The tune, an old one – 'Smoke Gets in Your Eyes' – was playing and I said to myself, I won't tell him yet. Not until the end of the dance – maybe even later, like a week's time.

He held me so close and he almost whispered in my ear, 'I'm glad your friend is gone back – I was nearly jealous of her.'

'Don't be silly now,' I said, 'and don't be too serious yet. Let's have fun tonight and we'll be serious when it's over.'

'I'm on,' he said.

And he was. We danced every dance and during the old-time waltzes he whirled me around so much I thought I'd twirl away out the door. I smiled and laughed and never left his side because I felt rotten that I had led him on when deep in my heart I knew he wasn't for me. Before the last dance I asked him to come outside. I told him that Joe would be picking me up and there mightn't be much time. He looked a little puzzled, and yet there was an expectation in his glance that maybe tonight things might even go a little further than a goodnight kiss. God love him, he was a bit on edge as we walked out into the sultry dark night. He knew it was early for Joe to be there, so we went over to the back wall behind the dance hall where it's usual for courting couples to go after the dance. I was surprised I felt so down about ending whatever it was I had with Denis. I would like to go on having him as a friend but I knew it wasn't what he wanted. He pulled me into his arms and kissed me on the mouth. I returned the kiss because I felt closer to him than I ever had. It was like people feel at a leave-taking or something.

'Look, Denis,' I whispered when we broke away. 'This is over. It really is.'

He looked at me in amazement. 'Sure what are you telling me, when just now I felt what I felt?'

He wasn't very articulate and I knew I would have a bit of explaining to do. 'Listen, Denis – it's over for me.' He was about to protest and I put my hand on his mouth. 'Hush, let me explain. I like you so much it hurts. I even love you, but it's not the sort of love you want. Denis, you'll meet someone who'll be so right that you'll wonder what you ever saw in a flippity-gibbit like me.'

'That'll never happen.' His eyes were puzzled, yet he knew this was serious.

'Look, love,' I said. 'I'm not much good. I'm very restless – so restless I want someone who'll be like me. I'd like to see the whole world, I'd like to travel – move to places no one has ever seen. When I fall in love I want it to be mad, heady, crazy stuff – but with you I would be safe, secure, peaceful. I want someone who'll attract me – someone very different from what I know. You think I'm mad. Maybe I am, love.'

He was silent for a while, and over across the way, where the crowd was coming out of the dance hall, we could hear laughter and shrieks and a few loud guffaws. But he just stood there and then he cleared his throat. 'I think you're a bit cracked all right – but I want you to know that I love you. That you're the girl for me. That I want a life with you and I want to take care of you because you are a bit wild.'

'I'm sorry,' I told him. 'Honestly, my love,' I said, 'you'll never know how sorry I really am.'

Then, dear diary, I stood up on my toes and kissed him on the forehead, on his eyelids, on his lips. He tousled my hear and I thought I heard him give a little sob. If he did, it was in answer to my own. Then I heard Joe coming along and I just ran away, knowing I had done what I had to do.

I'm lying in bed now, and the storm that threatened has broken. There are huge claps of thunder making the beams overhead positively shake. The room is bright as day when the lightning flashes. It's terrifying but I'm not afraid. It must be terrible on the gypsies down near Barrons Wood, so many of them under canvas and sacking. I wonder what Hugh Morena is doing there now. Is he lying there listening to the crashing storm, wet and uncomfortable, whilst I lie here warm and snug?

I'm so sorry about Denis that tomorrow, Sunday, I'll offer up my whole Mass that he'll meet someone nicer. Because it is

Sunday I won't go near the river. But I'll be counting the dragging hours until Monday, when I know that no matter what happens, I'll be there.

Today nothing happened after Mass, so I rode out Laddie and we went for a long gallop. I think he has forgiven me for putting him through the procedure of helping Anne to ride. I galloped through all the low fields and then on the by-road to Ross and back. I was tempted to go along the riverbank and even right up to the camp. After all, I told myself, what would be so terrible about it? I've done it often before. Anyway, I resisted and came home to a lovely tea of hot scones and raspberry jam. I'm in bed early now and the only sound I can hear is a dog barking over in Michael Kelly's place and a cat snarling and snapping because the love of his life is obviously reluctant to make love. I wonder what it really is like to make love to someone you adore? I hope the stars explode and the earth moves and the world nearly stops when it comes to my turn. Or will I be like the she-cat, reluctant and snarling and turning away? I don't think I will.

Goodnight.

I went to the river. I told Daddy I was going for a bit of a stroll. I called Judy, our dog, and she was all fussed and excited about the prospect of a walk. I even cut down a branch of a catkin tree as if I was all business, with nothing else on my mind only a walk with the dog. Walking out the gate Joe shouted, 'Take care now. The evenings are starting to close in.'

'I will, Joe,' I shouted back. 'Sure you can't kill a bad thing.'

He waved his hand and I went down the rutted land. I looked back, though why I did I don't know. Maybe I didn't want any of them to see me heading for the river.

It was cooler since the storm. I had put on my new white cardigan that matched my white sandals, telling myself it was just the cooler weather that made me wear it. The truth is, I fancied it because it was the new longer style and had pockets, and I knew it looked well. And, damn it, I wanted to look well. Before I got as far as the willow trees my heart started to pound. Say if he wasn't there? Say if it was only my imagination? What if the attraction I felt for him wasn't reciprocated, if it was all in my poor mind?

He was there, standing at the edge of the trout pool. He wasn't aware of me so I could look and look to my heart's content. He's tall, almost a head taller than I am. His shoulders were broad under the shabby tweed jacket. He was staring ahead with his back to me. I could see he was smoking a cigarette; the tiny red glow was visible as he lifted it to his mouth. Judy, running excitedly ahead through the bracken and the leaves, made him turn around. Even from a distance of twenty yards or more I could see he was pleased to see me. With my heart suffocating me I tried to walk up to him, all calm and jaunty on the outside and all screaming jangling nerves on the inside.

'Hello,' he greeted me. 'I'm glad you came.'

I was going to be stupid and say something cocky to cover up my panic – 'Sure I always go for a walk, I'm used to taking Judy along the riverbank.' But I didn't. 'I'm glad I came too,' was all I said.

He held out his hand and I took it readily. It felt warm and strong and smooth. Much smoother than poor Denis's. Then again, he hadn't to work and slave on a farm where young hands roughened and toughened before you were twenty. I remembered he was a writer – so I suppose writers have smooth hands. He looked down at me and my heart did a somersault when I met his eyes. The sun no longer made spider's legs of his lashes, but their length didn't hide the pleasure in the dark depths. My heart thumped, wondering was I the cause of the pleasure.

'Shall we go for a walk?' he said.

God above, I thought, bad enough looking like he did, but I would listen to that accent for ever. *'Shall we?'* I liked it. Denis would have said 'Will we?' I would have said 'Will we?' We walked along the river path with Judy scampering and panting excitedly beside us. He still held my hand and I made no attempt to withdraw it. We came to the edge of the far side of the wood. It was darker and cooler under the trees. We walked in and I wondered would I be safe with him. After all, who was he? A stranger who lived with the gypsies.

Aware of my slight reluctance, he said, 'Don't worry – you'll be all right. We'll sit on that log and you can tell me more about yourself. I want to know every single thing about you, Teresa Rodgers, did you know that?'

'There's so little to tell,' I muttered, and yet I followed him into the shadowy woods and like a child sat down beside him. He put his arms around me and I was glad because it was cold. Then he turned and tilted my child and looked straight into my eyes. And I swear, dear diary, if he had asked me to jump into the middle of the trout pool there and then I would have gone.

'Did you know that you are the perfect Irish *cailín* with that blue-black hair and those dark blue eyes and all those tiny golden freckles scattered across the bridge of your nose?'

'I hate freckles,' I muttered, 'and there's no cure for them.'

He laughed loudly. I could see his white teeth and again marvelled about how he could keep them so white living in a campsite.

'Maybe I should go home,' I whispered. 'My father worries about me –'

'I believe he does – because you are all he has.'

'Well, if you know so much about me, why do you want to know more?'

'Because maybe you could say I'm a very curious fellow.'

'I'm seventeen, I've left school. My mother died when I was six. Maybe she died of cancer or TB or something like that. But I've never really heard – no one talks about what took her away. I think people are ashamed to discuss these things. I went to boarding school and I have quite a few friends – you saw them, remember? And because of what happened that day I'm ashamed of my life.'

I stopped, feeling so young and vulnerable. He put his arms around me then and drew me into his arms and kissed me on the mouth so long, so really long, that I struggled for breath. My heart started to pound and I drew away, because I was terrified of the effect he had on me. If the feeling that swamped me was desire – oh Jesus, I desired him so much it was wrong. 'I must go,' I gasped. 'I must.'

'All right,' he said, brushing his lips across the top of my head. 'I'll take you home.'

'Oh, you can't do that. If my father saw me with a stranger he'd be furious.'

He kissed me again, gently this time. 'But if you were with Denis MacMahon he'd be pleased.'

'How do you know so much?' I asked, my eyes narrow with curiosity.

'I hear so much. The Sheridans tell me everything about the people in these parts. Then again, I think I'm psychic.' He smiled.

We walked back along the riverbank. Judy was tired and trailed behind panting. He bend down and picked her up, cradling her in his arms. 'Well, old girl,' he told her, 'we'll give you a bit of a rest.'

She nestled contentedly in his arm, her head resting on his tweed sleeve and her eyes looking up at him adoringly. When we came to the fork in the road he put her down and, looking straight at me, he asked, 'When shall I see you again?'

'Soon, Hugh Morena – soon,' I told him. 'I must remember to do my diary.'

He laughed. 'Well, Teresa Rodgers, will I be in it?'

'You will,' I shouted back as I started to run along the dark road home. And he is, dear diary, and I have a strange feeling that he'll be in it for the rest of my life. Now amn't I the fanciful fool?

I didn't see him at all today. I wanted to so much I was almost sick with the longing of it. But after tea Daddy told me I was to go to Waterford to see my Uncle Ned who is in hospital there. I know my Uncle Ned is very sick, so I couldn't refuse. Then again, I have to be cute – if I go for a lone walk along the riverbank every evening he'll smell a rat. Or Joe will or some of Máire's spies will.

On the way in to Waterford Daddy asked me if I had seen young Denis MacMahon lately. I told him out straight there and then that I had seen him a while back and that I didn't think I'd see that much of him again.

'Ah, don't be stupid, girl – of course you will. Sure he's as grand a chap as God ever put on this earth. I know that for sure.' He was smiling as he flicked the whip and the pony trotted gently along the main road. He was no doubt sunk in pleasant thoughts, happy that his hoped-for plan would end in success. I was silent, thinking it was well he doesn't know that I've ended my association with Denis.

When we eventually got to the hospital and were told what ward my uncle was in, we could see he was very ill. A screen was pulled around him and his breathing was rasping and laboured. He gave me a watery little smile and held out his work-scarred veiny hand and whispered, 'Nice to see you, Teresa girl.'

I held his hand – it was hot and dry, but I could see his eyes immediately turning to Daddy. Obviously he had things on his mind. I told him I'd go for a little walk and they could have a grand chat. Poor man, there wouldn't be any more grand chats. He was probably worrying about his farm in County Wexford. Because he is a bachelor, he will, in all probability, leave it to Daddy. So maybe what they say is true. I know they talk about me, saying I'll end up rich as I'm the only one left and will inherit everything from the two Rodgers brothers. Funny, money means nothing to me. Maybe it would if I didn't have it.

On the way home, Daddy was silent. I think he was sad because Uncle Ned's so ill. Maybe in his brooding silence he was thinking of the way it was when they were young – all the pranks and misdemeanours they got up to. Or maybe he was thinking of my mother and the few brief years he had with her. I was sad too. But, God forgive me, I wasn't thinking of sick people or dead people. I was thinking of Hugh Morena and how much I wanted to be with him. I'm lying in my bed now hoping that nothing interferes with my plan for tomorrow evening. God knows it's a simple little plan.

I want to meet him. I desperately want to meet him.

I met him this evening and we walked along the riverbank. When we got to the stile he held out his hand and helped me over, and we were at the edge of Barrons Wood. He continued to hold my hand and we walked together to the bit moss-coloured log. It was darker and cooler in the woods. We sat down side by side and my treacherous heart started to thump uneasily. God knows it isn't easy to be chatty and calm with this fellow, so I put on what I thought was my sophisticated air. 'I've told you all about myself. Now it's your turn to tell me all about you. Come on, tell me.'

He put his arm around me and laid my head on his chest. He started to talk and as he did so he kept running his hand up and down my arm. Whether it was the gathering dusk, the silence of the woods, or the mesmeric quality of his voice, I'm not sure, but I've never experienced such tranquillity, such peace – I was a bit like a small tossing vessel that had arrived in safe harbour.

'I never knew my father,' he started. 'He died before I was born, and I was brought up in my grandfather's house in Sussex. After I finished my education I worked as a cub reporter on the *Brighton Gazette*. But I soon wearied of that and I decided I'd travel. Restlessness is my middle name, Teresa Rodgers. I then went to the Continent and ended up in Spain. I think I walked some few thousand miles visiting all the little hamlets, haunts and hilly villages in the unknown parts. I wrote a book about it – a sort of travel book, *Hills and Haciendas of Spain*. It wasn't a particularly good book but I felt it was a beginning. There were rumours of war and Spain was still in the grip of post-war change after their civil war. I felt the time had come for me to go home. I did. I was at home for a few months. And on a weekend hiking trip I met Johnnie Sheridan and Neddy Connors and their families travelling around England, practising their tinkering trade. I joined them and enjoyed their way of life, and experienced a kindness and warmth I had not experienced before. When they returned to Ireland I came with them. I had decided I'd write a book about Ireland. I travelled around with them and my book is halfway there. I was about to return to England because I felt too guilty – like a coward hiding out in a peaceful green hideaway whilst my country is being devastated by war. I had made up my mind to return the day I went fishing and saw four young girls picnicking by the river. But it was the daredevil leader with the cloud of dark hair who held my attention. I fell in love with her there and then, and I knew I couldn't go back without her.'

I should have been upset about what he told me but I wasn't. The very thought of going away with him should have been so ridiculous that I should have burst out laughing. But I didn't. The thought of being left behind was more abhorrent. He bent his head and kissed me gently on the lips. I returned his kiss and he pulled me off the log. We lay on the pine needles in the forest. He kissed me with such passion and intensity that I should have pushed him away. But I didn't. I could feel the long eyelashes brushing off my cheeks, and the sensation gave me the shaky pins-and-needles feeling that if he wanted more I wouldn't be able to resist. He kissed me on the eyelids and on my neck, and I could feel how much he was aroused. After all, I wasn't born on a farm for nothing.

'No, Hugh – no. That's enough, please.' He stopped then and cradled me in his arms like you would a child.

My heart was thumping so loud I knew he could hear it, just like I could hear his. My thoughts were churning wildly too. Maybe he thinks I'm cheap, I thought. After all, he saw me running naked into a river, and no one has ever seen the likes of that in Ireland before. And here I am in the woods lying down beside him.

I sat up abruptly, bruising the pine needles from my hair. It was so dark now I couldn't see the expression in his eyes. 'Do you think I'm cheap?' I asked. 'You know, a forward sort of person?'

'No, my little madcap, I don't. Why do you ask such a stupid question?'

'Because of the awful way we behaved at our picnic. God, I'd hate you to think that sort of thing ever went on before. It was a sort of madness. Irish girls are brought up to be as pure as the driven snow. To be modest in their dress – to sit demurely with their ankles crossed and their hands on their laps. And here I am in the woods with you in the dark. And do you know what, Hugh Morena? I have a pain in my heart for you and that's a fact.'

He kissed me again and again, but tenderly – without the terrible hunger that was on him before.

'If you'd gone on your picnic and if you hadn't gone mad, I might never have met you. As for thinking you cheap, or forward as you put it, no. I think you're a beautiful young girl with all her hormones working perfectly.' He drew me into his arms again. He began running his fingers through my hair, gently trying to undo the tangled mass. 'I love you,' he whispered into my ear. 'I think of you every single solitary moment of the day.'

As I write these words, dear diary, I can tell you – just you – that he has no edge on me. Because I think of him every single solitary second of the day.

This evening after tea, when I said I was going for a walk, I thought Máire, who was putting the blue-patterned cups on the dresser, turned to look at me reproachfully. I dropped my eyes – I should have stared her out. Even Daddy was a bit suspicious.

'Where did you say you were going?' he asked.

'A bit of a walk. I thought I'd take Judy.'

'I notice you're roaming the roads a lot. I didn't think you were one for your own company. But sure you were always a bit restless. Be home at a decent hour – the evenings are closing in.'

I walked out, whistling for Judy who was over the way with Joe chewing on a bone. She came flying and barking excitedly. I bent down and patted her, feeling guilty knowing she was just an excuse. The guilt spilled over when I thought of Laddie. I've been neglecting him of late. I've been neglecting everyone of late. I walked over to the barn and went in. He gave an excited whinny, tossing his head and then giving it the little familiar shake. I went up to him, telling him that it was a terrible thing to be in love. Telling him I'd make it up to him.

Hugh was standing near the trout pool. As Judy ran through the leaves and bracken he looked up, and as I approached his eyes never left mine. The distance between us closed and I met his gaze as unfalteringly as he met mine. Looking at him, I wondered what it would be like to go what the girls called 'the whole way' with him. Would the earth move and the heavens explode, the way I jokingly told Denis MacMahon I wanted? He kissed me, a gentle little kiss. Obviously he had more on his mind than the earth moving and the heavens exploding. Then he asked me a peculiar thing. He asked me to go to the woods with him to meet the Sheridans and the McDonaghs and a young couple he had mentioned before, Neddy and Eileen Connors. I told him it was impossible, that if my father got a breach of it he'd have a stroke. He was so disappointed.

We just walked, holding hands, all around the river bank. He definitely seemed to have things on his mind and was obviously disappointed that I hadn't gone with him to the gypsies.

I cycled over to Kate Barron this morning and begged her to call me after tea. I told her it was a big favour but it would allay my father's fears. She said she would, but because I didn't want her for herself but as an excuse to go gallivanting after my handsome stranger I'd have to do her a big favour when she wanted it. When I went home I harnessed Laddie, telling him we'd go for a great gallop. He was so excited I even went further than I intended to because of guilt.

After tea I was hanging around waiting for Kate. Joe was fixing the hen-house door, adding a new plank of wood to the bottom where it had rotted. He looked up when he heard me approaching. 'Well, well, and where are you off to?' he asked.

'Nowhere, Joe, nowhere.' As Kate hadn't arrived, my lie could pass for innocence. He looked at me steadily and then glanced around the farmyard, making sure there was no one about.

'Teresa, girl,' he said, his voice only a little above a growl, 'I heard you were seen walking out with one of the gypsies. Jasus, child, if he ever found out it would kill him, so it would.'

I looked at him not surprised that we had been seen. That's the way it is in these parts. But there was something so worried and hangdog about his poor face and his eyes, which were looking at me so distractedly, that I went over and hugged him like you would a shaggy dog.

'Don't worry about it, Joe. It's not what it seems. He's really not one of them. And I can mind myself.'

'But I do worry. Sure you're all he has. And it's wrong, me girl, to be out traipsing with one of them.'

'He's not one of them,' I repeated, as if he was a child needing reassurance. The dogs went berserk then and I knew Kate had cycled into the yard. Poor old Joe stood there ruefully shaking his head. I blew him a kiss and ran to meet Kate.

I could see that Daddy was pleased when he saw Kate. He just smiled and nodded after asking about how her parents were. When we said we were going for a bit of a cycle he merely said, 'Mind yereselves now.'

When we were out of earshot she asked, 'What's this, for the Lord's sake? Where are we going?'

'Just to the riverbank, and then, Kate, you're going nowhere, just home. I'm meeting Hugh Morena – you know, the fellow we met the day of the picnic. I promise you, Kate, I'll remember this favour.'

'Why had I to come along?' She sounded irritable.

'Because my father is getting suspicious.'

'Why do you want to meet him so much that you must play games and such like?'

'Because I'm crazy about him.'

'Hm. Crazy about him. That is a fine how-do-you-do.' But then her curiosity got the better of her. 'Have you ever kissed him?' she asked.

'I have,' I told her.

'Have you – you know – you know what I mean?'

'No,' I said.

'Well, will you?'

'I might,' I said, laughing at the incredulous gaze in her round saucer-like eyes.

'Teresa Rodgers, if you get into trouble don't involve me.'

'No, Kate, I won't.'

'Get into trouble?' she whispered, her eyes awash with awe.

'No, you dope – involve you.'

When we met he just tucked my arm into his, saying, 'It's about time I introduced you to my friends.' There were two fires blazing and I could plainly see four or more brightly painted caravans and quite a few canvas tents near the edge of the clearing. Still holding my hand, we walked to a couple who were sitting near the first of the blazing fires. I recognised Johnnie Sheridan and his wife – haven't they been coming to Barrons Woods for years? In fact I hardly remember a summer that they didn't come. She had thick hair, greying at the sides, it flowed long and straggly on to her shoulders. I could see that one of her front teeth was missing. She wore a long black skirt with a thick brown woolly cardigan and strong black boots. Old Johnnie had an old tweed sports coat with corduroy trousers that had seen better times. And that greasy old cap he always wore. He had the thickest bushy eyebrows and the merriest brown eyes I ever saw, like two shiny nuts beaming at us.

'Good evening, Johnnie – good evening, Margaret,' Hugh greeted them.

'Well, Hugh,' Margaret Sheridan said, her eyes taking in every single thing about me, 'I see you've brought us a visitor.'

'This is Teresa Rodgers,' he told her. 'Teresa, this is Margaret and Johnnie Sheridan – very close friends of mine.'

'Pleased to meet you, Miss,' they said almost in unison.

'Would you like a cup of tea, Miss?' Margaret asked.

168

'No, thank you,' I muttered, astonished at the easy warm rapport between the three of them. I hadn't failed to notice the respect in his voice when he addressed them. I wondered why. After all, they were the tinkers, the gypsies, the people that most folk looked down on, now and then giving them a few shillings for their wares, more often than not out of pity at the state of the small children. But this was different. Hugh's approach was different. He introduced me to them as if it was an honour for me to meet them.

Margaret spoke and scattered my thoughts. 'Ah, sure child, you'll have a cup of foxy tay – sure 'twill lighten the road for you.'

'We'll both have a cup of your foxy tay,' Hugh told her. 'We'll be back to join you in a jiffy.'

Still holding my hand, he led me away from the firelight and the warmth and the dancing shadows. Wordlessly I followed him, his hand, warm and strong, dispelling my fear of these people and the fear of that place. We went over to one of the brightly painted caravans. It had its shafts resting on a log of wood so that we could enter it. Hugh removed a torch from his pocket and in the yellow glow I could see that the caravan was actually far more spacious than one could imagine. There was a mattress at the far end, with a neatly folded rug on top. On some shelves there were clothes folded neatly, as well as a stack of paper and some fountain pens, a bottle of ink and three or four folders which contained thick sheets of written work.

'Welcome to Castle Morena,' he said, and I could see he was grinning.

'So this is yours,' I whispered, my heart pounding so much – not only because of his proximity but because of the fact that he was showing me the simplicity and the intimacy of the way he lived.

'I want you to know, darling, that this is all I have to offer now. When we get married and go to England, you'll have much more – all the comforts you'll need.'

'You're crazy – quite crazy,' I whispered.

'No, I'm not,' he said, lifting my chin and looking straight into my soul. Through the gathering longing and the heavy thumping of my heart I thought, he knows. He knows the way I feel about him – the way I want him. He took me in his arms then and it was my turn to feel the wild thudding of his heart. When he kissed me hard on the mouth I opened my lips. I had never done that for anyone before, and I knew there and then that I will never do it for anyone else again. His need and rising passion matched mine and I thought hazily that, if right then he pulled me down on to the mattress, he could have me, terrible sin and all that it would be.

But he stopped kissing me then.

'We must wait until it's right,' he muttered – his voice husky too.

'When will that be?' I whispered.

'When we're married.' He nodded towards the fires. 'I've learned so much from them. They're a very moral people, young Teresa – did you know that?'

'I think I heard that,' I said. He was about to turn away. I grabbed him and, getting right up on my toes, I kissed him on his closed eyelids. I could feel the thick lashes brushing off my face.

'Hey, do you know what?' I said.

'What?' he asked.

'I wanted to do that since the first day I met you. That day the sun made shadow, and your eyelashes looked like spider's legs, but now they feel like a silky fringe.'

'Hey, do you know what?' He gave a good impression of my accent.

'No,' I said.

'I think it's time we had a cup of foxy tay.'

Dear diary, you should have heard the funny way 'foxy tay' sounded with his accent. We had the tea and it was fine and strong. I wondered how they got it, with all the rationing. Maybe the travelling people have the sort of contacts that farmers don't have. Afterwards I met all the other members of the clan: Eileen Connors and her husband and their new baby. Neddy Connors was as proud as punch showing me the little cot he had made for his new daughter. It was tucked as neat was you could imagine near their bed. I met Davy and Ellen McDonagh, and they told me they had six children who were all in bed. Margaret and Johnnie Sheridan introduced me to their four youngest children – they had ten altogether but some of them had settled in England and some of the older married ones had already moved on to Rathkeale where they wintered.

No one seemed any way surprised at meeting me. It was almost as if they had been expecting me. Hugh walked me back along the riverbank. He pushed my bike whilst I strode alongside. It was very late. The moon was riding so high everything was silvery, bright and yet so silent. The willow trees were so still in the moonlight, their weeping branches hanging down like giant tresses, unmoving and still as they rested on the undergrowth. I will remember this evening forever, I thought. When I'm old and grey with passion all spent, I will remember walking along here in the moonlight with this man I know will be my husband and the father of my children. Whether we end up in England or the other side of the world, I will remember this night. The campfires, the friendship of the gypsies, my first glimpse of Castle Morena.

As we walked in companionable silence, I thought of Denis MacMahon. It seemed an eternity since I had been with him and yet it has only been a mere few weeks. In my new-found happiness I said a small prayer that he would find someone who loved him and who would make him as happy as I am.

When we approached the laneway up to our house, he put my bike against the ditch and, pulling me in to the shadows, he kissed me gain. Oh God above, there was nothing gentle or tender about his kisses this time. They were long and hard and desperate. I felt my whole body tingling, melting, almost on fire.

'Not yet, darling – not yet,' he whispered. 'We must get married.'

'Are we getting married?'

'Yes,' he answered.

'When?' I asked, like a child who had been promised a treat.

'Soon – very soon,' he said, his eyes never leaving mine.

We whispered our goodbyes and I cycled up our land. I could see the smoke from the chimney, and it puzzled me that Daddy would have put on fresh turf at such a late hour. I also feverishly sought some excuse to explain away my lateness. *We went to Kate Barron's and had supper. Kate's brothers were there and we played cards.* The excuses were tumbling through my mind. Judy started to bark then, excited little barks to welcome me home. I even thought I heard Laddie snorting a greeting. Funny, I thought, everyone seems so wide awake. Maybe it's the bright light making everybody think it's day.

Daddy was standing near the dresser, his back turned to me. I saw Máire out of the corner of my eye and I could see she had an apprehensive expression on her face as she thumped and thudded with the heavy box iron, battling with the weekly chore of ironing. Like someone in a dream, I wondered why she was ironing so late. Daddy turned around to stare at me and I swear, I never ever saw such an expression on a human face. He looked like the devil incarnate. His eyes were blazing with fury and he was red and shaking like someone in a paroxysm.

'Where were you, you little trollop?' he shouted.

'Nowhere,' I answered. 'Just out with Ka–' I never even finished the sentence.

'Don't you lie to me,' he roared as he drew out his hand and hit me a hard blow on the face. I fell back against the wooden table, a vase of wild flowers a photograph and an ash tray came with me and all the bits and pieces fell on top of me and I fell to the ground. He bent down and lifted me up and hit me again. 'Jesus Christ, I know where you were. Out roaming the road with one of the tinkers, or maybe lying down with him for all I know. I was never glad,' he roared, 'that your poor mother is dead, but I'm bloody glad now, because if she wasn't this would kill her. And you turning your back on a decent lad to walk the roads with a nobody. Get up to your room,' he roared. 'And you'll stay there, Miss, under lock and key until you get sense.'

As I turned away I could feel the blood from my cut lip warm on my tongue. My eye was already starting to swell. In fact, dear diary, I'm writing this with one eye closed. How did he find out? How? Then again, why should I be surprised? Everyone eventually knows everything about everyone in this Godforsaken place.

I have my curtains pulled back and way over the hill I can see the outline of the woods, and as I write I persuade myself I can see the red glow of the camp fires. The moon is so bright it's like daylight. Its beams have crept into my room showing up everything. The Infant of Prague seems to look at me in a reproachful sort of way. Does he look reproachful because of the heartbreak I have caused my father who in his own way loves me? He must, I suppose. I should feel bad too when I

172

think of him buying Laddie, and even how he got my room decorated for my homecoming.

Glancing back towards the woods I can definitely see the glow from the fires. I wonder is he lying there in the caravan thinking of me? Maybe the moonlight is casting a spidery shadow on his cheekbones.

Oh God, I know I should be demented for what happened. And I ache physically from the blows I received from Daddy, but the hurt inside me is greater. I even feel more love for Hugh now than I do for my poor Laddie or for my father. That's what I'm going to call the man who hit me, from now on. Father. I'm too old to be calling him Daddy. I still love him, honestly I do. I'm tired, though. Oh, I wish I had been different. Why couldn't I be content with all I have? Why couldn't I feel the love I feel for Hugh for Denis MacMahon, someone I've known for so long?

Dear diary, I'm tired. What will I do, locked up in this room? I know I'm locked up because I heard the key turn and Máire's voice for a minute. But now it's all silence. Just you, dear diary, and me and the Infant of Prague and the pale silvery moonlight.

Today was the longest day of my whole life. I first heard Joe cycling up to the lane and the dogs greeting him. Then I heard my father talking to him below. Their voices were so muted I hadn't a notion what they were talking about. Maybe it was all normal stuff about the milking and the creamery and how good the harvest was despite the dry weather. Máire brought up my breakfast – two eggs and soda bread with the butter spread far too thick. She took away the loathsome chamber and came back with it. I nabbed her then and made her sit down and talk to me. She was reluctant and told me my father didn't want to discuss anything with me. I asked her had his anger died down and she told me it hadn't. She had never seen such fury on any man, she said. She scolded me and told me I was a terrible girl to cause him such heartbreak, as if he hadn't enough on his plate as it was.

I said to her, 'Máire, you're not too old. You must remember the way you felt about your husband when you first met him. Well, that's the way I feel about this man.'

'Sure I never heard such nonsense in my life,' she said.

173

'You must be crazy even to be seen with one of them gypsies. Love? There's no such thing. It goes fast enough in the struggle of life, I'm telling you. Hush, will you, for God's sake? Talking about something you know nothing about.'

'Oh I do, I do,' I told her, but she walked out the door carrying my tray.

God, it's dark already and I'll go stark staring mad if I have to spend a few days here. Thank God for my books. I'm reading a book by Annie M P Smithson, *The Walk of a Queen*. The heroine is a bit goodie-goodie in it, or maybe I feel that now that I'm so bad. If this imprisonment goes on much longer, I'll get out some way. That I promise you.

Today was just the same as yesterday, only worse. The terrible thing is, tomorrow will be the same as today. I kept looking out the window towards Barrons Wood. I thought I saw the firelight, or at least the rosy glow. The moon is full tonight also. It's making me so restless that I think I'll go mad. I wonder is it true what they say – that the full moon has an influence on the mind? I think it has – I feel quite peculiar. I even thought I saw Hugh over at the side of the stable.

I'm sorry, dear diary, that I have been neglecting you for a while – you, my best companion, who is so receptive always. I'm here with my beloved Hugh. It was easy enough. It wasn't a trick of the moon. He was at the stable. Just like I could see the glow of the campfires, he could see my lighted window. He came the following night in the small hours. A tiny pebble against the glass and I awoke. After softly whispering together I packed the few clothes that I thought I'd need in a pillow cover. I threw them down to him and I climbed down the rope he had brought, then dropped into his waiting arms. We just clung on to each other and then crept out the gate. But halfway down the lane I whispered, 'I can't go without saying goodbye to Laddie.' I thought he'd try to dissuade me, but he didn't. He understood. We went back and Hugh waited outside the stable door as I stealthily went in. Laddie was lying down and when he saw me he stood up. I was terrified he might neigh with pleasure. I think he knew he couldn't come, so he bent his head and nuzzled me, and kept pushing his lovely soft muzzle into

174

my neck, slobbering over my hair. I kissed him again and again. Then I whispered that I loved him, and asked him to forgive me for running away. He nodded his head up and down, up and down, as if he understood. With my eyes blinded with tears I kissed him on the nostril for the very last time, and then ran before I changed my mind.

It is all so easy. I slept in Hugh's caravan and he slept in a tent a mere few yards away. I haven't words to describe the rapture of our kisses when we knew we were away from all prying eyes. Today I met everyone and I heard that next Saturday they're breaking camp and moving to County Limerick for the winter.

Today I learned so much more about Hugh. He told me more about the book he's writing. I didn't know until today that he can already speak the gypsies' language. He is very close to them and they all love and respect him. It's very peculiar to hear him sit with the children and tell them stories about England and Spain. The fable of King Arthur is a favourite, and they love to hear of the legend of El Cid which they make him tell again and again.

I sat talking to Margaret Sheridan a lot today. She knows that I have run away to be with Hugh. I told her about my worry that my father would send the guards to fetch me. But she consoled me, saying that Tom Rodgers is a very proud man, that much more likely he'll play a waiting game, as she put it, 'Waitin' for you, young Teresa, to come to heel.'

Hugh has asked me to marry him when we get to County Limerick. He tells me that there is a priest that will do it. I asked Margaret about this priest – she told me that he is the holiest man she ever met, and said, 'He will unite ye as man and wife.'

Chapter Fifteen

Hugh and I left today. We are going ahead of the others and will arrive before they do. I love the caravan, and the journey was quite wonderful. The leaves are turning yellow and gold. I can see the blackberries starting to ripen. Keeping thoughts of my father and home out of my mind isn't easy. I play little tricks. When pictures of Laddie, Máire, Joe and of course my father come into my mind I switch them off, thinking of what it will be like to be married. What will our life be like when we go to war-torn England? Will I have children, and will they look as gorgeous as he does? I'm getting to be a dab hand at switching off.

We arrived in County Limerick today and camped beside a beautiful river, a tributary of the Shannon. Hugh deftly made a fire and told me he'd teach me how it's done in twenty seconds flat. Nell, our horse, is an amiable creature, but I don't want to make a fuss over her; I'd feel I was being unfaithful to Laddie. Hugh made a slap-up meal of rashers, eggs and sausages with thickly buttered griddle bread. After we rested for a bit, we went for a walk. The evening was quite warm, despite the fact that it's getting dark so early now. When I'm just walking beside him I'm still in a state of shock at what I've done, but when I'm in his arms and he's kissing me it's all so worthwhile. We didn't talk much as we walked by the river. It was a peaceful river and not fussy and noisy like the Barrow, with its wide sweep, its weeping willows, trout ponds and lovely weir. We arrived at the sheltered spot where it was deeper. We sat on the rocks and I could feel they were still warm with the retained heat of day.

'Well, young Teresa, this is where we bathe. This is our bathroom – big, spacious, with no grime. And no cleaning-up afterwards. Ladies first – in you go.'

'God, I can't,' I told him.

He lifted my chin and dropped a light kiss on my lips. 'Why ever not? It's not a new experience for you.'

'Will you remind me of my foolishness forever?' I asked heatedly, a steady blush rising to my face.

'I'm sorry, my love – I won't mention it again. But I'm going in now. If you are too shy, go up a few yards and get in – it's a heaven-sent opportunity after the journey. We'll wave at each other.'

He moved a few feet from me and I never saw anyone divesting himself of clothes so fast. One minute he had his hands raised, pulling off his jumper, the next he was naked, striding with an ease I could never have felt into the river. I could see his back was brown from the sun. His shoulders were wide. The tan ended at his waist; his bottom and legs were paler. Obviously he worked stripped to the waist whether he was writing or tinkering. He was swimming in seconds, waving and beckoning me to get in also. I moved away from where I sat, telling myself it was the modest thing to do. Anyway, I was shy – maybe thinking he might be disappointed in me. Maybe my breasts are too small – men like curvaceous breasts. Kate Barron has magnificent breasts and I'm sure every fellow in the parish knows it. But cold soon kicked all thoughts of sizes of bosoms off me as I swam in deeper. Hugh shouted not to go into the currents. I turned back and noticed the red path the sinking sun had made on the water. I decided I'd swim through the sun-kissed pathway, and suddenly I was beside him. I opened my eyes and his dark glance met mine, and suddenly we were in each other's arms and kissing passionately, kissing each other's eyes, mouth, breasts, chest. I could feel his hardness growing and I felt so weak that I don't know how I slipped from his grasp.

'Hey,' I told him, 'aren't you the one who told me we'll wait until we're married?'

He dived under the water and rose up behind me and the moment of weakness passed. 'Is it only for weeks or is it for years? Because I feel I'm waiting for centuries for you,' he whispered.

Treading the water, I suddenly felt stupid tears spring to my eyes and run down, mingling with the river water.

'Hugh, are we mad?' I sobbed. 'Is what we've done a terrible wrong? How can we know we're right for each other?'

I think he noticed the tears, although my face was wet anyway. He gently put his hand on my face and brushed them away.

'I know we're right for each other – I know these things. But now, darling, in and get dressed and up to Castle Morena to bed whilst I watch over you and write. Tomorrow the others will be here. We'll plan our wedding and next week I must start teaching you their language.'

So here I am, dear diary, lying on Hugh's comfortable mattress. He poked out the crispest whitest linen sheets I ever saw, so I'm enjoying their white cleanliness. I'm also enjoying thoughts of him, and I idly wonder are they bad thoughts. But if I switch off from thoughts of him I'll think of home. I can't do that.

I've missed three whole days writing in your soft pages and telling you all the exciting things that happened. We heard the others come, as they were expected to. Suddenly our own private little clearing was alive with noise, barking dogs and voices, some soft, some harsh. Children fought and Eileen Connors' baby was crying. I know she breast-feeds because she went in to her caravan to do it. Despite the intimacy of their lifestyle, there is a certain shyness between the gypsies. They are not clean; they smell of smoke and dirt. I doubt if Neddy Connors and Eileen get into the river together. I know they rig up canvas and wash behind it. When the winter comes I suppose Hugh and I will have to do the same. I cannot imaging him ever forgoing his daily immersion.

We sat for hours tonight with Johnnie and Margaret. Hugh told them we wanted to marry as soon as possible. Johnnie said he knew that, and that I was a fair ripe young woman. I suppose fair means pretty, because my hair is as dark as soot. As for ripeness, if it means what I think it means, I'm ripe. Afterwards they told us about a retired old priest who lived near us. He had performed the ceremony of marriage for many of the gypsy families.

'But Johnnie,' I said, 'maybe I'll need certificates of freedom and stuff. If I do I'm bunched.'

'No, 'tisn't bits of paper and writin' he wants. He'll come and he'll marry ye, and in the eyes of God you'll be as married as ever the folks were with the bits of paper. Did Christ talk of bits of paper? Did he, girl? Sure not a bit of it. Didn't he say what God has joined together let no man break asunder – that's what 'tis about.'

'And when will he come?' I asked.

'Tomorrow,' he answered.

Eileen Connors and Neddy and the baby came to the fire, and so did Frankie McDonagh and his wife Mary. Eileen had her baby in her arms asleep and peaceful…

'C'mon, Margaret,' she asked. 'Look at Teresa's palm and tell her fortune. C'mon, Hugh, cross her palm and Margaret will read it and sure ye'll know how many children ye'll have and will ye have a long and happy life.'

'Aye,' Johnnie urged. 'Sure tell the young miss her fortune.'

I held out my hand at Margaret's bidding, and she clenched it in her brown gnarled, nutty hand. She bent down, her long grey locks hiding her face. She seemed to have trouble seeing, because she peered closer and brought me nearer the leaping flames.

'I see great happiness for you and your fine man when you become man and wife. You'll know the kind of joy only few know. I see you will have a boy child. I see – I see –' Suddenly she stopped and gently put my hand from her. She looked up and I don't know if it was the shadows cast by the fire, but right then she looked as old as time. Her lips were in a tight grim line and her eyes were expressionless. 'I'm too old to see things now, son. Maybe I've seen too much in the past. Things do be clouded now.'

Suddenly I shivered and felt cold, as if someone had walked over my grave. 'Hugh, I think I'll go,' I whispered. He jumped up and we walked away, arm in arm. Suddenly the moon dipped under a cloud and a slight rustle from the river nearly drowned out Eileen's question. But it didn't drown out Margaret Sheridan's answer: 'After the boy child I saw nothing.'

I sat at the back of Hugh's caravan, reluctant to shorten the day when I'd be lying there alone thinking. Hugh sat beside me and asked, 'What's wrong? Surely Margaret's silly fortune-telling didn't upset an intelligent girl like you.'

'But you don't think she's silly. You've spent a year with them studying their ways, their language – they impress you. I know you don't really think she's stupid.'

'No, I don't. But if I were you I shouldn't take too much heed of her fortune-telling. I don't believe anyone can see into the future. Didn't Christ say, "Sufficient for the day is the evil thereof"? I think he knew what he was talking about.'

As I write I feel better. I doubt if she did see my future. And, dear diary, as for the boy child – I'll believe it when I see him.

We were married yesterday. It's hard to imagine being married at such short notice. The old priest, Father MacDonald, was in his eighties and long since retired. He was a great friend of Johnnie's and I believe a little too fond of the bottle. We were married at seven o'clock in the evening. I wore the most beautiful white dress I had ever seen. Hugh bought it in Limerick that day, with two wedding rings and a dark blazer and flannels for himself. The whole ceremony was so unreal I have to pinch myself now and then to see if it really happened. Hugh looked so handsome in his fine clothes that I hardly recognised him. My dress was mid-calf, and so frail it was almost transparent. The skirt must have had yards and yards of material because it seemed to have a thousand folds. The top was lined and moulded. I was glad of that. At least it was some way modest and hid my breasts. But my legs were visible though the folds of the skirt. I wanted to wear a slip but I hadn't one.

The Sheridans and the Connorses and McDonaghs had prepared a positive feast. There was drink galore and Hugh had bottles of whiskey. I was told it would be unlucky to see him on the day of the wedding, so I kept away. I bathed in the river and went for a walk and met quite a few people from Rathkeale who were out. They smiled and I wondered what they would think if they really knew what I was about. I was getting married in a tinkers' encampment by a priest who was old and maybe feeble-minded or even unfrocked.

Johnnie Sheridan had on a tweed suit that had seen better days, but he looked shaved and clean. He stood beside Hugh, so I knew he was the best man. Eileen Connors wore a full red flowery skirt and a snow-white blouse. When I walked into the clearing she flashed her white-toothed smile and walked towards me. I was shaking, although the two fires were piled high with timbers and the sparks rose and crackled so much I could hardly hear the priest.

'Do you, Teresa Rodgers, take this man to be your lawful husband, for better or worse, richer or poorer, in sickness and in health till death do you part?'

'I do,' I said and hardly recognised my own voice.

'Do you, Hugh Morena, take this woman to be your lawful wife, for better or worse, in sickness and in health, richer or poorer, till death do you part?'

'I do.'

His voice was loud and firm. We exchanged rings – then Eileen removed the circlet of wild flowers she had made earlier that day and had placed on my head, telling me I was the most beautiful bride she had ever seen. She also took my wild-flower bouquet, and she flung them both in the fire, throwing her two hands above her head and saying something I didn't understand because she spoke in her own language.

'What is she saying?' I whispered to Hugh.

'She's burning the flowers and any misfortunes that might befall us during our married life.'

'Oh,' I said. 'Well, that's all right then.'

He laughed loudly then, and swept me in his arms, and they all cheered and shouted, flocking around us, shaking our hands and wishing us well. Then the feast started, and the drink flowed and laughter and conversations got louder and louder as they, in all probability, forgot the reason for such merriment. Maybe they were more excited because we were different, and yet maybe they felt proud because we, as settled people, had adopted their ways. Hugh and I sat with them, making merry. We said goodbye to the gentle priest as he went his way. Maybe the ceremony had been unorthodox, but we were more conscious that we were a married couple than any couple on this earth. After all, we were brought up to believe that it was the couple that really performed the sacrament when it came to matrimony. We sat there and when things were going so well – like flutes playing and songs the like of which I had never heard before pierced the autumn air – Hugh whispered that it was time to go away.

I won't admit at this stage that I was shy or nervous or terrified of what would take place. After all, I had to be honest with myself. I wanted him more that I ever wanted anyone. Hadn't I given up my father, my home, my friends, and my beloved pony – all aspects of my old life – for him? It was funny that there were no sideway glances, no nudges, no slagging as we walked off. These people seemed to respect that we were going to be untied in a way they understood and respected. I couldn't help but imagine all the lewd remarks and nudges that the noisy young farmers would make if it was Denis MacMahon I had married and was going to share a bed with.

I had dreamed of this. I wasn't let down. To try and describe the rapture I felt when Hugh finally made love to me would be impossible. I had heard there was pain and breakage, and sometimes blood. But if there was, I didn't feel it. By the time he reached a climax I wanted him so much I felt it was almost wrong, almost wanton.

I am married two days and there isn't an hour that I want to be away from him. I had foolishly and childishly told Denis MacMahon that I wanted to be fascinated – I wanted the sky to explode, the very earth to move. And it did. After Hugh and I made love, I knew that all the tears I would weep in a future that stretched so unknowingly ahead wouldn't be for Laddie, for my father, for Joe, for my old way of life – they would be for me, if anything ever happened to separate us. Dear diary, I love him. I love him so much it frightens me.

See – it's two more days since I've bothered putting pen to paper. Dreamy days of autumn tranquillity and golden trees and swans in the river. We no longer swim with a modest hundred yards between us; we now swim together and we have made love in the river, and on the bank, and on the way home to Castle Morena. Sometimes, when we get back to the caravan, Hugh wants to write. He tells me he is almost finished his manuscript. He holds me in his arms and tells me he feels bad here in lovely Ireland while the war rages on in the rest of Europe. I know he feels he should be there playing his part.

So I let him work and I go over to Eileen Connors' caravan. We sit and chat. She tells me what it is like living always on the road. She shyly asked me if I was satisfied with my first night. I told her I was. I even told her I had no idea that it would be so wonderful. She nodded and said she was glad – very glad. She was pensive, I thought, as she looked at me. Then she laughed and wondered was the boy child started. I told her it was about the last thing on my mind, and definitely the very last thing on Hugh's mind. She smiled, and said maybe a delay would be a good thing. I watched her as she fed her baby. She seemed so adept at the job, talking away as she put her to her breast. The baby grabbed her nipple and settled down so contentedly. I watched and wondered what it would be like to have Hugh's child at my breast. Would a small child come between everything we have now, or would it seal our love?

Eventually I wandered back to my caravan. Hugh was waiting for me – obviously his writing was finished and packed away. He is so orderly and neat, really. Except when it comes to making love. He's not orderly then. All his Englishness leaves him and he gets so passionate and utterly carried away. I didn't think the sky would keep exploding, but it does. I love him so much it frightens me. Have I said that before?

The summer is over and the golden amber days of autumn are giving away to chilly days when the thin winds slip sneakily under the hinged doors of the caravan. Hugh has erected a canvas lean-to where I wash every day away from what just might be the prying eyes of the others. He still swims in the river. Last night he gave me a little tin box to put you, my beloved diary in. He said it was just in case the children broke in and might mess things. Today he looked at me thoughtfully and said, 'Teresa – you're as strong as a mountain goat – aren't you?'

'Why do you ask that?'

'Because it could take until spring to really finish the book. I'd like to stay with the families until then. But foremost on my mind is you and your wellbeing. I must take care of you – you've given up so much for me.'

'I was never sick in my life,' I told him. 'So stop worrying. I love it here, here I feel free and I love you.'

He seemed satisfied after that. This evening two more caravans came. They were the Sheridans' eldest sons with their wives and families. They had come from Abbeyfeale and were going to winter with us. They seemed nice and when we were introduced to them they seemed to accept us after the initial shyness. They had six children between them and Johnnie seemed to be very happy they were back. I suppose the bigger the clan the more important he feels. Yet I like him – I like the bright, nutty brown eyes beneath the thick busy eyebrows. He has a kind of impish little grin like a little boy who was thinking up all kinds of pranks. I don't think he ever washes and yet he doesn't smell dirty. He smells of smoke and turf, bracken and old damp leaves. I like Margaret too. She calls me Young Miss. Sometimes I sit at her fire and when she's alone I get her to chat some. Only this evening I asked her about the priest who married us.

'Margaret,' I asked, 'are we married at all? We didn't go to church or to Communion, and we have no marriage certificate – nothing to prove we really are married.'

'Sure Miss Teresa, he is the holiest man on this earth. Though he's no longer workin' and maybe drank too much in his day, he's the nearest thing to God and heaven I know, so he is. Yes, child, 'tis well married you are. Sure, when yourself and Hugh leave to go your way, what's to stop you getting married again if it'll ease your hearts?'

I was going to ask her what she had seen in my palm that made her stop telling my fortune but something held me back. Sitting there in the warm glow of the fire, knowing that Hugh was working away a mere cock's step away, I felt so suffused with happiness I didn't want any shadow to cross and block out, even temporarily, what I felt then. I walked back across the clearing to our caravan. Hugh had fallen asleep; there were papers beside him and the pen was still in his hand, as if he had been making notes. I gently removed it, not wanting to wake him. He was fully dressed, but I thought he might was well stay that way.

As I write, dear diary, I glance at him from time to time. He looks so handsome fast asleep. I notice his hair could do with a trim – the black locks are falling across his forehead. The absurdly long eyelashes are resting on his cheekbones – his firm mouth is closed as he breathes easily. I look at him, thinking that I belong to him and he to me. Sometimes I can't believe this is true; now and then guilty little thoughts intrude on my mind. A little voice tells me I belonged to a lot before I met him: my father, Joe, Máire, Laddie, my good home and its spread of acres – even my lovely bedroom with its new finery and the old chest of drawers and the Infant of Prague. I stifle the thoughts, dear diary, because I'm good at stifling them. Maybe some day I will go home. With Hugh and my – what did they call it? Yes, my boy child. And by then I'll have two little daughters with jet-black hair and dark brown eyes and thick long lashes. Or maybe one of them will have my eyes – Hugh tells me they are the darkest blue, most Irish *cailín* eyes he has ever seen.

Once recently, after we made love, he told me he couldn't wait to show me off when we get to England when the war is over. Then I can meet his mother and his friends. God almighty, I don't think I'd like that. They'll all have posh accents and mine is terrible. When I said this, he told me I should see myself. I asked him to explain himself, and he said that when he sees me tossing my hair and looking around me with that arrogant Teresa Rodgers look, he firmly believes I'm descended from the High Kings of Ireland. He's mad really – but that's why I love him.

I am married six weeks and my period is now two weeks overdue. I haven't told Hugh and he hasn't noticed. Why I hesitate I'm not sure. He has never mentioned children or the possibility I might have a baby. Yet I'm not barely eighteen and he's not quite twenty-three, and we make wild love so it's inevitable that this should happen. I'll tell him before the week is out.

It's cold now, and when we go for a walk we wade through masses of dried crunchy leaves. There is a long narrow country road stretching on and on forever. As we walk it hand in hand, I call it a tramp's nightmare and Hugh asks me to explain. I tell him there's no great explanation; it's a tramp's nightmare because it's never-ending. He tells me I have the most peculiar expressions, and he chases me as I run through the rustling, heaving dead leaves. Just today I told him it brought back Barrons Wood to me. He took me in his arms and asked me to tell him straight out if I missed my home and everything attached to it. I told him no, not one bit. But a little lump came to my throat and stupid tears came into my eyes. He noticed and kissed them away, and told me he would make it up to me.

One would imagine that I would have time to write oodles and oodles of stuff in my dear little diary every night. Instead, I'm merely hitting a page here and there in an odd erratic haphazard manner. Two days ago I told Hugh I thought that I was expecting a baby. I raked his eyes for any sign of shadow concerning my news. But there wasn't any. We were behind the caravan and I had just finished washing and dressing. I tried to be flippant, saying, 'We'll have to put an extra wing on to Castle Morena – because soon we'll be three.'

He was shaving in a small mirror he had hung on a hook at the back of the caravan. He had the long razor in his hand he stopped his operation, his hand suspended, and stared at me in amazement.

'What did you say?' he asked.

'A baby – you know, a little baby,' I told him.

He put down the razor, and it seemed to take a moment for my information to sink in. Then he gave a whoop, put down the razor and lifted me off my feet, swinging me around and covering me with lathery, soapy kisses. He was happy, deliriously happy. He put his hand on my stomach, his touch so gentle.

'Imagine, Teresa Rodgers, all that excitement that is going on in there.'

'Just imagine, Hugh Morena, and you were the cause of it,' I said, smiling like a drooling fool.

Then he sobered up and took me by the hand. We walked around to the swing door in the front. He hoisted me up, saying, 'I can't have you climbing stairs.' His grin took in the three steps to the opening. We sat on the bed and suddenly there was a serious air about him. 'Listen, darling, this has altered things. We cannot go on like this – living rough like we are. You'll need proper medical care, a good doctor, heat, warmth – good food. We must leave.'

It was my turn to get serious. 'And tell me, what about your book? You started your book before you ever met me. I'm not going to be the reason for you giving it up. Anyway, there won't be any sign or symptom of a baby on me for months and months. I'm as strong as an ox. I want to look on this as the greatest experience of my life. Eileen told me that Margaret has brought hundreds and hundreds of babies into the world. She also told me that young mothers come to her to have their babies because she has lucky hands.'

His eyes were full of doubts. I stood up in front of him and pulled his head into my breast, and rocked him to and fro, telling him I'd be fine. 'And after all,' I added, 'you tell me I'm a good writer, so maybe I'd like to write a book about it some day.' I think my positive approach eased his worries, because he jumped up, and told me I was going on a shopping spree with him to Limerick to buy winter clothes and particularly a warm coat for me. We asked Johnnie if we could borrow his pony and cart. He was more than agreeable. On the way to Limerick, Hugh sang 'It's a Long Way to Tipperary' and I joined in, and the pony, Nell, seemed to be keeping time, and I never felt happier in my whole life.

It's very cold now and all the leaves are gone from the trees. They look bare, like black lace against the winter sky. There's a tough of frost in the air. And at night sometimes, we linger around the fires before going to bed. I am now seriously learning the gypsies' language; I have just a word here and there, but Hugh is fluent. I'm quite jealous. They seem to laugh and talk for hours and I don't know what they're saying. He sees me looking a bit lost and translates. When we go to bed and after we make love, I ask him to teach me. He holds me in his arms and murmurs words I don't understand in my ear and then translates. And they are all words of love and tenderness. I heatedly tell him that I want to know how to talk to Margaret and Eileen and the Sheridans' sons. He soothes me then, and says we'll start lessons very soon.

I'm getting sick most mornings now. Margaret made me a herbal concoction. It tastes pepperminty but it helps. Now that it's dark so early, Hugh spends hours and hours writing in the caravan. Sometimes I lie on the bed looking at him. We have a large paraffin lamp, and the shadow of his head goes right up on the roof. In this warm world of cosy heat and shadows, I study his handsome profile and wonder, will my baby have his good looks? The dark, dark look and those amazing eyes?

I am glad of the winter coat. It's thick and fawn-coloured, with a hood and wooden toggles and deep pockets, where I snuggle down my hands when I walk the length of the tramp's nightmare road. Hugh has brought me a book on pregnancy. As he writes I read it. It's fascinating. I simply cannot believe that the child I'm carrying already has arms and legs and eyes and things. My waistline has thickened a little now. The zips of my skirt doesn't go up any more. I've sewn two tapes which I will let out as time goes by. Anyway, I read and read about cell formation and chromosomes and X and Y factors, and I'm getting fierce curious to know what this baby will be like.

Hugh tells me about his mother: he tells me she is quite a great person. He tells me he loves her, mostly because she respected his wishes and allowed him so much freedom. He keeps telling me that she will be crazy with happiness when she hears about the baby. He intends writing and telling her very soon.

Christmas is in the air and I'm told that the gypsy families will celebrate it just like people celebrate it the world over. Margaret plans that, instead of separate fires, we'll have just one big one. She'll cook some fine geese and hams. She tells me money isn't too scarce this year; what with the scarcity of stuff in the shops the tinkering trade went right well this summer. And so did the horse fairs in Galway, way back before they came to Tulla. The surrounding farms are very generous also. The families have received presents of turkeys and warm blankets, and even a few Christmas puddings. Because I have no money, Hugh has given me an allowance so that I can feel independent and can be in a position to buy what he terms my small necessities. He apologised that he hadn't thought of it earlier, reminding me that I was never short of anything. He is right, I wasn't.

Lately I'm not so good for switching off. Sometimes I think of my old life and how good my father was to me. He got me so much in his effort to keep me content. Now I can accept the fact that he went quite mad when he heard I was out with what he thought was one of the gypsies. Sometimes I'm surprised that he hasn't tried to find me.

Today we went to Limerick again. Hugh wanted to buy some small token Christmas presents for the Sheridans and the Connorses. He also wanted to send his mother something. The streets were full of bustling shoppers, and there was an air of Christmas about despite the rationing of foodstuffs. I was shocked to see myself in a full-length mirror in a shop where Hugh was browsing. First I wondered who the schoolgirl with the long mop of dark unruly hair and the fawn duffle coat was. Her face was so thin and there was a slight thickening of her waistline. I looked at her for a bit before I realised she was me. I rejoined Hugh at the jewellery counter. He glanced up and his eyes met mine, and he must have seen something in them that worried him, because he came over. 'What's wrong, love? You look like someone who has just seen a ghost.'

'I have,' I whispered, 'and the ghost is me.'

He looked puzzled for a bit and I pointed to the mirror. He immediately seemed to understand I was upset.

'Had you forgotten how lovely you are?'

'Oh God, I look terrible. How can you say that? You should be ashamed of me. My hair is like a tinker's.' Then I bit my lip because he looked upset. 'Oh, don't mind me. We just say these things.'

'But I do mind,' he told me. 'And I'm going to do something about it.'

He marched me out of the shop and up William Street until we came to a hair-dressing salon.

'Come on in.'

I did and stood there like a fool, and it seemed as if half the eyes of Limerick were on me. When the assistant approached me, I muttered something about a trim. Hugh smiled at her and I could see the way his charm was working.

'A shampoo and a trim by the best hair stylist you have.'

By the time we left, both of us had the works and I decided I didn't look too bad. Hugh told me I was beautiful, with my unruly locks someway under control. He said he could see my face again. Then he made me walk to the bridge whilst he did some shopping. I presumed it was something for me. When he was gone I ran into a bookshop and saw exactly what he'd like – a hard-covered book with the dying Cuchulainn on the front cover. Inside, beautifully illustrated, were the wonderful old stories of Ireland.

Christmas Day was different and very memorable. Maybe I'll have many more Christmases, but today will stand out. It was as black as night when we heard some of the children laughing.

'I presume Santa has come,' Hugh whispered in my ear. But it was so warm and cosy lying there beside him I hardly wanted the day to start. 'Our first Christmas,' he whispered as he kissed me. Then I got carried away and started to kiss him on the eyelids and on the mouth, running my tongue along his teeth. I bit his ears and the tip of his nose. He called me a brazen Irish hussy, and after we made love we lay there in the warm darkness and I wondered if I would ever enjoy a Christmas morning as much. Later Hugh got up and lit the big brass lamp and put the kettle on the methylated stove for an early cup of tea. He has got into the habit of doing this because he read that an early cup of tea prevents morning sickness. Afterwards, Johnnie Sheridan's grandchildren came banging on our door, showing us their Christmas presents. They had guns and cowboy hats, and one little fellow was dressed us as an Indian, complete with feathers, tomahawk and fringed trousers. They crowded on top of us, all excited, and I realised that happiness doesn't necessarily mean a conventional house with a thatch or a slate roof. I would think that Johnnie's grandchildren were as happy today as any children ever are on a frosty Christmas morning.

After they went Hugh drew a large parcel from under his shelf and handed it to me. He was smiling as he watched me open it. I drew out a fine tartan wool skirt with side buckles and leather straps, and underneath it a cherry-red wool twinset, obviously carefully chosen to match the skirt. I thought the buckles would be handy to let out and out as time goes by. He was grinning as if he was the cleverest fellow in the whole world. I told him I loved them; they were the nicest presents I had got since Laddie. I gave him the book. When he saw it he was like a small boy turning the pages of a Christmas annual with wonder.

We shared a lovely lovely day with all four families, the Sheridans, the Connorses, the McDonaghs and the Morenas.

*

Stephen turned the yellow pages, his fingers stiff from clutching the black-covered book with the faded golden date, 1940. There were no more entries except a few short lines on the last page of December 1940.

*

Tomorrow begins a new year. I wonder how it will go? I wonder what it will be like to be a mother, to have a baby suckling at my breast? Will it be so important for me that I might become a real Irish mammy, putting my sons before my husband, myself, everything? I haven't much experience of what a real mammy is like but I have seen the goings-on in friends' houses. Mothers like slaves for their husbands and sons. Funny, not so much for their daughters, though. I wonder was I better off living like I did, or did I miss out terribly? I'll never know. All I know is that I can't for the life of

190

me see any little baby coming before my love for Hugh. Ah no, that's not fair really on the little scrap; I feel him already moving inside me. If anyone told me this time last year I would be living in a caravan with an English man who writes books, surrounded by the gypsies we were told never, ever to go near, I wouldn't have believed it for a second. It's true – fact is stranger than fiction. Tomorrow, dear little diary, I will be putting you in the tin box and starting a new book. Hugh bought me one the identical same as you – I hope I will feel as good writing in it as I did scrawling in you.

January 1st 1941. Today, the first day of a brand-new year, started freezing. It was so cold I didn't want to go into the wash room, as we call the canvas lean-to at the back of the caravan. But of course we had to. Hugh always first heats the water on the methylated stove and goes first, and then it is my turn. The wind is whistling through the canvas now and when Hugh saw me standing there in my slip he had that lost and sad look that I know means I should be living in a nice cosy house, what with the baby and all. I know if I complain about the cold and the lack of hygiene and the confined way we live in our little caravan, he'll look at me and in the dark depths of those wonderful eyes I'll see a niggling worry that I shouldn't be in this place, that I should be in a warm house with decent, well-cooked meals and plenty of rest, because I'm such a young mother-to-be. He has aired his worries, but I know that if he hadn't met me he would have stayed happily with the gypsies, writing his book and completely soaking up their ways, living their life. I know we must return to civilisation after the baby is born. I tell him that his story will have bite if he gives an account of how his first-born son was born in a caravan amongst the people he has learned to know and love. That shuts him up.

But at times I do grow a bit fed up with things. The days are so short and the nights so long. Sometimes I feel I've forgotten what it was like before I came to live in this caravan. The nights are full of shadows where I lie reading, or watching Hugh with his dark head bent over his writing, the steady tap-tap of his typewriter breaking the silence. The glow from the lamp throws his shadow on the wall. Sometimes his head is bent; sometimes his profile is so distinct it's like an etching. I just watch and then he turns his head and looks at me. Sometimes he comes over and puts his arms around me and whispers that I have great patience for a wild Irish girl. I love it when I can tear him away from his work. I love it better when he decides he has done enough and he undresses and gets in beside me. He's always so cold, but I warm him up. Then he puts his hand on my swelling stomach in an effort to feel the baby move. When it does and he feels the flicker of life, he's like a child, all smug that he has created this small creature. I tell him his part was minimal and that I'm the important one in this drama-to-be.

These are the nice times. But sometimes I'm so bored during the day, when Hugh has gone into Rathkeale or even Limerick, and I wander like a lost soul, dropping in on Margaret and Johnnie Sheridan. I sit with them and ask them to teach me their language. They really seem to want to do this. Margaret has great patience and explains what all the words mean. I nag her at times, saying, 'Margaret, tell me what you saw in my palm. Remember, the evening you told my fortune? Come on, tell me.' She lifts her lined tired eyes from her little stove and, pushing back her long grey hair, she laughs hoarsely and says, 'Sure, Virgin Mary and her Blessed son, will you listen to the child? Sure the birds in the bushes know that it's all nonsense, so they do, so they do.' But I go home uneasy. At times I'm more than uneasy, I'm terrified. What do I know about babies? Sure at least I'm not like the girls in the boarding school, or the girls from the city, who have never seen animals mated or animals giving birth. At least I know where the birth channel is. Anna in school thought that they popped out through the navel. Maybe now she knows better. Maybe some day I'll see her and tell her everything first hand. I wonder will I ever see my friends again? Will I ever see my father or Joe or Máire. Will I ever rub Laddie's muzzle and kiss him on the little white star on his forehead? Is he gone, is he sold off at some fair in Waterford or in Kilkenny? Oh God, I'd better stop or I'll start bawling my stupid head off. And Hugh will look at me and my unhappiness, and I'll be in England with his mother, and his book will be unfinished and all this will have been wasted.

Tomorrow I'll go over to Eileen and ask her to teach me to make tin mugs. She's so good at them; she makes sweet cans also. I'm just an ornament getting bigger every day and getting more useless. Yes, tomorrow I'll start to be useful. Who knows, maybe when I'm in England I can make tin mugs and sweet cans, and Hugh might be fierce proud of me?

The baby has given me a right kick. Yes, I bet he's a boy. He feels as if he'll be a right strong fellow. Sometimes I can't wait to have him, and other times I'm terrified he'll come between this love, this physical love Hugh and I have for each other. I think if Hugh ever left me I would be happy to die. Now I'm morbid again. Off with me tomorrow to learn more of their language, and also to learn the trade of tinkering.

There was a winter fair in Abbeyfeale today and I went along with Hugh and the others. Watching Johnnie Sheridan selling a pony was about the funniest thing – all that nodding and spitting and walking away.

I said a few times to Hugh, 'Will Johnnie be raging because he's not going to buy?'

Hugh smiled his knowing smile and explained, 'He'll sell all right. You're only watching the build-up to the final transaction. It's better than a play in the Abbey.'

Eventually there was a settlement and the beating of sticks in the muddy road, and the money changed hands, and luck money was passed, and everyone went to the pub for a drink. Johnnie looked at Hugh and then at me, and I think he felt a bit sorry for us, because he asked the publican could 'the fine gent take in his child bride to the snug'. The publican looked at us and then nodded consent. Hugh said, 'Come on, love, I'll buy you a hot whiskey.'

I shook my head and asked him was he mad? I had never taken a drop of the stuff in my life.

He kissed me on the cheek and said. 'That is a decided gap in your upbringing when you think of all the mad things you have done.'

Knowing what is generally thought of women who frequent snugs, I looked to my right and my left before following him into the dark confined place. I thought the hot punch was really awful but I felt all warm and full of glow after it – in fact, so warm and so glowing that there would be no end to the things I'd have got up to if Margaret Sheridan and Eileen Connors hadn't been there. On the way out the publican said, 'Goodbye Mrs Morena, I hope we'll see you again soon.' The new name was so unfamiliar that I hardly knew he was talking to me. Mrs Morena – Mrs Morena. Teresa Morena – Teresa Morena – Teresa Morena. I'd better get used to it – it's very different to Teresa Rodgers, so it is.

*

Stephen read through all the entries in January, noting that Teresa was making progress at the language and at the tin-making, recording everything that was happening to her physically as her pregnancy progressed and writing of her increasing love for her husband. Her youthful exuberant spirits rose when the long cold winter gave way to spring.

*

February 20th. It isn't just the cock's step now – it's a decided stretch in the evening. There's a big house about a mile from here called Beechwood. Sometimes Hugh and I go for a long walk and today, when we passed the great big iron gates, I noticed that all up the driveway were drifts of snowdrops. I stood there looking at them. I wanted to pick a bunch of them and take them back to the caravan to remind me of spring.

'Don't, love,' Hugh advised. 'They would wilt with the old lamp. Let them have their day – everything and everyone should have its day.'

'Is this our day?' I asked.

'This is the beginning of a million days for us.'

'Talk about exaggeration,' I told him as I linked his arm in mine and we left the big house – the huge gates and the drifts of snowdrops untouched. I felt good and we walked home.

Hugh was in Limerick today. He brought back the news-papers. I read the *Irish Press* and was horrified to read about the terrible bombings in England. I asked him was he worried about his mother. He told me he wasn't, as she lived in the country, all the children from the big cities were sent to there for their safety. I found myself reading about the war with a great interest. Maybe because of our isolation, I wanted to know what was happening in the great world out there. I read about Rommel, the German general, landing in North Africa to fight in the desert. I read Churchill's speeches too.

I was lying in bed propped up on one elbow; I find this comfortable. And I decided I'd distract Hugh from his book. Secretly I'm getting a little sick of all the time he spends with it.

No – no, I'm not jealous, because when he's not writing he's always with me. It's just that I can't imagine that you'd have to spend such time writing a book.

'Isn't Churchill a great fellow with words?' I said to him. 'All those wonderful speeches about nothing to offer but blood, toil, tears and sweat. I love strong words like he uses.'

'I know you do – you're very good with words. Don't think I haven't noticed all the time you spend with your diary. I had a sneaky look. I know you'll be a good writer some day.'

I felt a glow from his praise. Sometimes I thought he might think me a stupid sort of girl. But if he thinks I'm good at words he musn't. I'll be eighteen on the 16th of March, and I'll be seven months gone.

I had a great birthday. The first thing I heard in the morning when I woke up were the children singing, 'Happy birthday to Teresa, happy birthday to you.' Hugh opened the caravan and there they all stood. Johnnie's little grandson Maurice had a bunch of daffodils in his hands. I looked at their bright yellow faces and saw the moisture was standing out in little drops on the petals. I jumped down and hugged him, ignoring his runny nose. 'Thanks, Maurice. I love them – I love them.' He was as pleased as punch.

After our breakfast Hugh handed me a little box wrapped in pale green paper. Inside was another box – a velvety box – and inside the velvety box was a gold chain with an unusual little pendant of a bunch of snowdrops, their little faces made of white enamel, their stems of gold.

'It's beautiful,' I whispered, 'beautiful. Where did you get it?'

'I got it made in Limerick by an old jeweller. I wouldn't let you pick the snowdrops, so I thought these would make up for my stupid objection to such a simple thing.'

'I'll wear them always,' I told him, 'Always.'

Afterwards, Margaret Sheridan gave me a warm knitted bedjacket 'for yer lying-in time', she told me. It was pale blue and very soft and beautifully knitted. I kissed her on her brown wrinkled cheek.

'Sure where at all did Tom Rodgers get the likes of you?' she said.

Strange words, but I suppose I know what she meant. My

father was never much of a one for showing anyone that he even liked them. Maybe I wasn't either until I met Hugh. Then again, half of Hugh is English and conservative, but the other half is Spanish and demonstrative.

Eileen gave me four little copper mugs and a copper ash tray. 'When yer livin' in a fine house across the water they'll remind you of me,' she said.

God, I'm so happy with these people mostly, and yet now and then I'm tired of the way of life – the cold and the draughts, the smell of smoke, the awful terrible business of going to the woods to go to the toilet, the canvas lean-to for a bathroom. My hair is a tangled mess of curls again. Tomorrow I'll ask Eileen to cut a lump off it. I won't tell Hugh until I get it done, because he'll object.

*

The next extracts in his mother's diary told Stephen that the eighteen-year-old Teresa rejoiced in the coming of spring and the lengthening of the days. He read of her impatience at her increasing girth when she could not longer jump the hedges and streams like she used to. The diaries highlighted little snippets of the war that raged on in Europe.

*

If Hugh is right and I am good with words maybe I should read more. Give him his due he keeps buying me books. He has some notion that I'm like Annie M P Smithson. I think he's bought all of her books for me. I like them but the heroines are so good and pure and stilted that I feel like an absolute sinner. Then again, my biggest sin is that I ran away. There's nowhere in the gospel or the catechism to say that you can't run away – so that mightn't be a sin. Of course, there's a lot about honouring thy father and thy mother. I didn't honour my father by leaving him – did I. But then, isn't there a lot about leaving thy father and thy mother and cleaving to your marriage partner. Well I want to cleave so much to Hugh that I even make the first move and when I do he can never resist. He still calls me a brazen Irish hussey, but I know that I am as important to him as he is to me. Last night he wondered should we make love now that I'm so near my time. I tell him there isn't a thing in the book he has given me that says we shouldn't. He laughs and takes me in his arms, and we go crazy for each other. I don't think the Annie M P Smithson heroines would agree.

I read the paper from cover to cover today. God above, how safe and snug we are in Ireland, with only rations to contend with, in comparison to the bombs and death that reigns in Europe! I read in the *Irish Press* today that London suffered its worst night of bombings since the beginning of the war. According to the report in the paper, five hundred and fifty planes dropped 200,000 incendiary bombs. That is on poor London alone. I also read that Yugoslavia and Greece have been defeated and are now occupied by Germany. Imagine if the Germans came here – and did the goose-step up and down Abbeyfeale or the main street in Rathkeale. Sometimes, after Hugh has combed the papers, he looks very depressed. I know he feels he should be doing his part, fighting for his country. When we go to England after the baby is born he'll join up. That I know.

I don't think things are progressing very normally right now. Today I saw some bright-red blood on the sheet after I got up. I didn't tell Hugh, but I asked Eileen if she had ever seen such a thing. She looked worried for a bit and then tried to console me, saying that towards the end there are often signs of bleeding. She then told me not to worry, and that Margaret had delivered hundreds of babies, 'in terrible weather too'. She told me, 'All the babies are healthy when they come. Sometimes they do get sick and die when they're little. But Teresa, sure that won't happen you – you'll be with your own then.'

I didn't tell Hugh about the bright-red blood. I stopped the flow by tearing up an old towel and packed it firmly between my legs. We went for a walk and if he thought I was like a bandy duck, he didn't say so. It was the most beautiful night, spring-like and warm. The ditches and trees had all come to life with growth and colour and movement. The odd rustle in the trees were from small birds who were nesting, 'a bit like me,' I said to Hugh. We stopped and he lay against the ditch and pulled me into his arms. He found it difficult to circle my girth but he managed.

'Teresa, there is something I want to tell you,' he started. 'I've arranged for you to go to hospital in Limerick to have the baby.'

I pulled away. 'But you can't do that. It's my baby and my

body, and you know Margaret is brilliant at this business. And you want to be there and write about it in your book, and in a hospital they won't let you within an ass's roar of me.'

'Forget all those things. It's for your safety and wellbeing – don't you understand that?' he argued.

'No, I'll be fine. I'm a young healthy person – sure Hugh, I've watched all sorts of animals giving birth on the farm. It's a natural event. Even the book you brought me says it's a natural event. No, love,' I insisted, 'I want you near me. I want Margaret Sheridan and Eileen, and when we have our baby I want all the others to come and see me. It'll be great.'

Today he didn't say a word about the hospital. Neither did I. The bleeding has stopped and I'm glad. If he knew about that I would be in there now, lying beneath clean sterile sheets, alone and terrified. Instead I'm lying here filled with wonderment at the strong kicking of my baby. I think he'll be a footballer anyway. As I write I'm watching Hugh with his dark head bent over his manuscript that is now as thick as six inches. I can't imagine what else he can put into it.

He showed me a letter he got from his mother this morning. He collected it in Abbeyfeale Post Office. She writes in the most elegant hand and on the poshest notepaper I've ever seen. She lives in Southway House in Essex. She tells him she is so anxious for him to come home. She has a number of evacuees in her home but the family maid and the gardener George are helping her to cope. She mentioned all her Red Cross activities, and the various fêtes she is organising for the war fund. She is happy for him that he has finally got married. She's looking forward to seeing his young bride. She's surprised that there's a baby on the way during such a difficult time, but she hopes that everything will go well, and she will be so happy to welcome me and her first grandchild into her home.

It was such a friendly letter that I know I will feel better about crossing the water when the time comes.

*

Stephen's fingers, cramped and stiff now, noticed that there were only three more entries in the diary. His heart quickened with a tangible fear. He knew he was reading about the last days of Teresa's life.

For some unknown reason he was tempted to put the book away so that he might foolishly stave off the terrible hour when Teresa's young life came to an end. He looked around her room. His head was so full of the events of eighteen years before that he had to shake his head to return to normality. Teresa had painted such vivid pictures with her pen that Stephen felt more at home with her and Hugh than he did with the grandfather who had reared him.

*

As I write Hugh sleeps beside me. His breathing is steady and his head turned to my side as I sit propped writing in my diary. The big fire outside is sparking and the flames are still leaping as the others sit around it, talking and laughing. I know that the time has come for them to pack up camp and move. I have a strange feeling they would be on their way sooner if I wasn't on my last legs. Now that my time is so near I hang around talking to Eileen Connors, and examining her fat, thriving little baby. The baby's gorgeous, all cuddles and folds. She lets her sit on my lap, or on the bit of lap I have left, as we talk in her caravan. She asked me today if I've seen any more bleeding, and I told her I haven't – or at least nothing as bad as I saw first. Just a little sign now and then.

Margaret called in to see us, and she asked me to lie down on Eileen's bed. I did and she ran her hands all over me, pressing hard near the pit of my stomach.

'Ah, young Teresa, sure you're in great form. The head is down. When the apple is ripe 'twill drop, so it will – when it's ripe 'twill drop.' She left then and I felt relieved that she hadn't noticed anything out of the ordinary.

Hugh was full of energy and high spirits when I came back to the caravan. 'I'll finish this book tomorrow or the next day, my love – then I shall give you my total attention.'

Tomorrow I won't nag him at all. I'll wander around and help Eileen with the mugs and the cans – I'm getting good at it. I'll even go over after our tea so that he'll finish the book. When I come back we'll go mad and celebrate. When I think of him there's only one way I want to celebrate right now – that is to make love, intense, passionate and hungry. God above, wouldn't it be a terrible thing if this diary was ever found and read by anyone other than Hugh? What would they think but that Teresa Rodgers was the craziest female ever to come out of the strait-laced village of Tulla? But it's only my husband that drives me crazy, so that must be all right. Maybe I'll go to confession before the baby is born and tell the priest all my sins. Then again, are they sins? Is it a sin when you're married? Wasn't I always on good behaviour with Denis MacMahon? Poor Denis, he could never have satisfied me. I told him I wanted the heavens to explode. And they did – they did.

*

The last entry was dated May 6th 1941.

*

I never thought I could hold a pen in my hand again. I never thought I could open the pages of my little diary again. I'm doing it like a mechanical dead thing. I have no feelings, only dead feelings. I'm not interested in living; I'm not even interested in dying. I just want to crawl into a black hole and lie down. It would be easier than dying. Dying might take and effort and I can now make none.

Hugh is dead. Hugh is dead. Hugh is dead. If I write it a dozen times, a hundred times, I might accept it. It won't really sink in. He's dead a week. Or is it more? Is it less? I'm not sure. I only know I'll never see him again. Never hear that beloved voice or watch those dark long-lashed eyes with their intense, sometimes brooding, look. Like the way he kept staring at me lately, worrying about whether I should go into hospital. Sometimes his eyes would be sparkling with life like a small boy's, like when we used run across the stones in the stream through the dry rustling leaves in the autumn. Of course I will mostly remember his eyes when they were filled with lust, love and passion.

Dear little diary, you'll want to know how he died. I went like I said, on the last day of his life, to idle the hours away, to make tin cans, to talk to Eileen and Margaret – to talk to Johnnie. I went to Eileen's cosy caravan last. She had lit a little stove. We talked and talked. She wanted to know all about my life as a young girl. She wanted to know what a real school was like, what it was like living in a settled community – what it was like never to feel hungry, cold, dirty, never to have to worry about money or health or storms or whether farmers would object to your staying on their land. I told her all I could – about my father's loneliness when my mother died, and how I had no one to talk to, only Máire and Joe. I told her about the picnic and us all going into the river in our pelts and she laughed so heartily the tears ran down her face. When I told her about the festooned tree and seeing Hugh afterwards, she kept gasping, 'You're a card, you're a card, so you are.' As we sat there talking in the dark with nothing to light the caravan only the glow of her little stove, the place suddenly lit up. It was almost as bright as day. I looked out and saw to my horror that our caravan was on fire. Already the flames were leaping to the sky, all yellow-red and ferocious. 'Oh Christ, Eileen, Hugh is in there,' I screamed. I could hear myself screaming more and more trying to break away and run into the flames. 'Hugh is in there,' I told them, but someone held me back with arms of steel. 'I must get him. Help me.' I screamed and sobbed, 'Please help me.' The arms held me like a vice but from somewhere I got superhuman strength and broke away. Screaming his name, I ran to the steps. I felt the heat and something scorching. I didn't know it was my hair and my clothes. I heard hoarse voices shouting, and then I heard no more.

The days went by and they told me I was there at the funeral. I don't remember clearly. I only remember when they put the coffin down. I wanted to hold him for all eternity, to soothe away the burns and the disappointment that he didn't live to see his son born and his book finished. I wanted to keep telling him it didn't matter, because we would be together forever.

Now I live out the empty days. Eileen told me that when the baby is born, Johnnie will take me to my father and explain everything to him. Or maybe I'd prefer to go to Hugh's mother in her fine house in England. I told her I had no interest in going to my father or to England to his mother. I told her I had no interest in living. She told me I would feel different when I held my baby. My baby. Our baby.

The poor little fellow is due in two day's time. I notice as I write that the red blood is flowing again. I wondered why I felt such crampy pains all day. Maybe the red haemorrhage is the reason. I don't know. I only know as I lie in this little makeshift caravan that I want something to numb me, to take away the loss, the terrible terrible loss that engulfs me.

It would be easy to stretch out my hand and knock over the lamp like he must have done in his sleep. But in my case it would be deliberate. But if I did that, I would take my baby with me. He must live and love and laugh like I have done until now. Oh God, for that I am grateful.

*

There was nothing else.

Stephen was overwhelmed with loneliness and emptiness. He lay clutching thze book between his big strong fingers. Somewhere down below a dog barked and then the cock crew. It was dawn, he thought, the start of another day. Cold and stiff, he wondered how her last day, or maybe days, had gone. It was obvious to him that she died of a haemorrhage when giving birth. He wondered if she had known her time was up when he had been delivered safe and well. Did she feel cold and weak when they failed to stem her life's blood? Did she get a chance to hold him, even for a brief moment, to her breast as she would have wanted, or did she slip away with a great thankfulness because her beloved Hugh wasn't beside her? He'd never know now.

Stephen found something wet on his face. He didn't wipe the tears away in shame. He knew Teresa so well now, maybe far better than most sons would ever know their mothers. He felt no impatience for the tears that had flowed for two young people who lost out on life when it was all beginning.

He guiltily stood up, putting the two diaries under the mattress. He would take only one person into his confidence. He would tell Aileen MacMahon all about Teresa and Hugh. He would want her to know. He intended marrying her if he had to go through hellfire and brimstone to do it. And it was only right that he should tell her about his parents.

He glanced in the oval mirror above the chest of drawers. Leaning over, he studied his face for the very first time. Maybe he had inherited some of the physical characteristics of his parents. He ruefully thought that a little more of his mother's zest and colour would have been a decided asset when it came to his own make-up.

Chapter Sixteen

'Happy birthday,' Niamh shouted, pulling Aileen into wakefulness. 'Come on, get up – today you're sweet sixteen.'

Aileen opened her eyes slowly. Niamh was already pulling on her beige lisle stockings, warbling softly, 'When you were sweet – when you were sweet sixteen.'

'Not much point getting excited about a birthday on an oul school day,' Aileen muttered. 'And did anyone tell you you have a voice like a crow?'

'Well, I like that and I trying to be nice and happy for the birthday girl. Anyway, I wonder will anyone remember your birthday? You don't deserve it if they do, you grumpy old woman, you. Still I got you something,' Niamh told her, thrusting a packet into Aileen's hand.

Aileen opened the present and saw that her friend had splashed out on a cachet of cosmetics containing a box of powder, a fluffy pink powder-puff and a lipstick called Whisper of Pink. 'Ah, thanks, Niamh – I love them. I'll knock them over when I go to the dance.' She put the present into her locker.

'You won't need that stuff for the fellow you want to knock over,' Niamh said soberly. 'Anyway, it'll be exciting to see what you get in the post – that's if, you ungrateful wench, you get anything in the post.'

During her break Aileen opened her post. Her parents had sent her a birthday card, and inside there was a postal order for five pounds and a letter from her mother.

Dear Aileen,
A very happy sixteenth birthday to you. I hope you will have a lovely day. Your Dad gave me the money to send you and I hope you will get something nice for yourself when you go to Dun Laoghaire on your day off. I won't tell

you what to get because it would take the kick out of it for you. Anyway, it's hard to believe that you are now sixteen.

I haven't much news really. Sometimes I see Ann and Maggie in town when I do the shopping. But I suppose they write to you and you know all the news. Maeve is working hard at school. I try to help her every evening with her homework. It will be great when you come home in June – you can help her with her work for her summer exam. Eddie has made a lot of friends in the secondary school in Ross. He plays football every Saturday now, and your Dad is pleased that he is also turning out to be a good hurler. I think he's hoping he will be picked for the under-fourteens for Kilkenny.

How is Niamh? Please give her my regards.

There isn't much more to say except have a lovely day. By the way, the little white cat had kittens yesterday, and she's not much more than a kitten herself. She had four – two white, two black and white. Maeve begged me to keep them, although Eddie had agreed to drown them. I gave in to her and kept them. Sometimes I'm too tired to argue.

Look forward to seeing you soon.

Love and best wishes, Mam.

Eddie's card had a scrawl on the back.

Dear Aileen,

I hope you have a lovely birthday. You are getting old now. There isn't much to tell you except that everyone in this place would drive you mad. Mam moans a lot about everything, and Dad is making me do so much work around the place that I asked him for a small wage. Mam blew up and wanted to know do I appreciate anything they do for me? Maeve gets worse every day. Her cat had kittens and I was going to drown them, but she went mad and Mam said she could keep them. I asked them could I drown her instead, but I got a right clout.

By the way, I saw Stephen Rodgers at Mass last Sunday. He was standing at the wall with the other fellows, and he was smoking. I went over to him and we got talking and I asked him for a few fags, but just when he was secretly obliging Mam looked up from talking to the women and shouted at me to come along. She looked at him as if he was the devil, and I was right fed up because I had to go home like a child.

Your fond brother,
Eddie.

Maeve sent a card with lots of love and several crosses.

She recognised his hand before opening his letter. Her fingers shook slightly as she tore open the envelope. She glanced at the bottom and saw the signature 'Stephanie'. Her heart hammered and she wasn't sure whether it was out of anticipation or fear in case he had changed over the months. People do change, her thoughts told her. In the long months since she had been with him, sometimes his face blurred and faded. She often lay in bed at night, trying to remember the sound of his voice, the surprise in the dark eyes, the absurd length of his eyelashes, the strength of his hands. Sometimes the memories came vivid, like pictures on a screen, sometimes, no matter how she tried, they didn't come at all. Maybe it was the same with him. Maybe she was fading from his mind too.

Dear Aileen,
A very happy birthday to you. I hope that you have a lovely day despite the fact that you are still in the process of being educated. I'm sure you are looking forward to your summer holidays, when you will have a measure of freedom to do what you want to do. I am looking forward to your homecoming and hope that we'll do all the things we planned. I meet Anne and Maggie from time to time and we exchange any news we have – mostly about you. I still see Richie Casey quite a lot and his friendship has helped to lighten the gloom of recent times. I see Eddie from time to time. He's grown so much, I hardly recognise the small talkative little chap who was going to build a raft and sail away to the end of the world. Sometimes I feel like doing the same, but I'll hold on and maybe we'll do it together. Incidentally, I've got some things to show you when I see you. No, on second thoughts, maybe I'll just tell you all about them.

I got two diaries from an old friend of my mother's. They have become very precious to me, and their contents

have torn away all the clouds and uncertainties that have
been part of my life until now. When I finished them it was
like walking into sunshine after years groping in the dark.

Now I've mystified you, but we girls are all secrets and
mysteries. I'll tell you more when you come home. I'll also
have a present for you for this momentous birthday in your
life.

All my love,
Stephanie.

She read and reread the letter and her heart lightened. Despite
the fact that he had kept up the pretence of being a girl in case
the nuns should open the letter, she knew he hadn't changed.
Sitting silent in the chatter and laughter of the other girls she
remembered their pact. *When I'm sixteen,* she had said. *Why
sixteen? Because at sixteen I'll be a woman.*

'Well, what did he say?' Niamh nudged her impatiently.

'Who?'

'Stephen, of course.'

'Nothing. Just that he was looking forward to seeing me
and that he had got some mysterious diaries or something, and
he was happy about them.'

'Is that all?'

'No – he's looking forward to my homecoming and he's
seen Richie Casey from time to time. That appeared important
to him somehow.'

'Well, I can understand that. Richie Casey is important to
me too.'

'Girls, the break is over – back to classes now and go as
quiet as possible.'

Walking back to the classrooms, Aileen wondered if
Niamh was serious about Richie Casey. She knew that they
had kept up some correspondence from time to time, but
Niamh was always flippant about it. 'Heard from Rita,' she
would say. 'She's great gas.' But she wouldn't say much more.

Aileen wondered if she and Stephen were more involved
with each other then they cared to admit. In a brief six weeks'
time she would be home for the long summer holidays and she
knew, as she sat down at her desk, that this summer there
would be no fobbing him off. He had agreed to her childish
pact and the time had come for her to face up to the fact that

she loved him – loved him so much she had to stand up to her mother's disapproval, animosity and even hatred. She would have to stand up to the fact that he was the victim of loose talk because his mother had run away and had married a nobody when she could have had anyone – maybe even someone as respectable as her own father. Aileen would have to pray for strength to face all of them.

Two weeks before Aileen was due home, Mary MacMahon went to see the doctor. Doctor Devane had a sizable practice in Ross, and Mary had hoped she wouldn't be sitting for hours in the waiting room, so she was relieved to see that there were only four before her. She wished she had an obvious physical illness to talk about – something like a bad hip or knee or even an ulcer. He'd probably look at her as if she were a head case when she told him that she couldn't sleep very well, and that she had a vague feeling that something terrible was going to happen – a sort of feeling of impending doom. There was a constant knot in her stomach and a lump in her throat. She couldn't eat and she had gotten thin. Sometimes, when she caught a glimpse of herself in the mirror, she was shocked at the scrawny neck and the lines at the sides of her eyes. Yet if anyone asked her what she was worrying about, she couldn't put a finger on it. She just worried about everything. About Denis in case he had an accident, out all days working like a demon; about Aileen, who was so attractive now; about Eddie, who was so wild and so downright bold at time; about little Maeve, who could be quite precocious but who was a loveable little one. For the last two years Mary had hoped that they would have another little baby, but it hadn't happened. Sure, she knew you have your number written up there in the stars.

Then Mary was plagued at times with vague things – stupid things that should be forgotten. Like, did Denis marry her on the rebound because he couldn't have Teresa Rodgers? Sometimes the thought tormented her. Sometimes she felt like screaming because she couldn't break the chain of thought. Betty Power, her best friend, always liked to talk about when they were all young. Mary would casually slot in a question about Denis and Teresa Rodgers. Betty was always consoling, in a way. She would say, 'Oh, sure Denis never had a chance – she was a mad, restless sort of girl. Anyway, they only went out for a few months together. A lot of people thought something would come of it, because he was going to get the farm and she was Tom's only daughter and would have got the lot. But sure it petered out. And then you came along and swept Denis off his feet.'

'Mrs MacMahon.'

The doctor's voice scattered her thoughts. She pulled herself together and tried to smile, but her face was stiff and her mouth felt sort of frozen.

'Well, well, how are you, Mary?' he asked when she had seated herself in his room.

'Ah, sure Doctor, I could be better. I hope you'll give me time to explain, because 'tisn't anything ordinary.'

'I have all the time in the world, Mary,' he told her, his eyes taking in her thinness, her nervous agitation, her worried look. As he listened with total attention, she plucked up courage and opened her heart about all the things that worried her, and how she was unable to stop panicking.

'Doctor, every day I say, tomorrow I'll stop worrying, and tomorrow I'll be my old self, but somehow tomorrow is as bad as today.'

'Don't worry, Mary. This happens to many women your age. It's part of the change of life, known medically as the menopause.'

He examined her heart, and Mary was glad she had put on her new peach slip. She hadn't been going to bother; it had been an effort to poke it out. He examined her lungs and nodded; they were fine. When he looked at her nails and pulled down her eyes to examine the whites, he told her she was a bit anaemic and that he'd give her some pills for her nerves.

Three weeks later Mary was in a nursing home in Waterford, recovering from a nervous breakdown, and three weeks later Aileen was home from school for the summer holidays.

Chapter Seventeen

'You can't have them in the house – you must put them in one of the sheds.' Aileen shouted at Maeve.

'Mammy told me I could have them in the house.'

'Well, I'm telling you you can't, because they're dirty. So, Miss, out with them – now,' Aileen ordered.

Maeve went out with her basket of kittens, muttering that she 'knew things would be rotten when bossy-boots Aileen came home and you wouldn't mind but she was the cause of all the trouble always.'

To Aileen's surprise Eddie cleaned his room without too much protest. She was gratified when she heard him clumping around sweeping under his bed, and gathering all his old comics and books and stacking them neatly on his windowsill. She sat on his bed. 'Tell me, Eddie, what actually happened to Mam? I mean, why was she shifted to hospital? Did she do anything queer or what?'

Eddie's freckles were standing out in fresh crops because of the fine weather, and his pale reddish hair stood up in spikes, in dire need of a haircut. 'No, she did nothin' queer like go runnin' round the house with a hatchet. She just got real quiet. She never complained, no matter what we did. She let Maeve keep the kittens in the house and didn't mind when they messed the place up – didn't give out yards about me bringing in mud any more. Remember in the evenins when she'd sit down knittin' and blatherin' away to Dad? Well, she didn't do that any more – just sat there like a lamb. Daddy sent for the doctor one day and he came and gave her an injection or somethin'. The next day she was found sittin' near the river and the day after that Daddy drove her into the nursing home.'

That Saturday, Aileen went to see her mother. The journey to Waterford was spent in silence and fear, wondering what to expect. Would her mother be as quiet and apathetic as they said she would be – or would she show any spark of her old self, asking questions about school, about the exams, about her friends, and particularly if Aileen had made any new ones? She sat beside her father, unmindful of the flashing hedgerows, unmindful of the young girls who were cycling three abreast, laughing and talking, a source of great irritation to her father who muttered, 'Do they want to be killed – do they?'

Aileen remembered the day they had gone to Dublin to get her uniform, and how excited her mother had been meeting her cousin, Peggy, and the lunch they had in the Capitol, and her mother nagging Peggy and wondering if there was any news. There had been plenty of news since – long gossiping letters to her mother every Christmas, and eventually a letter bringing the news her mother had wanted: Peggy had two small sons named William and Paul. Yes, Aileen thought, I must keep thinking about my mother and Peggy and things like that, because I don't want to think of him yet. Whenever Stephen intruded on her thoughts, she felt duty-bound to push him away, telling herself it was wrong, that her thoughts should be all for her sick mother. Yet she knew that deep inside she was sick with excitement and apprehension about seeing Stephen Rodgers the very next day after Mass.

'We're here.' Her father's voice broke into her thoughts as he turned the car into the gate of the nursing home. He sounded tired, making her realise how lonely he must be without her Mary. As far back as Aileen could remember, her mother had ruled the roost. Her decisions were the ones that were mostly accepted. Denis had worked hard, plodding his way down through the years, obviously content to leave well enough alone.

Aileen was shocked when she saw her mother first – she was thinner than she ever remembered and greyer; the fine tracery of lines was deeper around her eyes. 'Hello, Mam,' she greeted her, leaning over and giving her a kiss on the cheek.

Her mother's sad eyes seemed to roam over her, taking in her wind-blown hair, last year's faded cotton dress, the flat open-toed sandals which were decidedly the worse for wear.

'You look well, Aileen. I'm sorry you had to come home to so much work. I'm sure you're surprised to see me landed in a place like this.' Mary looked at her husband. 'Denis, we can't have her going around looking like that. She needs new summer things – please give her some money so that she can go shopping. She's grown up now and must meet the right people – she has to look like someone home from an expensive boarding school, not someone slaving around the place.'

Despite her mother's careworn appearance Aileen was relieved to see her sounding so normal, fretting herself sick about the small mundane things that had always worried her. She leaned over and took her mother's thin hand in hers.

'Everything will be grand. Would you believe, even Eddie is behaving himself? And Maeve is trying very hard to be good. So everything is fine.'

They stayed another hour, trying to dredge up little bits of news that would interest Mary, but after the initial normality of her behaviour she lapsed into silence, her nervous fingers plucking at the ribbon of her blue nightdress.

On the journey home, Denis was unusually talkative.

'A queer thing about your mother – she was always full of worries. She'd worry about worry if you could imagine such a thing.

'When you were growing up she was afraid you'd get to know the wrong people, terrified you'd be seen with the wrong fellows. You know, in a place like this a girl can get a bad name if she's seen with the wrong type.'

Aileen knew what he was leading up to and in a rare moment of sympathy – or was it love? – for her father, who never interfered, whose opinions never seemed to matter, she blurted out, 'Dad, you know I'm friendly with Stephen Rodgers, don't you?'

'Aye, I do.'

'You know that Mam hates him, don't you?' Her father was about to reply but she stopped him. 'No, Dad, let me go on. I'd like you to know how much I like him. He's different from the other fellows – he's sort of refined and educated or something like that. I really do like him, Dad.'

'Aye, I know, girl. I'm not blind. But it would be better you didn't.'

'Because of all that talk, that stupid talk about who his mother or his father was and what have you? I loathe all the gossip in this place. That's what so great about Dublin. People don't seem to care who your father or mother was. They seem to take you at face value.'

'I have no objection to the lad myself. He's a fine fellow and hard-working, I'll say that for him. But Aileen, he's not for you. I know you think I'm an old fogey who doesn't know what it's like to have the blood singing inside you on a spring day –'

'Oh, Dad,' she burst out laughing, 'you're getting poetic in your old age.'

He glanced at her and she could see something unfathomable in his blue eyes, as if maybe he was remembering a time when the blood did sing inside him on a spring day.

He didn't mention Stephen again and she was glad. She knew that even if she had promised not to see him, she wouldn't have kept her promise. All her father had said was that it would be better if she didn't. She was already looking forward to Mass when her starved eyes would get a first glimpse of him after so long.

He was standing at the far ditch smoking a cigarette. He was a few paces away from the group of men who always congregated after second Mass. He was alone. Always alone, she thought. Looking at him in his best navy suit, white shirt and brown tie that clashed a bit with the navy, she thought he looked so vulnerable, like a small boy waiting for something to happen. Because she had come out the side gate he hadn't seen her, so she could get an eyeful. Looking at the thick black hair, the unsmiling handsome face, his height and the width of his shoulders the thought came that he was far more handsome than any fellow she saw in Dublin, Dun Laoghaire, Kilkenny, Ross.

I'll make it up to him, she thought fiercely, for all the unhappiness, the loneliness, the feeling of being different and apart.

He glanced sideways as if aware he was under scrutiny. Her heart got up to its old familiar tricks when she met his eyes. From somewhere deep down the tears came, surprising her because he was there, a mere whisper away. 'Hello,' he greeted her, flinging his cigarette into the ditch.

'Hello yourself,' she answered, her voice sounding unfamiliar and croaky, her thoughts churning and chaotic. It's only a minute since I've saw him, she thought, yet I'm a sweaty, tearful, shaky wreck. I wonder will he have this effect on me always?

'Welcome home – what's it like being home from school? And more important still, what's it like being sixteen?'

'It's great being home from school, but things aren't all that great at home. My mam is in hospital. As for sixteen – that's a great feeling.' Aileen wondered if he would say anything about their pact. Could he have forgotten all about it, or worse still, would his feeling for her have changed?

'I heard about your mother. I suppose you'll be so busy you won't see the light of day?'

'It's awful about Mam, but everyone is being very helpful – even our Eddie – so I suppose I will see the light of day.'

'Will I see you tonight so?'

'I suppose so – where?'

'Would you like to go to the pictures in Ross? Richie Casey tells me there's a great one on there. *Bridge On the River Kwai*.'

'All right – how will we get there? Will we cycle?'

'No, my grandfather has softened somewhat in his old age. I can borrow his car.'

'Great. Where will I see you?'

'At the end of your lane.'

'No, that would be too near the house – I'll walk along the main road and you can pick me up.'

'All right – I'll do that.' His eyes held hers briefly before she walked away, feeling self-conscious because she knew he was watching her every move. Yet her feet hardly touched the ground. What had her father called it? A time when the blood was singing. The words were so uncharacteristic of her father, and yet she knew what he meant. Her blood was indeed singing at the prospect of a whole undisturbed evening with Stephen. She had heard that the film *Bridge On the River Kwai* was a long film – so much the better, she thought. And so much the better that Mam wouldn't be there with her searching inquisitive eyes.

God, she thought, what is he doing to me that I'm glad my poor mother is in hospital? That can't be right. She hadn't time to dwell on her sin because Maggie, waiting patiently for her, asked her eagerly, 'Well, are you thrilled to see him again?'

'I am.'

'Well, you're honest anyway. Isn't it a terrible pity about

your mother, so sick and worried and stuff?'

'What do you mean?' Aileen looked at her friend, puzzled in case she had heard something about her mother's condition that she was unaware of.

'Well, I believed she's very worried in case you'll end up with him. She's very worried about you and Stephen – maybe she said something to my mother. I'm not sure – my mother might have hinted something. Look, Aileen, I shouldn't be blathering like this. You know my tongue runs away with me. Don't let my oul talk stop you seeing him.'

'There's nothing on earth that will stop me seeing him.'

Eddie was playing a match in the afternoon and Maeve was invited to her friend's house for tea. As a salve to her guilty conscience over her uncharitable thoughts concerning her mother, Aileen was even more helpful about the place than usual. She helped her father with the milking, bringing the cows into the stalls and immediately getting down to the task. They were both silent as they worked. She was thinking of the evening ahead and how it would go, hoping that he wouldn't question her too much about where she was going and who she was going with.

Denis was silent too, thinking that maybe he should have put his foot down when Aileen had told him openly that she that she liked young Rodgers. He knew he was weak in situations like that – he wasn't much good in telling people, particularly his own daughter, what to do and who to befriend. He was a simple man in ways – he believed you should do your very best with your children, instil some bit of decency in them, then trust them. Maybe his way was a cop-out, but he believed in the old saying 'live and let live'. Mary didn't go along with that at all. She had a different way of thinking altogether. But her way mightn't have been right either – look where she had ended up.

Denis glanced at Aileen as she quietly and efficiently went about her work. There was no doubt she was a lovely girl. There was a sort of elegance – was that the word? – about her. She was the sort of girl people said would 'go places'. Yes, he thought, he should have put his foot down about Stephen Rodgers. But then again, he couldn't, because he liked the lad. He often wondered was it because he had been so attracted to his mother. But it wasn't right that the lad should be marked because of his mother's rash behaviour. Maybe Aileen was right – maybe it was only in the country that people remembered things like that. He couldn't imagine people in London or in Dublin holding something like that against a lad.

He thought of Mary and her unreasonable hatred. You wouldn't mind, only Stephen would be well off when he inherited Tom's place. Hadn't old Ned left everything to Tom years ago? That lad would end up cushy. Sure, he should be welcomed with open arms for a daughter if his father hadn't been a gypsy, or was it a traveller they called them now?

'Dad, can I go to the pictures to night?' Aileen   asked. 'It's a film called *Bridge On the River Kwai*. Everyone is going, Ann and Maggie and the Brennans – everyone.' She felt a momentary wave of guilt because she was giving the impression she was going with the girls.

'All right, I suppose,' he said looking at the anticipation in her eyes. 'But don't be too late. You know if your mother was here she'd insist on that.'

Eddie begged her to let him go to the pictures too. 'No, no, I can't this time, Eddie – another time, I promise.'

'Who are you goin' with?'

'Well, I'll tell you because I know you like him and I know you'll keep it a secret. I'm going with Stephen Rodgers.'

'Jasus, Aileen, if Ma hears there'll be blue murder. You know that.'

'I know, but I'm willing to take the chance.'

Later as Aileen was getting ready, Maeve, lying on her bed reading a book, watched as she plundered her wardrobe for something to wear. It was her first real date with Stephen and she wanted things to be right.

'Lord, you'd think you were going to a wedding you're so particular,' Maeve said as she watched her older sister gazing forlornly at her clothes. 'What's wrong with the dress you had on? You'd imagine you were going out with a prince or something.'

'The dress I had on I wore all day helping Dad and doing Mam's jobs while you were off gallivanting. I wore it milking cows, feeding hens and turkeys, slopping out pigsties. I've just washed from head to toe, and, Miss, I don't intend putting it back on again. So shut up and run away or something.'

Maeve subsided, muttering that if she could go to the pictures at night – night, mind you – she wouldn't care what she wore. Aileen ignored her and gazed at last year's dresses. Her mother was right – she could do with a few new clothes. She recalled the fashion that had hit Dublin before she left: masses of underskirts made of net which made your dress stick out like a crinoline of old. She smiled to herself, thinking of Stephen's shock if she appeared in one of those. He'd probably die of a heart attack.

Finally she decided on a blue simple linen dress with short sleeves, buttoned down the front. She remembered the woman in the shop told her when she was buying it that it was made for her. The colour was the same as the colour of her eyes.

Looking at herself in the mirror she thought the dress was too tight across the bust – it must have shrunk in the wash or something. She decided she'd wear a cardigan. No, that would look so middle-aged or something. She'd wear it across her shoulders – right casual, like some models did in magazines. She'd bring it anyway – she'd be more comfortable with it.

He was there before her, sitting in his grandfather's car at the fork of the road. Her wretched overworked heart started again as she walked towards him; as he opened the door she noticed he had changed the brown tie for a wine one.

'I thought something might happen to stop you coming,' he said, smiling as she settled in the seat beside him.

'No, nothing happened. I gave the impression I was going out with the girls – sure my poor father is easy to fool.'

I was never in such a confined place with him before, she thought as they drove in silence to Ross. She wondered if she should break the silence or just sit and wallow in the fact that he was so near at last. She thought of all the times she had lain in bed in school conjuring up his face, his slow smile, the black hair, the almost black eyes, the strong brown hands. And now he was beside her.

'A penny for them,' he said, glancing at her, his eyes warm with a sort of teasing look.

'I was thinking of school and things.'

'School on an evening like this – just when you've escaped? Just when your summer is starting?'

'Yeah – it's cracked, isn't it? Well, if you really want to

know, I was thinking of you.'

'Tell me, was it good or bad?'

'It was all right.'

They lapsed into silence again and suddenly the Barrow Bridge was ahead. He drove over and parked the car near the river, then got out and opened her door. Strange, she thought, he's not like any other fellow I know. She wondered where he had learned such things. Certainly not on a farm with Tom Rodgers or Joe Power.

There was a queue outside the cinema, and Aileen felt every eye was on them as they joined it. She was surprised to see Maggie and Ann up near the door with the Brennan boys. If Maggie had told her they had a sort of double date she had forgotten. She waved at them and they waved back.

Once in the dark cinema she was so conscious of his nearness that she found it hard to concentrate on the much-lauded *Bridge On the River Kwai*. About a half an hour through the film, when she should be getting the gist of what it might be like to be a Japanese prisoner of war in the Philippine islands she was conscious only of his thigh and of his knee touching hers as they sat in the Star's cramped uncomfortable seats. When he sought her hand and held it a in grip so tight it almost hurt, she knew they could build all the bridges they liked over the river Kwai and she would only be half-aware. I know him forever, she thought, and yet this was like a first date.

When the lights came on during the interval Aileen was again acutely aware of the people around them. She could see from the corner of his eyes that Stephen was rummaging in his pocket. He withdrew a brown paper bag.

'I'm not used to taking girls to the pictures, but I think this is part of the ritual,' he said. The bag was full of iced caramels, slightly warm from the heat.

'My favourites,' she whispered, not because they were, but to put him at his ease, although looking at him few would guess he was unused to taking a girl to the cimema.

After they ate some sweets he held her hand again and she could feel the strength and the hardness caused by years of hard work on his grandfather's farm.

When the picture ended they filed out in silence, listening to the praise and the talk of Oscar nominations and how outstanding had been the performance of Alec Guinness. They remained silent as they drove home. Aileen sat clutching the remains of her bag of iced caramels, her thoughts in a tailspin, wondering what he might do, wondering what her father would say if he knew she was with him in a car on a dark road, what effect the knowledge would have on her mother, who was sick and maybe incarcerated because of Stephen.

Before they came to the boreen leading to her house, Stephen switched off the engine, turning off the lights. She wasn't sure if she heard the thump of his heart or the thump of her own – she was only sure of the old familiar sensation washing over her.

He turned towards her and took her in his arms. His first kiss was hungry and passionate.

'You're hurting me,' she whispered when she got her breath back. 'Take it easy–'

'Jesus, Aileen, how can I take it easy? I want you so much, I'm sick with longing.'

'I know, I know,' she whispered softly, running her hands over his face, pushing back his hair.

Suddenly they were in each other's arms again and the terrible waiting and longing was over as they kissed each other wildly and with abandon – she kissing unfamiliar places like behind his ears, like his eyelids, where his thick long eyelashes tickled her lips. She kissed the stubble on his chin and then went back to his firm mouth. He kissed her on the eyebrows and below her ears, burying his mouth in her shining blonde hair before going to her neck to the top of her breasts. If he opens the buttons, she thought weakly, I won't be able to stop him. Whatever he does I'll have no willpower. I'm wanton when it comes to him.

Suddenly he stopped. Pulling her head down on his shoulder, he whispered huskily, 'Aileen MacMahon, I love you – you know that.'

'I do.'

'Will you marry me?'

'I will.'

'How will we manage it? The way people talk about me? Even your mother! Everyone.'

'I don't care what they say or what they feel. The only thing that matters is what I feel. And I feel I love you more than anything in the whole wide world. The nonsense about

218

your mother or who your father was means nothing, nothing to me.'

'When will I see you again?' he asked urgently. 'There are things on my mind. I told you about my mother's diaries – I'd like to tell you and only you about what was in them.'

'Thursday evening, down by the willow tree,' Aileen whispered. 'I'll have to lie low and visit my mother a lot this week.'

'All right. Thursday it'll have to be. Will I last till then, do you think?'

'Oh, you will. Haven't you lasted till I was sixteen?'

'I have, and it was like a million years.'

They kissed goodnight, a long tender kiss. She was the first to break away. 'I'll wait until you're home safely – God knows who might snatch you away from me.'

She waved before running up the boreen, pushing the small niggling worry that her father might question her to the back or her mind.

Mary MacMahon was six weeks in Maywood Nursing Home in Waterford before she was discharged. Before she left, the resident psychiatrist advised her to stay out as much as possible in the fresh air, to continue with her relaxation programme, to remember to take her pills and, most important, to get an outside interest, a hobby, something that would occupy her mind outside the home.

'I will try, Doctor Tierney – I will.'

'You're still a young woman, Mary. The day will come when your children leave home. At that stage you should have something to fall back on. So many women of your generation live their lives through their children, sometimes to such an extent that their own lives are pushed aside. Even the welfare of their husbands is secondary.'

'That didn't happen to me. My husband is very important to me.'

'I'm glad to hear it, Mary. I've made an appointment for you to come back to see me once a week in my clinic.'

'Thank you, Doctor, for everything. I will be sure to attend.'

When he had gone she sat in a pool of sunshine near her window. She'd be ready to go when Denis came.

She was certainly in a calmer frame of mind and her depression had lifted to a certain extent. She had some measure of control over her fears and thoughts. They didn't just jump out at her like a Jack in the Box and overwhelm her, making her weak. In a way she was very ashamed that she had had to be hospitalised for her nerves. She certainly hoped people wouldn't be pointing and whispering when she came out. Surely they'd understand that it was just her age? When a woman reached a certain age it was possible for her to have a breakdown – it had nothing to do with her family or anything like that. People were queer – they held all sorts of things in for you, so they did.

She smiled when she recalled the advice one young doctor had given her: 'Learn how to switch off and do nothing, and learn how to do nothing real well.' She had laughed, the first genuine laugh she had had in years. The priest had been wonderful too. Father Fergus O'Regan had come back from a stint in England to be a curate in the cathedral in Waterford, and had visited her a couple of times a week. Sometimes he just sat there and listened. She found talking to him very easy, and he rarely interrupted, as if he knew that talk was healing. He was also so handsome that she noticed the nurses tidying themselves up when he was due to visit.

Mary MacMahon opened her heart to the priest. She told him even her most stupid worries, like the one that maybe Denis didn't marry her for herself but 'maybe on the rebound, Father. At my age I shouldn't care about that – in fact I only heard about this other girl after I had married. Isn't it silly, Father, to worry about a thing like that?'

'Silly indeed. Your husband has proved his love for you in a hundred way over the years – working, providing, cherishing. So why worry about something that's over, water under the bridge? Sometimes when a man is young, love is mixed up with other things and it isn't love at all.'

'Like sexual desire, Father?' Her question amazed her – she felt she could talk to this priest about anything, and in doing so the knot inside her eased.

'Yes, Mary, like sexual desire, appetite, passion – call it what you like. Anyway, I'm sure your husband has forgotten this girl completely.'

'Well, Father, it's not easy do that. You see she had a son

and he lives around and that's a terrible worry I have too. Terrible.'

'Do you want to talk about it?'

'I'll try, Father. You see, I have a daughter, Aileen, and if I say so myself she's a lovely girl. She is a boarder with the Loretto nuns in Dalkey – I have a cousin there who's a nun and we sent her there thinking that it would be good for her – they would give her a good education and let her meet the right people, Father. You see, she's at the age when young men are attracted to her, and I'm terrified she'll go out with the wrong young man.'

'Is there some young man in her life now?'

'There is, and the terrible thing is, he's the son of the girl who was going with Denis. She ran away and married – oh God, Father, I even find it hard to tell you. She married a gypsy, or so they say, and when she died the baby was brought back and reared by his grandfather, and he's the one who Aileen thinks the world of. Oh, Father, I can't bear the thought of it even. Even when I see him something curls up inside me – he has a terrible effect on me. Isn't it cracked that a young fellow can do that to me? Anyway, nothing – nothing – can come of the attraction they have for each other – nothing.'

'Why, Mary, can nothing come of it? It's her life, not yours. Then maybe you worry unduly. It's probably an obsession all in your head – maybe it's just two young people who like each other.'

'No – it's more than that. I have a feeling about it. If I see him at Mass or in the town or anywhere, he looks at me, and there's a strange expression in his eyes, as if he owns her already. Isn't that stupid, Father?'

'I could make light of it,' he told her, 'and say mountains out of molehills, but I won't. I know what inner turmoil does to you.'

'Do you, Father? Do you? I didn't think priests knew anything like that.' She looked at him and for the first time she could see there was pain in his eyes and lines around his mouth, and she supposed that even priests had worries at times. 'I'm selfish, Father. I suppose everyone has worries, even God's priests.'

'Yes, Mary – even God's priests.'

They were silent for a while and. It must be hard, she

thought, a handsome young man living the lonely life of a priest.

Suddenly he smiled and held out his hand, taking hers in his firm grip. 'When Jesus in the gospel advised, "Sufficient for the day is the evil thereof," he had something there, Mary, do you know that?'

'I do, Father and I will try to remember it. It's not easy but I'll try.'

Suddenly Father Fergus was gone and she sat on, waiting for her husband, telling herself she would try and remember the lovely priest's advice. She'd do her level best to be a better wife to Denis when she got home. After all, she would have him when the children were gone. She didn't mind them going, as long as they went with the right partner. That was still of tantamount importance to her.

Chapter Eighteen

'**M**y mother is home – so I can't be too late.'

'I know, and if she knew you were with me she'd be in hospital again.'

'No, she's not as bad as she was. She's on tablets and rests a lot. She never rested before in her life – always last to bed and up first, so maybe she's getting a bit of sense.'

Stephen and Aileen were sitting on a large stone, partially hidden by the willow trees, near their favourite spot by the river. They hadn't met since the previous Saturday, and in the intervening days Aileen had thought of a million things to say to him. But now she was strangely silent.

'Niamh Turley wants me to ask her to come and stay for a few days. I'm not so sure, with Mam sick, but maybe it will be all right.' God above, she thought, why am I all stilted and strained, and I the one who went to Dublin to school? Shouldn't I be all polished and confident and stuff? She wished she could be like the Dublin girls who seemed to exude confidence.

'Niamh is a great girl – I know Richie Casey thinks so. It would be nice to have her here. Maybe the four of us could do wild things.' He was smiling as he put his arm around her. 'People did wild things by this river – do you know that?'

'Well, I've heard of the "Banks of my Own Lovely Lee" and wild daisies crushed and that stuff.'

He laughed, and drawing her closer, murmured, 'You're still a kid really.'

'Not so much of a kid now – amn't I sixteen?'

'Sure don't I know it – haven't I waited long enough for it?'

They were both silent then, listening to the river in full spate now, with strong currents swirling and circling as it sped its frenzied way. Aileen, glancing towards Barrons Wood, saw the rising smoke from the fires where the tinkers camped. She wondered if he was ever tempted to visit them, to find out a little more about his mother, or about who his father was.

As if reading her thoughts he said, 'Remember when I wrote to you, I told you I got something important, something that threw a lot of light on things for me?'

'Yes, I remember.' She wondered was this what he wanted to talk about. He had hinted that he had something important to tell her.

'I know you've heard all the old talk about me – my mother running away with a gypsy and leaving my grandfather heartbroken, and never coming back. Well, it's true in a way, she did all that.' He put his hand under Aileen's chin and turned her face around, looking at her with the dark intensity that always reduced her to a jelly. 'You know all that, don't you?'

'I don't care about these things – I told you that, didn't I. Didn't I?' She didn't even wait for an answer. 'I only care about you – not your father or mother or who or what they did all that old stuff.' She reached up and pulled down his head and kissed him firmly on the mouth.

As if it was a signal he gently pushed her down on the mossy bank and kissed her with such passion that she was afraid. She found herself returning his kisses with the same abandon, and suddenly he was kissing her neck, the hollow at her throat, the tops of her breasts – she could feel his rising desire and the hardness of his body. She was filled with a wild desire to throw away everything she had been taught and to have him there and then. And to have him again and again. it flashed through her mind what all the old gossips would say, 'Ah, sure what would you expect? His mother was a wild thing and his father was a nobody.' She could nearly hear them. 'No, love – no. We must wait – it wouldn't be right. Not here, not now. We'll wait, we'll wait till we're married.'

'In five years' time?' he answered huskily. 'I'll be dead then, Aileen MacMahon.'

'All right, what would you think of two years?' she murmured, as if she were consoling a child. She could see that the danger was past and they were in some control. He lay beside her and she ran her hands through his black hair running her fingers over his eyebrows and along the edges of his lashes. 'When I was in school, lying there in the dark dormitory and all the others thinking about their homework, I would think of doing this – just running my fingers all over your face. Wasn't that stupid?'

'It was when you compare it to my thoughts. I used to lie there in the dark and used to ravish you and then when I fell asleep all sorts of things happened to me and I used to ravish you again. What do you think of that?'

'I think you love me,' she answered simply.

'I don't love you – I adore you. If I thought we couldn't be together for the rest of our lives I'd walk into the middle of that river now.'

'Well, you don't have to get wet, because I adore you too. Anyway, enough about that – tell me what you found out about your parents.'

He put his arm around her and they sat leaning up against the bank. 'I was working in the low field when I saw old Johnnie Sheridan coming along. I watched him for a bit and there was something sort of purposeful about him, I had a notion he was looking for me. He came and handed me a brown paper parcel and muttered something about "I knew she'd want you to have it". I took the parcel and we spoke for a bit and then he told me he wouldn't be in the parts again, that a younger man was taking over the clan. We said goodbye and do you know what? I felt this peculiar warmth for him – after all, he knew both my parents – and the fact that I'd never see him again filled me with a sort of sadness. Watching him walk away, old and feeble, I felt sorry to see him go. It was like the end of an era – something like that.' Stephen stopped and looked over at the woods and the rising smoke. 'It doesn't seem right that he's not there any more.'

Aileen waited for him to go on. She knew he had waited to tell her his story for a long time.

'The parcel contained two diaries – for the years 1940 and 1941. I read them at night. Sometimes I felt like an intruder looking into the heart and mind of a seventeen-year-old girl. Yet I felt she'd want me to know. And, my love, I want you to know, my father was a fellow named Hugh Morena and was of Spanish and English blood. He was a writer and met the gypsies when they were in England, and came to Ireland to write a book about them, about their ways, customs, language – everything.' Suddenly he laughed and pointed to the old willow tree. 'See that old tree – the big one? Well, it was over there my father first saw my mother and her friends on a hot summer's day when they were picnicking. I won't tell you what they did because I don't want you to think I had such a wild mother – you might scare and run away.'

'Tell me – tell me,' Aileen demanded. 'Isn't that why I'm here?'

'Well, my mother and her friends must have been very hot – there was a heatwave at the time. Anyway they went into the river for a long cool swim – without a single stitch of clothes.'

'That must have taken courage twenty years ago,' Aileen answered, her brilliant blue eyes showing not a little awe.

'And before they did, they made an offering to the willow god.' Stephen pointed to the tree.

Aileen looked puzzled. 'What did they do?'

'They flung all their underwear on top of the tree.'

'God, she must have been a wild sort of girl.' Aileen's voice was filled with wonder. 'She makes me feel so dull and sensible.'

'You're beautiful and intelligent, and I certainly wouldn't want you making offerings to the willow god. There's more – do you want to know? I don't know if I should tell you – maybe I should let sleeping dogs lie.'

'Of course you'll tell me. You can't just make me fierce curious and then shut up like a clam. What?'

'Your father was in love with my mother.'

'You're joking,' Aileen gasped. 'My quiet, hard-working poor father in love with your mother? God almighty, I can't believe it. I suppose it was before he met my mother.' She was silent for a bit allowing the news to sink in. 'I wonder was he demented when she went away? I'll go home this evening and see him in a different light.' She turned to look at Stephen, taking in his jet-black hair, the shade of stubble on his chin, the broad shoulders, the sheer maleness of him. 'I wonder will something happen to break us up too?' she asked quietly.

'No, we'll go full circle. We'll get married and have ten kids. I sort of know these things.'

'Now, Stephen Rodgers, you can't be doing the crystal-ball gypsy act anymore. Your father was just a writer – not a romantic travelling gypsy.'

'Yeah – I know, isn't that sad?'

'Wouldn't my poor mother be fierce impressed if I told

her? All her worries would go away.'

'You're never to tell anyone – it's to be our secret.'

'Anyway,' she told him, 'you know how I feel. If your father was a drunken brawling tinker it would make no difference to the way I feel about you.'

Stephen didn't answer but tightened his grip around her.

The only sound was the rushing river tumbling over the weir. In the undergrowth a small restless creature tried to settle. Then suddenly, over at Barrons Wood, a baby started to cry noisily, demanding to be fed. With Stephen's strong arms encircling Aileen she listened to the sounds of the approaching night. His mother had been wild and rash, but she had married her equal. She had often wondered why Stephen was that bit different from most of the fellows in the parts – maybe he had inherited these traits from his father.

'Where did the diaries end?' she asked him, breaking the silence.

'The day before she died. My father had died tragically a week previously in a caravan fire.' He broke off, his dark glance taking in Barrons Wood and the rising smoke. 'It can't have been easy.'

'No, it can't,' she said softly, 'but God above I'm glad I have you, and I'm glad Johnnie brought you back. It's so sad I could cry, so I could.'

'Someday we'll give the diaries to our daughter to read. She might like to know about her grandmother and the times that were in it.'

Aileen looked up. The first star had come out. It twinkled small and silvery and seemed a million miles away. Yet she felt an affinity with the very universe itself – as if God and nature had stowed some sort of blessing on their love. 'I must go,' she whispered, 'my mother will be worried. I wish I could tell her – you know, about your father and things.'

'You must never tell anyone.' His tone was almost rough. 'These things shouldn't matter.'

'I know, but they do – to some people.' She sounded tired. 'But I promise I won't say a whisper.'

'And I'm sorry I nearly devoured you. But you understand I feel strongly about this.'

They kissed goodbye, long and tenderly. Aileen promised him she'd meet him on the following Saturday. 'Maybe I will ask Niamh, and you tell Richie, and the four of us will go wild and have a bit of fun. You know what, Stephen Rodgers? We could do with a bit of fun.'

'After we get married you'll have so much fun, you'll die laughing,' he said.

'Is that a promise?'

'Cross my heart.'

Niamh Turley came that Saturday morning, bringing a fresh salmon wrapped in several layers of newspaper and a beautiful plant from her mother for Mary MacMahon. She was only in the door when she told Eddie he was gorgeous, that the girls must be fighting like dogs over him. He blushed furiously at her bright outspokenness, but Aileen could see he was as pleased as punch. She gave Maeve a big hug, telling her she'd love to steal her and take her home, as she was sick living in a household of males. Niamh was such a ray of brightness that even Mary MacMahon showed interest, asking about her parents and her brothers, and how things were in Skerries.

Later when she was hanging up her clothes in the girls room, Aileen told Niamh that Stephen intended telling Richie about her visit. 'We're hoping that the four of us can do something exciting.'

'Richie knows I'm here – I phoned him last night and told him I was coming.'

'That's something. I wish I could do things like that, pick up a phone, make arrangements like a civilised person, instead of a few hurried mutters at the church gate after Mass. Anyway, we have no phone, I wish we had.'

'We wouldn't have one only for the lifeboat. Dad got it in because of that.'

'You have no idea how great it is having you here. My mother won't be sitting here like a pale ghost worrying herself to death about me. She'll be happy because I'm entertaining company – a girl from a fine school in Dublin.' They both laughed.

'Is she still as bad?' Niamh asked. 'She seems much calmer.'

'She is because she's on pills. But if she thought for one minute I was with Stephen, she'd break down again. I know she would. I'm amazed she hasn't heard. I think my father

228

knows and is staying quiet about it, hoping it will pass. We must have been seen by neighbours and people – but maybe they're not telling her because she has been so ill.' Aileen was tempted to tell Niamh about the diaries, but she remembered how anxious Stephen was to keep them a secret. Niamh would have enjoyed hearing all about Teresa Rodgers and her wild antics – marrying a writer instead of a gypsy. *Someday I'll give them to our daughter to read*, he had said. The thought of having a baby for him filled her with such a peculiar feeling of longing she thought it had to be wrong.

'What do you think of this creation?' Niamh's question woke her from her dreams. The dress was the latest fashion – a full skirt with flouncy petticoats underneath. 'Do you have one?' Niamh wanted to know.

'Lord, no – this isn't the big city. Since I came home, it's all go or all work or all blooming lies saying I'm with Ann or Maggie when I'm with Stephen.'

'Look, can we see a few shops or something? We could get you a petticoat and that'd fluff out all your dresses and you'll be in high fashion.'

'Dunno,' said Aileen wistfully. 'I think I'd feel a fool flouncing around in layers like that.'

'No, you wouldn't. You're so tall you could carry them off.'

'Maybe.' Aileen still sounded doubtful. 'Still, it's great you're here. I'll ask Dad for the money and sure maybe I'll be transformed with your city notions.'

The weeks that followed were the happiest Aileen ever remembered. Niamh's brightness brushed off on the whole family. Even Mary MacMahon was taken out of herself by the young girl from Dublin. Niamh prattled away to Aileen and her father when they were milking. When Aileen was too busy to accompany her, she went with Eddie to the river and tried her hand at casting, listening to him eagerly when he explained that river fishing was a different game to fishing in the sea. Sometimes she sat with Maeve in the sunlit yard over near the white-washed barn, playing shop or post office, and never begrudging her the time or showing an iota of boredom.

But for both girls the evenings were free. Richie Casey was working full-time for his father now, and every evening drove from Brennerstown to meet them and Stephen by the river.

Sometimes they were joined by Maggie and Ann, who were now doing steady lines with the Brennan brothers Jimmy and Davey. Sometimes they just sat by the riverbank, talking and smoking, listening to the ebullient Richie who told colourful yarns about the customers in the shop.

'God, Stephen, you should see this bird who came in last Friday – she had everything. Looks, figure, hair like a golden cloud.'

'God, I hate her already,' Niamh muttered and they all laughed as Richie went on:

'When she saw me behind the counter she went as scarlet as paint. "So what can I do for you, Miss?" I asks, putting on all the charm I could muster. Ah, the poor girl wanted a chamber pot. The stutters and stammers as she explained it was for her grandmother. I showed her six of them, flowers inside, flowers outside, plain-coloured, curved, big and small. When she finally chose one I spent about an hour wrapping it, and then I asked her would I personally deliver it. She ran out of the shop screaming. Then there was another day this fella came in looking for something to take paint off a greyhound. Seemingly he had painted the favourite, giving him white paws and a few spots to measure. Then he backed him to the hilt pretending he was an also-ran. Won a stack but the paint put an end to his antics. The poor dog was never the same afterwards.'

Niamh told them about how her father had been in the British Navy during the war, and how his boat had been torpedoed and he had clung to a plank for two days before being rescued. 'When he came back he discovered the very same thing had happened to his brother. After that they were known as the survivors. In fact, the first boat he bought for my brothers was called *The Survivor* and we still have it. Believe me, with that crowd of gangsters it has survived a lot.'

Davey told them about the land that his father had sold to a couple who came back from England. 'They built a fierce modern bungalow on it, all spit and polish, tiles and bathrooms and things. Anyway, they soon found out all wasn't well – the bloody house was haunted. Fires would start in the walls and on the ceiling, and not a match in the house. Word went out that the bungalow was built on a fairy ring and that they'd never have a bit of peace. That house had six owners in two years. Then this fine fat German and his fine fat wife came along and got it for a song. They're up there now, not a fairy bothering them, and they're laughing all the way to the bank.'

Aileen would sometimes steal a look at Stephen as he listened, smoking contentedly. She had never seen him like this. it must be good for him, she thought, to be completely accepted, no longer a subject for gossip. He didn't contribute to the yarns though; maybe he hadn't any funny memories to recall. With his arm tightly around her she vowed, not for the first time, that things would be different from now on.

'Well, would you say that you and Richie would do the long steady line?' Aileen asked Niamh that night as they lay in the bed before dropping off to sleep. This was the time they always held their whispered post mortems – somehow the velvety darkness made it so much easier.

'Yeah, I like Richie – I feel great with him. I don't know if it's love, but if another one put her eyes on him, I'd dig them out!'

Aileen bit the sheet, trying to stifle her laughter. 'God you're cracked, so you are.'

'Well, how would you feel,' Niamh asked sleepily, 'if someone stole your Stephen away?'

The question took Aileen by surprise. The thought that anything like that might happen would be so horrendous that she felt almost sick. 'It's simple – I'd die. I wouldn't be too good at tearing eyes out.'

'Ye're a right Romeo and Juliet, aren't ye? Love like that will never be my lot.'

'You'd never know.'

'Maybe,' Niamh answered, almost asleep.

As Aileen lay in the darkness this new dread, that he might meet someone else, filled her. After all, his mother had dropped her own father for a stranger. Could the same streak be in her son? Maybe some day when she was back slogging it out in school, he would walk into someone else. It could happen in Ross, or in Kilkenny, or in Waterford – something would ignite in him, like it had in his mother, and he would fall like ninepins. She felt physically sick. She found herself praying with an intensity she had never felt before. She hadn't even prayed for her mother's recovery with such feeling. She prayed that Stephen would never leave her – never love anyone else. She prayed that all the animosity of the township would go and that they could get married and be together for the rest of their lives. She tossed and turned until the dawn lit up the outline of the other bed with the peacefully sleeping Niamh, whose simple little question had robbed Aileen of all peace.

The evening before Niamh went home, they all went to the dance in Waterford. Aileen told her mother they were going with the Brennans, who had borrowed their father's car. Sometimes she surprised herself with the ease with which she lied.

'I know you'll both behave yourselves – your schooling has put you apart from the others and I know I can trust you,' her mother said, her eyes slightly glazed from the pills which had brought this unnatural calmness. Aileen could see that Mam had even put on weight, and that the lines had eased from her face.

'Of course, Mam,' Aileen told her, giving Niamh a surreptitious wink and at the same time asking God to forgive her for all the deceit. She was surprised once again that the gossips in the place hadn't told her mother she had been seen with Stephen Rodgers. It must be killing them having to refrain because of her mother's breakdown. I suppose I'm lucky, she thought – if my mother hadn't the nervous breakdown I wouldn't have been able to see him so much. But since Niamh had come, she and Stephen had not been alone together. Knowing the effect he had on her, she thought it better. After her sleepless night, when she felt so worked up in case she'd lose him, God knows what would happen if they were alone.

Crossing the yard in their bouffant layered petticoats, Aileen and Niamh had to run the gauntlet of Eddie's jeers. 'God, ye look like expectin' elephants.'

'Shut up,' Aileen told him heatedly, demented because she felt he was right. 'I feel a fool,' she whispered to Niamh as they walked down the boreen, 'in fact I feel just like an expecting elephant.'

'Better be dead than old-fashioned,' Niamh consoled her. 'Wait till you see Stephen's face when he sees you. You're like Grace Kelly only for the long hair.'

The van was at the crossroads and when they appeared Richie got out, pointing to the rug he had spread out in the back to protect their dresses. His exaggerated gestures as he helped them in, pushing in their full skirts, made Stephen grin. He looked at Aileen, his black eyes sparkling. 'Why didn't ye tell me? I could have saved ye money and made two hoops out of fence wire.'

Aileen felt the familiar blush; knowing how sensitive she was, he blew her a kiss and mouthed 'I love you', filling her with a sudden rush of unexpected happiness.

'You know,' Niamh said softly that night, 'I can understand how you're so much in love.'

'How?' Aileen whispered. They had whirled the night away, and when the excuse-me dances were announced, were amazed at the myriad new faces they brought. When they had sat out with a refreshing mineral the jokes and fun had been non-stop. Niamh's last night had been wonderful.

'I don't know – maybe it's that air of mystery. He doesn't go wild or mad, just looks at you with those eyes. Then again, I'm used to Richie prattling away, saying exactly what's on his mind. I couldn't ever imagine your Stephen doing that. God almighty, when I go home tomorrow I'm going to miss you all terribly.'

'We'll miss you terribly,' Aileen told her. 'I'll keep all the news to tell you when we go back to school.'

'It won't be too long now. God, I wish we were finished – wouldn't you?'

'Yeah, but what'll we do when we are? You'll get married, but I'm not sure. Maybe I'll become a teacher, I like bossing kids around. I like kids though, so I'd have to be nice to them too.'

The next day went by in a flurry of packing, farewells, even tears.

'Come on, Niamh,' Denis MacMahon shouted, 'you have a train to catch. Won't you be seeing each other when you're back at school?'

They stood in the sunlit farmyard waving goodbye. Even the strutting cock was quiet as Niamh clambered into the car. The whole MacMahon family waved and waved until the car

233

turned at the end of the boreen. When they wandered back into the house it was strangely empty. Eddie wanted to know when Niamh was coming back.

'I think you have a crush on her,' Aileen whispered, not wanting her mother to hear.

Eddie blushed scarlet, his freckles standing out like tiny golden moons. 'I hate girls, but she's not the worst,' he answered forlornly.

The next day Jack the Post handed Mary MacMahon a letter when she was at her breakfast. 'From your cousin Peggy,' he said looking at the English stamp.

'Aye, it is,' she said, seemingly indifferent to his prying curiosity.

'How is she?' Jack asked. 'She was always a great girl, always had the good word.'

'She's fine, Jack – fine. She has two little sons now, and her husband Bill is doing right well at the building.'

'Wasn't she from Dungarvan way? Sure I suppose she'd like to come home like so many across the water?'

Aileen thought how amazed people in Dublin would be if the postman came in and discussed what was in a letter or who it was from, and then calmly sat down for his cup of tea, departing only when duty called. When Stephen and I are married and living in Australia, she thought, will I sit at a table and wait for a letter bringing news from Ireland, maybe Niamh telling me she has a new baby girl, or Maggie telling me they bought a few extra acres, or Eddie telling me something outrageous, or Maeve telling me she met a lovely boy at the parish social?

Her mother's voice shattered her day-dreaming. 'She wants me to go over. She thinks the change will do me good.'

'And it will,' Jack the Post told her. 'I always liked that grand girl, 'twould do you good to meet her.'

'She even wants me to take Maeve,' Mary glanced at Aileen. 'What'll I do – do you think I should go?'

'Of course, Mam, you should jump at it. Sure, you're mad about Peggy, and with Maeve gone I won't have that much to do. Dad, Eddie and I can do everything. I'll mind your turkeys for you – you won't know them when you come back.'

'I wonder will I be able for the journey?' Aileen knew that

Mary was worried about her health and thinking of her breakdown.

'Of course you will, and anyway you could fly from Dublin. Think of Maeve driving us all mad boasting about her plane journey to London.'

'She's right – she's right,' Jack the Post said, 'just what the doctor ordered. Never look a gift horse in the face, I say – never.' He slowly got up out of the chair, swinging his bag over his shoulder and wishing Mary well, telling her to go and have a good time. 'You know, Mary, as well as the next, that there's no pockets in a shroud.'

Mary went to ask Denis in the milking parlour where he was clearing up. She looked at him. How strong and dependable he is, she thought, and I couldn't even stay the course. I had to get bad nerves and hospital treatment, making a show of us. He had never complained about her six weeks in hospital, and seemed happy to see her home, and here she was going off to London, mind you – on a holiday, if you don't mind. Sure holidays were for other people, not for farmers or their wives.

'I think it's a great offer, girl. It will do you a power of good. Sure isn't there enough of us to take care of things?'

So it was settled. The idea of their mother going on a holiday had Aileen and Eddie quite excited. As Aileen had predicted, Maeve was already impossible. Denis drove them to Waterford to do some shopping for their holiday. Maeve nagged them to death for one of the new zipped jackets with a hood; she told them she was the only girl in the country without one. They had high tea in Dooleys on the Quay, and Maeve was so excited that she just pushed around her ham and couldn't even eat her cream tart.

Denis MacMahon drove his wife Mary and his youngest daughter to the airport in Dublin for the first holiday of their lives.

When their flight was called he gave Mary a rough hug.

She clung to him, blinking away her tears. 'I wish you were coming too – sure you need a holiday more than any of us.'

He smiled. 'Now, what farmer do you know goes on holidays? Off with you and have a good time, and give my regards to Peggy.'

Looking at his wife departing nervously in her new suit and high-heeled shoes, he realised how important she was. She had brought such energy and enthusiasm to the farm and the rearing of their children. In fact, she had little or no other interests except himself, the place and the children. Watching her retreating back and the excited gait of his youngest, he knew he had held something back from his wife all the years. He had given her a lot, but he hadn't given her himself. When she was sick with all those irrational worries, had he really listened to her? Maybe that's why she had had her terrible breakdown. He'd make it up to her if God was willing. He wouldn't try to snatch at sunbeams and wonder what might have been any more. He'd be glad at what he had and never indulge in useless daydreams. Driving carefully through heavy Dublin traffic before clearing the city and heading for home, Denis made up his mind that things would be different.

Chapter Nineteen

It was Joe who noticed that Tom Rodgers was failing. He consoled himself; old age was ahead of them all. After all, Tom must be approaching seventy and had worked hard all his life. Joe noticed small things first, like Tom calling him Ned a few times. He had never done that before. Funny, he thought, how as you got older you went back instead of forwards. Then again, Tom Rodgers had been a horse of a man; no work had been too hard, no task too difficult, no day too long. Maybe all that had taken its toll. The old man depended on Stephen more and more, although the dependence didn't bring them much closer.

'Joe, I don't think he's well,' Stephen said one day when they were saving the hay.

'Strange, I was thinking that meself,' said Joe

'He's forgetting things. Called me Joe a few times lately. I even heard him call Máire Ciss. Sometimes I see him with a peculiar look in his eye, and then he shakes his head trying to clear it.'

'Sure boy, age gets us all in the end. I'm not getting any younger myself.'

'Ah, Joe, you'll go on forever – that I know.'

The two men worked in silence for a while, Stephen thinking that it was sad to see his grandfather's strength ebbing. The day might come when the unthinkable happened – when old Tom Rodgers wouldn't be able to work any more. Work had kept him going. Even after his wife's death and his only daughter's flight he had kept on working. His farm was one of the finest in the place – every acre utilised, nothing run down or neglected.

Joe was thinking along different lines. If anything happened old Tom, he knew, the lad would have so few happy memories. He recalled one occasion they were draining in the low field. Stephen had been little more than a baby. He had followed them, clutching a toy shovel, eager to help. He had sat on a ditch, watching their every move with his dark eyes. Old Tom had glanced up and, seeing the child, had gone over and picked him up, putting him down beside him. 'Come on, Stephen,' he had said, 'get at it – every little helps.' The child had shovelled away, content as a sandboy. 'The land is the thing, lad – you get out of it what you put into it,' Tom had encouraged him. Stephen had nodded his dark little head like a wise old man. It was one of the few happy memories that Joe had of them working together.

It happened in the middle of the night. Stephen heard the thud followed by the silence – no curses or mutters to show that his grandfather had fallen accidentally or stupidly. When he rushed in, Tom was lying on the floor and one glance showed Stephen that things weren't normal. Old Tom's face had a peculiar frozen look, and his mouth was drawn to one side, giving him an uncharacteristic grin. He didn't move or speak, yet his eyes followed Stephen, peculiarly aware.

'It's all right,' Stephen told him, picking Tom up in his arms and noticing that his nightshirt was wet, as if his bladder had failed him.

He knew something terrible had happened, and that his grandfather needed medical treatment immediately. 'Look – you'll be all right,' he told him, putting him back in the bed and tucking him in with an old patchwork quilt that seemed to have been there forever. 'I must get the doctor. You'll be fine – don't worry.'

He made the old man as comfortable as possible before running down the stairs, cursing once again the stupidity of not having a phone.

As Stephen tore across the yard, he heard the dog howl mournfully. Joe first, he thought, and then Máire and then off to the doctor.

When Joe opened the door of his cottage and saw Stephen, he knew something had happened. 'God, that's fierce, fierce altogether,' he said. 'I'll rouse Máire – 'tis on my way. You go straight for the doctor. I'll be with Tom in a jiffy.'

Joe found Tom lying in bed, covered to his chin with the old patchwork quilt. One glance showed him that old Tom would never be the same again. His face was pulled and crooked, his lips hanging loose with traces of spittle on his chin. His right arm hung from beneath the quilt, still and helpless. The old dog had somehow negotiated the steep stairs on his arthritic legs and was lying at the end of the bed, his eyes unblinking as he gazed at the master he had served so long.

Joe felt the moisture in his eyes. Jasus, he thought, I've never seen him helpless. Maybe heartbroken but never helpless.

The only sound in the room was Tom's rasping breath. Joe hoped that Stephen would think of the priest. Young fellows in the flush of health might forget. The next life to a young fella seemed very far away but to an old fellow like himself it was looming uncomfortably near.

Shep pricked up his ears before Joe even heard the car. Suddenly it seemed everyone was there. He could hear Máire's voice and Stephen coming up the stairs, talking lowly to the doctor.

Doctor Colfer looked grave as he examined the old man's heart, lungs and blood pressure. He looked into this eyes with a small light, switching it off again and again. When his examination was over he turned to Stephen, beckoning him out of the room.

'I'm afraid your grandfather has suffered a massive stroke,' he told him on the small landing. 'He's paralysed down the right side – his speech is affected completely. I'm afraid the prognosis is grave – he could suffer another stroke within the next twenty-four hours. I'll arrange to have an ambulance sent early in the morning. I think it would be too risky to shift him immediately. Keep him warm and let him sip a little water if he's able. I'll see that the ambulance gets here as soon as possible.'

After ten days in the hospital there was a slight improvement in Tom Rodgers's condition. A small movement of the right hand was noticed, accompanied by a few grunting sounds.

Both Stephen and Joe visited him, every evening. Both were aware that Tom seemed to know they were there.

Stephen would tell him things that would interest him, particularly anything that would relate to the farm, like the news that the sow had farrowed and the milk prices were going up, according to the *Press*. The harvest was the best ever, despite the shortage of rain. Joe was surprised at the lad talking to the old man, but he nodded his approval, telling him, 'You're right, boy, keeping him in the picture.'

Sometimes Stephen thought he saw a slight nod of under-standing and comprehension – maybe just a flicker in Tom's faded eyes or an almost imperceptible nod of the head – but most times the old man was helpless and silent.

A week later, driving back to Tulla, Stephen told Joe that his grandfather was being discharged from hospital. 'They can't do much more for him I'm afraid. They told me that an improvement could come with time but it's unlikely. Joe, do you think Máire might come full time for a while?'

'Sure she would – her children are done for, Willie is gone and I think at times she's lonely. She might be glad to give a hand. Hasn't she worked for old Tom on and off all her life?'

'I'll make it worth her while. Did you know, Joe, that my grandfather is a fairly rich man? I've been through the books because the accounts were coming in, though I felt I was sort of prying. I didn't particularly want to know.'

'Didn't I tell you a while back to let the hare sit and you'd be a wealthy man?

Stephen nodded but didn't answer.

Máire would help out the lad when Tom came home, Joe thought, although the job wouldn't be easy, with the man unable to answer the call of nature. Still, her own husband Willie had been like that in the end. She was used to such work. Jasus, he hoped the good God would take him before women – even nurses – would be mopping his arse.

Stephen was thinking he'd see Aileen after Mass tomorrow. He had met her very briefly in Ross a few days pre-viously. She had heard about his grandfather and he had heard about her mother going to England. Even the brief meeting had filled him with a aching longing. Even though his grand-father was seriously ill and he had sole responsibility for running the farm, he still thought about her constantly.

The next day was at his usual spot at the ditch opposite the church gate. Aileen didn't even try to be secretive and furtive. Accompanied by Eddie, she walked straight over to him. This is the way it's going to be, she thought. After all, if he was any of the well-known farmers' sons it would be normal to stand and chat for a bit.

'Hello,' she said, and added, 'I'm glad you're here.'

'And I'm glad you're here.' He was smiling and she knew he meant it.

'Is anyone glad I'm here?' Eddie asked, sighing exaggeratedly.

'I was never so glad to see anyone in my life.' Stephen gave him a cuff on the shoulder and Eddie returned it, and for a bit they indulged in a friendly little boxing match.

That's the way it should be, Aileen thought. Maybe when we're married that's the way it will be. 'How is your grandfather?' she asked.

'He's not so good. I think he'll be home soon. There isn't much more they can do. Máire Ryan is coming to stay full-time for a bit.'

'It's good to have her. It can't be easy – you'd never manage on your own.'

'Maybe I'm better than you think.' He was looking directly at her and she got the impression, as she often had before, that they were completely alone. She was also aware that there were shadows under his eyes, making them look darker than ever. 'Can I see you this evening?'

'Oh you can,' she laughed, 'I thought you mightn't ask me.'

'Oh, I'll ask you all right, Aileen MacMahon, but it will be lateish – after nine, when I come back from the hospital.'

'That's perfect. I'll have finished my jobs and this nightmare,' she gave Eddie a small push, 'will be under control.'

'No, I won't – I'm thinking of going to the pub for a few jars.'

The three of them laughed, sharing a warm feeling, a little akin to the one they had shared some years before when they had fished during the stolen, idyllic hours by the river.

She was there before him. She sat on the moss-covered stone waiting. She was calm, no longer ill at ease in case he wouldn't come. She looked across at the wide expanse of water, flowing swift and silvery to the noisy frolicsome weir. She thought of her brother and his boyhood dreams of making a raft and sailing away to God knows where. She hugged her knees resting her chin on them, listening to the sound of the river and the muted sound of the gypsies over near the woods.

Aileen was glad of the respite – it gave her time to think. She wondered if her mother would be anything like her old self when she returned from her holiday, fussing and worrying about all the ordinary things she always worried about. In a way Aieen half hoped that she wouldn't be, that the pills would have removed her raw anxiety. Would the day ever come when Mary'd cop on and accept Stephen? Aileen doubted it – even Saint Jude couldn't work that one, she thought ruefully.

'A penny for them.'

She hadn't heard him coming. He had taken a short cut and hadn't come along by the willow trees. She glanced up at him. 'I was thinking of all sorts of things. My mother, Eddie and his raft, school soon – lots of things.'

Stephen sat down beside her and she noticed that he had flung his grey tweed sports coat over his working clothes. She had never seen him like that before – he always had made a special effort to dress neatly when they were to meet. As if reading her thoughts, he said, 'Forgive the rakish look – I was rushed, I was afraid you'd be gone.'

She noticed the shadow of stubble on his face, the black hair visible on his chest where a button of his shirt was missing. 'I like the rakish look,' she told him, putting her hand to his face and running her finger along the black stubble.

He put his arm around her, yet seemed pensive and troubled. 'Remember, Aileen, you told me once that you didn't want to live on a farm here – that when you were grown up you'd prefer to live in the city? Remember?'

'I remember, and you told me you couldn't wait to get to Australia.'

'That's right. But walking over here, I was thinking that maybe I'll be caught like a rat in a trap. Maybe I'll have to stay here. My grandfather is coming home next week and he's helpless like a baby – I can't leave him like that. They tell me he could go on like that for years. Maybe I'll never get away. How could I expect you to marry me and live here with me? All the old gossips would continue to whisper and you'd be as shunned as I.'

'Maybe you could tell them the truth about your father.'

'I'll never do that – I wouldn't satisfy any of them. Let them think what they want to think.'

Across the way where the gypsies camped, someone

roughly ordered a child to come in. The noise started up the dogs, and in the barking commotion that followed a few more voices were raised.

'I suppose they'll be leaving soon.' Aileen broke the silence.

'After I read my mother's diaries I feel I know so much about them. I know they'll be travelling to County Limerick – or to the West. That's where they'll winter. It's a strange way to live.'

She could see he was restless, troubled. Maybe his grandfather's illness and all it entailed weighed heavily on him. She stole a look at his profile and the old brooding, unsmiling look was back. She leaned over and brushed back the wayward lock of black hair. 'Everything will be all right,' she murmured gently. 'I know – I know these things. Maybe I'll go into the crystal-ball business now, seeing that you're out of it.' She was rewarded with a laugh and suddenly she was in his arms and they started kissing, at first gently and easily, and then passionately and then with total abandon. All the terrible need and hunger rose to the surface. She could hear the noise of the weir above the thunder of their hearts, and the thought came that it would be easier to stop the mighty river than to halt what was happening now. He pushed her down on the moss-covered flat stones and awkwardly and clumsily opened the buttons of her coat. She pulled him to her, holding him close. His kisses were no longer confined to the places that had become familiar to him. He moved his mouth hungrily to her neck, to behind her ears and back to her neck again. His fingers were wildly fumbling, opening the buttons of her dress before burying his face between the soft mounds of her young breasts. Her own desperate need and hunger were unquenchable as she returned his frenzied love-making, kissing his mouth, his neck, her lips moving hungrily to the black hair on his chest. He lifted her head, his black eyes glittering with the unasked question. She nodded. Their hearts pounded so loudly that they were almost deafened.

Their union was rushed, hungry, inexperienced, demanding. When it was over, they lay, their bodies still together, their hearts pounding noisily. Somewhere across the way a curlew cried, and another dog barked. The first star appeared – Aileen could see it twinkling, small and yet somehow friendly, as if it wasn't too shocked.

'I see the first star,' she whispered. 'I must make a wish.' Her voice was still shaky with spent passion. 'I wish we could be together forever.'

'You shouldn't have told me, love – now it mightn't happen I'll pretend I never heard.' His tone was low and gentle and she noticed that his hands were shaking as he buttoned her dress. She met his eyes. An expression she had never seen before were in their dark depths. 'I'll never hurt you again – it will be better next time.'

'It was wrong, Stephen, wasn't it?' Her childish question seemed to need an answer.

'With anyone else, yes – but with you I don't feel it was wrong.' He helped her to her feet and they walked home slowly. She noticed that the first star had been joined by a myriad others. The whole sky seemed awash with starlight. Yet the trees in Barrons Wood were dark and forbidding. She could see the smoke rising in fitful puffs and the odd flame darting heavenwards.

Stephen was part of her now, and she knew she loved him more than life itself. Yet a strange loneliness descended on her, as if part of her youthful innocence was over, or maybe the loneliness was caused because they had very few days before she went away. She stopped and, reaching up, kissed him gently on the mouth. 'How will I get on in that awful school without you? Tell me, how?'

'How will I get by on that awful farm without you?' His tone was teasing but he sounded happy. She knew that giving herself to him had taken away all his restlessness, loneliness, discontent.

'I mightn't be able to see you before I go, what with getting ready for school, my mother coming home, your grandfather coming home.'

'What will I do so?'

'Write to me. Send the letter to Niamh's house – Pier House, Skerries. That way you can write with no fear the nuns will lay their hands on it. You can write what you want to write.'

'No, I can't.'

'Why?'

'Because I don't have enough words to tell you how I feel about you.'

244

Chapter Twenty

Two weeks after he had suffered the massive stroke, Tom Rodgers came home, silent and useless, to the farm where he had toiled in vigorous health for a lifetime. There was no indication that he was aware that Stephen, Joe and Máire were there to meet him. District Nurse O'Shea was there, no doubt looking for news but also to instruct Máire on the unsavoury aspects of the job she had so willingly taken on. The white ambulance looked strange, alien, in the yard. Even the geese and hens had scattered, screeching and squawking, as it swept in through the gate.

Stephen watched silently as they lifted Tom on to a stretcher. When they brought him into the kitchen, Shep jumped up, all excited, his plume-like tail wagging even more enthusiastically when he sniffed the occupant on the stretcher. He got no reaction – not even a kick.

The ambulance men looked at the steep ladder-like stairs in the kitchen. 'God, boy,' one of them addressed Stephen, 'we won't get the boss up there – he'd have to sprout wings.'

'We know that. He's to go in there.' Stephen pointed to the door at the far side of the kitchen, the unused parlour. Máire had cleaned and scrubbed the forgotten, forlorn room, washing and ironing curtains chosen a lifetime ago by Ciss, Tom's young wife, who had come into the place with high hopes and an awareness that new curtains were about the only change Tom would tolerate.

The place was ready and waiting now. After Tom was made comfortable in his own bed, with the patched quilt washed and repaired, they drank their tea in the kitchen while Nurse O'Shea gave them instructions. 'Someone will have to be with him most of the day. His swallow is just sufficient to allow him to have soft strained food. He is doubly incontinent and that will mean a lot of messy work, Máire. But thank God, you have a fine strong man in Stephen – he will help you lift him.

There's a list of what you'll need – sheets, towelling napkins, rubber undersheets, cream and Vaseline.'

'We have everything.' Stephen sounded abrupt. He almost felt the old man's humiliation as the nurse brightly discussed his necessities. He felt a certain sorrow for the man who had always been so private and independent, and who could no longer control his bodily functions. In all probability Tom would prefer to be dead.

Later, as they were bringing the cows in for milking, Joe said, 'Jasus, Stephen – promise me a good belt of a hurley if that happens to me, won't you now, boy?'

'Sure I might give you a belt of a hurley if it never happened.'

To their own surprise, on a day that was sad for everyone, they shared a smile.

They took their turns to sit with Tom day and night. Joe made light of his stint in the small hours: 'Sure I might as well be sitting with Tom as tossin' and turnin' in me own bed. When you get on, lad, you don't need as much sleep as a young fella. Sure the Pope himself only sleeps four hours in a day – if the Pope can do it so can Joe Power.'

So they drew up a timetable. Máire watched over Tom during the day, Stephen sat with him from teatime till after midnight, and Joe was there until dawn. They put a small bed in the room and Joe managed to have a little 'shut-eye', as he called it, during the small hours.

Sometimes, as Stephen sat with his grandfather, he thought of the last evening he had spent with Aileen. He wasn't ashamed or guilty that they had made love. He sincerely hoped she wasn't. As he sat in the room, the silence broken by his grandfather's rasping breathing and the ticking of the clock, he knew that it was her last week before returning to Dublin. Maybe she's down by the river now, waiting, he thought. Did she know that his grandfather was home and needed constant watching? Sometimes the old man woke and his eyes would look around the room with a lost expression as if he were trying to get his bearings.

Once Stephen saw Tom looking at him with sad and ravaged eyes, as if he had something on his mind. Stephen went over to the bed. 'Whatever it is, it's all right. There's nothing to worry about, the place is fine. I got the milk cheque and we're finished draining the field, and the new bull you bought from Dan Sheehan is worth his weight in gold.' He imagined he saw a flicker of satisfaction on Tom's face.

When the doctor made his rounds, Stephen asked him if it was possible that his grandfather understood what he was saying. He was told it was quite possible he did. Stephen and Joe agreed to tell the old man things about the farm or indeed any gossip in the parts that might interest him.

Halfway through the week, Stephen couldn't bear it any more. He simply had to see her. 'Joe,' he said, 'would you come along at nine tonight? I must go out for a bit. I'll make it up to you.'

'That's all right, lad – if I could lay me hands on a looker like that I'd want to go out for a bit too.'

'So you know?'

'Everyone knows except Mary MacMahon. I'd say Denis knows and I don't see him gettin' in a tissy. Funny how history has a way of repeatin' itself.'

She wasn't there. He realised that he had been a naive and hopeful fool to think that she might. Sitting on their favourite flat stone, he felt such a desire and hunger for her that he wanted to get up and run the three miles to her home and knock brazenly on the door, demanding to see her. He would like to confront Denis and Mary MacMahon and say, 'Look, I'm in love with your daughter and I want to marry her as soon as possible. I love her and will take the greatest care of her and she will never want for anything as long as she lives.'

He struck a match off a nearby stone and, lighting his cigarette, smiled at his fantasy. He could imagine the shock on Mary MacMahon's face. Maybe little Maeve would be thrilled with the excitement of it all, and he felt that Eddie would welcome him.

Once or twice he thought he heard a twig breaking near the willow tree and he looked over with expectation, hoping to see her shy smile. But except for the water tumbling over the weir, there wasn't a sound.

Nothing stirred in the silent world. Glancing towards Barrons Wood, he saw that the tinkers were gone. There was smoke spiralling towards the sky, no rosy leaping flames, no sounds of people talking or squabbling, or a young fellow crying because he had got the back of his father's hand. Since reading the diaries Stephen knew how they lived. He knew. He knew how his mother had been irritated by the lack of privacy, the lack of hygiene, the cold. But the minor irritations had been as nothing compared to the great love she had had for his father. At least he had inherited from her a capacity to love greatly. He hadn't inherited her wit, her way with words, her impetuous rashness. But they both loved greatly.

He stubbed out his cigarette, watching the tiny remnants of red ash flicker before dying away. How would it go for him? How long would his grandfather last? He would be twenty-one soon, and Aileen seventeen. The farm would be his – that he knew. Yet the old man could live for years and years. How could he walk away, leaving a well-tended place to rot while he made a life with Aileen, knowing he had walked out on the only relative he had? He wondered if he should pray. He wasn't much good at prayers. Even at Mass his thoughts strayed so much he might as well have stayed at home.

He heard a twig snap. He looked around, his heart thumping with expectation. There was no one there – possibly a rat or a badger on a late-night forage.

He walked home quickly, anxious to relieve Joe. We're a sort of family in a way, he thought, old Tom bedridden and helpless now, Máire kind and hardworking, Joe the friend and the father he had never had.

When they came in the door Aileen could see that the holiday had done her mother an enormous amount of good. Mary was on a high – talking animatedly about her cousin Peggy and all the things they did, and all the things they saw. Her words spilled out in a torrent of enthusiasm for the shops, the shows, the markets. 'Denis,' she told her husband, 'you have no idea the things you can buy. They have this great market full of hundreds of stalls, all packed with everything under God's sun.'

'It's called the flea market,' Maeve butted in, 'and honestly, we didn't see a bit of a flea, did we, Mam?'

'I hope ye didn't,' Eddie answered for his mother, 'we have enough fleas around here without bringing 'em in from England.'

After tea Aileen's mother unpacked her bags and cases to

dispense her largesse. She drew out a pair of knee-length fur-lined boots for Aileen, telling her they were all the rage in England. 'Peggy made me buy them for you,' she said, 'with your height you could wear them.' She had also bought her a blue jumper. 'Peggy said it would be right with your eyes.' There was a lot of underwear bought at the markets, and a special present for Aileen from Peggy. Aileen took the glamorous nightdress and held it up. 'Peggy thought it would be nice for your bottom drawer in years and years to come.' Even though the nightdress was lined, it was gossamer-light and almost see-through. Eddie gave a wolf-whistle and winked at Aileen.

'I can see you haven't changed much,' Mary said. But she obviously wasn't going to get into bad humour with him, and he was pleased with his two shirts and two books.

Denis MacMahon looked at his black shoes with no laces, secretly thinking they looked dandyish though he didn't want to hurt her feelings by saying so. The shirts and the cap were fine, and it was good to have her home. 'Tell me, how is Bob Fitzpatrick and how is he doing?'

'Things were never better. He's on the building site from dawn till dusk, and would you believe, he has twenty men working for him now? Peggy says he's saving his money and hoping to come back and buy a little business. Peggy has a hankering for Dungarvan, and I know she wants to bring up her lads there. She thought he might buy a shop or something.'

'And I could go there on holidays. I'd mind William and Paul and go for swims in the sea, not in an oul stream,' Maeve said.

'You can't mind yourself – both of then would be drowned like rats if you were minding them,' Eddie jeered.

'Look at you,' she snapped back, 'you were nowhere. I was in London and even Aileen was in Dublin, but poor you.'

Eddie reached out to give her a belt, but Denis intervened. 'Stop it now – can't you see that your mother is exhausted? Let's have a bit of peace for once.'

Later, when the younger ones had gone reluctantly to bed, Mary wanted to know if Aileen had organised some of her packing for school.

'Most of it,' Aileen told her, 'although I still need a few

things, I'll get them in Waterford on Saturday.'

'Of course, we'll do a bit of shopping on Saturday.'

'There's no need for you to come, Mam,' Aileen said. 'I can get them myself, you should rest a bit after your holiday.'

'Maybe you're right – I keep forgetting that you're nearly seventeen now.'

Aileen lay in bed, her mind full of churning thoughts and her heart racing. Somehow her mother's homecoming and Maeve's childish prattle had brought back the enormity, the sheer magnitude of what had happened at the river. The memory came back to torture her now. She knew what she and Stephen had done was terribly wrong, and yet she had never needed him or wanted him more. She had gone to the river twice to try and see him. She had sat there waiting, and every sound and every rustle was Stephen coming to meet her. She had been filled with all sorts of irrational fears. Maybe it was true what the nuns preached. Maybe a fellow did indeed lose interest in a girl who was free and easy. Maybe he thought she was cheap now.

Rocking to and fro in the bed as she had when she was a child, Aileen tried to remember the very last thing he had said, when she had asked him to write to Niamh's house: 'I'll never have enough words to let you know how I feel.' Her fears eased, and she knew she would have to see him again before she went away. She would be leaving on Sunday evening; she would see him after Mass. But he would maybe look dark and remote as only he could. And even if he wanted to speak to her he couldn't, because her mother's eagle eye was back. She knew his grandfather was very ill – perhaps dying; Stephen was obviously very busy. Would it be possible to contact him to say she would be in Waterford on Saturday?

She didn't want to go back to school without seeing him again.

Aileen wanted to be with him in a normal sort of way, where they'd talk and laugh and maybe exorcise their last meeting with all its hunger and passion and crazy helpless abandon. She wondered in a confused and childish way if they would ever be able to go back to the way they had been together, with some control over their emotions.

That night her sleep was filled with dreams. She was with

him in London. There was this big market, exactly as her mother had described, with endless, endless stalls all full of clothes, china, blankets and bric-à-brac. She and Stephen were walking hand, in hand and he was talking and laughing and pointing things out, just like she hoped he would. She asked him why was everyone looking at her, and he pointed to her dress. She looked down and to her horror saw that she was dressed in the flimsy nightdress that Peggy had sent her. Her breasts and legs were clearly visible. She was wearing the fur-lined boots. Distraught, she burst out crying, and shouted at him, demanding how he could let her out like that. Seeing her upset, he took off his coat and wrapped it around her and then he held her and kissed her passionately and he told her it was all right – all right. Waking up with a start, Aileen was surprised to feel the tears on her face.

At breakfast her mother wanted to know everything that had happened since she had gone away.

'Ah, there's not much to tell you,' Denis said, 'except of course poor Tom Rodgers got a stroke. According to Joe Power, the man is helpless like a baby, lying there as dead as the trunk of a tree. Joe and Máire Ryan are living there now, trying to give Stephen a hand. They say Tom has to be looked after round the clock.'

'Well, I'm sorry to hear it. But something was bound to give with that man. Think of the trouble he had with his wife dying young and his only daughter disgracing herself, and not knowing what he has on his hands with her child.'

'Well, they say that the lad will inherit the lot. Not alone Tulla but the money from the sale of Tom's brother's place. Stephen Rodgers won't be short.'

''Tis the like of him that'd get it – sure who knows what he would do with money like that? The bad blood could break out in him and he could drink and squander the lot.'

'Don't be stupid, Mam,' Aileen said. 'Stephen isn't like that. I don't think he even wants his grandfather's farm or money. He talks of going to Australia.'

'And how would you know what that nobody wants to do? Tell me that, Miss.'

'Mam, for God's sake, don't call him that. He's anything but a nobody – you don't know what you're talking about. Please don't call him that.'

'And how do you know all this? I told you before not to have anything to do with that young man. Isn't it well I'm back, and isn't it well you're off to school tomorrow?'

Aileen was sorely tempted to shout that she had seen him so often you wouldn't believe. *We're madly in love and can't wait to get away from here.* But she didn't. She'd bide her time. She had a childlike faith that their time would come. She glanced at Eddie, who had his eyes closed and was silently mouthing and wagging his finger, imitating their mother when she was giving out. His silent mimicry, when he didn't think he had an audience, made her smile. There would be plenty of time to tackle her mother in the months ahead. To try and see Stephen today was now her top priority.

'Well, I'm off,' Denis told them, rising stiffly from his chair. He glanced at Aileen. 'Well, young woman, I suppose you want money for your shopping in Waterford today?'

'I do, Dad – I'll get the one o'clock bus at the crossroads near Tulla. Is that all right, Mam?' She turned to her mother.

'I suppose it is,' Mary answered, some of the old apathy back in her voice.

Denis walked to the dresser and, taking down an old tin box, he handed Aileen some notes. 'Will you have enough?'

'I will, Dad – I will,' she said gratefully. She felt a rush of affection for him. They had become close over the weeks and months of her mother's illness. A lump came into her throat and tears weren't too far away as she realised how much she'd miss him when she was back at school. 'Thanks, Dad,' she shouted again as he was going out the door. He looked back a bit surprised, but then he winked and she winked back at him.

Denis walked out into the sunshine, shouting to Eddie to come and give him a hand with the fence in the lower meadow. Aileen was on his mind as he collected his tools in the store shed. She was a young woman now – a beautiful young woman at that. Naturally he had a fatherly pride in her and he hoped she could handle the young fellows who came snooping around. Although, in Aileen's case, there was only one, and it looked as if he already had a claim on her. He didn't doubt for a minute that Stephen Rodgers was a decent fellow, despite Mary's terrible, irrational animosity towards him. But the line had to end – if it didn't, it would indeed break Mary's heart. He would have a word with Aileen when she came home at Christmas. He didn't want to upset her now. He just wanted things to go on an even keel for a bit. Ah, he would have a word with her, but he'd bide his time until Christmas.

Aileen was getting ready for the bus when she heard Eddie shouting, 'Howya, Maggie!' Yes, that would be it, she thought excitedly. She'd ask Maggie to do it. Maggie wouldn't refuse – Maggie rarely refused anybody anything.

'Is Aileen around?' she heard Maggie shout.

'I'm up here,' she shouted down, sticking her head out of the window. She heard her mother say something to Maggie and then her friends footsteps on the stairs. 'Come in, for God's sake,' Aileen exclaimed as she nearly dragged her friend into the room. 'Maggie, will you be an angel and do something for me?' she whispered.

'Here I am, coming over like a dutiful friend to say goodbye before you go back to school, and I'm assaulted and then asked to do you a favour. What is it?' Maggie's eyes were cagey.

'It's nothing really – but it will save my life.'

'You look healthy enough, I must say.' Maggie was still suspicious.

'Maggie, will you call to Stephen's place and tell him I'm getting the one o'clock bus to Waterford? Tell him I'll be on my own, that I have to get a few things for school. Tell him I'll be at the crossroads where the bus stops. Tell him, Maggie,' she entreated.

'Is it that bad?'

'Yes, Maggie, 'tis that bad.'

Whether it was the simple honesty of her friend's reply or the genuine pleading in the intense blue eyes, Maggie softened.

'All right – I'll do it. I know his grandfather is on the flat of his back. If he wasn't, I'd be afraid of that cranky old man. I'll just tell him, is that it?'

'Yep, that's it and I won't forget this. I'll do the same for you some day.'

'We'll see,' Maggie answered with a rueful grin, 'we'll see.'

He was sitting in his grandfather's old Ford when she got to the crossroads. She silently thanked Maggie and offered up a prayer of thanksgiving. Was she being a hypocrite praying when she was guilty of the terrible sin of impurity? 'Hello.' She noticed he was still in his working clothes, with the good sports coat flung on hurriedly in an obvious attempt to look right for the city. She met the dark intensity of his look, and in an effort to defuse the emotion of their first meeting since they had made love, she grinned. 'So 'tis yourself that's in it.'

He grinned, getting the message. 'Aye, so 'tis at that.'

As she got into the car she found herself babbling, her heart already in ribbons.

'I know it was terrible to send Maggie, the nuns in the Loretto would call it forward. But I took a chance because I'm off tomorrow.'

'Isn't the knowledge branded in my brain? When she gave me the message I just dropped everything and came. Thus the ravaged look again.'

She was sitting beside him primly and maybe stupidly, pulling down her summer skirt, wildly hoping that he wouldn't mention anything about their last meeting. She watched his brown hand reach over to start the ignition and suddenly he seemed to change his mind. Instead he reached over and took her in his arms and kissed her long and tenderly. She felt the old familiar longing and broke away. 'Do you know, Stephen Rodgers, I only wanted a lift to town to buy vests and stuff?' If he kisses me again, she thought, it's me that won't be able to stop.

'Okay,' he said, starting the engine this time, 'vests it is.'

As they drove in silence she looked at him from under her eyelashes thinking, I won't see him for an age after today. Weeks and weeks of boring school, thinking, imagining and wanting him. She noticed a small bit of shaving cream near his ear. He must have rushed frantically when he got Maggie's message. Unexpectedly a lump came to her throat and she felt her eyes prickle with tears. As the old grey Ford rattled on its way she thought how wonderful it would be if they could drive on and on. Maybe they could go to Dun Laoghaire and get on the boat and go to England and be together for the rest of their lives.

'A penny for them.'

'I was just thinking about the price of vests.'

'No, you weren't. There's not a vest in the country that would give you the look I saw on your face right now.'

'Oh, all right, know-all. I was thinking, wouldn't it be lovely if we were going away somewhere together and not a bother in the world on us.'

'That's going to happen. I don't need a crystal ball to tell me that. I know it's going to happen. By the way, I don't like your hair tied in that ponytail. Take that yoke off. I want to remember it all loose and blonde and blowing all over the place.'

'So you're giving me orders now? Well, kind sir, if you want to know, this damsel is aware of a lump of soap stuck on your cheekbone. She wants to remember you without lumps of soap stuck on your face.'

Laughing, he brushed away the offending soap and she pulled the elastic band from her hair.

In silence he crossed the bridge into Waterford, going down the quay and parked outside the Imperial Hotel, opposite Reginalds Tower. Getting up and opening the door for her, he whispered, 'Forsooth, pretty wench – let's storm the castle and foray for suitable vests and then we'll banquet.'

'I have a long list, dope. It's not just vests – it never was vests.' She wondered if he was serious about having something to eat. She would love to sit with him somewhere nice and quiet and share a meal with him. But then again, if she wasn't home by the Ross bus her mother would be suspicious and would question her incessantly.

As they strode up the quay the young couple attracted a fair bit of attention. His dark swarthiness made a sharp contrast to her silvery blondeness. Several pairs of eyes watched them as they made their way to Hearnes shop, and idly wondered who they were. Strangers, undoubtedly. Maybe they were home on holidays from England. No, no – the young man looked far too dishevelled for a holidaymaker back from across the water. Everyone knew you dressed up to the nines when you came home from England, to show the folks how well you were doing. The pair didn't look like hikers from Dublin either, because there wasn't a haversack between them. Nor did they have the look of country people who came in every Saturday to do the shopping. One woman in the bus queue muttered to her daughter, 'You wouldn't know what you'd have blowing in these days.'

Aileen, aware of the interest they were causing, whispered, 'I hope we won't see anyone we know.'

'I hope we do,' he answered as he took her hand in a firm grasp. 'That woman is going to have to face it one day, she might as well face it now.'

'By the way, I don't want you coming into shops with me. I have to buy black stockings and shoes, and things in chemists, and I'd be faster on my own.'

'Okay. If it means I'll have more time with you I'll wait outside.'

After Aileen had finished the hastiest bit of shopping she had ever done, she joined Stephen at the agreed meeting place. Relieved of some of her parcels, he told her they were going to eat. 'We'll go to Dooleys Hotel – you look as weak as a gadfly.'

'Maybe we'll see people we know,' she protested.

'Maybe we won't. 'Tis a good place – my grandfather, Joe and I go there after the cattle mart.' He saw she was pale and tired looking. 'You could do with a rest, and a bit of nourishment wouldn't go astray.'

Once in the hotel, Stephen ordered steak and chips, tea, apple tart and cream. They demolished everything in sight. As they shared a big pot of tea, Aileen said, 'Do you know, this is the first time we've had a real meal together?'

'I was thinking the same myself. It's heaven for me to sit here and watch you. I said to myself, this girl, Rodgers, is going to sit across your table for the rest of your life. Aren't you the lucky bastard? Do you know, I've lain awake at night thinking what it would be like the next time I saw you? I was desperately worried about what happened. I asked myself a thousand times did I – did I force you? – did I hurt you? I went down to the river twice – Joe did the needful and stayed with my grandfather. You weren't there. I was desperate, darling.'

He had never called her darling before. It had a peculiar effect on her. She fought hard to stop the sensation of longing and the rising need for him. 'I don't want to talk about the last time,' she said softly. 'I thought we could talk about ordinary everyday things. Because if we don't, and if I keep thinking of what happened and the way I feel about you, I won't be able to go back to school at all.'

He leaned over the table and kissed her gently on the

mouth.

An elderly woman at the next table watched with disapproval. Haven't we reached a sorry state, she thought, when young men can't keep their hands off their girls in a public place where decent people were trying to have their bit? Still, she was a lovely-looking girl, and though he was a bit scruffy, he looked like someone in the films. Still, there was a time and place for everything, and Dooleys Hotel on a busy Saturday afternoon wasn't a place for kissing. You wouldn't mind, only the young girl had barely finished her tart. She had heard someone say that sort of thing went on in the cinemas, in the back row. Who was it that said it? Of course, it was the missioner at the retreat they had during Lent. He was talking about all the places that were occasions of sin for young people. He had emphasised that the back row in the cinema was such a place, not to mention dark ill-lit dance halls where young people danced so close together you couldn't put a penny between them. God knows what the young couple near her would do in a dark dance hall if he couldn't keep his hands off her in a brightly lit dining room in the heart of Waterford city. She had even read something in a magazine in the doctor's waiting room that specialists were working on a pill that would prevent a girl from having a baby. God and his Blessed Mother, what was the world coming to? No one would make her take that pill, that was for certain. Then she reminded herself that she was nearly seventy, and there would be no need for her to be worried about any pill. She sighed as she watched the couple get up. They had a lot of shopping, and yet they somehow looked too young to be married and doing a weekly shop. Despite the parcels the boy still managed to keep his arm around his girlfriend and open the door at the same time. She watched them through the glass door as they walked out into the foyer. Blessed Virgin, if they weren't in each other's arms again and half the city of Waterford looking on.

The wind-whipped run to the car didn't help. Both of them were having trouble with their breathing as they got in. She knew if they were down by the river near the mossy bank, what had happened before would happen again.

'Stephen, as I was saying a while back, I was hoping that today would be a warm, friendly, kind of day. I'd ask you

257

about your grandfather and how you're coping, and you'd tell me and then you'd ask me things about home or school – I wanted us to have that kind of day.'

'No, Aileen MacMahon, we can't have that kind of day because, though I know you for years, we haven't been together for a single month. Think of it. I'm right. We have a few snatched words at the dance, another after Mass, a lovely few days at the river – sure, if you put them all together we haven't been with each other one solid month. And when we are, you're afraid we'll be seen.'

'That's not true,' she said heatedly. 'I'm not afraid any more.'

'Now let me finish. Because your mother thinks I'm a nobody and unsuitable for her daughter, we have to sneak around hoping that no one will ever see us and spill the beans that Stephen Rodgers is on the prowl. If things were different we could spend all our free time together, like any courting couple. But the way it is, I'm afraid of losing you – terribly afraid that someone will come and spirit you away.'

Suddenly they were in each other's arms and devouring each other, kissing with the same hungry abandon and desperation as before. When it looked as if nothing would stop them, Aileen gained some measure of control. Holding him tight and listening to his hammering heart, she soothed him like she would a fractious child. 'No, love, no. People are watching, we must stop. No one, I swear, will ever spirit me away. Where do you get the words?' Her voice was almost a sob. 'Wouldn't you know your father was a writer? Spiriting me away, how are you?' She ran her hand through his hair, her fingers untangling and smoothing until he too had control. He looked at her and the thought came that she had never seen such unadorned love in anyone's eyes before.

'When will I see you again?' His voice was hoarse.

'I'll have to go to first Mass tomorrow – Dad is driving me up to Dublin after dinner. Maybe Mam will be there too. I mightn't be able to talk to you, but I'll wave to you – I'll wave at you three times.' Her blue eyes sparkled like a child's. 'The first wave is to tell you that I adore you. The second – let me see – is to tell you that I miss you, and the third is to tell you that no one will ever spirit me away from you. Okay?'

'Okay – I'll have to be content with three waves.'

He drove with his foot down hard on the accelerator as the old car devoured the miles. Aileen stared out the window at the flashing hedgerows and trees. Their leaves were turning gold and russet. Here and there, the blackberries were peeping black and shiny in the ditches. 'The summer is over,' she almost spoke to herself.

''Tis –' he glanced at her, and then his dark eyes concentrated once more on the road, 'and for me it was the best summer of my life.'

'And for me too. The very best summer of my life.'

Sometimes when he sat with his grandfather, Stephen got the impression that the old man wanted to say something. Tom's rheumy, faded eyes would burrow into Stephen's and he would try to raise his hand before letting it fall back helplessly with a slight grunt. Most times, though, he just stared out the lace-curtained window. Sometimes Stephen thought he could see a look of expectancy on his lined face, and wondered what on earth the helpless silent old man could be expecting. Was he hoping for death and the promise of eternal life, where he would meet his wife and daughter again? Did he dream during those fitful sleeps? Did Teresa come laughing through his confused disoriented dreams? Did his wife Ciss hold out her hand and beckon? Stephen now found it easy to forgive this helpless hulk of a man, to forgive all the harshness and resentment that had been his lot for so long.

At times Máire looked so exhausted that he insisted that he would help her change his grandfather's bedlinen and pyjamas when it was necessary. As Tom was doubly incontinent, the task was unsavoury but neither of them ever showed disgust, and did the job with gentle efficiency. Stephen told her she was never to do it on her own again. 'You're not getting any younger and he's too heavy – you're to give either Joe or myself a shout.'

'But I do give ye a shout – don't ye help me when ye're around? Anyway, the poor man would hate to be made a show of – Tom Rodgers was always such a proud man. Anyway, sure God be good to him, he's like a baby now – and you wouldn't be put off with a baby now.'

Sometimes, though, when it was obvious that his grandfather's bowels or his bladder had emptied, Stephen quietly went about the job of cleaning him up himself. Máire had cut up dozens of sheets and towels, and had them stored neatly in the sideboard along with towels, soap, pyjamas and face cloths; she had cleared out all the glass and china. Now, this evening, after putting the soiled garments and sheets in a bucket of disinfected water, Stephen was foraging for replacements when he caught the eye of a young woman in an old sepia photograph. She was tall and dark and smiling, holding a baby aloft, a bit like you'd hold a trophy. He knew the woman was Ciss, his grandmother, and he knew the baby in her arms was Teresa. I'm getting imaginative, he thought, but he could have sworn that the young woman's eyes were looking straight into his with an expression of grateful thanks.

As he lifted his grandfather, Stephen noticed that the old man's legs were no longer thick and strong, but frail and blue, with the flesh hanging down loose and flaccid, the blue veins standing out, knotted and gnarled. He gently dressed him, talking to him all the time, and went to the kitchen to wash his hands. Joe was there waiting.

'Now, you won't forget that belt of a hurley, will you?' he said.

'I won't, Joe – sure I have it on the ready.'

'Think of it,' Joe said in horror, 'your arse being cleaned like a baby.'

'Maybe when they're cleaning your arse, you won't know any more than he knows,' Stephen consoled him.

'Oh, he knows all right – sure don't I know the man like the back of me hand? He knows. Wasn't he tryin' to say somethin' to me the other night? His eyes were borin' into me own, but his poor crooked mouth couldn't get a word out.'

Nurse O'Shea, the district nurse, came three times a week and after examining Tom and helping Máire, she usually sat in the kitchen for a cup of tea and a chat. A gossiping woman in her middle fifties, she thirsted for news. 'When God calls him, and it won't be long now, I suppose Stephen will get everything.'

'And why wouldn't he? Isn't he Tom's only grandchild?'

'But because of what happened, sure he might be slow to do that. I knew a wealthy farmer out Brennanstown way who left all his money to the bishop. After all, Tom never knew who the boy's father was, and sure he only had the gypsies' word for it that the boy is Teresa's son.'

'That's nonsense – you need only have eyes in you head to see whose he is. Hasn't he a great look of her? And what's more, there's a look of breeding about him that's lackin',' Máire looked pointedly at the nurse, 'in a lot of people I know. Anyway, all that old story is water under the bridge.'

'Well, it's not water under the bridge that Stephen Rodgers is walking out with Aileen MacMahon. They've been seen down by the river, and, if truth be known, they're not all that innocent. Sure Máire, you know that it would break Mary MacMahon's heart if her daughter did a steady line with Stephen. The MacMahons have farmed the place for genera-tions and she wouldn't be happy with that.'

'If I may say so, Nurse O'Shea, poor Mary MacMahon has notions beyond her station. Wasn't she lucky to get Denis MacMahon and he with a fine place? From what I hear, she didn't bring much along with her either. She should be pleased if there's anything doing between Stephen and her girl – pleased she should be.'

'Well, she won't. Her nervous breakdown was brought on by the worry of the thing.'

'She'd be better off to count her blessings and not be courting trouble. Well, Nurse O'Shea, whatever about some of us, I have my jobs to do. I suppose you're so busy you haven't time to bid a body the time of day?' Máire's sarcasm was lost on Nurse O'Shea, who leisurely gathered her bag and bits as if well aware that in a district like hers there would be no shortage of titbits of gossip. Currently the silent watchers of the Tom Rodgers situation were wondering if the lad would get the farm and the money, or if the old stigma of his birth would deprive him of the lot.

Nurse O'Shea hummed as she cycled along the sunlit road. There was no doubt the situation was interesting. And wasn't it peculiar that Stephen Rodgers was walking out with Aileen MacMahon, seeing that her father had walked out with his mother? Now that would have been the match of the decade, so it would.

As the days shortened and the evenings darkened Stephen was swamped with a deep sense of loss. He only ever felt whole – complete – when he was with Aileen. He had seen her at first

Mass on the Sunday she had returned to school. He had sat far back at the men's side of the church so that he could feast his eyes on her. Her thick blonde hair was tied back in that stupid ponytail she found so handy. She wore an old grey beret she had obviously stuck on in a hurry – it gave her a rakish sort of look that was a bit out of character. He couldn't say a single prayer. He spent all his time watching her as she stood, knelt and possibly prayed. There was something awkward and self-conscious about her movements, as if she knew she was being watched. As she walked back to her seat from Holy Communion, he could see the familiar faint blush suffuse her fair skin. Somehow it made him love her even more. He knew how she hated blushing; she had told him how much only a few weeks ago. He had laughingly told her that it suited her, and she had heatedly replied that he wouldn't understand, that there wasn't a blush in the world that would get through his tanned hide.

He somehow caught her mother's eye before she filed into her seat after Communion. It was as cold as a dead fish. The woman loathed him, he knew that. He sighed as he knelt down for the final blessing. He wondered if there was any miracle out there that would make her accept him. He didn't think so.

Now, back home, sitting beside his grandfather, Stephen recalled his last glimpse of Aileen. True to her word, she had waved three times, and now he smiled in the sick room, recalling what the three waves meant. *One is to tell you that I love you, the second is to tell you that no one will ever spirit me away and the third one is to tell you that I'll miss you.* During the long hours of waiting and watching over old Tom, Stephen sometimes feared he would never see her again. The terror would engulf him, forcing him to walk out of the parlour and stand in the kitchen and smoke a cigarette.

One night, Máire ran into his bedroom and shook him into wakefulness. 'Get up, Stephen, your grandfather has taken a bad turn.'

He jumped out of the bed, and grabbed his trousers. 'I'll go and get the doctor immediately.'

'There's no need. Joe is gone. You're his only flesh and blood – stay with him.'

He could instantly see the change in the old man. The

pallor was gone, replaced by a bluish tinge which was more pronounced around his mouth. But there was something changed about his eyes. Was there an awareness that death was near?

Stephen pulled a chair near the bed and took his grandfather's hand in his. It was icy cold, and he rubbed it, trying to bring back some degree of warmth. Concentrating on his task, he was almost shocked to hear his grandfather whisper. Bending his head, Stephen tried to catch the words. But all he could hear was a low rasping sound.

'It's all right – don't try to talk now. Rest a bit. The doctor will be here soon and will fix you up. You'll be grand.' Stephen spoke as if he were consoling a child. The old man's eyes seemed to bore into his, and he could clearly see he was deeply agitated. 'It's all right,' Stephen repeated, 'all right.' He was suddenly surprised to feel his grandfather's hand tighten in his.

'Teresa.'

Stephen bent his head closer.

'Teresa – your mother – she broke my heart. I blamed you for her death. 'Twas wrong – wrong.'

Stephen could feel the old man's hand loosen and go limp, but Tom's eyes still held his. 'I wanted to make up – but I wasn't able. Not able.'

'It's all right now – all right. Where would I have been now without you?' Stephen whispered. He continued to hold his grandfather's hand, reaching out and wiping the sweat that had gathered on Tom's forehead. He tried to murmur consoling words as he rubbed the grey straggly bits of hair. He heard his grandfather trying to grapple once again with broken words that didn't make much sense.

'Proud of you – proud of you – couldn't tell you – wasn't able.' Stephen could barely make out the words.

Suddenly the door opened and Father Leahy, the parish priest, came into the room. He greeted Stephen and approached the bed. 'Well, Tom, I see you're under the weather.'

Tom gave no sign he heard. His eyes were still riveted to his raven-haired grandson. Máire could see that some communication had taken place between them.

Stephen was still sitting, with his head bent close to his grandfather. He spoke softly, and Máire was amazed that the old man seemed to understand what he said.

'There were times I wanted to tell you things too – like I was proud of you and that I loved you – but I wasn't able either.'

Afterwards, when Máire tried to recall the scene she thought it the biggest miracle that, from his death bed, Tom Rodgers had spoken words of affection to the grandson he had so often spurned. And there were tears in Stephen's eyes. Máire had never seen Tom Rodgers cry – not after the death of his wife, not after Teresa had run away. Neither had she seen Stephen cry since he was a small child. She knew somehow that their tears were tears of healing. At least she thought so. She always felt better after a good cry.

Chapter Twenty-One

Niamh handed Aileen the letter before supervised study. 'One from Rita for me, and one from Stephanie for you. My mother sent them on – she knew we'd be dying to hear from our girlfriends.' She winked at her friend and whispered, 'We'll compare notes afterwards.'

My dearest Aileen,

I'd love this to be a witty, hysterically funny letter to brighten the tedium of school for my lovely girl. Alas, it won't be. My grandfather died last week and was buried on Thursday last. The strange thing is I don't feel any relief after he has gone – sometimes I thought I would. A peculiar thing happened before he died. Remember, he was lying there like a helpless log, his eyes staring out the window or up at the ceiling, vacant and unseeing. But just before he went he became lucid and spoke to me. It wasn't easy to make out the words, but I did. He told me he had blamed me for my mother's death, and that he was sorry. He had wanted to feel close but wasn't able. I sat there holding his hand and a bit like a revelation, the sort of thing you read about in the Bible, I realised I loved him in a way it's hard to explain. When he died, darling, there was this great emptiness. It was as if everything was at a stand-still. Tom Rodgers was dead, and the farm and everything meant nothing.

Two days after the funeral the solicitor called, and it seems that he left me everything. So, my love, you won't be marrying a pauper. Enough about that.

By the way, Aileen MacMahon, I miss you so much it hurts. It's like a terrible pain I carry around with me all day. When will I see you again? I want to take you in my arms. I want to take that stupid elastic band out of your beautiful hair and watch it blow all over the place. After seeing you at Mass before you left I consoled myself all day with your three childish waves. By the way, I know you worried about what happened down by the river that night. Don't, love, don't. We're not the first couple it happened to, and we won't be the last. For any pain I caused you, physically or mentally, I'm sorry. I'll make it up to you. I know you'll be home at Hallowe'en, and I'm not just counting the hours, I'm now down to the minutes and seconds. It's strange here now. Joe and I do all the work, but we're sort of anchorless without Tom. Still, the show must go on, as they say, and the cows don't know he's dead.

By the way, your parents came to the funeral – there was a huge crowd from all over the place. I stood there with hundreds shaking my hand and saying the usual few words of sympathy. Your father came and spoke a bit, and your mother shook my hand. Hers felt like a dead fish. That woman doesn't like me – the understatement of the year. But Eddie was funny – he marched over to me when I was surrounded by the crowd after the burial. He shook my hand all business-like, and told me he was sorry for my trouble. He's at that awkward age, one day feeling like a man of the world, shaking hands at funerals all business-like and what have you, the next day down by the river wallowing in mud, feeling just like a boy. I'm glad I'm past that age. At least I know what I want – you, you, you.

Write, my love, give my regards to the ebullient Niamh. By the way, I see quite a bit of Richie now and it helps.

All my love,
Yours, Stephen

*

My dearest Stephen,
I got your letter yesterday. I was so happy to hear from you, and yet so sorry to read about your grandfather. I must have been awful for you sitting there for weeks and weeks and then, when things could have been better for you both, he died. Well, as my father would say, 'May heaven be his bed', and I hope it will. I should be very grateful to Tom Rodgers, because if he hadn't reared you I would never have known you. Imagine. What an empty world it would be without Stephen Rodgers.

So now you're a prosperous farmer – the sole owner of Tulla. If I fall out of love with you I'll still marry you for your land and money. Girls did that in my mother's day and are probably still doing it for all we know. You tell me you miss me so much it hurts. Well, I miss you too. In fact, I miss everything about you. And I mean everything. The way you smile, the way you don't smile. I miss the way you look at me for what seems like an age before you say a word. Maggie and Ann used to call it your brooding look. I miss them, but of course I have Niamh. If I hadn't I'd go cracked. I have other friends, but they've never met you so they wouldn't understand. And as for what happened by the river, I keep it a secret inside me. Sometimes I'm so afraid to think about it, and sometimes I'm weak with longing thinking about. Isn't it awful to be confused? I think I'm still wandering in that no-man's land you wrote about when you described Eddie at the funeral. You know, between girlhood and womanhood.

By the way, I'm sorry my mother's hand felt like a dead fish. Now you can't say the same for her daughter. Sometimes, Stephen Rodgers, I think you put me on fire when I was only twelve. Niamh and Richie are definitely doing the strong line. Different from us. He writes the maddest letters and she writes even madder ones back. They're sort of friends and can relax with each other. I hope we're friends too – or are we just crazy in love? I know I can't relax with you. How can you relax with someone you want all the time? It's a sin and I know it.

Now I've said it, and I didn't want to say it. I wanted to write funny innocent little things about the school and the girls and the wild things some of them get up to at weekends.

I think I'll have my hair cut and then you won't be whinging about my poor ponytail. I told you this is a stupid sort of letter. I'll be home at Hallowe'en. I love you.

Yours always,

Love, Aileen.

PS. By the way, I think I'm coming down with a bug – I feel peculiar. I hope I am. I'll get a few days in bed with matron fussing over me and I can wallow in uninterrupted thoughts of you. A.

*

267

Recently Stephen had noticed a new unfamiliar respect when people spoke to him. Men lingered after Mass now and discussed things like the prices the cattle and sheep were making or what the Common Market might mean to the farmers if Ireland joined, or even everyday things like last Sunday's hurling match. Sometimes he noticed the farmers' wives smile too. He wondered if inheriting a farm could blot out the past. Would money and land make them forget that his father was presumably a tinker, a nobody?

But there was no increased warmth from Aileen's mother. She merely acknowledged his presence with a curt not before going her way.

Things had changed in other ways too. Máire had moved permanently in now. After his grandfather had died she told him there was no point in her staying, that she didn't justify her wages. What with Tom gone, there was no great work any more.

'Is that what you want?' Stephen asked her.

'No, but 'tis what's right. There's little to do now with only yourself and Joe, and sure ye could do the bit of work yereselves.' She shrugged, not meeting his eye, and for the first time he noticed how thin and worn she had got. She had worked in Tulla all her life. She had slotted in marriage and children and still managed to give service to Tom Rodgers, his wife, his daughter and his grandson, and had finally given up everything to take care of him. Now she wanted to go because she felt her usefulness was over.

'Máire,' Stephen told her, 'I want you to stay. I know nothing about housework and I've no interest in hens and turkeys. Maybe you'd take these chores on and we'll split the profits.'

He was smiling at her and Máire could see the same pleading look she saw in his mother's eyes the very last time she had seen her. She had been squatting on her bed in a very unladylike manner. Máire recalled the girl had been desperate, locked up and isolated for her gallivanting. 'Máire, a *chroí*,' she had begged, 'please, please, please leave the door unlocked tonight. I can't stay here – I'll go stark raving mad. My father will never know – when he's fast asleep I'll creep away. Please, Máire, and I'll pray for you forever and ever.'

Of course Máire had refused – and thank God she hadn't

let the girl beguile her, the way things had turned out. Now she saw the same shades of pleading in the dark, almost black eyes of Teresa's son. 'Well, if that's what you want I'll stay and be glad to,' she told him. 'Larry Dalton, the lad over in MacMahon's, is getting married and he asked me if he could rent the cottage cheap.'

So she had stayed and seemed happy in her new role. She asked Stephen could she get in a handyman to do a bit of decorating. 'He's great at the papering and painting. We could get the parlour done – 'twould get rid of the feeling of sickness. And maybe your own room – 'tis a long while since anyone put a brush to it.'

Stephen told her that she could have a free hand, but, for some strange reason, when it came to changing his own room, he hesitated. He recalled that peculiar feeling of his mother's presence after he read the diaries. Even now sometimes he felt she was near – at times so near he could reach out and touch her. 'No, Máire, do what you want with the rest of the place, but let my room alone. I'm sort of used to it – maybe I'm getting settled in my ways.'

'All right so. Anyway, you'll be getting married in a few years – sure aren't you the most eligible fellow around now? Joe says from now on you'll be kicking the young wans away, so you will.'

'If I am,' Stephen laughed, 'you'll be the first to know.'

Sitting in her Church History lesson, Niamh gave up trying to concentrate on whether Martin Luther was a good Christian or an evil man, and let her thoughts wander. She was hoping that Aileen might go with her to Skerries for the weekend. Maybe they could go to the pictures. Everyone was talking about *The Robe*. It was supposed to be marvellous and even the Religion teacher, Sister Evangelist, had heard that it was worth seeing.

'Class dismissed,' the nun intoned after the lesson.

After tea, during the break before evening study, Aileen whispered to her, 'Would you come out for a little walk in the grounds? We can go down to the sea wall – I want to ask you something.'

'Okay, but why the mystery? Can't you ask me here? Oh, all right, we'll sneak away. You have me right curious now.'

They stole up to the dormitory, got their gaberdine coats

on and slipped out a side door. Immediately the strong wind gusting from the sea made them put up their hoods. They walked in silence, casting an odd glance backwards in case they were seen. When they reached the sea wall they could see right across the bay to Howth, with all the glittering lights in the houses that went halfway up to the summit. The necklace of light circling the northern coastline always entranced Aileen. 'I think it's the loveliest sight I've ever seen, with the exception of the weir at home.'

'God Almighty, you didn't get me out in a gale force ten to admire the view, did you?' Niamh sounded grumpy.

Aileen said quietly, 'No, I didn't. I want to ask you something.'

Niamh saw the worry in Aileen's eyes. 'What's wrong? What's happened?'

'Did you ever miss a period or go a bit late or anything like that?' Aileen's voice was barely above a whisper.

Niamh was utterly taken aback. Her heart lurched painfully. She tried to hide her astonishment and sound matter-of-fact, as if best friends were in the habit of asking such a thing. 'A missed period or a late period? Let me see. When I started first they went away all together for a few months, then when they came back they came sort of regularly. Why?' The horror of what her question might mean almost suffocated her. 'Jesus, Aileen, you're not really worried about what I think you're worried about, are you? You couldn't be, could you?' Niamh's own desperation made her voice shake. 'Could you?' she repeated weakly.

Aileen was silent for a while. 'I don't know,' she said at last. 'God Almighty, Niamh, I honestly don't know. It never entered my head that anything like that could happen.'

'What did happen? Did you – you know – put yourself in a position where it might?'

'You mean did we – do it? Did we make love? We did, but you won't believe this – it only happened once. Just once.' Aileen sounded so forlorn, so confused, that Niamh reached out and took her arm.

'Listen – I bet it's only a false alarm. Yes, that's what it is. I often heard my mother and her friends talking about false alarms. I was only a kid and they used to gather in our kitchen

270

and I would be there, playing with my dolls and they were always talking about false alarms. I didn't know what it meant then, but I do now. Don't worry. I read somewhere that stress and worry makes them go astray too.' Niamh's tone took on a positive tone. 'Maybe you have TB. Periods go away when you have TB.'

'No, I don't think I have TB – I just feel a bit sick at times.'

'Jasus, Aileen, if you're pregnant what'll you do?'

Aileen looked down at the churning waves hitting the rocks and sending a fine film of spray up to the night sky. 'Maybe I'll just throw myself in.'

'No, you won't. Remember the night years ago when we were in bed, the night the young husband was drowned? We made a promise that if ever one or other of us was in trouble the other would help out. So I'll have to think, won't I?'

The two friends stood wordless, the only sound the thundering sea below, as the enormity of Aileen's problem stunned them. Niamh was the first to speak.

'Richie says Stephen is nuts about you, that ye're a right Romeo and Juliet pair. Tell me,' her voice dropped so low that her words were nearly whipped away in the wind, 'was it wonderful, out of this world or what? I often imagine things but I have no idea.'

'It was sort of frenzied and passionate, and we were powerless to stop it. I'm the one who should have had control – but I hadn't.'

'You're madly in love with him, aren't you?'

'I've always loved him.' Aileen's voice shook and Niamh realised how disastrous it would be if her fears came to pass. She could only imagine the gossip it would cause in the country where the MacMahons were held in high esteem and where Stephen Rodgers was a household name. She recalled the awful hatred Aileen's mother had for Stephen – a peculiar animosity that was hard to explain. She tried to brighten Aileen up. 'Look, tomorrow the whole thing could have changed. You could wake up crippled with cramps in the throes of a period. If so, we'll go out and celebrate.'

Aileen didn't wake up in the throes of a cramp. There was nothing. Just the slight nausea, the lightness in her head and a slight soreness in her breasts.

*

After morning prayers Niamh handed her a letter addressed to Pier House, which her mother had sent on. 'Well, any news?' she whispered.

Aileen shook her head and Niamh squeezed her hand, muttering, 'It'll be all right – I'm going to light a penny candle. It'll be all right.'

Later, during study, Aileen surreptitiously opened the letter.

My dearest Aileen,

I got your letter and I've read it at least a hundred times – maybe more. I hope you're well over the bug and things. There isn't much news – things are quiet this time of year as you well know. Joe and I went to the mart in Waterford last week, selling and buying in. We had a drink in a pub up there on Ballybricken Hill and who did we meet but your father. He came over and talked to us for a long while. I must say he was pleasant, but then again he would be – didn't he father you? Anyway, he asked how things were since Tom died and I told him – a bit lonely. He nodded, and said they were lonely too since you went to school. He looked at me with your extraordinary eyes and I distinctly got the impression that he knew I was seeing you. I would have loved to have asked for your hand in marriage there and then. Imagine the shock. Looking for the hand of a seventeen-year-old girl, going to a posh boarding school in Dublin by all accounts. Sure the poor man would have collapsed on the sawdust-covered floor – not to mention the effect it would have had on your mother.

Richie and I went to the pictures in Ross the other night. We met some girls he introduced – that fellow knows everyone. Anyway, one of them was a friend of his sister's and she asked me to go to a hooley at Hallowe'en. Richie told her to lay off, that I was spoken for. Anyway, listening to him I got a warm feeling that I belonged to you and it was great. Ah, sure, I'm just writing words because there isn't anything else I can do. I can't take you in my arms and kiss you all over, and maybe much, much more. Stop, Rodgers, stop. You're getting excited, and she won't like that. God, Aileen MacMahon, I love you. I can't wait to see you again. By the way, the girl asked me to bring you along to her hooley when you come home. I said I would, but we won't if you don't want it.

Write, my love. Tell me everything and anything – I don't care what it's about.

I love you,
Stephen.

Aileen's hand trembled, rustling the letter. She felt a slight wave of resentment that he was living such an ordinary life, far removed from her mind-blowing worry. Then she dismissed the thought. It was unfair to him, and she was becoming a cranky old bore. How could he possibly know of her predicament? And yet, why had it never entered either of their heads? Both of us are reasonably intelligent, she thought, both of us were brought up on farms where mating is an everyday event nearly always resulting in young.

She reread Stephen's letter and when she came to the part about the girl at the pictures she was amazed at the jealousy which swept over her. She was often surprised that she had Stephen to herself for so long. He was so handsome, so different, and girls in the towns didn't give a tinker's curse about who his father was or what his mother did. Then again, she was the only one who knew that his father wasn't what people thought. If it came out that his father was a writer it would give him such a romantic aura that ever girl in the place would want him.

She reread Stephen's words of love and his desire to be with her, and once again dismissed her awful thoughts. She was turning into a jealous, resentful, pregnant nag.

Could it be possible she was pregnant with his baby? If she was she couldn't tell him. At least not for ages and ages. She wouldn't tell him at Hallowe'en – she might tell him at Christmas. Maybe at Christmas she would show. She closed her eyes, blotting out the unthinkable horror of her mother's reaction when the news would eventually break. No, no, she could never tell her mother. Never. Never. Maybe she was getting carried away with the whole terrible prospect. Her second period was due now, and maybe it would come and all her terrible fears would be for nothing. Niamh lit a candle for her every single day, and Aileen prayed in front of the Tabernacle in the oratory. She didn't think that God would

273

answer her prayers because of the terrible sin, yet still she prayed.

After her bath that Saturday she had surreptitiously examined her stomach. Flat as ever. No sign of change. Her breasts might be a little bigger, but she had been well endowed since she was thirteen. But had those blue veins zig-zagging through her white skin always been there? She wasn't sure. She wasn't sure of anything.

Dearest Stephen,
I was glad to get your letter. I was envious to see you're having a nice, easy grand time and here we are studying our heads off for the Leaving Cert. I was glad you met my father after the mart – it somehow made me feel good you could stop and chat and talk. The other night I was lying in bed thinking of all the old stuff. In a way wasn't it pre-ordained – is that the word – that your mother and my father didn't marry? If they had, we wouldn't exist. Now isn't that the most bleak thought? Imagine neither of us existing.

So, you're having a ball going to the pictures and meeting pretty girls who ask you to parties and things. I was a bit jealous when I read it, but I wasn't when I reread it. Like you, I wish we could be together. I want to run my hands through your black hair and my finger over your brows, and feel the roughness when you need a shave. I want to hold you tight and keep you from being picked up by stray girls who might wander into the picture house. See – I am becoming a jealous bore. Do you ever see Eddie after Mass or after a hurling match or anywhere? If you do, tell him to write to me. I want to get one of his funny, mad letters so that I can laugh. Write, my love. Tell Richie I was asking for him. Write.
   All, and I mean all, my love,
   Aileen.

Darling Aileen,
I got your letter and as usual it turned an ordinary muck-slogging farmer's day into something special. It was my turn to be jealous that Eddie could make you laugh and I can't. Why am I not witty or funny? I envy the Eddies and Richies of this world, fellows who can make my beautiful

girl laugh. I'll have to do a course or something in Dublin on How to Make a Girl Laugh. Joking aside, did I perceive (nice word) something sad or pensive about your letter? Don't be like that – soon we'll be together. Hey – crystal ball – remember, I know these things.

By the way, I see Ann and Maggie from time to time and they seem to be doing strong lines with the Brennan brothers. They tell me you write to them, so I'm sure they write back and you know all about them.

A sad little thing happened last week. Old Shep died. I don't think he had any interest in life after the death of my grandfather. He just lay there staring into the fire. If he heard someone coming up the boreen he would perk up and then, when it wasn't old Tom, the life would go out of him. I didn't think a dog could die of a broken heart but Shep did. Of course, if I couldn't end my days with you I too would die of a broken heart – there isn't a doubt in the world about it.

I love you,
Stephen.

*

Four weeks later Niamh, who had left the classroom to run an errand for Sister Xavier, came back into the room to find it abuzz. The French teacher hadn't come in yet, and the girls were in a tight knot.

'What happened? What's all the commotion about?'

'It's Aileen,' Stella O'Keeffe told her, 'she just keeled over and fainted, hitting her head off the desk. They carted her off to the sick bay. No end to the excitement and the blood – she looked awful.'

Niamh's heart froze inside her, yet she tried to appear casual. 'Maybe she's getting the flu or something.'

'Maybe. She looked like death itself, the lucky sucker. Wouldn't I give my eye teeth to faint and hit my head off the desk and be carted off to be fussed over, and miss all the bloody study?'

Niamh's thoughts were in a tailspin, imagining Aileen on the broad of her back being examined by a matron who could instantly detect something as simple as a period cramp. Would they call a doctor? Would her condition be diagnosed? Could a simple examination with a stethoscope show that a girl was pregnant? Niamh knew Aileen had long since missed her second period; when Aileen had told her, it had been Niamh who had broken down and cried uncontrollably.

The next day Niamh approached Sister Evangelist and asked could she visit Aileen. She was quietly but firmly told no; Aileen was quite run-down and anaemic and needed a lot of rest. Niamh stood there, small and determined. 'When will visitors be allowed?' she stubbornly persisted. 'You see, Sister, she's my very best friend and I would love to see her.'

'We'll let you know, Niamh, in a few days.' Sister Evangelist swept away, leaving behind the peculiar nun's smell of soap and serge.

That night sleep eluded Niamh completely. She listened to the sea tossing and tumbling down below as she tossed and turned, distraught over Aileen's dilemma. She prayed that they wouldn't detect what was wrong with her; she prayed that Aileen would get her period; she prayed that Mary MacMahon wouldn't go completely berserk if the unthinkable happened. She just prayed. She fell asleep finally, and when she woke up with the worst headache imaginable, she told herself that Aileen couldn't be feeling much worse than she was.

After lunch, Niamh sauntered over to the sick bay, hoping she'd catch a glimpse of the matron, who seemed the motherly sort who might let her in. Instead she met Sister Martha, a lay sister. 'Hello, Sister Martha,' she greeted her – airy, casual, all brightness. 'I was just dropping in to see Aileen MacMahon.

'You must wait there like a good girl and I'll see if it's allowed,' the nun said in her lilting Cork accent, leaving Niamh fidgeting anxiously, hoping that her casual approach might succeed.

A few minutes later the nun emerged from the sick bay. 'Sorry, Niamh, but Aileen isn't allowed any visitors for a while.'

Niamh, utterly frustrated, trailed away. How could she be expected to go on in a school where her best friend was held captive until they decided her fate? She would have given her right hand to talk to someone but there was no one she could trust with her friend's unwanted situation.

Wandering in to the little chapel, Niamh prayed like she had never prayed before. Two elderly nuns were kneeling in front of the altar, heads bowed. Looking up at the sanctuary lamp, red and flickering slightly, at the immaculate white altar cloth with the gold thread embroidery, at the beautifully arranged chrysanthemums, Niamh thought it might be great to be a nun. Away from all temptation and certainly away from the sins of the flesh. Thou shalt not commit adultery – oh God, Aileen and Stephen had committed the sin which caused so many girls to nudge, wink and whisper, their imagination spiralling out of control, wondering what on earth 'it' would be like. How had Aileen put it? *It was frenzied and passionate and we were powerless to stop it.* Dear Blessed Virgin, help them. You see, I know them and they're very good really, despite what happened. The red sanctuary lamp flickered momentarily – maybe it was the draught or maybe the movement meant that someone heard her distracted prayer.

That night sleep was once again slow to come. The next day was Friday. She'd make another effort then, Niamh vowed.

The other girls in the class were getting quite curious about Aileen, wondering and whispering about the contagious illness she must have picked up, that visitors weren't allowed.

If she couldn't see her tomorrow she would look for permission to go home for the weekend. Maybe a break from the terrible worry would bring some peace. Maybe in a roundabout way she could talk to her mother and get advice. Niamh thought of Richie and in some way found a small measure of calmness. He was such good company, so funny and always in good humour. He seemed keen on her. They had kissed, warm – funny, kisses, that's if kisses could be funny. He called her his tomboy because of her cropped brown hair, and she called him Mister Paintseller because of his job. She felt so good with him, and yet the thought of going as far as Aileen and Stephen was unthinkable. But the thought of anyone else going out with him was a bit unthinkable too. Her last thought before falling asleep was *maybe I'll see Aileen tomorrow. Maybe she'll be fine and her symptoms were a false alarm.*

Yes, she thought sleepily, I'll see her tomorrow if it kills me.

She didn't.

Niamh Turley never saw her best friend again.

Chapter Twenty-Two

Jack the Post delivered the letter on Wednesday. In vaguely familiar handwriting it was addressed to Mrs Mary MacMahon. Mary didn't want to open it then, knowing that Jack's pervading curiosity would try to glean some information about its contents.

In the lonely years that were to follow, the memory of that morning often came back to her.

Mary put the letter behind the third plate on the shelf. Had she a sense of foreboding even then? She remembered thinking that the old willow-patterned dinner service needed a good wash. It was old and belonged to Denis's mother. She remembered saying to Jack, 'I'll read it later. I enjoy it better if I have all my jobs done.'

'I see it's from County Dublin too. Ah, sure Dublin is such a big place, sprawling all over the place. Young people trying their luck up there all the time,' he told her.

'True, Jack, true.'

He knew that if he stayed there a month of Sundays he wouldn't find out what was in that letter. A close woman was Mary MacMahon. A good person, but not a chatty woman. Still, if Denis MacMahon was happy with her, who was he to complain? 'I'll be on my way, Mary – thanks for the tea.'

When he was gone Mary took down the letter, her movements curiously slow. It was from her second cousin, Sister Philomena, in the convent where Aileen went to school. It was a short, nicely written letter, telling her that Aileen was indisposed and that it would be better if she had some rest at home. Would they come to collect her as soon as possible? Mary's heart started to race, and a knot of fear tangled her stomach. Not well – *indisposed* – rest. Jesus above, why would she be coming home for a few weeks unless it was serious? *Indisposed.* What did *indisposed* really mean? God in his heaven, what could be wrong with a seventeen-year-old girl who was never, ever a day sick in her life?

278

She'd have to talk to Denis. He wouldn't be able to throw much light on the subject, but just to talk to him would help. Later maybe she'd ring from the post office to the school and find out more.

She found her husband hosing out the milking parlour. There was a stolidness about him, and his everyday action brought some measure of calm to her churning thoughts. She even tried to remember what the doctor in the nursing home had told her to do when panic struck. *Take deep breaths – break away from what you're doing and do something else,* he told her. It was a small exercise that had proved helpful to other patients. Well, she was doing something else – hadn't she run helter-skelter out to find Denis? But she wasn't breathing deeply. She simply hadn't time.

'I got a letter from the school. It's Aileen. She's not well. My cousin, the nun, Sister Philomena, says she's indisposed – she wants us to take her home for a bit, to collect her as soon as possible. God and his Blessed Mother, Denis, what could it be at all?'

'Sure there's nothing terrible in that. Maybe it's a girl's ailment – anaemia or something. Don't worry, we'll go up tomorrow. Isn't she due home next week anyway? She'll be game ball soon, don't worry.'

Sister Philomena greeted them warmly and brought them into a room that looked like a parlour. There was a round table and leather-covered chairs, and an uncomfortable horse-hair sofa. The room was a place of pale walls and a few framed holy pictures, with a baby grand piano over at the wall away from the tall marble fireplace. The room was heated to take the chill away.

'Sit down, Mary, Denis, make yourselves comfortable. Sister Martha will be along with tea soon. We won't discuss anything until you've had a nice cup of tea and some scones. You must be exhausted after the journey?'

Mary MacMahon had no appetite for the tea or scones which were obviously nice, seeing that her husband managed to devour four of them. When they had finished the nun spoke. Mary wondered if it was her imagination, or was there a reluctance to talk on her cousin's part?

'The Reverend Mother decided it was better if I told you. It was also decided that Aileen shouldn't be present. She fainted during class and knocked her head off the corner of the desk – just a bad bruise, nothing more.'

Why is she going on about a bit of a faint and a bruise, Mary thought. Surely they didn't drive all the way from County Kilkenny to hear of a faint and a bruise.

She could hear her cousin's soft modulated tone as if from afar. 'She was taken to sick bay and examined by matron, who came to the conclusion that she was anaemic.'

Anaemic, she thought. So Denis was right, God love him, and funny he never hit the nail on the head before. Anyway, Aileen was hopeless when it came to vegetables, particularly cabbage. Everyone knew there was iron in cabbage, but you couldn't make that girl eat it for love or money.

'The matron decided she'd get the doctor to have a look at her when he was visiting another girl. He suggested some blood and urine tests.' Sister Philomena stopped then and her kind grey eyes scanned both their faces, aware of how distraught and agitated her cousin Mary was. Her husband Denis looked solid and calm, and yet, in his rather startling blue eyes, there was concern. 'The results of the tests showed that Aileen is pregnant.'

The silence that followed was like a curtain that descended, enclosing them in a frozen time warp until the shock of the news sunk in. Mary was the first to speak.

'Nora, there must be a terrible mistake. She couldn't be – pregnant.' Mary's voice was a terrified squeak, and in shock she didn't realise that she had called her cousin by her own name.

'Pregnant.' Denis had found his voice. 'She can't be. Sure she's just a child.'

'I know.' The nun's eyes were full of sympathy. 'I know, Denis, what a shock this is. Such a lovely girl, so bright, with a good future ahead of her. She could have gone on to training for the teaching.'

The nun's calm discussing of what her daughter's future might have been was enough to snap the taut spring inside Mary. She jumped up and, thumping the table, screamed, 'Pregnant – I don't believe it! It isn't true. It can't be. It can't be. Tell her, Denis,' she screamed, 'that somebody is making this up – someone who hates us. Tell her.' Mary flung herself on to the sofa, loud sobs wracking her thin frame, her shoulders jerking and moving as she wept uncontrollable tears.

Denis walked over to her, putting a hand on her shoulder. 'Take it easy, girl, take it easy. It isn't the end of the world. Easy now.'

She continued to sob, in wracking heart-rending sounds. Denis looked at the nun and then back at his distraught wife, only too well aware that all Mary's carefully laid-out plans for Aileen were over. Her dreams were in dust. Mary lifted her ravaged face and looked at her husband through her drenched eyes. 'We're destroyed, Denis, utterly destroyed,' she whispered. 'We can never lift our heads again.'

'Don't be silly, girl.' He sounded unconvincing. 'Of course we can. Sure, it'll be only a nine-day wonder – she isn't the first and she won't be the last.'

'Don't say that!' Mary broke into fresh wild hysterical sobs. 'Don't say that about our Aileen. Other girls, yes – but not Aileen.'

She started to moan softly, rocking to and fro and staring ahead with wild terrible eyes staring into a future where her daughter's life lay in tatters. Sister Philomena whispered to Denis, 'The shock must have been too much for her. I'll go and fetch the Reverend Mother – she might be able to help.'

Denis and Mary were left alone as she went to get the nun. My girl is somewhere in this building, Denis thought. She knows what's going on. Then again, is she my girl any more? Isn't she used and defiled now?

Of course he knew who the father of the child was – Stephen Rodgers, the young man who could inspire the sort of hatred in Mary that you'd have for the devil himself. He had known there was something serious between them. He had seen them talking after Mass – he knew that Aileen had met him on those summer evenings when her friend Niamh was down. He had given his daughter too much freedom when Mary had been in hospital. He should have been stricter, more of a listening father instead of the plodding workhouse he had become. Jesus above, what would become of the child?

Child? She wasn't a child any more, but a young woman who knew what it was like to have a man. It was unthinkable – yet couldn't he still recall a time, long ago now, when young wild blood went singing through his veins on a summer's evening.

Sitting in the nun's parlour watching his shocked wife rocking to and fro, moaning softly, Denis saw Teresa Rodgers. She came with her beguiling look and her black mop of hair, with her taunting, teasing smile. God, if he was honest, wouldn't he have taken her just like her son had taken his daughter if she had given him half a chance?

'Good evening.' The Reverend Mother entered quietly, taking in the harrowing scene of the demented, moaning woman and the troubled fair-haired man. Putting her hand on Mary's shoulder, she shook her gently but spoke firmly. 'Do try and pull yourself together, Mrs MacMahon. I appreciate what a shock this is to you, but we must be sensible, and think and plan ahead.'

Mary raised her bloated, tear-stained face and gazed at the nun wordlessly.

'If you both wish, we can make arrangements for Aileen to go to England until after the baby is born. No one need know. According to the doctor, she's less than three months pregnant, so perhaps she could live with a relative in England before going into a special facility where she will wait until after the baby is born. It has happened to decent girls before, and things have turned out quite satisfactorily. After the baby is adopted, Aileen can continue her education if she so desires. I know of one case where the parents explained their daughter's absence merely by stating that she had gone to a finishing school in England. I need not mention the importance of total secrecy, and needless to say, the young man responsible should never be told.'

The possibility of a cover-up for Aileen's disgrace – the chance that the neighbours need never find out – brought a small measure of sanity to Mary MacMahon.

'I have a cousin in England – a cousin who is very close to me,' she said hopefully. 'I'm sure she might help until – until–' Mary couldn't bring herself to say 'baby'. She felt if she put words on her daughter's condition it would become reality. The terrible realisation that all her plans for her daughter were in tatters was slowly sinking in. She daren't even think of the young man responsible – if she were to dwell on him for a single second, it would be to wish him dead. As long as night followed day, Mary would never, ever forgive her daughter for what happened. How she could have let herself down and behave like a common cottier or a city factory girl, Mary couldn't possibly imagine. As for Stephen Rodgers, she had known from the first day she had seen him he was trouble. She knew it was wrong – sinful – to feel such hatred, such inexplicable animosity, for someone who had never wronged her. She had even asked herself if her loathing could have spring from an irrational jealousy. Once, she had admitted to it in Confession, and the priest had told her to say an aspiration when the thoughts came. There was no aspiration in the whole wide world that would make Mary feel better now. She hated Stephen Rodgers. She hated him so much she could kill him. His mother had played around with her husband, and her son had now destroyed her lovely daughter.

With a start she realised that Denis and the Reverend Mother were staring at her and she grappled with herself to regain composure. 'Reverend Mother,' she brokenly explained, 'I don't want to see Aileen. If she could stay here, maybe until I contact Peggy, my cousin in London, and then go straight over, it would be better. You see, we have a small daughter and a young son, and I think it would be best if they didn't see her. If she could stay here, I would be grateful.'

Denis stared at her. How could she not want to see her own daughter, her own flesh and blood, the light of her eyes? 'Mary, we must see her.' His tone was gentle. 'You don't think I came all the way up here to go home without seeing her? She's our girl – we can't just dump her now.'

'You can go, Denis, but I won't.' Her voice shook, but she had made up her mind.

'Perhaps, Mary,' Sister Philomena suggested, 'you should go with Denis. Put yourself in the girl's place. She's young, and she needs support from her mother in particular. I advise you to see her.'

'I agree with Sister Philomena, Mrs MacMahon,' the Reverend Mother advised. 'As for her staying here for an extra day or two, there is no problem.'

'Thank you, Mother,' Mary whispered between lips that were dry and cracked.

Denis MacMahon, sitting in the convent parlour in County Dublin, with the smell of beeswax and camphor, never felt as uncomfortable in his whole life. He felt unreal. Maybe it's a dream, he thought. Maybe I'll wake up and hear Eddie and Maeve squabbling and the dogs barking and the cows lowing, waiting to be milked. But no, he was still in his new Sunday suit and his white shirt and his best tie, talking to two nuns who had told him that his beloved eldest daughter was pregnant. His wife looked like death, and he realised if bad news could kill, she would undoubtedly be dead now.

'Come on, girl,' he coaxed, 'of course we'll go up and see our Aileen. Sure we must.'

Mary ignored him and started to cry again, quietly this time, as if all her energy had been spent in the first torrential outpour. 'I can't, Denis, I can't. Please don't make me. Please. You see, I want to remember her the way she was,' she said brokenly.

'You're not making sense, talking about her as if she was dead.'

'She's dead to me,' Mary told him quietly.

'All right, Mr MacMahon,' the Reverend Mother said, 'if your wife feels so strongly about it, perhaps it would be better she didn't see Aileen. I'll take you up to see her. You see, she's expecting to be going home with you, so the change in plan may upset her. Then again, it may not.'

Aileen was sitting at the side of the bed, her blonde hair in the familiar ponytail. She was dressed in her school uniform; there was a suitcase at her feet and her gaberdine overcoat was folded neatly on her lap.

Denis MacMahon didn't consider himself an emotional man but somehow, looking at her sitting patiently, her pallor obvious, he felt a lump in his throat which nearly choked him. 'Hello, girl. Sure how are you?'

His words were exactly what she expected from her father. No shouts, screams or recriminations. Looking at his beloved face, she felt tears prickle her eyes. I won't cry, she told herself. Not now – not yet. Her father looked so uncomfortable and miserable, as if he was the cause of all the trouble. She never remembered loving him so much as she did this minute, now that her time with him, as they both knew it, was over. Over, because she had, according to all the accepted social rulings, disgraced herself.

'I'm sorry, Dad. I know I've let you and Mam down. I'm really sorry.'

He walked over to her side of the bed and awkwardly sat down beside her. Putting his arm around her, he hugged her close. He didn't try to minimise or make light of her situation. 'Ah Aileen, 'tis a terrible pity so it is. Your mother is like a madwoman down there in the nuns' parlour. She put such a store on you, so she did. She wanted nothing only the best – the very best for you.'

'And now I've let her down. I've let all of you down.'

'Aileen, there's worse to come.' Denis seemed to have difficulty going on. His worried blue eyes, so like her own, roamed over her face, then dropped and hurriedly looked away as if he'd seen something he didn't want to see. 'She doesn't want to see you – doesn't want to speak to you. I tried, but she's like a rock. She says she wants to remember you the way you were.'

The shadows deepened in her intense blue eyes as she bit her lip. 'So, Dad, what'll I do? I can't make myself invisible. If I go home, she has to see me.'

He cleared his throat and she could see how nervous he was. Whatever was coming, she could already see her father was unhappy about it. 'Look, love, the plan is that the nuns will keep you for another day or two. Then you're going to London to live with Peggy – you remember Peggy. That's it for now – well, until –'

Aileen could see how embarrassed he was and tried to help him. 'Until my trouble is over, Dad – is that it?'

'Then you'll come home and things will be the same.' He tried to persuade himself that it would happen.

'I won't, Dad, and you know it. No matter how you and Mam cover up, people will poke out the situation and start adding two and two together. If I came back it would be to nudges and whispers and pointing fingers – you know that. I can never come home.'

'So what do you suggest?'

'Maybe Stephen and I could get married. We love each other. I know this sounds corny, Dad – but you'll never know how much. I never thought you could love anyone so much.'

'Jasus, Aileen.' He looked around almost fearfully, as if his taking of the Lord's name could float down through the ceiling into the nuns' parlour below. 'If your mother heard you even suggesting such a thing she would drop dead. He's the last person in the whole of Ireland she would tolerate. It would surely kill her.'

'Because she hates him! Her hate is a sickness, Dad – you know it is. It's a sickness,' she repeated.

'Don't say that – it's not right to say things like that about your mother.'

'But it's true. And you like Stephen – you like him in your heart, I know you do. You knew his mother and you liked her. Maybe you even loved her, so you can't hate her son, Dad – can you?'

'Shush, love – that's all in the past. I do like the lad – he's a fine, hard-working fellow. But stop, don't even think of marriage. If anything like that happened it would kill your mother, the same as if you put a knife through her. Look love, I never asked you to do me a favour, did I now?'

'No, Dad,' she said. 'You didn't.'

'But I'm asking one now. I don't ever want you to see him again. Ever. He must never be told about this. These things happen to young people and you'll both get over it. When it's all over, you can get on with your life, go on with your education. I'll see you right financially – but girl, you must promise me now.'

'Dad, I could say yes, but I mightn't mean it. I love you, Dad, I really do. But Stephen is my life. Honestly, it's hard to explain, but maybe I wouldn't want to go on without him. It's terrible but that's the way it is,' Aileen whispered as she looked at him, her blue eyes glittering with tears.

Suddenly her steady-as-a-rock father started to cry, hard, unfamiliar, tearing sounds wracking his solid frame. He drew her near and they hugged each other closely, their tears flowing uncontrollably, as if their hearts were broken.

Chapter Twenty-Three

Like someone in a trance, Aileen embarked on the journey to London. Sister Philomena brought her to the boat in Dun Laoghaire. Her case was packed with clothes her mother had sent on to the school. Her uniform was left behind in the school to be sent on home – 'You'd never know, it might come in handy for Maeve.' Maeve, her little nosy, precocious, demanding sister who seemed to live in a different world now, with Eddie and his mad plans and funny ways. She mustn't think of him or Maeve or Niamh or any of her friends.

And she mustn't think of Stephen.

Her mother would die, her father had told her. *Die.* Did normal mothers die because their daughters did wrong? Aileen doubted it. Then again, her mother wasn't normal, that was part of the problem. In the past Aileen heard of girls who got into trouble and who took the boat, and who were never heard of again. It happened because the men in their lives dumped them, didn't want to know. But it was different for her – Stephen loved her. What had he said? *I think I've loved you forever.* If he knew about her he would, in all probability, be very happy. He'd consider the baby a bond between them that even her mother couldn't sever.

She mustn't think of Stephen – if she did she'd probably die. She wasn't sure if people died of longing – the only thing she was sure of right now was that she was on a boat that was ploughing across the Irish Sea, taking her to England. She had plenty of money; her father had seen to that. She also had written instructions that the boat would arrive in Holyhead at half-one in the morning and she was to get on a train to London which would arrive at a place named Euston Station at half-past six. She was to make her way to a café named Lyons which was situated in the station, and there she would meet Peggy, who would take her to her home in Islington.

"'Tis a calm crossing – we're lucky.'

Aileen glanced up and saw a young man with fair hair and a freckled face. "'Tis, I suppose,' she said. 'Maybe we are lucky.'

'Have you been across before?'

'No, this is the first time.'

He had been watching her for nearly an hour now, sitting there, her hands in her pockets, her long blonde hair tied back, her lovely face cold and indifferent. He could see she had little or no interest in the journey, almost as if she was a habitual traveller. Yet she had said that this was her first time. She was some looker all right. He had been trying to pluck up courage for half an hour to put his talk on her.

'Are you looking for a job?' he asked.

She looked at him as if seeing him for the first time and wondered how she'd get rid of him. Yet he looked harmless enough – maybe if she talked to him the journey might be less boring. And, more importantly, she wouldn't have time to think. 'No, I'm not going to work – I'm going to visit a cousin in London.' For a second a shadow of a smile played around her mouth as she wondered what he would do if she told him the truth. *I'm banished to London because they tell me I'm expecting a baby, and that has happened because I made love once – just once – with someone I absolutely adore. But that someone is bad news to my poor sick mother, so I'm on the boat. Even now, that someone thinks I'm winging my way home for Hallowe'en.* She wondered what Eddie and Maeve would think when she didn't turn up. Would they torture her parents with questions? Stephen would wait for her outside Mass and then outside the dance hall in Ross, and would go away, puzzled because she wasn't there. What would Niamh be thinking? She was the only friend who knew her terrible predicament.

'I'm working at the building sites in London for three year now,' the young man was saying.

She wondered had he been talking away whilst she was sunk in thought. 'I believe there's a lot of money to be made in England at the building.'

'Aye – but it's not what it was. After the war and in the early fifties, some made a fortune. But things are not too bad. I'm savin' to buy a cottage and maybe a small holdin' when I come back. By the way, my name is Johnnie Davis – I'm from County Meath.' He held out his hand and she took it in hers. The thought came that it was thinner and smaller than Stephen's but the hardness and the calluses were there just the same.

'I'm Aileen MacMahon and I'm from County Kilkenny –

I'm a farmer's daughter and I do know a little about holdings and things.' They laughed; the ice thawed a little.

Jasus, he thought, she's a beautiful young wan altogether, but a bit dead in herself. And little or no smiles like most other young wans you'd meet. Then again, some of them would be lookin' for somethin'. And she couldn't be feeling sick, because the Irish Sea was like a duck pond tonight. 'Would you like a cup of tea?' he asked.

'Thanks, I'd love one.' She watched Johnnie go for the tea and noticed that his raincoat was shabby but his shoes were well soled and shining. His fair reddish hair was cut short and close to his head, and he wasn't tall when he stood up.

When he came back he was carrying the cups carefully so as not to spill a drop. She sipped it wordlessly. 'Would you like more sugar?' he asked.

'No, it's fine.' She actually thought it was about the worst cup of tea she had ever tasted, but she didn't want to hurt him. She even accepted the plastic-wrapped fruit cake as if she were eager for plastic-wrapped fruit cake. They sipped their tea and ate their cake and she felt she was lucky she had met him – if he did nothing else he would at least shorten the journey into the unknown.

'There are ten of us,' Johnnie told her, 'living in a two-bedroomed cottage on twenty acres. I'm third down the line and sure the mice in the fields have morn' us. So there was nothin' but to cross the water and make a livin'. I have a brother and two sisters over there, and they're makin' out too.'

Aileen felt it was right she should tell him a bit about herself and not be too mysterious. 'I'm the eldest of three – two girls and a boy. We have a farm – I think it's a hundred and fifty acres.' She heard his impressed whistle and continued, 'Having a sizable farm doesn't mean you have much money. My father works like a slave and we help him a lot. My mother slaves too – we have only one labourer so Dad does most of the work himself.' Thinking of her father brought the treacherous little lump to her throat. She swallowed it quickly and went on, trying to sound bright. 'I have a brother and he's fourteen, so I suppose he'll inherit the lot. He's welcome to it. I honestly think a farmer's wife has a terrible life.'

'So you won't marry a farmer?'

He saw her hesitate. A faint blush highlighted the blazing blue of her eyes. I've said something, he thought, I've said something to make her uncomfortable. He wondered if he would say what he liked to this girl. On the boat they could share confidences that weren't possible at a dance or a hooley or some such place. People who met crossing the Irish Sea were indeed ships that pass in the night. They never met each other again. he knew. He had to put his talk on so many people going over and back to England. 'As I was sayin', you won't marry a farmer?'

There was a questioning look about Johnnie's smile and Aileen warmed to him, thinking once again she was lucky to have met him. 'You're fierce curious, Johnnie Davis, so you are.' She was smiling slightly and he could see her white even teeth. The thought came involuntarily and out of the blue. What would it be like to kiss a girl like that? She had a sort of class about her, a kind of quality – God Almighty, wouldn't he be boasting about it until the cows came home?'

'Maybe I am,' he said, recovering, 'but sure 'tis curiosity that keeps the Irish going. The English, sure they never want to know a thing about you. The again, they think most of us are dirt – *no Irish, no Italians, no dogs*. God, sure you'd see that on the ads when you're looking for digs.'

'That's terrible, so it is.' Her blue eyes showed a puzzled sympathy, as if she had never heard such a thing before. 'Tell me, have you a girl?'

'Now it's you that is fierce curious. But I haven't – not now. But if you ask me in two weeks' time I might have. The Irish girls are lonely over there, and 'tis easy to pick 'em up.' He was smiling broadly, his pale blue eyes meeting hers, and inside her she felt the terrible weight she seemed to be carrying for months now thaw and lighten. 'So have you a fella?'

'I have, and he's a farmer but he doesn't want to stay farming. He wants to go to Australia – some notion he has.'

'And what will he do with the farm, and will you go with him?'

'Maybe I will – if things work out.'

Suddenly she tried to stifle a yawn, and Johnnie could see the exhaustion in her eyes. The girl plainly had something on her mind.

'I'm sorry, I haven't slept much lately,' she apologised. She didn't want to give to much away, and added, 'I go to boarding school and the girls chatter a lot in the dormitory – it's not easy to sleep. I believe we have a five-hour journey to London?'

'Aye – we have a hoor of a journey to London, that I can tell you.' He watched as she tried to stifle another yawn. Without thinking, he put his arm around her and gently pressed her head on his shoulder. 'Rest now – you'll be okay with Johnnie Davis.'

Aileen closed her eyes and in minutes she was asleep. Johnnie tightened his arm around her protectively. He was so curious about this girl. She was obviously well off. Her clothes weren't the sort his mother bought in the cheap shops in Drogheda. He could feel the soft wool of her coat and noticed that her long, shapely legs were encased in pale tan nylons. She wore flat-heeled shoes and he could see they were a good-quality leather, brown and laced, a bit like a schoolgirl would wear. Then again, she had told him she was at a boarding school. There was something wrong – maybe she would confide in him on the long train journey.

As he sat getting cramped and cold, but patiently holding her, he hoped that the few snatched hours of sleep would take away her obvious exhaustion. Her mouth was slightly open, her breath soft on his neck. He watched her breasts rise and fall inside the shapely coat. One thing he knew as he looked at her: unlike the ships that pass in the night, he wouldn't forget her.

'Wake up, wake up – we're here.'

His voice came from the edges of fragmented dreams. Cramped and cold, confused and disoriented Aileen looked at her companion. 'We're here,' he told her gently. 'We're in Holyhead and we must get a dacent seat on the train. Sure, God love you, you don't know where ye are.'

Aileen sat up swiftly. 'You'd better go to the ladies' now – twould be better than on the train,' Johnnie advised.

'Thanks,' she nodded, and made her way to the Ladies' where a short queue had already formed. Glancing at herself in the mirror, she told herself she looked like an old hag. Suddenly, without warning, she started to retch violently into the wash basin. As her terrible vomiting continued, a sympathetic woman near said, 'Terrible for you, love. Still, it was a good crossing, although some people need only know they're on the water and they'll get sick.'

Aileen ran the tap and smiled shakily at the woman as she wiped her mouth with one of the linen hankies her mother had sent her.

'Anyway, love,' the woman whispered, 'sea-sickness is good for you – it cleans you out.'

If only you knew, Aileen thought, this isn't sea-sickness and it won't clean me out.

Feeling shaky and weak, she went to find Johnnie Davis. He was standing in a queue with her suitcases and his own. 'Are you okay?' he asked anxiously, noting the pallor and the shadows under her eyes.

'I've been sick,' she explained and then bit her lip. Her sickness would have him puzzled – the sea was calm as a mirror; he had even pointed that out. No one should get sick on a crossing like that except a girl who was pregnant and puzzled, and knew little or nothing about the nausea of the first four months of pregnancy. 'I'll be fine now, I'm not used to travel,' she told him.

Suddenly it was all bustle, with people shouting to their companions as the boat shuddered and docked. The passengers trooped out into the chilly darkness, the wind somehow fresh and welcoming after the confines of the boat. Aileen stayed close to Johnnie, once again grateful that she had met him. It meant she wouldn't have to think – he would lead the way and she would follow.

The ticket checkers and porters had queer lilting musical accents – of course, she realised, she was in Wales now. Then there were more shouts and confusion as the crowd made their exhausted way to the train. She could see Johnnie was anxious to get a good seat – he ran ahead of her and she could barely make him out as he ran carrying her large case as well as his own bags. She saw him open the carriage door way down near the noisy hissing engine and look around, waving wildly at her as she ran to join him. They were lucky – the carriage had only three other occupants, two men with raincoats and caps, obviously returning to work in England, and a young man, probably going in search of work. Johnnie had kept the window seat for her, whispering, 'You won't see much in the dark, but when it gets lighter you'll get your first glance of John Bull.' She smiled at him as she sank gratefully down beside him. The train revved and shunted and pulled noisily away, obviously on time because one of the men nodded at his gold watch approvingly as the train gathered speed.

Aileen was glad he didn't put his arm around her now. It had been all right on the boat but now things seemed different. 'Tell me more about yourself,' she asked when they had settled, 'about your brothers and sisters, about County Meath. I know nothing about it except Tara is there, and isn't there a prehistoric tomb at Newgrange?'

Johnnie smiled indulgently. 'That's the County Meath the Americans want to see. We know about these places, but that's about it. I told you there were ten of us, and we were poor as church mice. My father was a drunkard who drank every penny he earned. My poor mother's life was hell. Strange, though, when he hadn't the drink in him he was all right – but when he was drunk he was a monster. 'Tis a terrible thing the drink, that's why my brothers or sisters don't touch it. We saw what it does – he's dead now and I should be charitable, but I hope he's roastin'. It's wrong to feel that, I suppose?'

'I suppose it is.'

'That's all to tell about Johnnie Davis. But I have a notion that you've had a more interesting life.'

'No, I haven't. The usual life on a farm – then I was sent to boarding school in Dublin like a lot of farmer's daughters. Now I'm going to visit my mother's cousin for a bit.'

'A quare time to be goin' visitin' and we nearly into the winter. Why now?'

'Because she has two small sons, and well – she's sick.' Suddenly Aileen felt uncomfortable with the lie and she was glad the light in the carriage was poor so that Johnnie couldn't see her telltale blush.

''Tis strange that your cousin had to send to Ireland for help – there's plenty of help over there. Listen, Aileen girl, is it what I think it is?'

She looked at him in amazement and she noted that his eyes were full of genuine concern – not the village type of nosy curiosity that she hated. He looked kind, even caring, as if his question was asked for the best of reasons. Did she dare take this stranger into her confidence? Oh God above, what a relief it would be to share the burden with someone young – someone who might understand. It seemed years since she had spoken to Niamh. Since then, she had been so much alone, a pariah – someone outside the fold. She lifted her eyes and met his gaze steadily. 'Yes – it's what you think.'

His sympathy was obvious in his kind eyes. Taking her hand in his hard, callused grasp, he said, 'You can always change your mind and come with me. I'll take care of you and the nipper too, when the time comes.'

Her eyes filled with tears – tears she had kept at bay since her father had left her. 'Thanks, Johnnie.' Her voice was more like a sob. 'But you see, I'm spoken for.'

'And tell me, where is he now when you'd be wantin' him?'

'At home on his farm. He doesn't know – he hadn't an inkling. In fact, he's probably lying in his bed wondering why I didn't turn up for the Hallowe'en dance. He can never know – if he did he'd come and get me. It's a long story, Johnnie.' She sounded so weary, as if she had been over the ground a thousand times before. 'I made a promise to my father – you'd like my father. He's great. Anyway, I promised him I wouldn't ever contact the father of my baby.' Baby. *Baby*. The word was out. There was a baby. Stephen was the father and she the mother. They were a family, and they were sundered by a narrow confined society riddled with hypocrisy and double standards. Stephen was going about his work in Tulla, at home, his mind in torture, and she was on a train roaring to London, a place where she'd be tucked away from all curious eyes, where Mary hoped she might get swallowed up and they'd never meet again. She felt strange – weak.

Johnnie's question scattered her thoughts. 'Do people think he's no good?'

'No, no, it's not like that. It's something to do with his past – his father, mother, stuff like that. Anyway, my mother loathes him.'

'His father, mother? How could anyone hold somethin' against a fella because of his father? Sure I told you about mine – sure no one in their right senses would take it out on us because he beat me mother when he was drunk. Could they?'

'No – but everyone isn't in their right senses. My mother certainly isn't. She's sort of sick when it comes to Stephen.'

'So the bloke's name is Stephen. Well, I wish I was Stephen. How long do you know the fella?'

'Since I was four.' A whisper of a smile played around her mouth as she wiped the remainder of her tears with the back of her hand.

'That's a while now. I couldn't compete with a fella you've known since you were four.'

Johnnie was still holding her hand. For the first time since she had discovered she was pregnant, the icy lump inside her began to dissolve and Aileen felt almost normal.

She must have dozed off, because now Johnnie was asking

her if she wanted a sandwich with her tea. She insisted on paying this time – she told him she had loads of money. Munching her utterly tasteless cheese sandwiches, she glanced at the unfamiliar flashing landscape in the gathering light outside. 'It's every bit as green as Ireland, and the sheep look just the same.'

He was glad to see her smiling, 'Well, the sheep wouldn't have a cockney bleat, would they now?'

She laughed and her whole face lit up, the sparkle touching her vivid blue eyes. Johnnie had never before spoken to a girl like her – she was the loveliest-looking girl he had ever met. He even thought if he had met her at home and she a big farmer's daughter, she would have been nice to him – she seemed that kind of girl. Her parents must have been mad to send her away all alone, a prey to any of the shady characters she might meet on the journey.

For the rest of the journey, Aileen and Johnnie talked as if they had known each other all their lives. They played cards – Johnnie told her he always carried a deck in his pocket. A man opposite watched them quietly all the time. Could they be a young couple doing a bunk? They certainly looked happy together, and seemed to be able to talk to each other, although he couldn't hear their undertone. Still, they didn't look right for each other. He looked like a building labourer, one of the hordes of lads working in England. She was a different kettle of fish altogether. There was a look about her – a look of comfort, of money. Whoever they were, he wished them well in this country, where too many Irish eked out a living and never felt at home.

'Aileen, this is it – we're here.' Johnnie pulled down her cases. 'I'll stay with you until you meet your cousin – 'tis a terrible confusion out there.'

Standing beside him in the station, looking at the rushing columns of people like busy ants on a hot summer's day going helter-skelter about their business, Aileen realised how lost she would have been without him. He propelled her through a ticket barrier and then looked around to get his bearings. 'There's a seat – sit down for a minute. I want to give you my address, and you give me yours. You'd never know, it might be handy when you need a friendly hand.'

They exchanged addresses, scrawling them on a notebook he had in his pocket. Aileen, glancing at his small, almost printed words, saw that he lived in a place called Shepherd's Bush; she wrote Peggy's address, 19, Rugby Avenue, Islington, London N1.

'Now I must get you to Lyons café and deliver you safe and sound,' he said and she smiled at him gratefully.

Peggy was waiting, accompanied by a small broad-shouldered brown-haired man. She looked exactly as she had looked the day in Dublin – the day they had bought her uniform, a thousand years ago.

Peggy saw the young couple approaching. God, Aileen had a worried apprehensive look on her face, as if she was wondering how she would be received. 'Aileen, oh Aileen,' Peggy cried as she warmly embraced the girl. 'Sure it's great to see you. Aren't you the right lady now! I wouldn't have known you.' She introduced Aileen to her husband Bob, and the girl found her hand clasped in the tight friendly grip of a man she didn't know but who was willing to give her a home when her own mother couldn't bear to look at her.

'You're welcome, girl,' Bob greeted her, and his eyes were smiling as if he really meant it.

Aileen turned to introduce Johnnie, who stood there a little lost, a little apart. 'This is Johnnie Davis from County Meath. I met him coming over and we made the journey together.'

Peggy and Bob greeted Johnnie warmly, then Peggy told Aileen they had to go home soon as their little sons were with a neighbour and they didn't want to delay. On impulse Aileen hugged Johnnie closely. 'Thanks a million for everything. It was great to talk to you – you'll never know how great,' she said softly. She didn't want Peggy to hear, though the milling throng and the public-address system made listening impossible.

'Remember,' Johnnie told her, 'if ever you need me, you know where I'll be. Just whistle and I'll come.'

'I'll remember.'

He was gone, lost in the swirling masses, and she was being led away by Peggy, who was chatting as if everything was completely normal.

Chapter Twenty-Four

'A letter for you over there,' her brother David told Niamh when she arrived from school. 'It's from the lover boy with the hardware shop.'

'Ah, shut up, will you? I hope you won't drive me mad during my break.'

David looked at her, surprised – it wasn't like Niamh to be so uptight and cranky on her holidays. She was normally so bright and bouncy – almost euphoric – when she came home from school. 'Well, somebody got out of the bed on the wrong side today. Anyway, tell me, how is the beautiful blonde culchie?'

'We don't call her that any more,' Niamh said shortly.

'God, excuse me for living,' he snorted before walking away.

'Oh, David, I'm sorry. I am, honestly – 'tis all the studying, the nuns have us mad.'

'Well, don't take it out on me.'

'I won't,' she shouted to his retreating back.

'I forget to tell you that was waiting for you,' her mother said, nodding towards the letter.

'Mum, I'll read it in my room after I do my bit of unpacking.' Her mother glanced after Niamh as she climbed the stairs, and wondered what was wrong. Niamh was worried about something – Helen Turley didn't have to be Sherlock Holmes to know that there was something playing on her daughter's mind.

Niamh sank down exhausted on her bed. She was weighed down so much with her private worry that she wondered how she'd survive the weekend without telling someone. But she had made her promise to Aileen, and there was the problem of Aileen's mother – a woman who would presumably go stark raving mad if there was a leak about the situation. She hadn't seen her friend since the morning she had fainted. She had come up against such a solid wall of evasiveness when she enquired that she had finally lost her patience and had confronted Sister Philomena, demanding outright to know how Aileen was.

'Aileen has a virus and is going home to recuperate.'

Home. Niamh recalled her panic when she realised they had found out that Aileen was pregnant. Home. Aileen's mother had such a sick horror of scandal and an even worse horror of Stephen Rodgers that home would be the last place Aileen should go. But of course Aileen wouldn't show her condition for so long; maybe she could go home for a spell before going to those horrible places that girls went to have their babies.

*

Dear Niamh,

No bright epistle in the door to tell that you love me. *Niamh smiled for the first time in days at the unorthodox start to his letter.* I was hoping that you would be invited to Aileen's for the Hallowe'en but no word filtered through so I was disappointed. I haven't seen Stephen for a while – he's very busy, well-heeled from what I hear. Old Tom turned up trumps and left him all his worldly goods. Pity he wasn't a bit better to him in life – but there you go, that's the way. How are you anyway? I'd love to meet you soon – or I'll forget your cropped hair, your wide grin, your sparkling eyes and that Dublin accent which you insist you don't have, but which you have, me girl, and there's no denying it. I was wondering if I took off to Dublin to see you, but I know Saturday is your day off, and sadly Saturday is my busiest day. You see, you Dublin jackeen, that's the day the farmers take off, and that's the day the open their tightly closed moneybags so the merchant prince Richie must be on the job. Niamh, alannah, I'm sorry this is all about me, but I haven't heard from you so I can't write about you. I hope you're well and that the study isn't driving you and Aileen up the wall. Talking about Aileen reminds me of her other half. That fellow is besotted – really besotted (isn't that a descriptive word?), and she is too, if the truth be known. I wonder will oul Ma MacMahon soften now that Stephen is no longer an unwanted grandson landed on an old man's doorstep? Or would anyone soften that woman and give her a bit of sense? Anyway, it's you I'm besotted with, so write.

Yours, Richie.

Niamh clutched the letter like a lifeline. Dear Richie – so funny and warm and different from so many fellows she knew around Skerries. Tears ran down her snub nose. Maybe I'm besotted too, she thought, wiping them away. The burden of her secret was so heavy that she wondered what would happen if she took someone into her confidence. Richie? Her Mother? Or her brother? Anyone trustworthy. Suddenly a shaft of light came and she knew what she'd do. She'd go to Confession and she'd ask the priest's advice. Niamh had always been a bit religious. When she was at national school she used get up every morning and go to Mass; her father and her brother used to joke about having a little nun in the family. Her enthusiasm for that had long since gone, but she still went to Confession every month.

'Niamh, come down,' she heard her mother shouting up the stairs, 'there's some hot soup for you.'

She put away the letter and took off her school coat, shouting down, 'Okay, Mum, I'll be down in a sec.'

She hoped the strain didn't show on her face – she'd have to put on a big act to pretend everything was normal. 'Well,' her mother said as they sat in the cosy kitchen, every corner warm from the hot range, 'tell me all the news.'

'There's not much news, Mum. We're studying like demons, the nuns keep nagging that we must remember the money our parents are spending on our education and that the least we can do in return for their goodness is get a good Leaving. This is dinned in every day.'

'I suppose they're right. A good result will help when the time comes for you to think about what you'd like to do. How's Aileen?'

Niamh felt the blood rising to her face. Let me appear normal, dear God, do now, she prayed. 'Aileen's okay. She had a cold – a virus or something – and had to stay in bed.' The lie slipped out easily enough and the uncomfortable minute passed.

She told him her sins and had got her absolution and was just finishing her Act of Contrition when she decided she'd better get in fast or the grid would close.

'Father, there's something I want to ask you.'

'Yes, my child?' His tone was gentle and encouraging, and gave her the courage to go on.

'I have a very close friend, Father, and she's in terrible trouble.'

'Yes, and what form does this trouble take?'

'She's going to have a baby, father. She's only seventeen and she loves her boyfriend very much and he loves her, but her mother is totally against her having anything to do with him. I just know she'll be sent away to one of those awful homes and never be heard of again.' The words came out in a rush.

'How long do you know this girl?'

'We both attend the same school, and as I said, she's my very best friend.'

'Are you the only person who knows about this, other than the girl's family?'

'Absolutely, Father – she confided to me some weeks ago.'

'That's hard on you, child. But you must not in any way interfere. The girl's parents have her welfare at heart. They know what is best for their own child.'

'But you see, Father,' Niamh insisted, 'they don't know Stephen. He's twenty-one and very responsible, and has his own farm and he loves her.'

'If that is so, what objection have they to a possible marriage?'

'It's something stupid about who his father was – something foolish and ridiculous and in the past.'

'I see, my child. I know how it all seems to a young girl like you, caught up in the whole business. But you must be strong and keep this to yourself and pray for your young friend to give her strength in her ordeal.'

'Thanks, Father,' Niamh whispered, her heart plummeting. He had no magic formula that could help her.

'I'll pray for you, child, and for your friend also.'

'Thanks, Father,' she repeated, suddenly depressed, knowing that in the months ahead she would have to keep quiet when she'd be tempted to splutter Aileen's secret all over the place.

'I'm surprised I haven't heard from Aileen. Not a single word for weeks now. Did Niamh say anything in her letters?'

They were sitting in their favourite pub across the road from the dance hall in Ross. 'Well, sure boy, I was hoping

Niamh would be visiting Aileen this weekend. But sure there's an old flu going – every man, woman and child was coughing up their lungs in the shop yesterday.'

'Maybe – but I still think it's strange.'

'Look boy, will you stop worrying? 'Tis a well-known thing that true love never runs smooth. I wrote to Niamh the other day and I'll hear from her soon. That young one can't keep a bit of news to herself, and if I hear anything I'll let you know.'

Stephen and Richie drank in silence before going to the dance for what Richie called a bit of diversion. Stephen had little interest but went along nevertheless. The place was full and over the way he saw Richie's sister Noreen with some of her friends. When the haunting strains of 'Mister Wonderful' filled the hall, he decided to ask her to dance.

'Where is your girl tonight?' she asked mid-dance. 'I thought all the schools had a mid-term break.'

'I thought she'd be here. I expected her home.'

'Well, there's plenty more fish in the sea.' She was smiling that mischievous smile that was so like Richie's.

'I know there are but maybe I'm a faithful sort of fool.'

He was smiling and when his black eyes held hers for a few seconds, she wondered what it would be like to be in his arms, not just for a slow waltz but for a blooming good court, a session she could boast about to her friends. 'You're wasted, so you are – you should spread yourself around.'

Just like Richie, he thought, she says exactly what comes into her head. No inhibitions – no embarrassment. If he wasn't so worried about Aileen he would have enjoyed her company.

He didn't dance for the next two, just stood smoking and leaning on the balustrade, watching the dancers twirling and wheeling about. He noticed Richie dancing and laughing with a girl who seemed to be bent double at something he had said. He wished – not for the first time – that he could be different, happy, extrovert, with the ability to make people laugh.

A Ladies' Choice was announced, and there was a tap on his shoulder.

'Ah, sure I thought I'd ask the faithful fool out to dance,' Noreen smiled. She was rewarded with a genuine laugh. His white teeth were in marked contrast to his dark looks, she thought. She thought of Aileen MacMahon, a girl she hardly knew, and felt a wave of envy. She would give her eye teeth to have a night out with Stephen Rodgers. If even now he asked her to the wall outside the dance hall where young couples courted, she would run ahead of him.

He held her closer for this dance, and she hoped he wouldn't feel the beating of her heart through her thin silk dress. The song was 'Save the Last Dance for Me'. Sure, she would save the last dance and every other dance for him, if she had him. Suddenly she was filled with jealousy for the tall, blonde, innocent-looking Aileen MacMahon. Wouldn't it be great if she stayed up in her boarding school in Dublin and never, ever set foot in the place again?

When the dance was over, Stephen said his goodbyes to Richie and Noreen, and told Richie that he would call over soon. Driving home he noticed that the roads were bathed in pale moonlight. All the old familiar landmarks stood out: the narrow boreen leading to the MacMahon house, the old oak tree with the swing. The rope was still there, hanging motionless, a bit worse for wear now. He recalled the trio as they had been on that summer's day, Aileen already showing burgeoning signs of the beauty she was to become, Eddie, freckled, bored and discontented, and Maeve, small and demanding. A feeling of desolation swept over him. Why hadn't she written? What hadn't she come home for Hallowe'en? Every secondary school in the country had a break then. Could her mother's disapproval finally have gotten to her? Could they have been seen at the river that fateful evening when they had finally succumbed to their desires?

The desolation was replaced by an overwhelming longing to be with her. He decided he couldn't go home just yet. He drove to the river, parking the car near the stile, and walked down the familiar path. He didn't have to look where he was going – he knew every inch of the way. He came to the old willow tree and ducked under the weeping, bare branches. Walking to the mossy bank where they had made love, he sat down and let a cigarette. He looked at the tree and a smile briefly softened the grim outlines of his face. He recalled his mother's account of the picnic and what she described as a bout of midsummer's madness when they played homage to the willow tree. It was near here that she had met his father. Such a strange encounter, on that was to bring so much sorrow. Yet Teresa had loved his father – loved him so much she had given up everything to be with him. Her descriptions of her physical need for him had been so revealing. Yes, he had inherited that physical need – he knew what it was to love like that. He would have to plan. The farm and the money in the bank was his now. Old Tom had been frugal in many ways. Certainly since his daughter had left him, there had been no impulsive purchases like a pony for Christmas, no notions like getting someone in to decorate a bedroom for a homecoming. Any money Tom had spent had gone towards keeping the farm one of the finest in the county.

Staring across the moonlit river, Stephen knew that he couldn't end his days in Tulla. He and Aileen would get married. Because of her mother's hatred for him, they would have to go away. He would sell up and amply compensate Máire and Joe for their years of unselfish service. They would go to Australia and buy land and maybe build a house – the sort of house Aileen would love. They would have children and grow old together in the new world, free of gossip and ignorance and the raking-up of old wounds.

A shadow briefly crossed the moon, bringing the unwanted thought that the cloud was a sign that his dreams might never come true. Glancing at his watch, he saw that it was very late. Máire would probably be still up and waiting.

The kitchen light was still on. Máire had snoozed off in the old armchair that he had taken in from the parlour for her comfort. She opened her eyes suddenly, and saw Stephen standing there looking at her. 'Lord, you gave me a fright for a minute – I must have dozed off.'

'Máire, how many times have I told you to go to bed and get your rest? There's no point in staying up.'

'Ah, sure I don't sleep as much as I did. Anyway, I like to be here when you come in. There's some hot griddle bread on the dresser for your supper.'

'You're a terrible woman, so you are.' Though Stephen was smiling, Máire thought he looked troubled. Maybe the dance had been a disappointment. If that old busybody Nurse O'Shea was right, he had set his heart of the young one of the MacMahons. She was a lovely girl, with no airs and graces; still, her mother was a bit of an upstart with terrible notions. She wouldn't let her daughter go lightly, particularly to

Stephen. 'Was the dance any good?' she asked casually, as if she wasn't really interested in his answer. But she was – she cared for him more than he'd ever know. She remembered how, when he had been a little child and she'd bring him the bag of sticky sweets, he'd fling his arms around her and be so grateful that he'd run off to eat them in his own little den. God knows it hadn't been much of a treat – if anything, it highlighted how little he had got during his childhood growing up with old Tom. Yes, the boy had been hurt enough, and God help anyone that would hurt him more – as long as she had a breath in her body, anyway.

''Twas all right – I met Richie and his sister Noreen there.'

'You were so late I thought you might have gone on somewhere for a hooley, the night that was in it.'

'No such luck, Máire.' He sounded weary. 'I actually went for a walk to the river.'

'Sure you could have got your death of cold down by that old river, and God knows what you'd see on a night like this.'

'I saw nothing – no ghosts, banshees, not even a friendly little witch.'

He didn't tell her that he had sat in the moonlight planning a future in a sunlit world thousands of miles away.

Chapter Twenty-Five

It was just as if she were on holiday. Peggy and her husband Bob couldn't make Aileen more welcome. She had her own room with a single bed, modern teak furniture and matching curtains and bedspread. in fact, everything in her room looked new – she wondered if they had been bought specially for her stay. The red-bricked house was tall and narrow with bay windows, and it looked like hundreds and hundreds of others in lslington. Peggy's little boys, aged four and six, were friendly little fellows who seemed pleased with the visitor from lreland. Every time they spoke to Aileen she found their English accents entrancing.

Everything on the surface seemed so normal, so acceptable, that the only hint given that she was the girl in trouble from Ireland was when Bob Fitzpatrick put his arms around her, and said, 'Don't worry, girl – we'll take care of you.' Peggy, a bit red in the face, nodded in eager agreement.

After a week Aileen had settled into a routine. In the morning she helped Peggy with the housework. Sometimes she went with her to the school to collect the boys. Usually they walked up the steep hill, past all the identical lace-curtained bay-windowed houses, listening to the little boys relating all the happenings of their school day. But routine or no, Aileen went through the first three weeks in a daze. Sometimes she persuaded herself that it was all a dream. I'll wake up in bed with Maeve beside me or in the dormitory with Niamh giving out about being woken at such an unlikely hour, she told herself.

But at night, when the little red-bricked house was quiet and in darkness, Stephen would come to her in the small lonely hours between sleep and wakefulness. She had no trouble remembering him – the slow smile that didn't come too easily, the look in his dark, almost black eyes, the pressure of his lips on hers, the wild thumping of his heart against her breasts. The feel of him – the feel of his clothes, his rough tweed jacket, the smooth feel of his good suit, the feel of his thick unruly black hair, the feel of him when they finally made love. His terrible worry he had that he had hurt her. He didn't know, and now it was unlikely that he would ever know, that their one night of frenzied passion and love had done much more than hurt her. It had created a new life inside her – a growing small thing that had banished her from everything she had known: her home, her parents, Eddie, Maeve, her friends and Stephen himself.

Sometimes when she was undressing, Aileen would look at herself in the mirror. She looked the very same as she had looked before – her stomach was still flat. Maybe her breasts were a bit bigger; they certainly were a bit sore, and were those dark circles always around her nipples? She wasn't sure – she was never examined herself before. The only thing she was sure of was that she would die if she didn't see Stephen Rodgers again. She had indeed promised her father that she would keep everything a secret because of her mother's mental state. She had promised the priest in Confession too. Promises. Promises.

Lying in bed, Aileen decided she couldn't go on like a mechanical dead thing, smiling, helping, talking as if nothing was wrong. She made up her mind that she would talk to Peggy the very next day and discuss the situation like two rational human beings.

''Tis freezing out there, a real November fog,' Peggy said the next morning. 'We'll have a cuppa and sit down nice and cosy for a bit – there's no one on us.'

Aileen decided that this was the time. When Peggy had poured out the tea, she would discuss her situation with her. Peggy herself seemed a bit on edge, and the thought came to Aileen that she had the same idea – that the time had come for the airing of Aileen's problem.

Aileen became aware of some crumbs imprisoned against the tubular steel bar that surrounded the table. She had never seen a plastic red table like it before. Peggy had told her they were all the rage – so easy to keep clean, a lick of a cloth, not that constant scrubbing like you had to do with the wooden ones at home. Funny, the things I'm thinking about when, in a few minutes I should know what plans they have for me, what's been said behind closed doors, what earnest discussions have gone on about my position. She noticed that her own hand was shaking as she poured out the milk.

'Peggy, I must talk to you.'

'I know, love, I know. 'Twould be better you got it all off your chest.'

'I wish it was as easy as that,' Aileen answered, and for no reason at all they both burst out laughing. In fact, Peggy laughed so much that the tears had to be brushed away. 'Oh God, Aileen, if we could get it all out with a bit of a chat, wouldn't life be great for women?'

When they both recovered Aileen asked simply, 'Peggy, tell me what they have planned. What's going to become of me? Sure, I can't go on as if nothing was wrong.'

'Of course you can't, love. I was going to broach the subject again and again myself. But I found it hard. I'm glad 'tis yourself that's bringing it up. You're to stay here until you're six months gone. Then the nuns have arranged for you to go into a house that's run by the Sisters of Charity for the last three months.'

'I see. That'll be about February.'

'About then. Listen, Bob and I would love to have you – we don't want you to go anywhere. But the nuns in Dublin and your parents have made all the plans, just in case anyone over from the home place might see you and word would get back. Then again, the lads – they're curious little fellows and they might ask questions when you're near your time.'

'I see.'

'Oh, Aileen, you don't see at all. Do you? You hardly know what's happened to you. God almighty, 'tis terrible on you, so it is. If you want to talk about it that's what I'm here for – to listen. Do you know that?'

'I do, Peggy,' she said gratefully. 'I could start to talk and tell you things, but the only thing I want to talk about is Stephen and I can't talk about him because he's taboo or something.'

'You can talk to me about him till the cows come home. The walls haven't ears and I'm here to listen. Tell me what you want.'

'Now that I can tell you I find it hard,' began Aileen. 'You see, I can't sum it up in a few words. I'm mad about him, Peggy – I've been mad about him for years.' The older woman listened, her elbows on the red table. Looking at the young girl sitting upright on the uncomfortable tubular chair, so far removed from Ireland and its narrow conventions, Peggy felt a closeness and a love for her just as if she was her own daughter.

'Even when I was only fourteen I knew he had such an effect on me it was wrong to be with him. We made a sort of pact that we wouldn't go out together until I was sixteen, and Peggy, we stuck to it – we did. When we did start to go out together, things got easy for us – Mam got sick with her nerves and she was in hospital, and Dad was so easygoing, not watching my every move, so I had more freedom. We had a lovely summer, and towards the end of it we were both depressed – I was going back to school and his grandfather had had a stroke, and Stephen was very worried about him. The second-last time we met we were so happy to be together. We had missed each other time and time again. Anyway we got carried away and it happened. Just once.' Aileen stopped and Peggy could see a faraway look in her blue eyes as she recalled a summer evening when two young people who were madly in love had committed what was generally accepted as the greatest sin of all. 'I didn't think it was as easy as that to have a baby – sure I should have known better.'

Peggy took a time to answer. 'Ye were unlucky, that's what ye were. Sure they're out there doing all sorts of things. Up to all the tricks of the trade. Do they get caught? Not on your nanny. Tell me, love, about your Stephen – sure I've only heard bits and pieces.'

Aileen's face became animated, her words rushed and eager. 'He's lovely. He's tall, strong, dark. He's very dark – sort of stands out. He's worked on his grandfather's farm since he was a young kid. He left school after his Leaving Cert. In fact, everything is right about him except what his mother did. She's supposed to have run away with a gypsy and lived with them, and when Stephen was born she died and the baby was brought back to his grandfather and everyone remembers and holds it against him. At times I wish I was like his mother, wild and impetuous. She got exactly what she wanted and conventions didn't stop her. I'm so dull, Peggy, at times I wonder what he saw in me.'

'Dull? You're anything but dull. You're kind and you're

lovely. When I used to mind you when as a baby I wanted to take you back to Dungarvan with me and roll you around in your pram and show you off to everyone. You were the light of their eye. Your mother used to look at you and say almost in wonder, "Where did I get her, Peggy?"'

'And now I've let them down. And I'm supposed to stay here and let them plan my life for me. I'm not supposed to have a say in anything. Not to tell Stephen, not to tell Niamh, my very best friend, not to write to a single soul. Peggy, I can't do that, can I?'

'It's hard, I know. There is something else. Arrangements have been made for you to go to a secretarial college from the fifth of January until Easter. You'll be learning something, and your mother will feel it's a sort of finish to your education. I'm also taking you to see a doctor next week to find out exactly when your baby is due. Sometime in May, they think. These things have to be done, Aileen.'

'So it's all been taken care of. What if I don't agree to this? Say if I don't care if my mother goes stark raving mad? Say if I want Stephen more than I want anything? What'll they all do then? Can you tell me that?'

'I know how you feel, Aileen,' Peggy sighed. 'But right now, maybe what is happening is best. God almighty, I don't want your mother ever to know I said this. Maybe it's not all over between you and Stephen. I've heard of young couples before having babies and getting them adopted and then getting married much later and having a happy life together. You're only a child, and he's just got the farm and everything – it would be better give yourselves a chance. If your mother could hear me, she'd kill me stone dead.'

'Even the thought that we could be together makes me feel better.' Aileen's voice broke. 'You don't know how much I love him. If you did,' she sobbed, 'you'd help us, you really would.'

Peggy got up from her chair put her arms around the sobbing girl. 'Maybe I will,' she whispered, 'maybe I will. But right now, love, let things be. Let the hare sit, as they say.'

Chapter Twenty-Six

November had come in so cold and frosty that the usual Sunday gathering after Mass dispersed swiftly. Even neighbours who hadn't seen each other for a whole week greeted each other only hurriedly before going their way. Stephen stood in his usual place opposite the gate, hoping to see Eddie. In the long empty weeks since Aileen had failed to turn up at the mid-term break, he had been in hell wondering what had happened to her. Why hadn't she come home? Why hadn't she written? Why were three of his letters unanswered? He had even written to Niamh, friendly outgoing Niamh, and had received no reply.

Richie had tried to console him, saying, 'Ah, sure you know the way 'tis with birds, they go through little phases – you'll soon hear words of undying love and all your troubles will be over.' But he hadn't heard. As the empty grey days had gone by there wasn't a word. That Sunday in November he decided if he didn't waylay Eddie and get some sort of information he would have to take drastic action. Now, through the smoke of his cigarette he glimpsed Eddie coming out of the church with Maeve. His face was set in the scowl that was now familiar to Stephen, as he strode down the steps of the church, his hands plunged into the pocket of his tweed overcoat.

Stephen stubbed his cigarette on the church pillar and strode over to him. 'Hello Eddie – long time no see.'

The boy looked up, startled, and a veiled look clouded his blue eyes. His normal boyish greeting was absent, replaced by an unfamiliar closed expression that sat uneasily on the extrovert Eddie. 'Hiya Stephen,' he muttered as young Maeve raked the older man with a frightened expression in her blue eyes – eyes the exact replica of Aileen's.

'Come on, Eddie,' she urged, 'Mam said we're not to loiter.'

'Shut up, will you?' Eddie snapped at her.

'I was wondering about Aileen.' Stephen looked at Eddie. 'I haven't heard from her. I haven't seen her. I was wondering how she is.'

Eddie looked uncomfortably at the pain and puzzlement in Stephen Rodgers's eyes. He knew he couldn't stand there after Mass with all the old nosy women and blurt out his own worries. He had heard the muffled and the heated words at home when his parents thought he was asleep. He had seen his mother's red-rimmed eyes and her ravaged expression. He had noticed his father's longer-than-usual silences. He knew something was wrong. When he had asked his mother outright why Aileen hadn't come home for the mid-term break, he had been told that she was at a finishing school in London and it wasn't his business really. He could see that his mother was ill again – he noticed she was swallowing pills and resting in bed. But on a few occasions, when she was supposed to be resting, he heard her crying. His father had got a woman in to help with the work, but she just came and went after her chores, doing little to lighten the melancholy that seemed to pervade the house.

Because he had spoken to no one about the situation, Eddie was only too eager to talk to Stephen. 'She's living in London now. She's going to a finishing school or somethin' like that. I haven't seen her myself in ages.'

'A finishing school in London?' Stephen tried to hide his panic – he didn't want the boy to close up like a clam. 'That's unusual, I thought you went to these places after your Leaving. Eddie, have you her address?'

The boy, knowing how close Aileen and Stephen were, felt a strange sorrow that he was powerless to help. 'Jasus, Stephen, the secrecy is fierce – fierce. But if I get it I'll definitely give it to you – honestly.'

'Come on Eddie, come on. Mam will kill us.'

Stephen, glancing down at the young girl, knew that they had been told not to talk to him.

'Hello, Maeve,' he smiled.

'Hello,' she answered, still tugging at her brother's sleeve.

'You'd better go, Eddie,' Stephen told him, 'and thanks – maybe I'll see you again.'

'Yeah, you will,' the boy told him as he went, the impatient Maeve still dragging him down the road.

A finishing school. A finishing school. Certainly Stephen had heard of such places but never knew anyone who went to one. Why? Why had they taken her out of the school in Dublin and sent her to England? Her mother must have got some inkling of how close they had become. Maybe this was her way of trying to end their relationship. A finishing school in London had all the stamp of Mary MacMahon's notions.

As he drove home, Stephen's thoughts tried to grapple with the scrap of information. But even if she was in London, why hadn't she written? She had always written. Why hadn't Niamh written? Did Niamh know about the finishing school? Did Ann or Maggie? As he drove up the lane to the farmhouse, Stephen saw that the muddy rutted lane was hardened by frost. For the first time he noticed the mantle of frost everywhere. It blanketed the fields, and brushed the bare trees and the hedges with its sparkle. He remembered that when he was small, a frosty day like this would remind him of Christmas. He would spend hours kneeling in front of the fire between his grandfather and Joe, drawing Christmas cards with big fat robins perched on snow-laden branches, listening to the men talking about cattle prices, the latest football match or which field would lie fallow the next spring. On such Sundays he would feel good, for a bit anyway, until the loneliness would descend and he would wish that things were different, wish that he had a mother and a father, brothers or even a sister, and a home like most of the boys at school.

He was a man now, and the frost still reminded him that Christmas was coming. If he didn't hear from her before Christmas he would have to go and find her. If he had to face the wrath of her mother and possibly her father, if he had to go and demand what happened, if he had to move heaven and earth, he would have to find out what had happened.

In the farmhouse, Joe had finished the milking and was sitting in front of the fire reading the paper. Máire was bustling about, already preparing the dinner. The black kettle was singing on the hook, ready for the pot of tea she made every Sunday when Stephen came in from Mass.

Joe, glancing up, saw the pensive worried look and knew that the lad had something on his mind. Maybe he was missing young Aileen MacMahon. The girl was still away at some school or other. What they wanted with all that schoolin' was a mystery to him. In his day the three Rs were all that a body needed. Still, times were changin'. Women were doctors and solicitors and things now. God Almighty, the day could come when women would be doing the jobs of men all over the place. He was the first to break the silence.

'I was readin' about the murder in County Limerick. The fella with the hotel who murdered the wife. The paper is full of it – a good looker too. Probably the drink – although women would drive a body mad, so they would.'

He was rewarded with a smile. ''Tis true, Joe – they'd drive a body mad.'

Máire handed them the steaming mugs of tea. She poured herself one and sat down at the well-scrubbed wooden table. 'I was talkin' to Nurse O'Shea at first Mass this morning. Do you know what she told me? She said that Mary MacMahon was bad with the nerves again and that young Aileen was gone to a school in London – some posh place. Did ye ever hear such nonsense? That poor woman is losin' the run of herself. The MacMahons were always a down-to-earth crowd – none of that nonsense about them at all, at all.'

'Yes, I heard something about about it from her brother Eddie – it seems a peculiar choice to have made.'

Stephen didn't elaborate further, and as Máire watched him drinking his tea, his face gave nothing away. But she well knew he had been sweet on the girl for so long now. And if Nurse O'Shea was right, they were very close indeed. God love him, but she didn't want any daughter of Mary MacMahon's breaking Stephen's heart. He had had enough of that in a way. But the letters weren't coming in either. Not a screed of a one. Maybe that why he was so quiet and into himself these days.

Now and then Máire'd think it would be nice to be young again. Young with an unlined face and a nice trim figure and not a vein in your legs, with your hair flying as you cycled along the roads. But when she recalled the pain you'd have inside you when you'd fancy some fellow that didn't fancy you, she wouldn't want to be young again at all.

She glanced at Stephen again. He was staring into the fire, his dark eyes inscrutable, as if seeing things no one else could see. She wanted to go over to him and put her arms around him like she had when he was a small boy. But he was a big strong man now. 'Anyway,' she murmured half to herself, 'everyone knows that true love never runs smooth.'

Later that evening Máire recalled the way he had glanced up, surprised, at her words; yet there had been warmth in his glance. Maybe the surprise was that no one had been talking about love at all. If anything, Joe had been rambling on about a murder in County Limerick. Stephen had looked at her with a sort of gratitude as if her harmless little remark had touched and lightened some fear he had inside him.

The first week in December, a few letters came. Sitting at the breakfast table with Peggy and her little boys, Aileen immediately recognised her father's handwriting on one. There was an English stamp on the other.

'Aileen got some letters, Aileen got some letters,' the little boys chanted. Paul, the leader of the two, said, 'Perhaps they're Christmas cards from Ireland.' The first signs of Christmas were appearing in the shops and the little lads were already excited. She could tell that letters from Ireland were a big part of Peggy's life, and her small sons knew it. Aileen's hands trembled as she slit open her father's letter and drew out a money order attached to a one-sheet letter. 'No card, I'm afraid,' she said to the two expectant little faces. They soon lost interest in Aileen's post and began chasing each other around the kitchen, foiling all their mother's attempts to get them ready for school. Before Peggy left with them, she advised Aileen to make a fresh cup of tea before reading her news.

Dear Aileen,

I should have written sooner, I know that. But I've been very busy, as you might expect. I hope you are keeping well. I know that Peggy will be good to you and she will see that everything will be all right. I'm afraid your mother is sick again – she had a relapse of her nervous trouble and is attending the doctor again and is on medication. I got a woman in – Nora Pender from Glenmore – to help with the housework. Needless to say, Aileen, you are on our minds. I know that your mother is worried sick about you, and Eddie is very curious about why you never came home. Your mother has let it be known that you're going to a school in London, and they seem to have accepted that. We have made arrangements for you to do a two months' course in a secretarial college in London after Christmas. The nuns suggested it and it will fill in your time in a valuable way until your trouble is over. I'm enclosing fifty pounds for your use. I will send you more soon. Do take care of yourself, Aileen. Needless to say, I miss you all the time.

Your loving Dad.

She could imagine how strained Denis had been writing the letter. There was no definite mention of her condition, only veiled good wishes. Aileen hadn't for a wild moment thought he would mention Stephen – but there might have been some reference to her friends. Yet there had been no recriminations, no judgmental tone. Poor old Dad, she thought, it's not easy for him. It's the last thing you expected to happen, the last thing I expected to happen. She wondered if he would ever quite get over it.

She opened the second letter and gasped in delight. It was from Johnnie Davis.

Dear Aileen,
I decided to write to you. I'm sure your relations wouldn't like me calling on you. I hope you are keeping well and keeping your pecker up also. I often lie in bed at night thinking of you and your trouble as they say. If ever I can do anything to help, please let me know. Maybe your Stephen would like to visit you. If he does, he can doss down with me. That is, if you tell him about yourself. Just remember that, because I mean it. Aileen, I hope we meet again.
    Your fond friend,
    Johnnie.

She reread the two letters. If anything, Johnnie Davis's brought more comfort. She felt a warm glow that he hadn't forgotten her – that somewhere out there in the seething masses she had a friend. She was glad of her father's letter too – and grateful for the money. Although Peggy had been the soul of generosity, Aileen needed pocket money. Her gaze wandered around the small basement kitchen, so different from the one at home. She looked at the red formica-topped table, the tubular chairs, the black and white tiled floor, the barred window passed by a variety of legs every so often. When she had first come to Peggy's house, the procession of legs passing by the bars of the basement window had helped pass the time. Even now a pair of thick lumpy legs were going by. She supposed they belonged to an elderly woman with varicose veins.

Was there a single thing in this little kitchen reminiscent of home? Yes. Over there in the corner was a picture of the

Sacred Heart with a small unlit lamp in front. She supposed Peggy had run out of paraffin oil. She looked at the gentle eyes of Christ in the picture, and the prayer that she had heard a thousand times came easy. *Sacred Heart of Jesus, I place all my trust in Thee. Sacred Heart of Jesus, I place all my trust in Thee.*

The idea came like a shaft of light.

Niamh.

Her very best friend. She recalled the childish promise they had made that if ever any one of them as in trouble the other would reach out and help. She had promised her father that she wouldn't get in touch with Stephen, but she had said nothing about Niamh! Why hadn't she thought of it before? Had her untenable position clouded all reason? I will do it now or I'll change my mind, she thought. She was only too well aware that the numbness that had held her in its frozen grip was out there waiting to take hold again if she didn't get down to it now.

*

My dear Niamh ,

Forgive me for not writing sooner. I desperately wanted to, but I couldn't. What can I say about my life now? It's like a nightmare and any minute I expect you or Maeve to shake me awake. How can I tell you what has happened since the night we stood listening to the sea crashing off the rocks below? All I can do is try. I'm living here at my cousin Peggy's house. I believe there is a word out that I'm attending finishing school, whatever that is. Anyway, I'm here to stay, and after Christmas I'm doing some sort of secretarial course before I go to a home for unmarried mothers run by the Sisters of Charity. I was with the doctor a while back and the baby is due in May. Arrangements are being made to have it adopted, and then I will continue with the course in typing and English and get some sort of diploma. And then they're all hoping that everything will be forgotten and poor Aileen can get on with her life trouble-free and unscathed.

Niamh, you won't believe this but my mother never saw me after word broke about the baby – she wanted to remember me the way I was. As if I was dead. I know even as I write that I will never return to Ireland. When Stephen and I went out first, he had a habit of saying, 'I know these things.' It was a sort of joke between us because of his supposed gypsy blood. But in my case I'm just psychic. I know I will never go back.

Now that I've mentioned Stephen and now that I'm thawing out from my numbness, the pain of being without him is indescribable. I promised my father almost on the Bible that I would never, ever tell him about my – what will I call it? – condition. Yes, I'll settle for condition. My father told me that if I contacted Stephen it would kill my mother. What a strange burden to put on me. Kill. Thou shalt not kill. When I learned the Catechism I never knew that telling someone you loved that you were going to have his baby would kill. Jesus, Niamh, now that the shock of the whole thing is easing and now that I can take a more objective view of everything over here, I realise that I want him. Because I love him. That's it. Where will I go and what will I do without him? I think you, of all people, know what I mean. God, what must he be thinking? Have you heard from Richie? What sort of conjecturing is going on? Do they really think I'm at bloody finishing school? Maybe they do, knowing what kind of woman my poor mother is.

By the way, I met a nice fellow coming over on the boat. His name is Johnnie Davis and he works on the building here and he's from County Meath. He kept me company on the long journey and at the end we were like close friends. I got a letter from him this very day and he told me if he could do anything to help me he would. I know, Niamh, that you're probably shocked that I told him – but it's a long story. We swapped addresses in case I'd ever need him. He lives in Number 37, Weighbrook Street, Shepherd's Bush, London W12. Honestly, if I didn't love Stephen with all my heart and soul, I think I'd get the Underground and a couple of buses and go to him. He was that kind of fellow – he showed no horror about my 'trouble'. By the way, it's not that Peggy isn't nice – she's an angel, and her husband and her two little sons also. They're grand little chaps with English accents. Peggy and Bob are saving up – they want to rear their sons in Ireland, in Dungarvan to be exact.

Please write, Niamh – PLEASE. I'm starving for news.
Love,
Your banished friend,
Aileen.

Chapter Twenty-Seven

'That lad is sufferin', I'm tellin you, Máire. He's goin' about his work with his mind a million miles away.'

Joe was taking a break for his morning mug of tea. It was icy cold outside; black frost had been forecast and even the new dog Sam, young and frisky as he was, seemed glad of the roaring fire.

''Tis young Aileen MacMahon,' Máire finally said. 'The lad has been in love with her – always, as far as I can make out. Sending her off to England to school was a notion that Mary MacMahon got to keep her away from Stephen. Where that woman got her high-falutin' notions I'll never know. Didn't I often say that her father was struggling on thirty acres over in Pucane in County Tipp all his life? And a houseful of them in it too.'

'True, true. Then again, maybe we're too interested in him. 'Tis many a woman he'll fall in love with before he chooses.'

'He won't. It's Aileen or no one. Joe, there's something I want to tell you.'

Joe looked at Máire in surprise. She never made a song or dance about telling him anything before. One thing about Máire, she wasn't a secretive woman. For a minute he wondered if she knew something about Stephen – maybe something she had heard from the other women after Mass.

'I was cleaning out all the place the other day. Thought I'd give it a good scour for Christmas, get rid of all the old clothes and stuff, maybe give them to the Vincent de Paul. Anyway, there I was rummaging in Stephen's chest of drawers for any old stuff he'd never wear again. In the bottom drawer under some old shirts and jumpers I found a paper parcel. God forgive my nosiness, but I had a look. God, Joe you know what was in the parcel?

'I don't but I'm goin' to know now – so I am.'

She ignored his good-humoured sarcasm and went on, 'If they weren't two diaries – written long ago by poor Teresa,

318

God be good to her. I knew then that was what Johnnie Sheridan had brought him last year. 'Twas good of him to keep them for so long, and you wouldn't mind only they looked as if someone flung them in the fire to burn them and then maybe changed their mind and poked them out. I was tempted to read them, but sure if he wanted us to know he would have told us.'

Joe sipped his mug of tea. He was not a curious man, but he would have given his eye teeth to read what was in the books. Hadn't he loved Teresa as if she was his own? Not only when she was a little girl tugging at his sleeve and driving him mad, but when she was grown up, talking animatedly to him as she brushed down Laddie or sat on the three-legged stool, her slim fingers going like flash lightning as she helped him with the milking, telling him all about the school or the parish dance or whatever she had on her mind. Sometimes in the summer after the thrashing when everyone would be gone home, she'd sit on the ditch looking at the stubbled fields and ask, 'Joe, I wonder where I'll end up at all?' Yes, yes, he'd be curious about her diaries, but like Máire, he wouldn't dare infringe a young girl's privacy, even though she was under the soil way over in Rathkeale in County Limerick. But he felt he owed it to her to see her son content and settled. Strange how he, an old bachelor, had got caught up in Tom Rodgers and his family. Still, if he hadn't he'd have missed out on so much.

'Here's Stephen,' Máire whispered. 'Not a word about my find. He'd be annoyed, I know that.'

Stephen came in, bringing in a gust of icy cold. 'A seasonal day,' he greeted them.

'Where did you go?' Máire tried to sound casual, because she knew how he hated to be the subject of people's discussion.

'I went to Brennerstown to see Richie Casey. He told me about a new anti-rot paint he's got in. I thought I'd get it for the new fences down near the road.'

She said nothing, just glanced at Joe, who nodded his head imperceptibly. They both guessed that that he had gone to Richie's because he was desperate for news of Aileen MacMahon.

The day Niamh Turley came home for her Christmas holidays, her mother knew there was definitely something bothering her only daughter. She would most certainly tackle her when she had packed away her clothes and thawed out from the icy cold that had the whole country in its grip. There was something wrong, there was no doubt about it. That troubled look in Niamh's brown eyes, the slightly pinched look around her mouth, were unusual, and the girl wasn't as forthcoming as usual with all her titbits of school news.

Later that day, putting on the almond icing on the Christmas cake, when the house was nice and peaceful with all the boys out, Helen Turley thought the moment opportune. She saw Niamh was desultorily eating all the little bits of almond icing that she had pared off, but her mind seemed a million miles away.

'Niamh, what's wrong? Would you like to talk about it?'

Niamh glanced up, startled, a tiny fragment of icing still clinging to her lower lip. She's little more than a child, Helen thought. She shouldn't be burdened like this.

'Mum – oh, I dunno if I can tell anyone, anyone at all.'

Niamh's voice was so low and forlorn that her mother decided to take the bull by the horns. 'Well, you're going to tell me, and I promise I won't tell a single soul. You can trust me.'

'It's Aileen,' Niamh blurted out, and then, to her mother's astonishment, she burst into uncontrollable crying. Knowing the relief they might bring, Helen gave her daughter the luxury of tears before she asked, 'What's wrong with Aileen?' Though the question tripped lightly off her tongue, her heart sank like a stone. What she knew might be wrong with Aileen was the thing most women dreaded happening to their daughters.

'She's going to have a baby, Mum – and it's terrible, terrible. She has been sent to England to a cousin, and then she's going into one of those places where girls have babies. Would you believe, Mum,' Niamh sobbed, 'her mother couldn't bear to look at her. She wanted to remember her the way she was, just as if she was dead. Oh Mum, it's awful – there's whispering about her in school and no one believes the story about a finishing school in London.' Her sobs subsiding as she looked at her mother with tear-drenched eyes.

'How do you know all this? Did Aileen tell you?'

'She did – I'm her very best friend. She wrote to me last week and she's so unhappy and confused – but I even knew before she went away.'

'The father of her baby is Stephen Rodgers, the young man you talk about so often – Richie's best friend. Am I right?'

'Oh Mum, of course you're right,' Niamh wailed, 'how could it be anyone else? They're crazy about each other, they have been for years, since she was a kid. He must be demented – up the wall, God help him.'

Niamh broke down again and Helen, looking at her shaking shoulders, tried to imagine how she herself might have felt if her very best friend at school had met the very same fate. She would have been devastated. 'What else did Aileen tell you in the letter?'

'She told me that she was living with Peggy, her mother's cousin, and Peggy's family in a small house in a place called Islington in London. The baby is not due until early in May. Nobody talks about it, but they're very good to her. She also told me how much she loves Stephen, and how much she needs him now, but she promised her father that she would never ever tell him, because her mother is a mental wreck and it would kill her. Her mother hates him, has always hated him, you see. God, Mum, she's in exile – you'd think she had committed a murder so you would.' As the words tumbled out, Niamh already felt the great weight she had carried for so long lifting off her shoulders. 'Stephen should know. If he did he'd go and get her even if she was in – in Russia. All that old stuff the nuns go on about, a fallen girl and what have you, Stephen wouldn't think like that. They love each other, and another thing – oh, maybe I'd better not tell you. Anyway, it doesn't matter.'

'Tell me, it does.'

'Oh, I suppose I will, seeing that I've told you everything else. Aileen said it only happened once. And I believe her, Mum, I really do.'

'I would too, love. Once was enough, God love them – they were unlucky. Has she told you to keep it from Stephen or Richie?'

'Yes. You see, her mother is a peculiar nutty sort of woman. She hates Stephen because of his father being a nobody or something. She's full of peculiar country ideas, and had high hopes for Aileen. Her father told her that if it got out it would kill her mother – she has bad nerves. I don't know how it would kill her, the old bat.'

Helen had to hide her smile – Niamh already sounded like her old self.

'Don't call the poor woman that. Maybe it would kill her.

Some people are like that in this world. Maybe her father is right. She is their eldest daughter and a lovely girl, and maybe they do have her interests at heart.'

'Oh God, Mum, how could you say that? The girl is over in England, banished. Her heart is broken because she adores Stephen Rodgers. Even her own mother looks on her as if she's already dead, when in fact she should marry Stephen – he's rich now, owns a big farm and stuff. This is one shotgun marriage that would work, I know that much.'

'You don't know, love. You just don't. If it's God's will they'll marry. The story will break, but I wouldn't advise you to be the one to break it. I'll pray for both of them over the Christmas – I have great faith in prayer over the Christmas.'

Eddie looked upwards, hoping for snow, and wondrously, from a leaden sullen sky, it came, turning the countryside into a Christmas wonderland. Denis MacMahon, only too glad to escape the gloom of his house, was happy to help Eddie and Maeve with a sleigh they were making. Eddie, nearly fifteen now, didn't want Maeve's involvement. But she shrilly insisted, and for the sake of peace he allowed her to come along.

The barn was considerably more cheerful than sitting in the kitchen looking at his zombie-like mother who spoke little now, who lived down her days doing only bits of work with little or no interest. In fact it was their father who had taken them into town to do most of their Christmas shopping, and who had insisted that they get their mother something special. Eddie had asked Denis about Aileen coming home, only to be told that she was doing a special course over there and it started again immediately after Christmas and it wouldn't be worth her while to come home. They had sent letters and cards to her, and she had sent letters and cards back, but Eddie knew for a while now that something fishy was going on. If Aileen was only in England doing a course and learning things, why was Mam so miserable? Why, at night when he was in bed, could he hear their troubled conversations in the kitchen? Why wasn't Aileen writing to Stephen Rodgers who was soft on her? She used to write to him when she was at school in Dublin. Stephen had asked him twice about her and he couldn't tell him a thing. Pakie Duffy in school had guffawed when Aileen's name had come up. Eddie had told him she was in England doing a course and Pakie wanted to know was it a nine-months' course. Eddie had blushed scarlet and had thumped him hard. Pakie had gone away with a bloody lip and there were no more guffaws, not in Eddie's presence anyway.

But it had got him thinking. Say if Pakie was right and Aileen was in trouble? And it couldn't be anyone only Stephen Rodgers who'd be responsible. There was some talk last year about a girl in Glenmore and she was gone just like that and wasn't seen since.

'Now Eddie, the sleigh's finished.' His father was trying to sound hearty and cheerful, but there was a terrible weight on him really. 'Don't get killed now. Stop the blooming thing before it hits the wall.'

Maeve was frantic with excitement – she had dressed herself in her warmest coat and boots and had searched the house for her red woollen cap with a pompom. She had flung her scarf around her shoulder and Eddie knew she was trying to look like the girl in the *Girls' Crystal Annual 1959*. Eddie had seen her studying it when they were shopping in Waterford. They lugged the sleigh down to the field near the road. That was the one with the sharpest incline – the one where they had the swing. Getting to the brow of the hill he shouted, 'Come on, Maeve – sit on the back, hold on like hell, and when we get to the bottom of the hill I'll swerve.'

'Okay, Eddie,' she cried, delighted, 'I'll hang on for dear life so I will.' She sat behind him clutching his thick jacket and he set the sleigh in motion. It started slow and then gathered speed as it sped over the impacted snow. Eddie gave a big whoop and Maeve screamed with sheer terror before he swerved and came to rest a mere whisper away from the stone wall.

'You should turn sooner,' she told him. 'I thought I'd be broken to bits, so I did.'

He told her if she was going to whinge, she could go home and play with her doll; she decided she'd stay quiet. They enjoyed the novelty for another hour. The bracing air and the glittering snow had dissipated Eddie's worries. Maybe everything was fine. Maybe Aileen might surprise them by coming home for Christmas after all.

He was about to pick up the homemade sleigh and drag Maeve home when he heard a car pulling up on the road. Glancing over the wall, he saw Stephen Rodgers get out.

'Hello, Eddie,' Stephen waved. 'I wish I was young again.'

''Twas great, why don't you come in and try it?'

'If I was a few years younger, there'd be no stopping me.' Stephen's voice dropped as Eddie came over to the wall. 'Any news of Aileen? Any hope of an address?'

'Honestly, Stephen, I'm kinda in the dark too. She sent Christmas cards and we sent her some back, but Mam took them off us and said she'd put them in one big envelope. She's supposed to be going to a finishing school and then doing a secretarial course, or somethin' like that.'

Maeve didn't tug impatiently at Eddie's sleeve. In fact, she had changed her mind about Stephen Rodgers. She thought he was very handsome – far more handsome than some film stars and the school head boys in the *Girls' Crystal Annual*.

'Look, Stephen,' Eddie told him, 'I'll go snoopin' round and if I get the address I'll give it to you after Mass. That'll be after Christmas now.'

Eddie looked so anxious to help him that Stephen grinned and reaching up, rewarded him with a playful cuff. 'Thanks, Eddie – I won't forget.'

On the same day that Stephen Rodgers spoke to Eddie MacMahon, Niamh Turley got a parcel in the post from Richie Casey. Her brother David joked that he hoped it wasn't presents from men and she still in a convent school. Her mother, seeing the look of anticipation in her eyes, was glad that there was something to take her mind off her friend's plight. 'Open it – let's see what's in it,' Helen told her, showing more enthusiasm than she felt.

Niamh tore off the brown paper wrapping and the Christmas wrapping. Inside was a flat white box, and inside that was tissue paper which she unfolded carefully. She withdrew an angora cherry-red jumper and a matching scarf with tassels. There was an envelope on which she recognised Richie's handwriting.

'It's a beautiful, classy present,' her mother told her, 'perfect for you. I couldn't have chosen better myself.'

'It is lovely, isn't it?' Niamh's eyes shone with excitement as she held it up against her. 'I didn't send him anything, only a card – he'll think I'm a right Shylock, won't he?'

'Ah, sure we all know 'tis the culchies have all the

country's wealth – imagine me buying that for a bird,' David said.

'Don't mind him – go up to your room and read your letter. I know you're dying to see what's in it.' Helen Turley gave her daughter an understanding wink – she knew how anxious Niamh was to know if the story about Aileen had broken.

As Niamh flew up the stairs, her brother's voice followed: 'If it's a proposal, say yes – we could do with a bit of money in the family.'

She sat on the edge of the bed, her hands trembling as she tore open the envelope. Inside was a Christmas card with a fat jovial Santa perched on a snow-covered chimney, and inside the card was the letter.

Dear Niamh,
I got your card and the seasonal greeting. I was glad of them, mind you – if it hadn't come I would presume you were dead, just as Stephen thinks Aileen is dead. Did the pair of ye get fed up with the pair of us and didn't want to tell us or something? Did ye meet two handsome sailor boys in Dun Laoghaire on your free Saturday? I'll tell you what, young Niamh Turley, you'd better not get fed up with me, because if you do, I'll be up there with a fine blackthorn stick to beat the behind off you. Why don't you write to me? I'm desperate to hear from you, not just anything or everything but words of undying love. Yeah, undying love. *Niamh's eyes blurred with happy tears and his handwriting danced and misted, making it difficult to read until she blinked a few times. Dear Richie – so funny, so nice, she thought.*

Niamh, I really miss you and I'd love to see you. After Christmas I could take a run up to Dublin. Things will be as quiet as the grave here. I could meet you in the city and we could go to the pictures and maybe have a bite to eat afterwards. Let me know if it's on?

About the lovely Aileen. Why did they send her away to a school in England? At least that's the story here. Why isn't she home for Christmas? Why the secrecy? Stephen is quiet – he doesn't go around with her heart on his sleeve, but I know he's distraught. He hasn't heard one single word from her since early September. Niamh, allanah, if

you can help him or if Aileen has written to you, forward
the address to him please.

Let me know if we can meet after Christmas; sure me
poor bloodshot eyes are sore for a look at you.

All my love – absolutely, Richie.

Have a lonely Christmas without me. R

She read the letter again and again. Her heart warmed that
Richie seemed to care for her, and yet it bled for Stephen. She
heard her brother David going out, banging the front door,
yelling his goodbyes. She heard her mother sweeping the yard
below, and the dog barking by the back gate, obviously frustrated that David had left him.

Her thoughts confused, she remembered Aileen's letter. *I
promised my father almost on the Bible that I would never tell
Stephen – my father said if I contacted him it would kill my mother.*

But Niamh hadn't promised Aileen's father anything. The
priest had told her not to interfere – so had her mother for that
matter. interfere. Would it be interfering if she helped her best
friend, if she helped two young people to find happiness?
Then again, Stephen Rodgers was an intelligent fellow – why
hadn't it entered his head what might be wrong? Did fellows
talk and gossip like girls? When Stephen told Richie that he
hadn't heard from Aileen, had he confided that they had gone
the whole way, the way girls might confide in each other?
Maybe fellows didn't talk like that. Then again, if Aileen
hadn't become pregnant, would she have told Niamh what
they had done? She might have eventually, when they had got
a chance to chat. She recalled Aileen's question about the
delayed period. She thought of her now, over in London with
her few Christmas cards and maybe some money presents.
Exiled in a way. It wasn't right – it certainly wasn't Christian.
Where was the love-thy-neighbour-as-thyself business? God
forgive her, but she would write to Stephen and of course to
Richie.

Niamh glanced at her watch. It was early enough. If she got
the letter off she would catch the post and Stephen would get it
tomorrow, Christmas Eve. Maybe it would be a terrible shock
to him, but it would give him all the answers.

Before she changed her mind, Niamh got paper and sat
down to write the most difficult letter of her life. She found
herself saying an aspiration that she was doing the right thing.

Dear Stephen,

I sincerely hope this arrives safely. I got a letter from Richie telling me that you are very worried about Aileen and not hearing from her. I'm writing this to you against all advice – advice from people I have taken into my confidence, like my mother and the priest in Confession. I know this will shock you, but maybe it will bring a certain relief too.

Aileen is pregnant and is expecting a baby sometime in the late spring. She is living in Islington, in London, with her mother's cousin Peggy Fitzpatrick and her family. Her family and I suppose it was Mrs MacMahon who told everyone that she is attending a finishing school (it sounds posh) and that she is also doing a secretarial course and so can't get home for Christmas. Aileen was worried that she might be pregnant in September after we came back to school. Then she fainted and hit her head off a desk and was put in the infirmary, and there she had tests or something and they found out. I never saw her again. She was banished almost overnight to England. She made a promise to her father, and you know how much she loves her father, that she wouldn't tell anybody because of the terrible effect it would have on her mother. Some question that it might kill her. Maybe it would, because she's a peculiar woman and thought the sun, moon and stars of Aileen. I'm surprised she not dead already.

Aileen wrote to me a while back and told me every-thing. She misses you – she misses you desperately. I honestly don't know what you can do. I'm sure the cousin Peggy has instructions to shoot you on sight if you do appear.

God, Stephen, this is the queerest Christmas letter I ever wrote. I haven't her address – if I had, I'd most certainly give it to you.

I will be thinking of you over the Christmas and wondering how I can help.

Your loving friend,
Niamh.

Jack the Post brought the letter at three o'clock on Christmas Eve. It was amongst a few Christmas cards, some for Máire from cousins in England, and a few for Stephen. He saw that the letter was closed and the handwriting unfamiliar; there was a Dublin postmark.

'I'll be glad when this is over and I can put my feet up. You'd imagine with the price of a stamp gone up they'd be scarce with the post cards, but 'tis worse they're getting.'

Máire gave him his usual mug of tea, and Stephen went to the press and drew out a bottle of whiskey and poured a glass with heavy hand into it. Jack already smelled a bit merry; there was no doubt every house in the parish had offered him a glass of Christmas cheer. 'Well, the cold is gone anyway,' Jack said to no one in particular, 'but it put paid to a white Christmas.'

'I'm glad,' Maire answered, 'sure no one only the children wants the snow.'

As they sat chatting, Stephen noticed that the light was already going out of the day. Joe had gone to Ross for what he termed 'a bit of business'. Both Máire and Stephen knew that he had gone for a bit of a pub crawl. Stephen didn't begrudge him the hours; he had given him a Christmas bonus, advising him to paint the town red.

Jack heaved himself reluctantly out of the chair, complaining that he still had a few more hours to do.

'By the way, Máire, do you know who's not a bit well in herself?'

'No,' Máire asked, all ears. She was a bit starved for news recently; Stephen had got so quiet in himself and Joe hadn't ventured too far with the snow.

'Mary MacMahon. Skin and bone she is, the poor woman, and she hasn't a word to throw a dog. And wouldn't you think the eldest girl would be home for Christmas instead of staying over there with John Bull? Anyway, happy Christmas to ye. Tell Joe I'll see him in Twoomeys on Saint Stephen's night.'

'We will, Jack, we will, and a happy Christmas to you too.' Stephen heard him go, grumbling about the post he still had to deliver. He decided he'd read the letter in his room. He had noticed that the handwriting was neat and square – a girl's handwriting. His heart thumped heavily in his chest, and a peculiar feeling of foreboding assailed him as he tore open the envelope.

He read the letter, and read it again and again.

He sat unmoving for so long that Máire below wondered had something happened to him. Suddenly her heart jumped as he tore down the stairs and rushed into the kitchen. She could immediately see that something had happened to upset or excite him. His dark eyes positively glittered with such excitement that for a minute he looked like his mother had when she was conjuring up one of her mad plans. He completely astonished her by putting his arms around her and giving her a warm, uncharacteristic hug. 'I must go to see Richie Casey,' he told her. 'I must go now. I've just heard something.'

'Is it bad news, lad?'

'No, Máire, it's the best bit of news I've ever had.' Suddenly he bent down and dropped a light kiss on her wrinkled cheek, leaving her amazed and wondering what in God's name he could have heard to work such a miracle.

'Lord, you'd imagine you won the Sweep.'

'What I heard is better than the Sweep.'

Suddenly he was gone and she could hear the sound of the engine as it revved noisily in the still day. She listened until the sound got fainter and fainter and there was nothing left only the sound of the ticking clock. Staring into the red embers of the fire, she wondered what had happened to make Stephen go quite mad. He wasn't given to excited outbursts. It must be something in the letter. The thought filled her with foreboding. The feeling seemed to pervade her whole being. She looked at the picture of the Sacred Heart. Dear Jesus, she prayed, don't let any harm come to him. Whatever has happened, let it be good, let it turn out as he'd want. I place all my trust in Thee.

Richie Casey was marking time before the shop shut. The previous week had been hectic enough as people made last-minute touch-ups to their houses, buying paint, new curtain rods and fairy lights. Now his head was bent over a string of the said fairy lights bought by a young married woman who was new to the area. She had just returned them, saying they were blinking on and off when she wanted to them to stay on all the time, and now he patiently tested each tiny bulb.

He heard the door and looked up and saw Stephen. 'Will you look at what the cat dragged in?' he grinned.

'Richie, when will you be finished? I must talk to you – 'tis urgent.'

Richie immediately knew that something had happened. There was a terrible suppressed excitement about Stephen and he looked pale, his eyes blacker than ever. 'I have to get these fixed, and then if no one comes in I'll close and meet you in Lynch's pub in half an hour. Will your news hold till then?'

'It might,' Stephen answered. 'I'll wait for you there – I'll buy you a pint.'

He flew out the door and Richie wondered if it had anything to do with Aileen. Maybe he had finally heard from her.

Suddenly the lights flashed into a steady colourful glow. 'Ah, that's where the trouble was,' he smiled at the young woman, giving her a few spare bulbs in case of a blackout.

John Lynch's only concession to the festive season was the red-berried holly he had behind the mirror at the back of the bar. But even so, the pub was noisy with a fair few early Christmas revellers. Stephen was waiting at the far end of the bar, his pint almost untouched. Richie could see that Jamie Hart had put his talk on him, so confidences in his presence were out. One might as well tell the local press.

Richie strode up purposefully, as if he had stolen a minute from a very busy day. 'Stephen, I want you for a minute. I have a message for you. Do you mind, Jamie?' Richie walked over to an empty table at the far end of the bar, near a roaring fire, and they sat down. 'Well, for Christ's sake what is it? What made you come in like a lunatic?'

'I had a letter from Niamh this morning. She sends you her love.'

For once Richie Casey was at a loss for words. Why would his Niamh write to Stephen and not to him? He accepted that the fellow was so handsome he could attract a haggard of sparrows, but he didn't think his little Niamh would become one of them. 'What else did she have to say?'

'She told me Aileen is pregnant.'

Richie looked at him in amazed consternation and let out a long, low whistle, 'Jasus, boy, but the cat is amongst the pigeons now.'

'Niamh told me everything in her letter. The baby is due in the spring. Aileen is in England – she was sent over when the news broke. Richie, I must go to her and take her away from all of them. Christ, I must if it's the very last thing I do.'

Chapter Twenty-Eight

It was the most mud-spattered car she had ever seen, but there was something familiar about it. Coming up to the house, Niamh stopped in puzzlement. She tried to jolt her memory. It couldn't be, could it? Not all the way from County Kilkenny to Skerries just like that. She went around to the back door, her heart thumping so heavily she thought she'd faint. She had gone down to the harbour with her brothers to watch the Saint Stephen's Day swim. Her two brothers had met their friends, and she had decided to come home after the event. Pushing open the back door, she felt as if her chest was filled with her thumping heart.

Sitting at her mother's well-scrubbed table, looking completely at home and drinking from the everyday cups, were Richie and Stephen. Richie was grinning at her as if to say, Aren't we great we found you? Stephen looked as if he hadn't slept for weeks, yet it was only two days since he had received her letter.

'Hi.' She tried to sound casual and at ease. 'Look what the full tide brought in.'

Helen Turley felt a sorrow for the tragedies of youth. She was glad she was forty-three and past a time when emotions were so high that every day could either be heaven or hell. 'Niamh, I made the young men some tea. They declined to stay for lunch, but if you can persuade them all the better. I'll let you have a chat; I'll wander down to the harbour and see what's happening. The bit of fresh air won't go astray.' As she waved at them before going out, she thought that Stephen's black eyes were the most intense and extraordinary she had ever seen.

Stephen got up abruptly and hugged Niamh close. 'Niamh, I'll never, never be able to thank you – never.'

'It's okay, okay,' she whispered, the tears springing to her eyes as she put her arms around him.

'Come on, come on, let's sit down and plan,' Richie

ordered, clearing his throat and trying to defuse the situation.

She told them most of the things they knew already. She told them of Aileen's initial concern, her faint, her parents coming, her mother refusing even to see her, saying that she wanted to remember the way she had been. 'Imagine saying a thing like that to your own daughter!'

'She was always a batty woman,' Stephen answered, running his hands distractedly through his hair. 'Jasus, of all the morons and idiots in Ireland, I must be the worst. Why it never struck me that she could be pregnant shows I'm an unimaginative fool.'

Richie and Niamh were silent. She felt embarrassed to be with two young fellows who were aware of what happened down by the river. She was afraid that Stephen might mention that it had happened only once on that fateful evening, but he didn't.

'Niamh, I have to have her address. I'll go over to England tomorrow. I must see her, I must be with her now.'

'But she didn't give it to me,' Niamh said.

'Sure even if you knew where you were going, you couldn't run off like a March hare and show up at her relatives' door – you'd get short shrift, I'm telling you,' Richie warned.

Niamh, thinking hard, said, 'There is someone who might be able to help.'

'Who?' Stephen asked urgently.

'When she was going over on the boat she met a fellow who was very friendly and helpful. He kept her company all the way on the boat and train, and stayed with her until she met her cousin.'

'Who is this paragon?' Stephen asked abruptly, obviously upset and disturbed that a stranger could help when he had been so obviously left out in the cold.

'His name is Johnnie Davis – he's from County Meath. He's working on the building sites in London and they actually swapped addresses. She even sent me his address – he must have been a nice fellow. Maybe he would help you reach her,' Niamh said, the excitement showing in her eyes at the prospect of a solution to the frustrating situation.

'The very thing,' Richie agreed. 'You'd be like the proverbial lost soul in London. You'll need someone to give you your bearings. If the bloke is that nice he'll put you up – he'll tell you where to get to her. It's a good idea, you know.'

'Maybe,' Stephen said, 'maybe.'

'What'll you do when you get there?' Niamh sounded more like her old self than she had for a long time. Her brown eyes showed the relief that the terrible burden was no longer solely hers. In her mind's eye she could see Stephen doing a Sir Galahad, sweeping Aileen off her feet, taking her away from the small red-bricked house identical to all the others in London. His answer didn't disappoint.

'I'll take her away from there, we'll get married as soon as possible. I'll sell up the farm and we'll get away from that gossip-ridden gloomy place and hopefully go to Australia.' The expression in his black eyes was almost frightening in its intensity. 'Christ, imagine treating her like that because she's going to have a baby.'

'It's happening all the time, you know, there's nothing new about it,' Richie told them.

'Yes, but you never think it's going to happen to you. It's always someone else.' Stephen smiled for the very first time. 'Look here, I'm a proper gobshite, taking over all your lives. Look, Niamh, we'll drive somewhere and I'll buy you both a bite to eat. Then you can go off somewhere and catch up – I'm sorry I'm such a selfish bastard, but I'll always be grateful to you both. You'll never know how much.'

Richie winked at Niamh, looking appreciatively at the cherry-red jumper and matching scarf that she wore so well. 'You liked them, huh?'

'I loved them,' she told him, 'and I felt a right meanie sending you nothing.'

'Sure won't you have fifty years to make reparation?' he grinned.

Niamh wrote a note for her mother, telling her she was going for a spin. She poured out a saucer of milk for the cat who had jumped up and was purring on Richie's lap. 'There's one member of the family who likes me anyway,' he said to nobody in particular.

'Any port in a storm,' Niamh smiled at him.

They drove to Howth and settled for a small restaurant which had opened only a few months previously. They chose turkey and ham, 'because of the day that's in it,' Richie said.

Niamh was never as glad of Richie's constant chatter. Stephen was quiet, obviously thinking of the journey that lay ahead, and she was drained and yet happy to be with them.

After they finished the meal, Stephen told them, 'Off with you both for a bit. I'll just sit here and drink more tea – you don't want me doing the gooseberry.'

'Before I go, have this.' Niamh handed him Johnnie Davis's address. He reached out and took it, his eyes already devouring the little scrap of paper.

Niamh remembered the lovely summer and the fun all four of them had had, and realised that things were going to change so drastically. She'd probably never see either Aileen or Stephen again.

Impulsively she bent down and kissed Stephen on the cheek. Her lips touched the faint stubble and she wondered if he had forgotten to shave in his hurry to get to Dublin; maybe he simply had to shave twice a day.

They walked out the glass door. Her red scarf caught the wind and blew up, a cheerful banner of defiance. Richie reached up and caught it, and tucked it around her neck. Suddenly they were in each other's arms and kissing hungrily.

Richie whispered against her dark curls, 'Despite how awful it is for them, it was a great opportunity to see you, love.'

She caught hold of his hand and held it tightly as they walked down the summit road. They were silent, each wondering what each other was thinking, yet aware of a strange new contentment washing over both of them.

Chapter Twenty-Nine

It was the strangest Christmas for Aileen MacMahon. Though the Fitzpatricks did everything in their power to make it a good one, she had never felt as alone. She pulled crackers and donned a paper hat and read out the little riddle from the red paper crackers.

'What's green and hairy and hairy and goes up and down all day?' she asked William.

'Let me think, Aileen, let me think.' He screwed up his little face in the throes of concentration. 'A caterpillar in a green cabbage,' he shouted happily.

'No,' she told him, 'a gooseberry in a lift.' The two little fellows roared in merriment and she joined in as if she was having a wonderful time. Try as she might, though, she couldn't drag her thoughts from what would be happening at home. She could see that the dusk was descending in the street outside. The next-door neighbour, an elderly man, was taking his dog for a walk. The little Yorkshire terrier was yapping with delight.

She thought, If I was at home now, Dad would be at the milking, complaining that the cows don't know it's Christmas Day. Stephen would be helping Joe with the milking too, and afterwards he might go for a walk down by the river. Maybe even now he's standing at the wide river, looking down at Barrons Wood, thinking of me. The leaves would be all gone off the willow trees and the empty branches would be swinging and stirring in the whispering wind. All the branches in the old trees would be bare and look like black lace against the wintry sky.

I mustn't think like this or I'll go stark raving mad. I must don a paper hat and pull crackers and laugh and joke, and not think that there is a baby growing inside me, and that I'm beginning to show and I even think last night I felt it move. Could I have felt it move? Maybe I could. Who will I ask? Do girls who are unmarried ask questions like that?

The doctor at the clinic had been business-like, as if a girl from Ireland who was having a baby was the most ordinary thing in the world. He had just asked her routine questions, like when she missed her last period, examined her stomach briefly, and had given her iron pills and told her to come back in six weeks' time. Peggy had been kind and gentle on the way home, but Aileen got the impression she hadn't wanted to talk about it – a case of the least said the soonest mended.

She couldn't bring herself to say to Peggy, 'I feel the odd twitching inside. Could that be the baby moving or could it be a simple case of indigestion?' On Christmas Night she lay in bed and indulged herself in utter and complete fantasy.

She was with Stephen by the river. It was warm and sunny and the gypsies were back in Barrons Wood. She could see the smoke rising from the fires and the sound of children playing. They were sitting on their favourite moss-covered stone near the bank. She was obviously pregnant, and she told him she felt the baby moving. She had never seen him so happy. He placed his hand on her stomach to see if he could feel it too; she put her hand on his and the sun glinted on her wedding ring. She and Stephen were married and everyone was happy about it, even her mother. They were living in Tulla and both Máire and Joe lived with them and she never tired of listening to stories about when Stephen was a little boy. They even told her stories about his mother Teresa and the antics she got up to.

Suddenly she was swamped with a clammy fear that as sure as night followed day, this particular dream would never be realised. The tears came, and her throat became so restricted that she could no longer restrain her sobs. She put a pillow over her head so that Peggy and Bob wouldn't hear.

'Dear Jesus,' she prayed aloud, 'please, please help me. Please let me see Stephen again. That's all I ask now. I want him to know how much I love him. Please. Please.'

She finally fell asleep, exhausted, and dreamed she was boarding the boat leaving Dun Laoghaire, waving goodbye to Sister Philomena. When she turned to go up the gangplank Stephen was waiting at the top, wearing his open-necked shirt and tweed jacket. She didn't care that he hadn't his good suit on – she ran up and threw herself into his arms, and he held her as if he'd never let her go. She led him to the seating area and got him a cardboard cup of tea, and it seemed they weren't going to England at all but to Australia, where he had always wanted to go. Johnnie Davis came along and shook hands with Stephen, and told him if he hadn't turned up he would have run off with her himself. Stephen laughed and tightened his grip on her. Then it all got blurred and she was with Johnnie on her own and they kept looking for Stephen all over the boat.

She woke up with a violent headache and then, feeling dreadfully ill, rushed into the bathroom and became violently sick. Kneeling on the cold black and white tiles, her head bent over the toilet bowl, her hair in disarray, she thought she heard footsteps. She looked up after a particularly bad bout of retching and saw Peggy standing there.

'Are you all right, Aileen?'

Stiff from kneeling, she got up and flushed the toilet.

'I'm sorry, Peggy, I woke you up and the day that's in it you could do with a rest too. I don't know what caused this.'

'Sure you do, you poor lamb, you know what caused it and so do I. You won't feel it now that Christmas is over and the spring will be coming.' Peggy reached out and held the girl's icy hand in hers. 'Come on – we'll make a nice cuppa. A bit of dry toast will fix your stomach.'

In the kitchen Aileen watched Peggy fill the kettle from the tap, and to her surprise saw that Peggy's shoulders were shaking, as if she were crying also. 'What's wrong, Peggy – what is it?' she asked.

'Oh, Aileen,' Peggy sobbed, 'I was just thinking that today at home would be fabulous, with all the wren boys going around, singing and dancing and looking for money for the wren. And here we are stuck in this awful place, and they calling it Boxing Day, and no one will bother with us at all. And there you are, a lovely girl in trouble, and we don't know what's going to happen to you either. You think I don't know what's going on in your head at times? Well, love, I do – you don't think I'm a stone, do you?' Peggy sobbed louder.

Aileen put her arms around the older woman. 'Shush, Peggy, you'll wake the lads and they'll think you're mad, bawling for the wren boys they never heard of.'

Suddenly, like the sun coming from behind a cloud, Peggy smiled and then started to laugh. Then they were both laughing, and their laughter grew as they sat on the tubular steel chairs in a kitchen in an alien city where wren boys on Saint Stephen's Day were never even heard of.

He had never been on a boat before. He was surprised there were so few travellers. He presumed that the emigrants who came home for Christmas wouldn't be returning yet. As the boat pulled away from the dockside in Dun Laoghaire, Stephen noticed a few strollers were waving. He waved back and then looked around, feeling a bit foolish waving at people he didn't know and would never see again. As the boat headed for the open sea he wandered down to the lower deck where at least it was warm.

The last few days had been hectic. He had sent a telegram to Johnnie Davis, explaining who he was, and asking if he could meet him. He had received one in return telling him to COME OVER STOP – I WILL HELP YOU STOP. He had told both Joe and Máire that he was going to England, that something urgent had cropped up and he felt it essential that he travel. They had tried to hide their astonishment, as if running off to England was something he had done before. Later Joe had said, 'Well, Stephen, I'm sure you know what you're doing.'

Stephen had felt it unfair not to take him into his confidence. 'Joe, I have to make arrangements about something. I don't know how long I'll be – I'll take enough money to see me through. I want you to get in help if you feel you need it. I'll leave enough money for you and Máire to carry on. The milk cheques are behind the tea caddy on the dresser, I've signed them in case you need them.'

'Listen, lad – 'tis the girl, 'tisn't it?' Joe had asked. Stephen had said nothing. Now, sitting on the boat with its engine throbbing and groaning as it made its way across the Irish Sea, Joe's face came back to Stephen. He had looked so anxious and had had such a troubled look in his faded eyes that Stephen had realised he should tell both of them what he was doing. He knew they would rather die than spread stories about him.

'It is, Joe, it is. I must see her. I heard on Christmas Eve that she's expecting my child. I promise I'll tell you everything when I come home. But right now she needs me more than anyone or anything else.'

'Jasus, Stephen, isn't it quare that Mary MacMahon failed to keep ye apart? They'll be hell to play when she finds out you're gone to meet her daughter.'

'I don't care what hell she feels – it's what her daughter feels that I'm worried about.' Stephen sat remembering how his rushed departure was – how demented Máire had been, brushing his navy overcoat and telling him to mind himself in that heathen place. She had packed some clothes in a bag she told him had belonged to his mother Teresa when she was going to boarding school. The money he had taken out of the bank was stuck in his breast pocket of his good suit. He had Johnnie Davis's address tucked safely away also.

He noticed a woman and a young lad drinking something out of paper cup; they seemed to have brought their own packed sandwiches. He decided he'd go in search of the tea, and when he stood up he ruefully acknowledged that he hadn't sea legs. The floor seemed to be tilted at a strange angle, and he marvelled at how well some travellers seemed to take that peculiarity in their stride. He eventually found a white-coated fellow with a peculiar accent who was selling cups of tea behind a plastic counter. There were cheese and ham sandwiches wrapped in plastic paper and he bought some, telling himself he needed something to down the grey liquid that passed for tea. He thought of how Aileen had made this same journey. Had she sat there feeling disgraced and ostracised because of what he had done? Had she felt resentment, or had she merely been confused and puzzled at the hasty plans that had been made for her? Christ, he thought, why hadn't she written? Why had she put her mother's and her father's wishes before the love they had for each other? Could she have changed? Could the probing questions of the nuns and the doctor who had eventually found out about her condition have upset her? He thought of her tall, leggy figure, the extraordinary blue look of her eyes, the thick blonde hair in her ponytail, or loose and blowing across her face. He remembered the way she smiled when he was there before her at a planned meeting place, the way she laughed when they shared a joke. He became so overwhelmed with the memory of her that the old familiar longing in his groin became so uncomfortable that he had to concentrate on the tasteless tea to dispel it.

He was flabbergasted by his arrival in London. He had never seen so many people in his life, people of all ages and colours, all rushing frantically on their way, as if some major event was taking place and they had to be there to save their lives. He had never seen anything like the traffic either – Dublin was bad but there was no comparison to London. The taxis were big and black, like undertakers' cars at funerals in Ireland. He felt slow and awkward as the milling, rushing throngs sped by. Carrying his bag and putting up the collar of his coat against the east wind, he approached a man standing at a newspaper kiosk.

'Excuse me,' he said, 'I'm looking for a taxi.'

The man glanced up from his newspaper and quipped, 'I'm not stopping you, mate.' Stephen laughed out loud. The man looked at him in narrow-eyed suspicion and walked away. I'm making a bad fist of this, Stephen thought, as he slotted away his first encounter in London to relate to Aileen when they met. Glancing down the busy street he noticed a taxi rank and a long queue of people. Walking towards the queue, he became aware of the noise, the constant roar of trundling traffic, the red towering double-decker buses. People waited behind railings for lights to change before plunging across the road to the safety of the opposite footpath. He wondered how they lived in such an environment, and decided there was something in the old saying that it takes all sorts to make a world.

The taxi driver didn't speak one word after Stephen gave Johnnie Davis's address in Shepherd's Bush. What sort of fellow was Johnnie? Would he be as helpful as his telegram suggested? The taxi was held up in the knotted traffic for so long that Stephen wondered if he would ever get to find out. Eventually they turned down quieter, gloomier, more shabby-looking streets.

'Here, mate.' The taxi driver nodded towards a derelict-looking red-bricked house in a row of similar-looking houses. Stephen got out and asked him how much he owed. The driver nodded towards the meter, a small luminous dial, and Stephen paid him eighteen shillings. Carrying his bag, he walked up the steps and rang the bell on the faded, peeling door. He could hear its strident ring, but the sound was having little or no effect on its occupants. Was there anyone there, or had he made a mistake? His strained ears were finally rewarded with a woman's voice, muttering that you'd think a body could have a bit of peace or a lie-in seeing that it was still Christmas time.

The door opened about six inches and two grey, watery eyes peered at him. 'Well, what do you want? If you're selling anything go away – I have all I'm likely to want.'

'No, I'm not selling anything. I'm looking for a fellow named Johnnie Davis from Ireland.' She opened the door another begrudging two inches. 'What would you be wanting him for?'

340

He had recognised her Irish accent the minute she opened her mouth. 'I just want to see him. He's expecting me in a way. I would be grateful if I could speak to him.'

'Well, you can't, because he's working, so he is. And where are you from, if I might ask?'

'You might,' he told her, thinking that the curiosity of the Irish was as strong in the suburbs of London as it was in any village in Ireland. 'I'm from a townland called Tulla in County Kilkenny. I'm just here for a day or two, and he's expecting me, I think.'

She blinked at him, the curiosity narrowing her faded eyes as they raked his good coat, his white shirt, his tie, the handsome features and the dark eyes that would make your heart turn over, she told herself, if you were young and foolish. But it was a long time since she had been young and foolish – forty years keeping a boarding house for Irish lads in London knocked all that out of you, not to mind losing himself nearly twenty years before. 'Come in – you can wait for Johnnie in the sitting room. He'll be home at four o'clock. The light is gone then, and the building ends when the light goes.'

He followed her into a small room crammed with sofas and chairs, hard and uncomfortable-looking, and protected with arm covers and the white lacy things at the back. He thought he had heard Máire once call them antimacassars and even then had wondered where they got the name. The sideboard was covered with ornaments and sepia photographs, old and faded now. Maybe they were pictures of people the landlady had left behind in Ireland, or maybe brothers and sisters who were scattered all over England. There was a picture of Patrick Pearse, his familiar handsome profile looking at bit strange in a cluttered sitting room in the heart of Shepherd's Bush. On the opposite wall was a picture of the Sacred Heart with a small lamp burning in front and a branch of withered palm stuck behind, battling for space with an equally tired sprig of holly.

'I can see you're taking it all in,' she muttered, nodding towards the picture of the Sacred Heart. 'My self and himself, God rest him, didn't lose our values when we crossed the water. Some of them become heathens, so they do, when they set foot on British soil.'

He smiled at her, noticing now that her grey eyes were kind. He guessed that she probably had a soft spot for the Irish lads who came over looking for work and digs. 'Yes, I can see that.' He nodded towards the picture.

'I'll get you a cup of tea. Sure travelling at this time of year is terrible. There's a washroom down the hall if you want it.' Suddenly she was gone and Stephen removed his coat and sat down. It must have started to rain, because the sound of the traffic was different now. He could hear the tyres hissing off the wet roads. He felt alien and strange sitting there in the cluttered room. Had Aileen felt the same, out of place and confused, when she had first come to London? He glanced at the picture of the Sacred Heart and felt its eyes looking at him. Closing his own, a broken prayer came to him that they could be together and that he would make it up to her for the rest of his life.

'There's a hot cuppa now.' He opened his eyes and saw that the landlady was looking at him, puzzled. 'I brought you a bit of my Christmas cake – now, 'tisn't every one of Johnnie's friends I'd give my good china or my cake to, I can tell you. And tell me, what'd be bringing a fine fellow like you over here this time of year? 'Tis a bad time to be looking for work.'

'I'm not looking for work. I'm here to see somebody.'

'A relation, would it be?'

'No, not exactly – someone who's not too well.' Even to his own ears it sounded stupid. He hoped she'd go away soon, because he was suddenly overwhelmed with weariness and he remembered that he hadn't really slept since he had got Niamh's letter. Putting the cup to his mouth he idly wondered what the woman would say if he told her the truth. *I'm here because I'm looking for the girl I love, who is pregnant and supposed to be at a finishing school, because that's what her mother has put out. Her said mother hates me and would probably prefer her daughter dead than married to me.*

He didn't have a chance to wonder too long, because she peered through the curtains and said, 'Ah, here's Johnnie now. They must have knocked off early because of the rain.'

She got up and went out into the hall. Stephen could hear their muffled voices, and suddenly a red-headed young man walked into the room. He wore an old shabby raincoat over his working clothes, and though he was damp and obviously cold, he scrutinised Stephen carefully, the look in his eyes wary, curious and calculating. Whether he came to a satisfactory

342

conclusion or not, Stephen wasn't sure, but he stuck out his hand and said, 'You're welcome.'

Stephen took it in his firm grip. 'Thanks, Johnnie, I'm very pleased to meet you.'

The preliminaries over, Johnnie asked him to come up to his room, 'That is, if Mrs Finnegan wouldn't mind.' The whimsical grin directed at his landlady gave Stephen the impression she didn't mind at all.

"Tis the brazen English hussies I object to, you know that – not a decent lad from home.'

He followed Johnnie up three flights of stairs. 'Sittin' on a gold mine she is,' Johnnie said over his shoulder. 'Owns the place outright. Has ten rooms let out and there's talk of the council widenin' the road, and if they do she'll get a fortune from the powers-that-be.'

He stopped at a door and led Stephen into quite a large room. There was a bed in the corner with a chest of drawers and a large sofa in the other end; tucked away to the window there was a cooker, kitchen table, two chairs and a sink. 'Look, sit a bit and I'll get the gas fire goin'. After we have somethin' to eat, or better, still drink, I'll tell you all I know. First I'll have a bit of a wash.'

The instant heat from the spluttering gas fire was welcome and helped to take the chill out of the high-ceilinged room. 'Look, have a read of this while I'm havin a wash.' Johnnie Davis tossed him a paper. Stephen sank into the armchair gratefully and glanced at the front page. There was a picture of the Queen, accompanied by Prince Philip and their two children, Prince Charles and Princess Anne, returning from Balmoral where they had spent Christmas with the rest of the royal family. There was a picture of the Shah of Persia and the empress Soraya, who were to separate because of her inability to produce an heir. He thought of all the Irish women who had babies year after year, ending up with an unwanted ten or twelve, and there was one of the richest couples in the world, and they couldn't have one single son.

'I'm ready now.' Looking up, Stephen saw that Johnnie had washed and put on a warm woollen jumper, and seemed ready to go somewhere. 'We'll go to the café around the corner and have a feed, then we'll talk.'

Only when the last mouthful of steak and the last chip had

been swallowed did Johnnie sit back and give the impression he was anxious to talk. Stephen understood his hunger – he had known an appetite as great, if not greater, after a day in the fields.

'To be honest, I was curious. In fact, I couldn't take me eyes off her. She didn't look like the usual bird you'd meet on a crossin'. It took me a long time after we got talkin' to twig there was somethin' wrong. A good looker like that, dressed right respectable, so tired she slept like a log, her head on my shoulder, for most of the journey. Jasus, it was terrible to let her off like that – she could have met Jack the Ripper for all her folks cared.'

Stephen was filled with all sorts of emotions: jealousy for this young man who had accompanied her, whom she had taken into her confidence, who had taken care of her on such a long journey into the unknown. Gratitude that he was a decent sort, thankfulness that he and Aileen, two young people who had little in common, who were going in different directions and who would probably never meet again as long as they lived, had done such an unlikely thing as swap addresses.

Johnnie Davis, aware of the pain his account was causing, tried to lighten the moment. 'You're a lucky bugger – she's a gorgeous girl and must be an idiot about you to have ended up the way she did.'

Stephen nodded. 'Johnnie, 'tis a long story. But if I hadn't been such a thick fool, she wouldn't have been on that boat. I would have stormed that convent in Dublin where they found out what was wrong. I got this letter from Niamh, her friend, on Christmas Eve. Up to then I had heard nothing from Aileen and was frantic. Would you believe I was in heaven when I heard about her being pregnant? No one could keep me away now. I made wild plans, got some money, made arrangements for the farm. I drove to Dublin for the second time in two days. I got your address and here I am.'

'Look, you need a bit of kip. You can sleep on the sofa. I'll tell you how to get there. It's not that far, but for a redneck like you Islington might as well be on the moon. You'll get up in the mornin' fresh, and go to her with a clear head to make your plans. She'll be there in the house. That woman she met looks like a dacent sort. I bet she won't kick you out – she looks like a woman with a soft heart.'

*

Stephen had heard about London Underground. The thought of going down into the very bowels of the earth to catch a train would have intrigued him if his mind hadn't been filled with Aileen, and the terrible new fear that he mightn't find her. Johnnie had written out the instructions carefully and clearly, and Stephen had set off full of hope, hardly aware of the milling throngs and the constant roll of traffic as the great city, with its heaving millions, went about another day. Even his early astonishment at all the coloured people working in the cafes, buses and on the Tube was diminishing now. He stood up for most of the journey, his eyes glued to the route plan on the opposite side of the carriage. He tried to edge near the door, afraid that if he didn't jump off when the train came to his destination he would be whisked away to God knows where. He had to change at Kings Cross, and suddenly he was there – the Angel, Islington. There was nothing to tell him it was any different from any of the other stops except the wild thumping of his heart. He alighted and followed the crowd up the escalator, almost unaware that he had never been on one before.

Outside the sun was shining as he read Johnnie's instructions. *Cross the road and walk to the bus stop. Join the queue and when the bus comes along with the name of her district, Rugby Avenue, get it and get off when you come to it. Then walk along for two hundred yards and turn right and go up a steep hill. She lives up there in number 19. It's a red-bricked house with bay windows and a basement barred kitchen window – the very same as hundreds of others in the area. In there you should find her.*

When Aileen saw the bright, crisp winter sunshine she was almost sorry that she hadn't gone to the clinic with Peggy for the children's dental appointment. She felt restless and uneasy. She had slept badly the night before, tossing and turning, hoping that sleep would bring merciful relief. She had lain awake, aware that the small movements inside her were indeed the first flickerings of her baby's movements. She had looked at herself in the mirror after her bath and had been aware that her stomach had swollen quite a bit over the past few weeks. Her skirts no longer zipped up with ease. She had bought some large safety pins; her jumpers came down over the gap and no one seemed to notice, although yesterday young William had told her she was getting fat. She had laughed and answered she had eaten too many mince pies.

Her ten-week secretarial course was to start the following Monday. She hoped that the other students wouldn't notice her condition.

Although Peggy and Bill and the kids couldn't have been better, the long days of inactivity were driving her mad. But the long sleepless nights were worse. The dark silent hours were filled with memories of Stephen and her despairing longing to have him with her now. Sometimes she thought of her parents – her father who was surely unhappy, her mother who must be distraught. Eddie, she thought, must be very puzzled and Maeve so curious that she must have driven them all mad.

After she finished tidying the house, Aileen decided she'd make a cup of tea and have one on the ready for Peggy when she returned. Sitting waiting for the kettle to boil, her eyes on the blue dancing gas flames, she thought she heard the doorbell ring. After a bit it rang again. She wondered who it could be. There were few callers to the house – in fact, a visitor was a rare event. She lowered the jets and went to open the door; catching her reflection in the mirror of the hall stand, she noted her pallor and the fact that her hair needed cutting.

She could see the dark shape of a man through the frosted glass door and for a wild, heart-thumping moment, her imagination ran away with her. Was there something familiar about the height, the black hair, the general outline? Her knees weak and her hands shaking, she tentatively opened the door, telling herself she was mad, expecting someone who lived in the heart of rural Ireland to be standing at a door in Islington in London.

He looked just the same as he had in all her dreams. His black hair was tossed and a bit unruly, the collar of his coat up as he always wore it. His eyes so dark, often so unreadable, were readable now. He was looking at her with such love, such hungry longing, that she knew she must be dreaming. Maybe she was sick and hallucinating. But there was nothing dreamlike about the way he took her in his arms, so tightly she thought she would smother. Then he started kissing her, kisses so wild and so hungry, kisses she returned with a terrible searing longing that matched his own. In their wild embrace they had backed into the hall. He closed the front door with his foot. They continued to embrace, kissing wordlessly and passionately, as if they were afraid to let go, in case one or the other of them might disappear.

Stephen, lifting his head, was the first to find his voice. 'Thank God I found you. Why did you do this to me?'

She saw the desperation in his eyes and felt traces of tears on her cheeks. She wasn't sure if they were his tears or her own. 'I couldn't tell you. I promised my father – you know the way my mother is –' She didn't get a chance to go on because they were kissing again. His mouth was now on her neck – his head bent to kiss her on the breasts and her slightly swollen belly. When he lifted his head he looked at her with such longing she knew she wanted him. But unlike the first time, the wild, hurried first time when there had been no way they could prevent what happened, she wanted to lie with him and watch those eyes as they made love. She wanted to lie together afterwards and talk a little and hold each other, and make love again and again. As if he could read her thoughts, he asked, 'Can we go somewhere?'

She reached up and brushed his hair back. 'I was thinking the very same thing myself, love,' she whispered, 'but we can't go anywhere now. Peggy is due back any minute – she's just gone to the dental clinic with the boys. She'll probably die if she sees you here.'

'She can die away – no one will ever take me away from you again.'

'I believe you,' she nodded, her blonde hair falling down in front of her eyes.

He took the long silky locks in his callused hand and fingered them. 'It's like silk – and have you given up the ponytail? Are you trying to drive me mad altogether?'

She hadn't time to answer, because they heard the gate opening and the footsteps on the narrow tiles pathway outside. 'Stephen – it's Peggy, she's here. What will I say to her?' There was genuine fear in her blue eyes.

'You don't have to say a single thing, love. I'll do all the talking. It's simple, don't worry.' Their lips touched briefly as they waited for Peggy Fitzpatrick to turn the key in the lock.

The door opened and William and Paul, their young eyes round with curiosity, gazed at the black-haired stranger. The expression on Peggy's face gave her away. Aileen knew that she recognised Stephen from all the stories she must have heard.

'Peggy, this is Stephen Rodgers – I told you about him. Stephen, this is my cousin Peggy, and these lads are her sons William and Paul.' Aileen sounded so normal, as if introducing Stephen was the most natural thing in the world, but he could see the worry in Peggy's eyes as she held out her hand.

'I'm very pleased to meet you,' the older woman said, and Aileen heard him respond in similar vein.

Aileen could almost imagine the thoughts going through Peggy's head. *So this is the ogre that has destroyed Mary's peace of mind. This is the son of Teresa Rodgers who ran off with a tinker, who was born at the side of the road, who, according to Mary MacMahon, has ruined her daughter for any decent man.* Aileen realised that even in the months since she had been with Stephen, he had matured and developed. He exuded a confidence that had not been there before. Glancing at Peggy, she could see the puzzlement in her eyes. Was there also a fleeting look of admiration there as she studied the handsome face, the dark sculpted looks that had always made him stand out in a crowd?

'I can't see anyone stopping us from making a pot of tea, can ye?' she said, confounding both of them with her acceptance of the situation.

'Yes, I'd like a cup of tea all right,' Stephen told the woman who had given Aileen a home, who had been prepared to give her support and strength until after his child was born.

'Give Aileen your coat, and sit down and make yourself at home. Sure you must be right confused, not knowing London or whether you're going or coming.'

'You can say that,' he smiled, obviously pleased at the way she was handling the situation. The young couple sat down on opposite sides of the table, their eyes locking again and again so that the very atmosphere in the small kitchen was charged with their happiness and love. The two small boys looked at Stephen, their eyes round with curiosity at the sight of the stranger.

'Are you from Ireland? My mammy is also,' William told him, his eyes unabashed and staring. 'My mammy says Ireland is nicer than England, and we're going to live there soon.'

'No, silly,' Paul said, 'when Daddy has enough money saved up.'

'Shush, will ye?' their mother told them. 'Be good little boys and run into the parlour and play with your toys and let us grown-ups have a little chat.'

Reluctantly the two little boys left. William stuck his head cheekily back through the door. 'Are you Aileen's sweetheart?' he asked, his eyes round with childish curiosity.

'I am,' Stephen told him, smiling.

'You're like the prince coming to marry her, so you are.'

'Will you get married?' Little Paul, not to be outdone, stuck his own head around the door.

'I most certainly will and you know what? You'll come to the hooley.'

'What's a hooley?' William wanted to know.

'Will you get out of here fast,' Peggy shouted, 'or I'll kill both of ye.'

Suddenly the kitchen was filled with an uncomfortable silence. Peggy was the first to break it. 'I have to tell ye, I made a promise to your mother, Aileen. I promised her if Stephen ever came here I wasn't to open the door to him. And I didn't, did I? You were here when I got home, weren't you?'

'He was,' Aileen answered, 'and now that he's here things are different.' Peggy could see the young girl's eyes were filled with tenderness. 'Now that he's here,' she repeated, 'we want to talk, to plan.'

'Mrs Fitzpatrick,' Stephen interrupted, 'I'd like to talk. I've been out of the picture to such an extent I think I should.'

'Please call me Peggy. Mrs Fitzpatrick sounds awful.'

'All right, Peggy it is. I want to marry Aileen as soon as possible. Certainly way before the baby is born. You see, Peggy, it's simple really – I love her and she's the most important thing in my whole life. Nothing else matters.'

'She's very young, Stephen.' Peggy suddenly sounded tired, as if she already knew that trying to argue with him would be useless.

'No, I'm not, Peggy,' Aileen answered her, 'I feel very old.'

'You've been through a lot for a girl of your age, but sure what am I to do but put up all the objections I can think of? Your mother will have me burned at the stake for letting you even see Stephen.' Peggy thought the young man looked so

349

acceptable, so responsible – and so handsome he'd make you weak at the knees. Maybe poor Mary was truly cracked to have objected to him so much. Maybe 'twas her very objections that had them in the situation they found themselves in now. 'Stephen, even over here, marriages have to be arranged. You have to get letters of freedom from the priest at home and what-have-you.'

'Peggy, I'll arrange everything. We all know that these things can be rushed, well – because of the situation. You will help us, won't you?' It wasn't as much pleading that was in his dark eyes as pain. Peggy realised how much he must have suffered not knowing what had become of Aileen. And he must really care – hadn't he rushed helter-skelter over as soon as he heard?

'Come on, drink up your tea and eat my scones – I can imagine how much ye have to say to each other. When ye're finished, why don't you take him down to the shops, Aileen, and go in somewhere and have a chat? I can imagine how much ye have to talk over.' They looked like excited children at her suggestion. 'Oh, I feel like an accomplice or something – don't ask me now, but I feel I'm doing the right thing.'

Aileen jumped up and gave her a warm hug. Stephen, his dark eyes filled with gratitude, said, 'Thank you. Joe who lives with us at home in Tulla has a habit of saying "You'll have luck for it".'

'I don't know,' said Peggy. 'I might never be able to set foot in my own country because of ye.'

Aileen found a table over near the window and he followed her, awkwardly carrying a brown plastic tray. Several pairs of eyes had tracked Aileen as he walked. He had never seen her look so beautiful. Her leggy height, the thick blonde hair, the animation and sparkle in her blue eyes, made her so desirable that he wanted to dump the laden tray and take her in his arms and out of this dreadful place to a safe haven where they could be alone. When they sat down she smiled. 'I know you're not used to places like this. No self-service in Ross yet, no queues, no sandwiches wrapped up in plastic, no food behind glass. England is different to home. I'm hungry – Peggy's tea and scones didn't fill the void.'

'I'm hungry too,' he told her, 'but for more things than food.'

She didn't answer but she knew what he meant. Their healthy young appetites made quick work of clearing their plate. When they were finished, Aileen went up and got two iced cakes and two of the tiniest pots of tea he had ever seen. After they finished he held her hand in a tight grip. 'We must talk – we must plan. We haven't all that much time.'

'I don't want to think about that yet,' she said. 'I'm so happy to have you here. You see, I used play games all day long. There wasn't much else to do. I used imagine that you'd come and we'd be together and I just want to have it like that for a bit.'

'I know, love, I know, but there's so much to get out of the way before we can be together always. I must go back and make arrangements for the sale of Tulla.'

'You'll sell the farm?' She looked surprised that the land that had been Rodgers land for so long would now pass out of his hands.

'Of course I'll sell it. I'll fix up Máire and Joe so that they won't want in their old age. With the rest we'll start a new life in Australia. I've been thinking of that for so long. You know, I've never been really happy at home. There was that feeling that I didn't belong.'

She tightened her hand on his. 'I know, darling, I know. But it was their ignorance, and sure there was no one as ignorant as my poor foolish mother. It was Niamh, wasn't it, that told you? Tell me how she is. How is Richie? Are they still in love? Come on, tell me everything.'

The eager questions pouring out of her mouth made him laugh. Suddenly he looked younger and she was reminded of the boy on that memorable day at the river when he showed her how to cast a fishing line.

'Talk about being bombarded! Well, I'll do my best. Yes, it was Niamh – she wrote to me and told me. She and Richie are in love. I think it will last. So now, Miss, you know that much.'

'And when you got the letter, were you surprised?' Her question was serious this time, and some of her early shyness was back in her voice.

'I was the happiest person alive. Poor Máire thought I had gone mad. I jumped into the car and drove over to Richie. We drove to Dublin on Saint Stephen's Day, and I was so grateful to that young Niamh that I love her nearly as much as love you.'

'Over my dead body.' She was grinning now. 'But come on, tell me more.'

'She didn't have your address, because of course you didn't send it. But she had Johnnie Davis's address. I came over, hoping that he'd help me. I wasn't wrong. He's a good lad.' He let her hand go and poked out two small bits of paper out of his breast pocket. 'See, Aileen MacMahon, these saved my life – his address and the instructions he gave me on how to get here.'

She watched as he tore them up into small shreds and put them in an ash tray. 'That's silly. You'll never find your way back. What did you do that for?'

'I don't need bits of paper – I have them memorised. Anyway, with my gypsy blood, I need only gaze into a crystal ball.'

'You fraud. That's why I fell in love with you – I thought you were a gypsy.'

They fell quiet as realisation came that their time together was coming to an end. The city was now ablaze with lights and the heavy traffic rolled along the main road in a never-ending line. It had started to drizzle, the fine rain obviously making the driving more hazardous. Stephen glanced out at the unfamiliar scene, the lights of the cars momentarily dazzling his eyes before they turned the corner. He looked back at Aileen, her chin resting on her hand, her eyes never leaving his face. She looked so young and vulnerable, so expectant, as if his coming had lightened her terrible burden.

'Aileen, is there anywhere we could go – to be together? You know what I mean.'

'No, my love, no. Being with you today was like it used to before – before–' Suddenly the old familiar blush was back, heightening the extraordinary blue of her eyes.

'Before the baby,' he prompted.

'Yes,' she whispered. 'I know it's a bit late, but I'd like to spare myself, as the nuns would advise, until we get married. Then it will be all brand new and lovely again. Won't it?'

Her eyes held his and he could see how important it was to answer her childish question. 'All right, but if you hear of a black-haired sod from Ireland exploding on the boat going home, you'll know it was me.'

Together they walked into the gathering dusk. Holding her

hand, he glanced back at the neon light flashing on and off over the restaurant.

'I'll always remember Lyons Corner Café.'

'I just hope you'll remember Johnnie's address.'

'Thirty-seven Weighbrook Street, Shepherd's Bush, London. If I could go as the crow flies I'd be there in minutes – but with all this traffic both over and under the ground, and more people than I've ever seen in my life, it will take me hours. I'll take you back to Peggy's – I don't want you rambling in your condition all over the place.'

Words – words again – and sad little silences. Anything to put off the moment when they'd part.

'There's no need,' she said. 'See that bus stop across the road? A bus will come there any minute and it will take me right up to the end of Peggy's road. Anyway, you have to get going. Aren't you going back to Ireland tomorrow, selling farms and things and coming back to make an honest woman of me?'

'Oh God, I am.' Suddenly they were in each other's arms, oblivious to the noise, the traffic and the people passing. He kissed her with a bruising intensity, raising the odd eyebrow among the passing crowd.

'I love you, Aileen MacMahon,' he whispered into her damp hair. 'I'll never love anyone else as long as I live. Why did I fall in love with a scrawny silver-haired nymph in a school yard a million years ago?'

'Because you thought you were a gypsy and could see into the future. Oh God, Stephen, please don't delay too long selling farms and things. Promise?'

'I won't. I promise, I'll be back quicker than Johnnie wrote the note.' He kissed her again, slowly and tenderly this time. They were indifferent to the rain that drenched them. Her blonde hair was darkened and plastered to her head; his looked even blacker than usual. One raindrop had fallen on his cheek and was coursing down towards his mouth. She reached up and brushed it away.

'Just like a tear.' She choked and suddenly she fell, sobbing, into his arms, her tears mixing with the murky London rain flowing down her cheeks. He caught her hand and led her away from the lights of the café into the darkened doorway of what looked like a closed office block. He removed a handkerchief from his pocket and slowly wiped her tears.

'Don't cry, Aileen. All our troubles are over – it's all ahead of us now, darling. Peggy will think I beat you. Please stop or I'm finished.'

She took the handkerchief from him and wiped her eyes, blowing her nose like an obedient child. She stuck the handkerchief in her pocket. 'It will remind me of you.' She touched his face, tracing her finger over his eyebrows, lightly touching his eyelashes, her fingertips running down his nose and across his mouth. 'When I'm in bed tonight I'll tell our baby what his father looks like. I talk to him at times. He moves a bit now. I didn't know what it was at first but now I do.'

Again they were in each other's arms, and in the darkened shelter of the doorway she unashamedly returned his kisses with an abandon that matched his own. She could feel his rising need and knew that if they weren't sheltering in a doorway in the heart of London, nothing would restrain them from their mutual passion.

'Maybe it's a girl,' he whispered.

'No, it's a boy – I'm sure.'

'I bet it's a girl. I know these things.'

A woman passing with her small dog on a lead wondered how anybody could be laughing on a drizzly, icy day in January.

'Go or I won't let you go,' Aileen told him.

He poked in his top pocket of his suit, and pulling out a roll of notes, peeled away some of them. 'Take these. You'll need money – you're my responsibility now.'

'No, I don't need it. My father sends me some, and Peggy is very good to me.'

'Aileen, take it – I'll feel better.'

Reluctantly she took the proffered notes. 'All right, I'll start buying the trousseau for my wedding.' She watched him shoving the rest of the money back into his pocket. 'You should have a wallet.'

'Farmers don't have wallets. You should know that.'

Wordlessly they kissed for the last time.

'You know where to get the Underground?'

'I do.'

'Mind yourself.'

'I will. Take care of yourself and our little girl till I get back.'

'Boy!' She was smiling now, all traces of her recent tears gone. She gently pushed him towards the intersection, and waited until he joined the crowd waiting for the lights to change before crossing the road. He stood head and shoulders above them all. He waved and she waved back until she could see him no more.

Standing on the platform with the milling throng around him, Stephen felt the rush of hot air and knew the train was coming. Stepping into the lighted carriage, he once again marvelled at how this great city could provide a living for so many people. He thoughts went to Johnnie Davis, probably sitting in his bedsit in front of the spluttering gas fire, waiting for news of his meeting with Aileen. He realised that despite all he had to do, he had never been as happy in his whole life. She was his now. No one could take her away ever again. Not her narrow-minded mother or the father who had extracted such a stupid promise from her. Not the nuns or the priests or any living person. He would never be separated from her again.

Joe and Máire would understand when he told them. With the exception of Niamh and Richie, they were the only two other people who mattered to him. Strange, he thought, he could count the people he loved on one hand. His mother's rash act and the presumption that his father was a nobody had kept him apart from so many.

Automatically he changed trains and with his eyes scanning the Underground map, discovered he had reached his stop sooner than he expected. He got off with the surging crowd, his mind full of Aileen. Her smile, her rain-darkened hair, her lovely face, even lovelier than he remembered. Her young coltish look was gone because of her advancing pregnancy. He thought of the way she had shyly told him that she talked to the baby at night, the way she felt it move, the way she looked at him so trustingly as he outlined his plans.

He didn't hear the woman scream – he didn't see the restraining hand trying to pull him back. He saw only the red towering bus, so near it looked like a great wall. He felt the sharp thud and then there was nothing, just a blur of yellow lights and a repetitive screaming sound he didn't recognise as an ambulance.

He thought he heard a man's voice saying, ''E went right under. Right under, 'e did.' There was something wet – ah yes, it had rained – but it felt different to rain – sticky and warm. And before the great wall of darkness descended, his last thought was for the girl who had loved him despite all the stupid, ignorant, narrow-minded, opposition of others.

PART THREE

Chapter Thirty

'Ah, hello, love.' Peggy Fitzpatrick looked up in surprise as her daughter quietly walked into the room. The girl looked pale, preoccupied. Peggy wildly wondered had she heard the heated and somewhat troubled discussion between herself and Bob. Her husband was already on his knees, raking out the hot ashes from the fireplace, a simple exercise he embarked on every night. Had he seen Ciara's troubled expression? Was he making more noise than usual to stave off any possible trouble?

'Mum – why didn't you tell me? Why, for God's sake, keep me in the dark all these years?' Ciara whirled around to face her father, who was still in a half-kneeling position near the fireplace. 'Dad, for God's sake tell me it isn't true. Go on, tell me.'

'Is what true, girl?'

'You know. What I heard Mum and you discussing now. That I'm adopted. *Adopted.*'

Looking at the distraught, terrified eyes searching his face for an answer, Bob cursed himself for doing a bad job in his own house. When he had partitioned the huge room over the shop, turning it into a kitchen and sitting room, he obviously hadn't insulated it enough. Certainly, by the look on the child, she had heard himself and Peggy. Bob rose from his knees and walked over to his daughter. Putting his arm around her he could feel she was shivering. 'Your mother wanted to tell you again and again, but I was the one that kept putting it off.' He shrugged helplessly, taking in her young dark beauty. 'I was a stupid man, afraid if you knew we might lose you.'

'So it's true, Mum, it's true. Why didn't you tell me? I had a right to know. You know I had!' Ciara was sobbing now, her slim shoulders shaking. 'And who in God's name is this Aileen?' she cried brokenly.

Her father patted her helplessly. 'If you sit down, girl, we'll tell you. 'Your mother will fill you in on everything, so she will.' He glanced at Peggy, who stood looking somehow older than he had ever seen her before.

'Ciara, love,' she entreated, 'please sit down. It was terribly wrong, I know that, but as your dad said, we were afraid, so we were. Will you sit down and let us tell you everything?'

The girl looked from one to the other, and sat down on the little stool her mother sometimes used to rest her legs, wiping her tears with the back of her hand. 'So it's true.' Her voice was little more than a whisper.

Peggy Fitzpatrick would have given the sight from her eyes to tell the child it was just a terrible, terrible mistake.

'Bob, will you sit down too, and if I forget anything help me out?' Her husband sat down like an obedient child. ''Tis where to start, where to start,' she repeated, almost to herself, like someone who had long since pushed away the truth. 'Your mother's name was Aileen MacMahon. Her mother was my first cousin. I knew Aileen since she was a baby. I used to go to the farm where she lived to give Mary a hand when her kids were small. I was only a schoolgirl then but I loved going to their farm in County Kilkenny – it was a change from Dungarvan.' Even as she spoke the rushed agitated words, she noticed that the stillness in the room was uncanny. Ciara was sitting so still, so pale, expressionless, like someone in a dream. She noticed that Bob had put fresh coal on the fire – it had already caught, and the small flames darted erratically as if they wondered why the habit of a lifetime was broken and fresh coals put on and it nearly midnight.

'Mary O'Regan was my cousin's name, and when she married Denis MacMahon she was over the moon. He was considered a great catch – young and easygoing with his own place, every girl's dream. She had three children – your mother, Aileen, was the eldest, there was a son Eddie, who was a bit wild, and another girl, Maeve. The children were all like the MacMahons, very fair and very blue in the eyes. I know it's hard for you to imagine, but you're as different from your mother as chalk is from cheese.'

Ciara sat more unmoving than any statue. The girl should have heard all this a long time ago, Peggy thought, and if she had it wouldn't have been so dramatic.

'Mary MacMahon doted on her children. There was

nothing too good for them, particularly Aileen. She was a beautiful girl – certainly take the eyes out of your head. She was sent to a boarding school in Dublin – some notion her mother had that it would give her a better education and a better polish than the school in Ross. Of course there was another reason too. There was a young man in the parts. He lived with his grandfather, who had a sizeable farm. His mother was an only child who, according to what I heard, was the apple of the old man's eye. But she did a terrible thing – it was the talk of the place, I believe.'

Peggy hesitated, wondering if she should go into things so thoroughly. But an encouraging nod from Bob and a tight-lipped 'Please go on' from Ciara made her continue. 'Well, seemingly when she was seventeen or so, she ran away with a fellow – they say he was a gypsy or he lived with the gypsies. Anyway the girl Teresa – that'd be your grandmother – died in childbirth and the gypsies brought the baby home and gave it to her father. Tom Rodgers reared the child, and he was named Stephen and he was your real father, Ciara. Seemingly Aileen was taken with him always, and Mary was demented she'd end up with him – 'twas sad in a way that the thing she feared most happened.'

'Did you ever meet him?' Ciara asked, her voice subdued.

'Do you want me to go on, love? Or would you like to wait and let that much sink in? It might be easier on your head.'

'Of course I want you to go on, Mum, if it takes till dawn. Maybe I'll never be easier in my head about it, but I must know every single thing. Haven't I waited a long time for it? At least you owe me that.'

'I do, I do. I know that. Well, I did see your father just once. He came to see Aileen when he found out where she was. When the nuns and her parents found out she was pregnant, she was sent across here. Her father asked me to take care of her until her time came to go into a house run by nuns for girls who were unmarried. Her mother Mary was so distracted that she had a recurrence of a nervous breakdown. Wouldn't even say goodbye to the child – didn't even want to see her. It was all so stupid when you think of it. Anyway, she stayed with me and your dad there – I suppose you'll still want to call him that?'

'Of course.' There was an edge of impatience to the girl's words.

'There were more plans for Aileen – she was to go to a top secretarial college for a course to learn office skills, and when she returned home she was to say she had been at a finishing school. That way she might explain her absence. That's it, Ciara – more or less. If there's anything more I can tell you, I'd be only too glad.'

'There's a million things you can tell me, a million. When she knew that this Stephen wasn't going to come back, was she up the wall – demented like I'd be?'

'No, Aileen wasn't like you. She was a quiet, restrained sort of girl. As the weeks became months she got quieter and quieter. During the night she would be feeding you; often when I went down when I'd hear her in the kitchen and she'd be crying. I used to try and console her. But she only wanted him and I couldn't bring him back.'

Ciara sat with her eyes closed as if shutting out the picture of a seventeen-year-old mother who cried for someone who never came. 'Did she write to anyone? Did she try to find out things?'

'She did. I remember she used go posting letters.'

'Did she ever hear from her parents? She had to have heard from them at least.'

'Of course she did. Denis was mad to have her return home. He wrote several letters to her. He wrote to me, asking me to help her change her mind. Her brother and sister wrote also. I don't know about Mary – she became a complete recluse and died five years after you were born.'

'Maybe my father changed his mind – maybe he didn't want to marry her in the end.' Ciara's dark eyes, with their incredible long, black lashes, stared unblinkingly at her mother. She's so like him, Peggy thought – dark, good-looking – yet the little she remembered of Stephen he had seemed calm, solid, quiet-spoken. He hadn't come across as hyper, restless, excitable like Ciara.

'It wasn't Stephen. It was her parents who didn't want them to marry. When Stephen Rodgers had heard she was pregnant he came right over. I was at the dental clinic with the lads and Aileen was at home on her own when he came. I nearly dropped dead when I saw him. Mary had led me to believe he was a nobody – a bit of a tinker, if the truth be known. He was one of the finest fellows I ever saw – dark as

360

the night, and he spoke in a very educated way. When he used to look at Aileen I knew she was everything for him. It was sort of peculiar seeing them together – you could almost feel the way they felt for each other.' Peggy swallowed as she recalled the day so long ago when she had sat in her small kitchen and made tea and buttered scones and had felt so modern with her red formica-topped table and her tubular steel chairs. She had never seen a love like it in any man's eyes. In the terrible months that followed she had had to take the girl in her arms and console her and rock her like a child. At times like that she used be demented wondering what had happened. Why hadn't he come back?

'Go on, Mum, go on,' Ciara urged as if she could never hear enough.

'Sorry, where was I? Ah, well, when he came I forgot all my promises to the MacMahons. I told both of them to go out for a bit so that they could be together. It was the thirtieth of December 1959. I remember it well – I still have the appointment card from the dental clinic in an old bag upstairs.'

'Where did they go, I wonder?'

'Just down to the shops and to Lyons Corner Café. She came home all glowing – it had poured rain and she was wet to the bone, but she didn't care. She couldn't even wait to get her coat off before she told me everything. He was going to sell the farm and they would get married and they would go to Australia – seemingly he always had a hankering to do that. She was like an excited child telling me everything.'

Leaning over, Peggy picked up the poker and broke up the coals in the fire. The flames leaped for a minute, casting a red glow on the faces of the listening young girl, and the man and woman who were so obviously caught up in the past.

'What was she like? What did she look like?' Ciara asked quietly.

'She was tall, with thick fair blondy hair. She had eyes that were as blue as the sky and a lovely figure. I often thought she would have made one of those models. She was like a child at times, one minute playing with William and Paul and making them screech laughing, and the next minute all quiet, maybe thinking of the baby. She rarely discussed her condition – sometimes I don't think the girl knew what was happening to her.'

'I wonder why he did a runner?'

'It was the greatest mystery. If ever I saw a genuine fellow it was him. Of course we made inquiries. He had stayed with a lad the night before but he never showed up there again. He never turned up on his farm in Tulla either. Aileen remembered he had a lot of money on him and got this wild notion that he might have been murdered for the money. We never found out.'

'That's incredible,' Ciara breathed. 'How could someone disappear without trace? What had the police to say? Did Aileen get in touch with the hospitals? Did you and Dad try? Did you, Dad?'

Bob Fitzpatrick spoke for the first time since his wife began her long story. 'We tried, Ciara. England was a different place in the fifties than it is now. It was choc-a-bloc with Irish people all going over in droves looking for work. Stephen Rodgers wouldn't have known a single soul there. It was possible to disappear – we don't even know if he had any identification on him. Aileen remembered he had his money thrust in his suit pocket. She said most farmers carried money around like that. She also remembered that he had torn up an address he had with him. If he hadn't we might have heard something.'

All three fell silent. The only sound in the room was the ticking of the grandfather clock, a fine piece that Peggy had inherited from her home place. Bob Fitzpatrick wondered what it would be like to hear you were adopted. He wondered if he would have cared as much as his beloved Ciara seemed to. He recalled how Peggy had refused to let Aileen go into any home for unmarried mothers for the last three months. She had kept her in the house until her time came. She told the MacMahons that the child had suffered enough; Bob had been surprised that they had agreed so readily. Denis MacMahon was apathetic in a way – but then rumour had it that Mary had tried to drown herself in the river. Imagine being that ashamed of a baby being born out of wedlock!

Now, nearly twenty years later, looking at the hurt and shock in the dark eyes of the child, he felt disturbed that the mistakes people made so long ago still had the power to hurt.

'Why did she give me up? Didn't she want me?'

'Of course she wanted you, love. You were so beautiful and perfect – everyone in the hospital said you were the nicest baby there.'

'How old was I when you adopted me?'

'About four months. She stayed with us until then and did every single thing for you herself. She'd get up so early and never said a word, but I knew she was waiting for the postman. She used get so still when the letters would drop in – I think every day she hoped to hear something. She eventually did that secretarial course, and when she was at that school she got very friendly with a girl called Jane Harris. She was an English girl, and she used to invite Aileen to her father's house in Surrey. Aileen wouldn't ever want to go, because she couldn't leave you. But we made her go a few times, telling her she could do with a break. Eventually this girl made arrangements to go to America, to Chicago, to work. She had lots of good contacts there and said they could get great jobs. She came here to visit us and told us to get around Aileen. I think Aileen decided to go knowing that her life was over in a way. Stephen had been her life and he was gone. The morning she was due to fly out, she dressed you in a pink brushed wool suit. Then she changed her mind and put on a pale blue one. She had you lying on her bed, and when I went in she was tracing her finger along your tiny eyebrows. She said blue suited you better. It was as if she was taking you out for the day, but really she was saying goodbye to you forever.

'The place was like a morgue after she went. I think if we hadn't you, we would have packed up there and then and gone back to Ireland.

'She wrote regularly for a bit and was happy to have us adopt you – signed the papers and everything. It was so straightforward. Then she stopped writing and moved away to a different job. It was as if she didn't want any part of her old life to intrude.'

'Wouldn't you think she'd want to know how I was getting on? How I was growing up? Maybe what I looked like? Wouldn't you, Mum?'

'Listen, love – it wasn't that she didn't care. She absolutely loved you. Maybe she thought it better to cut adrift for our sakes – for your sake. Maybe her own too. I don't know.'

'I can only guess how terrible it is for you to here all this now,' Bob Fitzpatrick intervened. 'It was wrong to keep you in the dark for so long. If you knew how it all happened, you might understand. Your mother there – I suppose you'll still want to call her that?'

Ciara nodded in total agreement.

'She was told she couldn't have any more children. She was right upset. She wanted a little girl. I used to have to drag her away from shop windows full of baby stuff, pink fluffy things. When you came along it was like an answer to all her prayers. No real mother could have done more for you, girl – that I know.'

Suddenly the tears Peggy had valiantly tried to keep at bay spilled over and she started to sob. Ciara saw her heaving shoulders and rushed over to her putting her arms around her. 'Don't, don't. Of course I understand – I do now, honestly I do.'

'Oh Ciara, I loved her. She was like a sister to me.' Glancing over Peggy's head, Ciara noticed that the brown hair was now streaked with grey. Her dark eyes met Bob's and she could see how upset he was.

'Listen, both of you. I can never repay you for the love you've given me. You'll always be my real mum and dad. But you know how restless and curious I am. Would you mind if I tried to find out what happened? There's no way I want to replace you. It's just my curiosity. I'd like to meet them just once. Maybe they're dead. It's possible, particularly my father.' Her dark eyes revealed a trace of excitement. 'Would either of you mind if I tried to trace them?'

Relieved that Ciara appeared more like her normal self, Peggy nodded enthusiastically. 'We wouldn't mind at all, love. Now that you know, it's like a great weight off my shoulders. Anyway, I reared you and I know you, and I feel that you'll always be ours.'

'Don't doubt it for a minute. I'll be around to torture you for another few years at least.'

That night Ciara lay awake, trying to come to terms with the new knowledge that she was adopted. Jumbled, churning, chaotic, frightening thoughts went around and around. Aileen MacMahon, a blonde blue-eyed schoolgirl, banished to England to have a baby so that her family wouldn't be disgraced at home. Stephen Rodgers, a young farmer with money and with some sort of stain as far as his parentage was concerned. Yet when he had heard about her, he had come over in the depths of winter to be with her. God, should she think of Peggy as her mother now? Or should she just think of her as Peggy? Oh God, she didn't know. Anyway, Peggy was absolutely sure that her father had been genuine. Hadn't she recalled the extraordinary love he and Aileen had for each other?

There was something fishy about the whole situation, Ciara thought. It simply couldn't happen now. Fair enough, the fifties might have been a time of recession and poor communication or whatever, but if a young man walked out of a house with all sorts of plans and was never heard of again it was still undoubtedly peculiar. Had Aileen been right to wonder if he had been murdered for his money? Had he been killed in an accident? Or had he simply changed his mind and decided he didn't want to burden himself with a pregnant young wife?

God, what would Peter say when he heard that she was adopted, if he knew that her father was supposed to be the son of a tinker? Ciara couldn't help but smile at the thought of his mother's reaction. As it was, she wasn't too enamoured that her eldest son was going out with a shopkeeper's daughter, a shopkeeper who had made his money on the building sites in England.

When she eventually fell asleep, Ciara's dreams were broken and confused, and she woke up exhausted with an unfamiliar headache. For the first time in her life she didn't want to get up and face the day. She wanted to sink down amongst the warm blankets and stay there and never, ever, have to face the truth that she wasn't the natural child of the couple she loved and always believed were her real parents.

'Why didn't either of ye tell me? You both knew all the time. Why all the secrecy? Were ye afraid I couldn't take it?'

'What's so wrong with being adopted?' Paul asked.

'Why can't I say I'm adopted? I am adopted – why can't I accept it?' she cried.

William stubbed his cigarette on to his saucer – a habit his mother deplored. 'So they finally got round to telling you. I wondered if they ever would.' His grey eyes saw her terrible upset. Though a week had passed, Ciara obviously hadn't come to terms with the unwanted information yet.

Paul added, 'Mam discussed it with us last summer. We

365

advised that it was essential you knew – and that it was time. We told her that knowing what kind of nut you were, the news would roll off you. I see that it hasn't.'

They were in the kitchen after tea on Saturday evening. The three of them always shared the job of tidying and washing-up after the evening meal, now that both brothers were working in Dublin. Peggy had gone to the October devotions and Bob was milling over the accounts in the shop below. Ciara thought the time right to accost her two brothers – or the fellows she thought were her brothers.

'Talk about secretive, furtive, terrified old biddies. Wouldn't you think you would have come out with it all the years we played and fought and told each other all sorts of things?'

'We simply couldn't have gone against their wishes. Paul and I wanted to hundreds of times. But now you finally know, what's the panic? Hundreds of kids get adopted – it's happening every single day. Why blow your top?'

'It's easy for both of you. And I don't *know* why I'm so upset so I don't. All I can say is that it's not easy. It's hard to describe. I feel peculiar. Like I'm on the outside looking in. How would you both feel if it happened to you?'

Paul answered, 'I'd probably be shocked for a bit. Then I'd think about it, then I might even look on it as interesting – then I'd probably forget it.'

'Well, I can't.' Ciara still sounded distraught. 'What would you think if I tried to find them – my real parents?'

William, her eldest brother, the one whose advice she had always sought, told her to sit down 'and stop murdering those unfortunate dishes.' She did exactly as he told her and accepted the cigarette he offered. After he lit both their cigarettes he waited a while before he questioned her. 'When did they tell you?'

'Last Sunday, and it was by sheer accident. I was out with Peter and when I came in full of the joys of spring, I heard both of them talking. First I thought they were having a row – I knew Mum was upset – and then I heard of someone named Aileen and then I heard I was adopted. I went right in and accosted them and I heard the whole story. We were up half the night. It was sad.'

'We were only small fellows – but we remember a bit about

it. Mam doted on Aileen. I vaguely remember her – she lived with us for a long while before you came along,' Paul told her.

'God, I hate you both in a way, but I suppose I'll have to forgive and forget.' Ciara watched the smoke rising from her cigarette, her large dark eyes filled with her own thoughts. 'They said they wouldn't mind if I tried to find them – my real parents. I really want to do that – I want to know what happened.'

They could see Ciara's familiar, determined, stubborn look. When she got it into her mind to do things, William and Paul knew it was impossible to stop her, and over the years they had given up trying.

'There are private detectives up in Dublin who do this sort of thing. I've already made inquiries.'

'You can stay in my flat when you come up,' Paul said, grinning. 'I'll always have a bed for my little sister.'

'But I'm not your little sister.' She was almost on the brink of tears. 'I'm no one.'

'Shush,' William said. 'You'll always be our bothersome sister – nothing will change that. Anyway, now you know why you look so different – dark and foreign and mysterious.'

'Oh, shut up – dark, foreign and mysterious, my eye,' she muttered.

Suddenly the phone jingled into life and William took up the receiver. 'Oh hello, Peter. Yes, she's here. Cold? Flu? Yes, I believe something like that. She's in fine fettle now. Here she is.'

William and Peter listened to Ciara's bright rejoinders which sounded as if she hadn't a trouble in the world. 'That's fine. I'll be ready. Here at eight-thirty. Bye – see you.'

'Have you told him yet?'

'No, I couldn't face him. I pretended I was sick. He's calling this evening, and his mother's invited me to dinner tomorrow night. It's his father's sixtieth birthday, so I'd better practise an instant smile. I'm getting good at it. I'm grinning at Mum and Dad all week like a gargoyle, trying to pretend I'm not put out.'

'What's so awful about telling Peter?' William wanted to know. 'It won't make a whit of difference to him. He's sound.'

'I don't know. I feel a peculiar reluctance to tell him. Isn't that kind of totally stupid?'

*

367

The social evening in the golf club was in full swing when they arrived. Peter had been late calling for her, apologising that something had cropped up at his office and had needed his immediate attention. Ciara was glad – it meant they had to rush and few words were necessary. When they arrived she saw that the Murray family were well represented. Peter's father was there with his golfing friends; according to Peter his father's Sunday fourball was the highlight of his week. The fourball was made up of himself, the doctor, the chemist and the bank manager – four successful men who were generally considered the top echelon of high society in Dungarvan. Ciara liked Peter's father – there was a kindness in his glance and under the bristling brows he always seemed to look at her with approval.

She couldn't say the same for his mother. Beth Murray was years younger than her husband, who was celebrating his sixtieth birthday the next day. Though she did her best to look disdainful and a bit above it all, it was obvious that she wallowed in her position and rarely a week went by when her picture wasn't in the local paper. She was usually pictured at the annual dinner of the Bridge Club, the Lady Captains dinner at the golf club, the Law Society dinner or the myriad charitable functions that went on in the area. Ciara found it difficult to like her and she felt in her heart that Beth Murray didn't much like her either. She would obviously prefer any of her cronies' daughters as a match for her eldest son; many of them would inherit what was generally referred to as 'old money' – money made and stockpiled in the old days when the chasm between rich and poor was very wide.

Peter put his hand on her shoulder. 'Come on over and we'll say hello to the folks before we join the others.'

Ciara was glad she wore the new dress she had bought a few weeks before when she was up in Dublin on a buying spree for the shop. It was Laura Ashley, cherry-red and covered with tiny flowers. It had a scooped neckline and was the new fashionable midcalf length. When she had tried it on, the shop assistant had told her it was perfect with her black hair, her dark eyes and her dusky skin.

'It's perfect – perfect. If you were going for Miss Ireland you'd walk away with it.'

Ciara had laughed and told her she was mad, but had

bought the dress anyway, knowing it was right for her. That evening Peggy had told her she looked lovely, and William and Paul had whistled together She felt good in it herself – it somehow helped to ease the feeling of vulnerability that had swamped her the previous week.

Peter's smile took in his parents' friends as he briefly made the introductions to the ones who didn't already know Ciara. 'Ciara Fitzpatrick – Joan and Harry Tierney, Adrian and Paula Dunne.'

Smiles and handshakes all round, but Ciara was aware that Beth Murray was appraising her, aware that this girl was seriously in the running where her eldest son's future was concerned.

When the introductions and the necessary small talk were over, Peter put his arm around Ciara and, leading her away, said, 'See you all later – we'll find out what's new over here.'

Tim Murray called after him, 'It's good to see you have the excellent taste I had when it comes to choosing women.'

There was general laughter but Beth Murray merely smiled a tight little token smile at her husband's harmless, genial remark.

When they joined the younger set, Ciara was glad to see that Peter's brothers, Noel and Dave, were there with their current girlfriends. 'Hi, Ciara, you look ravishing,' Noel greeted her with a wink. 'When you get tired of big brother there, let me know.'

'Gee thanks,' Rose Power grinned, pretending to be hurt.

The night flew as Ciara and Peter danced a lot, sometimes changing partners, sometimes sitting out for a drink. During the slow waltz Peter held her close, whispering that she was the belle of the ball and telling her that he loved her. She felt so reassured in his arms that the events of the past week eased and blurred a little. Maybe she was worrying too much. Maybe William was right – hundreds of people were adopted every day and it didn't make a whit of difference to their lives. Why should the knowledge have devastated her so much?

The strains of 'Save the Last Dance for Me' filled the air before farewells and promises to meet again were made and she was in Peter's car, driving the two miles back to her home. In the dark confines of the car she felt safe and close to him. The lights of the occasional car passing in the opposite direction highlighted his handsome profile, his fair hair – he was physically like his mother, but she was glad he seemed to have inherited his father's friendly comfortable way with people.

He glanced at her, taking in the black curly shoulder-length hair, the pale oval of her face, the dark, long-lashed eyes. 'You know,' he said tenderly, 'you were the belle of the ball tonight. You never looked lovelier – don't ever wear that dress for anyone but me.'

'You like it?'

'I love it. It made you look like – wait now, let me think. Yes, I have it, like a Romany gypsy princess.'

Her heart thumped uneasily. Why, she thought, can't I just snuggle up to him and say 'Here, there might be some truth in that. You won't believe what I'm going to tell you – you'll be fascinated. I'm not who you think I am. I'm adopted. Yes – adopted.' Imagine. But she couldn't. She wondered at her reluctance. Peter was one of the most open-minded people she had ever met.

Outside her father's shop, he parked the car and, taking her into his arms, kissed her long and passionately, whispering that he'd better go before he ravished her.

'I'll call for you tomorrow evening. Wear the same dress, darling.'

'I certainly won't if makes me look like what you said. I want to impress your mother,' she told him. 'I don't think she likes me.' She sounded a little lost.

'My mother is simply not the enthusiastic type,' he tried to reassure her, 'but she loves you, we all do.'

'Well, had you a good time?' Peggy asked, as she always did, over breakfast before Mass. William and Paul were still in bed and Bob was reading the Sunday papers in the sitting room. Ciara knew she loved to hear any little titbit of gossip, and, over the months, she had regaled her with anything that might interest her. But today she was strangely reluctant to chat. As she played with the toast crumbs on her plate, she idly wondered if she would ever be the same again. Would she be able to put away the knowledge that she wasn't Peggy and Bob Fitzpatrick's daughter, that she wasn't who she thought she had been for nearly twenty years?

She sighed, 'Yes, Mum, it was great – everyone was there.'

'Did anyone admire your dress?'

'Aren't you nosy now? But if you must know, they did. Peter raved about it.'

Peggy knew Ciara wasn't her old exuberant self. She knew the questions about Aileen and Stephen Rodgers would flow again. Even as a little girl, Ciara had had an inexhaustible curiosity – the day hadn't been long enough to satisfy it. Even as a little toddler, she would nod again and again when told things, and then run off, only to be back again in minutes looking for more answers. There was no doubt that the girl wouldn't rest until she knew what had happened to her parents. Ciara was like that – she had an extraordinary tenacity. She certainly wasn't like Aileen in that respect, yet she must have inherited her impulsiveness, her restlessness, her heightened awareness, from someone. Who? Peggy remembered when she was young and helping Mary MacMahon in the summers, the stories she had heard about Teresa Rodgers, the lovely restless madcap who had run away with a tinker and had broken her father's heart. Oh God, it was all so complicated and she felt so tired at times. Maybe the errors of her ways were coming to roost – she should have told the child long ago. To a little girl it would have been like a fairy story. Now she was a grown woman in love with Peter Murray, and the late telling would have obvious repercussions.

Timothy Murray patiently lifted his eyes from sports pages for the latest news on the golf circuit. 'You don't have to go to all that trouble, dear – there's no need.'

'Of course there is need. It's a very important birthday. You'll never be sixty again.'

'Maybe I don't want them to know I'm sixty. Would you like everyone to know you were sixty?'

Beth Murray gave an exasperated sigh. Men – it was so hard to understand what went through their heads. She knew that Timmy didn't care who knew his age, and now there he was pretending that he did. Still, it was true – she wouldn't get too excited about being sixty. She was glad she was only forty-eight; she enjoyed being twelve years younger than her husband. 'If it's any consolation to you, you don't look fifty,' she told him, sweeping the crumbs off the white table cloth on to a brass crumb tray. And he certainly didn't act his age either; he still had the old flirtatious way of talking to women. And how they lapped it up! He couldn't keep his eyes off the girl who was going out with Peter. There was no doubt she was a pretty girl, extraordinarily dark. Not a bit like her parents or her two brothers really. But what was her background? Not much. Her father was a pleasant enough individual, and indeed so was her mother. But what had they? A shop. Word was that it was a very successful shop since the girl had taken a hand in the running of it – but still it was a shop. Beth sighed. She hoped her son's infatuation would pass away and he might pick up with someone more suitable. 'I've invited them to come at seven-thirty for eight. Are you happy with that?'

'Whatever you say, dear – dinner parties are your department.'

'Would you like to know what's on the menu?' she asked.

He nodded, but his mind was already gone on to the fourball. In fact he would be teeing up for it in two hours' time. He'd better not have his customary drinks after it. If he did, he'd nod off in the middle of her dinner party and she'd be furious. He wouldn't hear the end of it until Christmas.

'Tell me,' he asked, trying to show some enthusiasm. He heard her droning on about beef Wellington and a grapefruit sorbet between the game soup and the main course – she had been served that at a dinner party she'd been at a while back, and it was very nice and rather different. He wondered if his approach shot would be as disastrous as it had been recently. Tom Downes told him he was coming up off the ball, slicing it because he was so anxious to see the end of the shot. He'd have to remember to keep the head down. 'Hit and spit' – wasn't that the advice he had got when his father brought him for his very first lesson?

'You're not listening to one word I'm saying,' his wife accused, 'not one word.'

'Oh I am, dear – sorbet and soup and things.'

'Oh, go away and get ready for Mass – if we don't get ten o'clock Mass, you'll be rushing for your golf. Sometimes I think that's all that matters to you now.'

He gave her a playful slap on her still-slim bottom as she walked away, twitching with exasperation.

*

372

'Well, am I all right?'

Bob and Peggy were still browsing through the Sunday papers, sitting in their customary chairs at the side of the fire. They glanced up simultaneously. 'You look fine enough to eat,' Bob told Ciara. Peggy, looking at the white linen blouse with a touch of lace at the neck and cuffs, wondered, not for the first time, where Ciara had got her good taste when it came to buying clothes. The blouse was perfect with the black velvet trousers, its whiteness enhancing her darkness.

'Are you sure, love, a trouser suit is right for a dinner party?' she asked. 'Now I know it's beautiful, but I just wondered –' Her voice trailed away, edged with doubt.

Ciara glanced at herself in the mirror over the sideboard. 'Well, she can like it or lump it.' Her words sounded brave, but she had given a lot of thought to what she'd wear for her first dinner-party invitation to the Murrays'. She couldn't wear the red dress again. Trouser suits were coming into high fashion; the black velvet one was a recent purchase and she felt good in it.

The doorbell shrilled into life, and with another hasty glance in the mirror, Ciara ran down the stairs to open the door for Peter. 'Come on up and say hello. They're up in the sitting room.' She knew that Peggy liked to meet Peter – in fact she was quite proud that her girl was going out with the young up-and-coming solicitor.

Peter shook hands with the Fitzpatricks and they talked about the weather and how Christmas was tearing in, and how the local football team had fared in the day's match.

Back in the car he looked at her, his eyes blazing with admiration. 'You look incredible.'

'I was worried about the trousers – maybe they're wrong for a dinner party.'

'They're perfect. They'd all be wearing them if they looked like you in them, although it's a shame to hide those lovely legs.'

'Stop, will you? By the way, I brought your mother some liqueur chocolates – will they do?'

'They'll do. My father will guzzle the lot of them – he's nuts about chocolates.'

'I feel quite nervous. I think your mother is getting worried I'm running away with her son.'

'Don't be – her son wants you to run away with him, okay?'

'Okay.'

The Murrays lived in an old house in its own grounds about two miles from the town centre. Ciara had no idea it was so magnificent. The hall was large and spacious with an old Victorian fireplace and a fire, even though the evening wasn't that cold. The old heavy brass fire irons were gleaming, and the uncharitable thought came to Ciara, as Peter led her into the drawing room, that the hall fire was lit to impress.

Everyone seemed to be already there before: his parents, brothers, their girlfriends, two older couples who were introduced as Timothy Murray's brothers and their respective spouses. Ciara felt distinctly nervous, and gratefully accepted a dry sherry from the proffered tray. She didn't particularly like sherry, but she could see that all the women were drinking it. After the initial introductions, she and Peter gravitated towards the younger crowd. She had become quite friendly with Sara Doyle, Dave's girlfriend.

'Not easy,' she whispered, nodding towards the well-dressed women and the dark-suited men.

'Easier after you have half a dozen of these.' Sara glanced towards the maid bearing down with replenishments of dry sherry. Ciara grinned; hurriedly gulping down her drink, she followed Sara's example, took another and began to relax. She saw Peter talking to his uncle; he looked across and met her gaze, rewarding her with a wink. She felt a sudden rush of love for him. He looked so relaxed, so right in his surroundings. She looked around the room with what she hoped was casual interest. She had never been anywhere so beautiful. The concealed spotlight highlighted the fine oil paintings on the wall. The furniture was mostly antique, what era, though – or was it circa they called it? – she wasn't sure. She only knew she hadn't seen anything like it before. She heard Beth Murray's thin tones informing her sister-in-law that she had got a pair of Georgian occasional chairs at an auction in Ivy Hall in Birr recently. So she was learning, Ciara told herself. Georgian – not that old, though they still probably cost a bundle. She thought of her father – yes, yes, she told the inner little voice that had a habit of taunting her recently, he'll always be my

374

father, kind, caring, and good – and the way he had worked in on buildings sites, even in sewers, in London for over twenty years to earn the sort of money to achieve his ambition and to make Peggy's dream come true. Home to Ireland and enough money to buy a little business. Ciara doubted if the people who laughed and chatted in this wonderful drawing room would consider a little shop great reward after a lifetime of hardship.

'Well, I see you're taking my advice,' Sara giggled, noting that Ciara was on her third glass of sherry.

'I wasn't thinking – my mind is on all sorts of things.'

Sara glanced at Peter, taking in his tall handsome good looks. 'I wouldn't blame you – he's a bit of all right.'

The buzz of voices was getting louder and louder – the laughter of the men noisier as yet another golf story was told and embellished. Peter came over to her and took her jacket; she was grateful; the room was getting warmer and warmer and the meal was obviously going to be long.

On the way in to the dining room, he whispered that he loved the blouse.

'And the red dress,' she grinned.

'And you,' he answered.

She was placed beside Peter's uncle Tom, and opposite Peter. Tom Murray was friendly and interested, asking her all about her young years in London and about how she felt when she came to live in Dungarvan. He asked about the shop. How was business? She answered readily, and told him how she loved the business, how her father had expanded so much and now she had to attend toy fairs as early as February to get a notion as to what the kids would want for Christmas. She told him all about a little brown furry toy, called a Chipmunk, that was going to be the biggest seller at Christmas since the Davy Crockett hat. He was amused and poured her out another glass of wine, which she seemed to get rid of all too easily. He was more than helpful, pouring her another and even topping that up. She felt heady and peculiar but she drank it. She wasn't quite sure when she felt removed from the gleaming white table linen, the heavy silver cutlery, the handcut crystal glass – someone had said it was old glass, as if the new Waterford crystal wasn't in the same league. Voices and more voices, the odd guffaw of loud spontaneous laughter, more muted polite dinner-party laughter, someone addressing her directly and her words careful and enunciated, the little inner voice telling her, *Take it easy now, take it easy. Smile and nibble your dessert, and nod and comment on the superb meal, because if you don't they'll know you're drunk, drunk, drunk. Yes, drunk.*

From a distance she heard Peter's mother's mincing tones. 'Tom, you must know her. She's one of the Boyles from County Clare – near Killaloe. Her father bred White Star which won the Derby a couple of years ago. He's very well known in racing circles.'

'And my father was known by all the gypsies in County Kilkenny.' She hardly recognised her own voice. She sipped her coffee, hoping that it might stop her but the little ploy didn't work. She knew there was a terrible irrepressible impulse telling her to go on and shock them. She'd give that smug lot something to talk about.

'Ciara.' She heard Peter's amused tone. 'Ciara, you're getting mixed up – your father hardly set foot in Kilkenny.'

'I'm adopted – you didn't know that. My mother was a girl named Aileen from County Kilkenny. She actually became pregnant when she was at school and sent off on the boat. My father's name was Stephen and he was the son of a tinker or a traveller or an itinerant or whatever they call them now.' She smiled a glittering bright smile, her dark eyes slowly taking in each and every one of them. 'So there – isn't that interesting?' Her voice sounded slurred and thick and she wondered, why, for a wild moment, she felt exultant and free. Then everything became a blur and even Peter's puzzled face disappeared from her view.

Chapter Thirty-One

John Kenny glanced down at the busy street before tackling his Monday-morning workload. A typical November day, he thought, foggy and damp, and now he could see a slight drizzle starting to fall. He remembered that when he was growing up on the farm in County Clare, his mother had always referred to the month of November as the Holy Souls month. When it drizzled like it drizzled now, she would say, 'It's the poor Holy Souls crying for prayers.' Looking at the traffic streaming along Dame Street, John recalled it was a long time since he had thought of the Holy Souls, or indeed his childhood in Clare. His mother was still alive and living on the farm with his brother and his brother's wife. He realised it was time he paid her a visit. Since he had started up as a private investigator he had got so caught up in his work and all its underlying problems that his trips home were few and far between.

It was five years since he had left the Gardaí and set up his own business. He was thirty-two now, unmarried, with ten people on his payroll. He remembered his first small office in Harolds Cross, when he had started his new career on a bright frosty January morning. His mother told him he was mad, resigning from the guards when all the young fellows in Ireland would give their eye teeth to get into the force. Steady, sure money and a good pension, and she reminded him she had never known a poor guard in her life.

'Is it gone in the head you are?' she had argued heatedly. 'A detective? You went to too many pictures and read too many detective books. Sure 'tis well your poor father isn't here to see you make a fool of yourself.'

She had gotten quieter as his business had grown over the years. John Kenny was now considered one of the best at his game, specialising in a vast range of activities, including workplace investigations, research on employers and employees, tracing natural mothers, missing persons, adoption tracing, finding bad debtors, insurance investigations, custody and family-law investigations. If he failed in his investigation, his fee covered only expenses; if he succeeded, his clients paid up readily. His team were top professionals when it came to the use of the very latest in electronic surveillance instruments. Yes, he felt he had come along way from the infertile rocky farm in County Clare and from traffic duty in O'Connell Street. John Kenny had earned the respect of his competitors and clients.

Walking away from the window, he glanced at his appointments book for the day. A married couple named Tracy looking for a missing son; three insurance investigations of fraudulent claims; a Mrs Doran wondering where her husband spent his evenings; a search for some stolen paintings; and a new client named Ciara Fitzpatrick, anxious to trace her natural parents. Just another routine day, he thought. In a way he was glad. He had just brought to a satisfactory conclusion an unsavoury case where a father, an extremely wealthy landowner, had abused his children physically, sexually, and mentally in a most cruel and savage way. Despite his political pull and his enormous wealth, his case had crumbled when John Kenny obtained concrete proof of his heinous crimes and the terrible suffering of the mother over the years. The mother was now about to start a new life in the States and the father was languishing in jail. When a case ended as satisfactorily as that, he felt happy – fulfilled.

It was ten-thirty before Ciara Fitzpatrick sat in the chair opposite him. At first glance three things struck him. She was very young, very tense – taut like a coiled spring – and very beautiful. He hadn't seen blue-black hair like that since he left County Clare. But her long-lashed eyes were the wrong colour for hair like that. They were dark brown – almost black – far darker than the bogs he had worked on as a young fellow. He smiled at her to put her at her ease.

Her answering smile played briefly around her wide mouth and then disappeared. 'You know why I'm here,' she said.

'Yes, I have all the particulars. You found out you were adopted in the late fifties, and you would like to trace your parents.'

'Yes, I would.'

'Why?'

She found his direct question and the steady gaze from his clear grey eyes disconcerting. 'I just want to. I only heard about a month ago that I was adopted. I was shocked and found the whole business upsetting.'

'Hearing it at this late stage can be a bit of a shock.'

'It was. Seemingly my parents – well, the two people I thought were my parents – kept putting it off. I think Peggy had persuaded herself I was her own. And by the way, they couldn't have been better or kinder or more generous.' He could see she was losing some of her initial apprehension about discussing her situation with him. Her tone had become more confident and her dark eyes never left his face. 'But trying to find Aileen and Stephen, my natural parents, has become a compulsion – almost an obsession.'

'Sometimes,' he told her quietly, 'the search for natural parents can end in hurt, disillusionment – even heartbreak. I must tell you these things. When a woman makes her mind up to have her baby adopted, incidentally a decision she hasn't come to easily, she usually decides to get along with her life.'

'I accept that, but I have a feeling – a sort of premonition – that it won't end like that for me. It's just a feeling I have in here.' He watched as her gloved hand tapped the lapel of her camel coat.

'All right,' he said, 'start at the beginning. Tell me everything you have been told. Everything you feel I should know.'

John Kenny listened as she related everything Peggy had told her. How her mother had been only seventeen, attending a boarding school in Dublin, when her pregnancy had been discovered. How her father had extracted a terrible promise from her that she wouldn't tell the child's father. How her boyfriend had been considered a nobody because his father had been a traveller, a gypsy. His name was Stephen Rodgers and he had inherited a farm from his grandfather; he had eventually heard about Aileen's condition from her best friend, a girl attending the same school. When he had heard he had immediately come to England, and the young couple made plans to marry. He planned to return to Ireland, sell his farm and tie up his affairs. 'Peggy said he was a fine fellow, and Aileen my mother loved him – in fact, Peggy says she had never in her life seen a young couple so much in love. After leaving my mother on a corner in Islington, he walked away and was never seen or heard of again.' She shrugged her slim shoulders. 'People don't just disappear. Something terrible must have happened. I want to find out.'

'I will certainly take on the case – there's no problem there,' John Kenny told her. 'But I don't want you walking out that door thinking that everything will be fine, that there will be a fairy-tale ending. The end result of a successful tracing can be fraught with frustration and disappointment. You can build a dream inside your head and then see it crumble. The people involved could be dead; they could have married and have families now. The burning love affair you've heard about could have been a youthful fling. For you to turn up in their lives now could be an embarrassment. I'll take the case on, but I must warn you, it could be expensive and could end in frustration.'

'I want you to take it on,' she said firmly.

He nodded, holding out his hand and taking hers. 'May I call you Ciara? First-name terms are best in this business. You call me John.'

'Agreed.'

He was relieved to see she was smiling and that some of the tension had left her. 'The first thing I want you to do is to get me the names and addresses of all the people who knew your parents in the area where they lived. The school friend with whom she corresponded – she would be invaluable. Friends of Stephen – maybe labourers he had employed on the farm. Your adoptive mother will help you there. I find they usually turn up trumps at a time like this. When I make contact with those people, it would be better you saw them. I will accompany you if it would make it easier.'

'Thank you – I would like that.'

Ciara got up from the chair and held out her hand. He took it, thinking she was taller than he had first thought. She was so lovely; he was sure that she was spoken for, as they used to say down in Clare. When she walked outside the door she waved and smiled. He waved back, realising only then he was in danger of breaking the rule he constantly preached against – involvement. He was getting involved. He had suggested he would accompany her to meet people who might have known her father. More than likely, the poor bastard had panicked when confronted with a pregnant girl, knowing the disapproval he caused in her family. It was the most likely explanation. Yet there was something – undoubtedly there was something that didn't quite add up.

Ciara felt a strange excitement, coupled with a feeling of satisfaction, as she sat on the train home. She was glad she had met John Kenny, and glad she had started the ball rolling. She liked him too. He came across as a solid, no-nonsense, down-to-earth kind of guy. Then again, he wasn't that young. He must be over thirty and maybe you became down-to-earth and solid at that age.

She liked his clear grey eyes and his dark lashes. She also liked his deep voice and that Clare accent. Just as well – she might have a lot of contact with him during his search.

She thought of Peter, and finally and reluctantly she dragged her thoughts to the evening she had disgraced herself. It was over two weeks ago and it was only now that she could bring herself to even think about it. She wondered if she were mad. Why had she picked his father's birthday party to tell everyone what she had found out? She had blitzed Beth Murray's carefully planned evening. What mad impulse had possessed her? Was it Peter's mother and her high-and-mighty ways, her snobbish, stupid name-dropping? Was it the feeling that maybe the Murrays, even Peter, thought they were above everyone else in town? Then again, maybe she was guilty of the same things. Was part of her attraction for Peter the fact that he was a successful young solicitor who would eventually take over the old and trusted firm? Could that in any way be the reason she wanted him? No, no, it wasn't. She remembered when they had gone out together first how wonderful everything had been, how her heart had sung all day, waiting for the witching hour when she would be with him. Had something changed since that dreadful dinner party?

He had taken her home. He had firmly, even a little roughly, helped her with her jacket and walked her down the steps to his car. Through a haze she recalled she had made her farewells, and had been aware of a cold calculating look in Beth Murray's eyes. Sara, Dave Murray's girlfriend, had muttered, 'Good for you.'

Peter had kissed her only briefly when he had said

goodnight outside her door.

Peggy had been preparing to go to bed and had glanced up from setting the table for breakfast, something she insisted on doing no matter how tired she was or how late the hour – the Fitzpatrick breakfast table had to set the night before. She had seen Ciara's pale face, her dark eyes glittering with the devil-may-care look she knew heralded trouble.

'You're home early,' she had said quietly.

'I told them,' Ciara laughed.

'You told them?'

'Yeah – I got sick and tired looking at them, so smug, polite and polished, so I told them, I did.'

'You told them what?' Peggy wanted to know. 'And you're not making much sense. I think you have too much drink taken, so I do.'

'I told them I was adopted and that the old lineage wasn't too good – that there was a bit of a gypsy in me, so there.' Ciara's words had slurred slightly; she had been aware that she had never seen Peggy so upset.

'I think, Miss, you'd better go to bed, and maybe in the morning you'll be more normal and not go around disgracing yourself, your father and me.'

'But he's not my father and you're not my mother, so you needn't be disgraced because I'm not your flesh and blood, am I?' Ciara had started to cry like a few drunks she had seen – stupid melancholic tears when the drink was losing its high.

Peggy had caught her arm and promptly led her into her bedroom. She had silently helped her undress, muttering, 'Maybe it was the shock of it all – maybe that's what it was.'

Now Ciara looked at her reflection in the window of the railway carriage and noted how serious, almost grim, she looked. She recalled her headache the following day. William and Paul had joked about her getting locked in Murrays', of all places. She had even thought that they looked at her with a new-found respect.

Peter had called for her the following evening, and they had gone for a long drive. They had driven almost to Mount Mellery before he stopped the car.

'What's all this nonsense about you being adopted, and throwing in the tinker for good measure?'

'It's not nonsense – I am. And I didn't make up the tinker

bit either. I heard it from Mum and Dad a few days before your mother's party. I don't know why I blurted it out – a lunatic impulse or something.'

'So it's true – you're adopted.' He had sounded quite incredulous.

'Yes, adopted. Seemingly my mother's name was Aileen MacMahon and my father was Stephen Rodgers. They were from County Kilkenny and my mother was a second cousin of Peggy's. That's why she adopted me.'

'Why in heaven's name didn't they tell you before this? Why did they take so long? That was stupid.'

'They didn't think – they just kept putting it off, maybe thinking they'd never have to do it. I agree it was stupid in this day and age.'

He had nodded with a quick intake of breath, as if he couldn't comprehend how anyone could have lapsed to such an extent. He had been silent for a bit, letting this unpalatable news sink in.

'And what's this about a tinker?' he had asked finally. 'Were you just trying to be dramatic, to take a rise out of my mother?'

She had told him what she had heard and how it was generally accepted that the man who was her father was supposedly the son of a tinker.

Peter had let that sink in for a while too before he replied, 'You could have told me when we were together. You didn't have to pick Dad's birthday to unburden yourself, did you?'

'I suppose I didn't. I like your dad, and someday I hope to apologise. Let's face it, Peter, I was drunk. Bloody drunk. The sherries and the wine went to my head. That, and maybe the shock of the whole business unhinged me. I don't know.'

He must have felt sorry for her then, because he had taken her in his arms and kissed her again and again. 'It doesn't really matter,' he had told her. 'It's not the end of the world, and I understand it must have been a hell of a shock.'

'Will it make a difference?' she had asked. 'You know, about us getting engaged and what-have-you?'

'Of course it won't, you little nut. I love you; I'm not interested in who your parents were.' She had relaxed in his arms, but later that night there had been a niggling doubt that his voice hadn't held that much conviction.

Now, as the train plunged through the dark countryside, past isolated farmhouses with lights in the windows and small villages where nothing stirred, Ciara recalled the night she had told Peter that she was going to try to trace her parents. He had taken the news quietly, merely wondering if Bob and Peggy would be upset. She had explained that they were all for it, and had told him she had already made an appointment with a private investigator in Dublin. He had listened politely, and had even suggested that he accompany her to Dublin, but she had insisted that she wanted to do this thing on her own. She had animatedly told him everything Peggy had told her about Aileen, her mother, attending a boarding school in Dublin. About Stephen Rodgers, who had inherited a substantial farm in a place called Tulla in County Kilkenny. About how Stephen had rushed over to London when he heard what happened. How Peggy had been very impressed with him, and how the young couple had planned to marry when he had tied up his affairs in Ireland. How he had walked away from Aileen and how she had never seen him again. Peter had listened with the professional attention he probably gave any of his clients.

She had seen him only once since, when they had gone to see the film *A Touch of Class* with Glenda Jackson and George Segal. Now, putting out her hand to wipe the condensation off the carriage window, Ciara recalled that he had held her hand, as he always did, throughout the film. They had gone for a meal afterwards and he had been teasing and tender; he had kissed her with his usual urgency and passion when they said goodbye, and he had wished her luck with her private investigator in Dublin. So why, why did she think that things had changed since he had heard she was adopted?

Two weeks later Ciara was in the shop with Bob and the two assistants. They had received the first of the Christmas orders and were packing the shelves and discussing the seasonal window display when the phone rang.

'For you, Ciara,' Bob shouted.

The deep voice and matter-of-fact tones of John Kenny told her that he had arranged for her to meet Niamh and Richie Casey, who were married and living in Kilkenny, where they had a supermarket and hardware store. He had also made arrangements for her to meet Eddie MacMahon, her mother's brother, in Ross. He had also found out that Joe Ryan, who had worked on her father's farm, was alive and well, though over eighty years of age now. The old man lived in a thatched cottage three miles from the Rodgers place in Tulla. John wondered if it was possible for her to meet him two days later in a pub named the Punch Bowl, in the main street in Kilkenny.

She held the phone tightly, wildly excited, wondering if he had untangled the mystery of her father's disappearance and her mother's whereabouts.

'Now I did warn you,' John said, 'that you could be opening a hornet's nest. If you want to change your mind at this stage, there's no harm done.'

'No, John, I don't want to do that. I'm more excited than you'll ever know.'

Putting down the phone, she was glad that Peter was in Dublin on a week's business. Without him and his disciplined mind, she had time to wallow in wild flights of imagination. Maybe things would work out – maybe she would find her mother – maybe the mystery surrounding her father's disappearance would be solved.

That evening, Ciara asked Bob for a loan of his car, telling him that she had an appointment with John Kenny in Kilkenny in two days' time.

'I don't mind you having the car,' he told her, 'but tell me, Miss, what am I going to do with a partner who's haring around the country instead of looking after the shop?'

'Dad, I'll promise I'll make it up to you. The Chipmunks and the Cabbage Patch Dolls are already walking out. Wait till you see the returns on Christmas Eve – we'll be laughing all the way to the bank.'

He smiled. 'I hope so.' He could see the restless excitement in Ciara's eyes, her inability to relax or sit still for any length of time. He loved the child; had loved her from the moment Aileen had brought her home. He wasn't really worried that if a miracle happened and she was successful in this business of finding Aileen, they would lose her. Indeed, it would be strange if Aileen was to come back into their lives. God, she had been a grand girl, and he hoped she had found some measure of happiness.

Looking at her daughter, Bob thought it strange that she had inherited nothing from her mother. Aileen had been a lovely girl, with quiet accepting ways about her. She hadn't been madly impulsive or full of Ciara's restless energy. The girl must have inherited all that from someone on Stephen's side of the family. Only the other day he had read an article in the *Irish Press* by one of those psychiatrist doctor fellows, which had said that children were the product of four grandparents – puzzling, all that stuff, but he supposed, those fellows knew what they were writing about.

Chapter Thirty-Two

Ciara was relieved when she saw John Kenny standing at the bar, reading a paper and drinking a beer. There was a calm assurance about him. She hadn't realised he was so broad-shouldered and tall. Then again, she recalled that he had been a garda, and most of them were physically fine. His hair was more auburn than brown, she thought. He was sitting in a pool of winter sunlight, and she noticed that a faint scar ran from the side of his well-shaped mouth down to his chin. Maybe he had acquired it in his young years, or during the course of his work. As if aware that he was being watched, he put down the paper and met her gaze.

Glancing at his watch, he smiled. 'On time – I like my clients to be punctual.'

'I'm glad you're here – didn't fancy sitting in a pub on my own.'

'Somebody might run away with you?'

'No – it's not the done thing in the country. Girls in Dublin might get away with it, but not down here.'

'Well, is it the done thing down here to have a drink?'

She hadn't had a drink since the catastrophic evening she had ruined Beth Murray's dinner party. 'I've discovered I'm not the best to drink – it blows my mind – but I'll risk a glass of beer.'

Over a simple roast-beef lunch Ciara congratulated him on the progress he was making.

'Easy so far,' he said. 'What I have done is routine. Wait until we get out into the big world – the States, maybe Australia. Wasn't that where your father intended making a fresh start?'

Ciara nodded, thinking how impossible it must be to try and find the whereabouts of anyone in vast countries like America or Australia. Her dark eyes clouded at the thought. 'Do you have much success in cases like mine? It can't be easy.'

'We have ways and means, my child.'

The thought came to her that if anyone had told her six weeks ago that she would be sitting having lunch with a private detective she had hired to trace two people she had never known existed, she simply would have told them they were stark raving mad. John Kenny looked so completely different from the popular conception of a detective. There was no sleazy raincoat, no pulled-down hat, no rapidly fired questions; there wasn't even a cigarette. He looked like a successful businessman, or maybe a teacher or a prosperous farmer in his best clothes.

'Are you married?' The question was out, impulsive and breathless, and she couldn't take it back. 'I'm sorry, I wasn't thinking. I shouldn't have asked.'

'I'll forgive you. I'm not married, never got round to it – too busy, too preoccupied or something. Maybe in my business you see too much of the bad side. And you – are you spoken for, as they say?'

'I am. At least I thought I was. No, I still am – God, it's confusing. Maybe we shouldn't complicate things with our personal lives.'

'You started it.'

She liked his smile – it was sort of quizzical and teasing, and his teeth were white and even. 'I'm going out with a fellow named Peter Murray. A solicitor from Dungarvan – his father and grandfather before him were at the same game. They are very wealthy, and have a fine house, and they belong to the best clubs, and he's considered a great catch. I'm supposed to be a very lucky girl.'

'I'd say he's probably a lucky fellow.'

'Not any more.' She surprised him by bursting out laughing. 'I did a terrible thing at a dinner party in his house a while back.' She outlined the evening, describing how the conversation had got round to some of the top families in Ireland. 'I don't know what got into me, some terrible impulse. What did I do? I blurted out that I heard I was adopted and that my father was the son of a tinker. God above, talk about shock tactics. Even Peter was furious. I know he was – he pretended he wasn't, but he was.'

John Kenny looked at the mobility of her lovely face, at the restless movement of her hands, the amazing length of her black eyelashes, and felt a strange attraction, more than a hint of the early hunger that used to assail him when he took a girl out on a date. 'People recover,' he said, 'and it will be only a nine-day wonder. Anyway, Ciara, we must get going – we have business to do.'

She jumped up, running her hand agitatedly through her black hair. 'Do you know what, I'm terrified.'

'It's too early to be terrified, now we're only untangling. When we find what we're looking for, then I'll allow you to be terrified.'

The bright and modern shop had the name Richard Casey & Sons on the sign above the premises. Outside the hardware section was a sizeable display of goods. There was a happy buzz about the place, as if indeed Richard Casey & Sons was a successful enterprise. John Kenny had parked his car at the end of the street, and as they walked into the shop, Ciara whispered, 'Are you sure they know we're coming?'

'If I couldn't organise this, I'd be better off back on the beat.' He put his arm around her, as if to alleviate her nervousness, as he led her into the hardware shop, which didn't look as impersonal as the supermarket. It had an old-world look about it, as if it carried everything from the proverbial needle to the anchor. Up at the far corner was a youngish-looking man with a receding reddish hairline. He was dressed in casual slacks and wearing a Fair Isle jumper, and was obviously very much at home as he joked with a customer.

'My mouth is gone dry – I think I'm going to drop dead,' she whispered. But John Kenny didn't appear to be listening. He walked over to the red-haired man, held out his hand and introduced himself.

Ciara saw the owner of the shop glance up, and she could see his utter astonishment as he came over with outstretched hand, taking in every inch of her. 'Jasus, you're the spit of him so you are,' he greeted her, taking her hand in a firm, warm clasp.

Then it was all confusion and action. Richie Casey shouted to a young lad who was down at the paint section, 'Peadar, take over for a bit – I'm taking these people upstairs to herself.'

He led them through the stockroom, warning them not to break their necks over the buckets and basins, telling them he was a poor man and couldn't afford the insurance. If it had been another time, Ciara would have been looking around at everything so she could to tell Bob about it when she got home. As it was, her heart was thumping loudly and her mouth was like the Sahara. Was this a dream? Was she really walking behind a close friend of her father?

When they got to the top of the stairs, Richie Casey opened a panelled door, leading into a large, bright living room. They could hear the sound of a vacuum cleaner; way down behind a sofa, a dark-haired woman was working busily. Ciara wondered if this was Niamh, the school friend her mother had taken into her confidence.

The woman looked up and switched off the cleaner . Her brown eyes were warm and friendly. There was no formal handshake – instead, after a quick appraisal, Niamh put her arms around Ciara and hugged her close, saying, 'God above, I can't believe it – I can't.'

It was as if the two woman had known each other all their lives. When Niamh finally let her go, Ciara could see she had a trace of tears in her eyes. 'We'll just have to sit down or I'll fall down.' She glanced towards a door. 'I have a few bits and pieces ready – I only have to make the tea. Come on – out here it's bright and cheerful.'

They followed her out into a large kitchen, warm with late winter sunshine and the heat from a large range with an assortment of brightly coloured saucepans on top. 'When I was young, living in Skerries, we always ate in the kitchen. I think it's much nicer than a dining room – I think dining rooms are the gloomiest rooms in any house. Ciara, I'm just prattling away to cover my astonishment, I can't take my eyes off you. Richie what do you think? Did you ever see the like of it?'

'I didn't – I told her that already. The spit of him – the very spit of him.'

Over a huge pot of tea, some buttered scones and a large cream sponge, they got down to the business that had brought them together. John Kenny briefly explained about the case and how important Aileen and Stephen's close friends were to them. Ciara couldn't take her eyes off Niamh Casey. She looked so young in her red polo-necked jumper and jeans, with her cropped dark hair and her lively, dancing eyes. Richie couldn't do enough for them – he plied them with food, and though Ciara wasn't a bit hungry she made an effort to eat, not wanting Niamh's efforts to go unacknowledged.

'Of course I'll tell you everything I know,' Niamh said. 'Aileen wrote to me at the time, before you were born, Ciara. We were very close friends – she was the sister I never had. She had taken me into her confidence in school about the possibility she might be pregnant. Shortly afterwards she was gone, vanished, exiled. I'll never forget the way I felt – lonely and demented, because she had made me promise I wouldn't tell anyone.' Her brown eyes raked every line, every plane of Ciara's young face. 'Do you know what? She would be fierce disappointed that she didn't pass on a single thing to you. She was so fair – a real blonde with the bluest of eyes. In school they used call her the blonde culchie. Funny thing, it never annoyed her. She used laugh to it off, although all the country girls hated to be called culchies.'

'Ah sure, 'tis the culchies that are running the country. I keep telling that to that Dublin jackeen I married.' Richie was grinning at his wife, his devotion very obvious.

'What I would like to know,' John Kenny asked, 'is did she write to you after Stephen Rodgers came to London? What were her impressions at the time?'

'Yes, she wrote all about it, every detail. I told you we were very close. Stephen stayed with a Johnnie Davis in a bedsit in London the night before he went to see Aileen. She described their meeting in detail. They were only with each other for a few hours – he was mad to get back to Ireland and sell up, and then they'd get married. The last time she saw him was when he waved at a pedestrian crossing before getting the Tube.' She stopped, remembering it all as if it were yesterday. 'Listen, Ciara. I knew your father. He would no more leave Aileen MacMahon in the lurch than he would kill an old woman. He worshipped her. She worshipped him. When he got my letter it was Christmas Eve – he was up in Skerries on Saint Stephen's Day. He wanted to rush over there and then. Something terrible must have happened to him. I believe he had a lot of money on him – maybe he was murdered or something. It had to have been something as dramatic as that.'

'And after Aileen went to America?' John Kenny prompted.

'I heard from her a few times after she went to Chicago –

she was working for a newspaper. She went to the States with a girl she met at a secretarial college.'

John told them, 'At the Smith and Harrington School of Commerce. I've found out all about that. She left in October 1959.'

'Well, I did hear from her a few times after she went to the States but then the letters stopped. I was sorry, but I understood that her old life was very painful and maybe she wanted to cut herself off and start again.'

'And you, Richie?' John asked. 'What is your opinion of the whole business?'

'I lived twenty miles from where he farmed, within cycling distance from each other. We used to cycle over and back to each other.' Richie grinned and rubbed his slight corpulence, 'I don't know if I could do it now, but we were young then.' He sobered up and closed his eyes in an obvious effort to recall what might be important. 'I won't go into every single little fiddle-faddle fart you know already; all I can say is he was my best friend. We were at school together, we went to matches together, we had a few pints together, we went to the dances together. He wasn't much of a fellow to shift the birds, because he had only one girl in his life, Aileen MacMahon. He knew her since he was knee-high to a grasshopper, but they could never do a normal line like others did. There was some old scandal about him and who his father was, as if anyone would give a shit – begging your pardon – who his father was when they could see he was such a decent sort. Anyway, he was brought up by his grandfather who left him everything – money, farm, the lot. I think that shut up some of the old biddies in the area – they wouldn't have minded landing him for their daughters then.' He looked at Ciara and nodded. 'And if God was good and if Stephen was standing beside us now, he couldn't deny you. Because as sure as God made little green apples, you're the very cut of him – I never in my life saw the like of it. He had the same eyes and those bloody long lashes – the girls were mad for him. I had a sister, and she and her friends had me pestered about him. But he had only one interest – Aileen.'

'What were the rumours in the area after his disappearance?' John Kenny asked.

'Oh, everything broke then. The story got around that

Aileen MacMahon was pregnant and that he had done a runner. In fact, Aileen's mother never got over the scandal. She hated the very ground he walked on. 'Twas peculiar. She died young enough – they say she never got over the fact that her daughter had a baby for a fellow she considered a nobody. When Stephen didn't return, the farm got run down with only Joe Power and another lad running it. Stephen Rodgers was a big fellow and could do the work of three. About five years after he disappeared it was sold – all arranged by a firm of solicitors, in England of all places. Joe and Máire, two people who lived with Stephen, were taken care of and set up comfortable. After the place passed out of the Rodgers name, the talk eventually died down. I suppose life goes on, but now, young Ciara, you've brought it all back. You've certainly brought him back. Sure girl, we'd move heaven and earth to help you if we could.'

Her husband's words seemed to have upset Niamh, because she cleared her throat audibly before adding, 'Richie is right – if there is anything we can do, we will. I have an address of the fellow he stayed with that night, and I wrote to him a few times. He wrote back, but he only knew as much as I did.'

'May I have that address, Niamh? It's a small thing, but you never know in this business.'

'I have some old photographs – would you like to see them?'

'You have no idea how much,' Ciara told her.

Niamh obviously had the photographs ready, because she was back in minutes. The two packs were old, faded, black and white, obviously taken with a box camera.

Ciara's dark eyes devoured the pictures one by one. She saw young people by the river – they seemed to be picnicking on wide flat stones with old weeping willow in the background.

'Would you look at the state of me?' Niamh laughed, pointing to a slim dark-haired girl with a big grin who was waving a cup at the camera. 'That's Aileen.' She pointed to a blonde girl who was kneeling beside her, her pale hair in a thick plait falling over her shoulder. She too was smiling broadly, as were the three other girls, who were obviously enjoying their day. 'They were Aileen's friends from around her area. I stayed with her that summer and we had a ball.'

There was another photo of two young men. Ciara immediately recognised Richie and the tall, broad-shouldered fellow
beside him must have been Stephen, her father. 'I remember
Aileen took that,' Niamh said. 'She shouted at him to smile,
telling him he looked like a fellow who had buried all
belonging to him.'

There were many more pictures – young couples arm in
arm, smiling obligingly as their lovely day was recorded.
There was one of Stephen and Aileen, he laughingly trying to
undo her plait. 'He hated it,' Niamh said. 'He was constantly at
her to take it out. He loved her with her hair blowing all over
the place. You can have a few of the photos if you like.'

'I'd love to – just one and I'll treasure it forever,' Ciara told
her with feeling.

She and John stayed a little longer, and they heard that the
Caseys had three sons, the eldest fifteen and the youngest
twelve. Richie told them they had bought the shop and had
expanded it eight years before.

'Barely keeping the wolf away from the door,' he told
them, grinning. Ciara told him to get along with it – he had the
signs of prosperity if ever she saw them. She told him all about
the shop in Dungarvan, and how they too had expanded and
made it a worthwhile venture. She told them all about Peggy
and the boys, William and Paul. She explained how she had
heard she was adopted and how badly it had affected her.
Niamh asked her if she had a boyfriend, and she told her all
about Peter Murray.

They left with promises that if there was any breakthrough
in the search, Richie and Niamh would be the very first to
know. The Caseys asked them to keep in touch one way or
another. 'Now that we've found you, don't disappear again,'
Niamh asked.

'I won't – I promise,' Ciara told her.

'Where now?' she asked, getting into the car.

'To see a close relation of yours. An uncle, in fact. Eddie
MacMahon, Aileen's brother.'

'You mean I'm going to the very place where she lived? I
don't know if I could do that. Don't ask me why.'

'You don't have to. Seemingly Denis MacMahon, Aileen's

father, has had a bit of a stroke, and Eddie thinks meeting you might be too much for him. This Eddie chap seems a nice guy, and he said he'll see us in a pub in Ross. We have an appointment in an hour's time – if we step on it we'll make it.'

The Drop Inn was almost empty, with the exception of two old men sitting up at the bar drinking pints and talking dogs. The publican asked them if they were passing through. John told him they were, more or less.

Ciara saw Eddie first. He came through the door, looking around as if he had an appointment. He was a well-built man with a shock of fair reddish hair, and was dressed in cords, with a tweed sportscoat over a polo-neck sweater. She thought he looked like a successful farmer. She could see he had the most startling blue eyes.

Without the slightest hesitation, he walked over. 'I was going to ask were you the people expecting me but I don't have to.' He examined Ciara from head to toe, a bit like he might have looked at a young colt at a bloodstock sales. 'Boy, you're the blooming spit of the fellow. Do you know that? And am I glad to meet you.' He held out his hand.

Ciara took it in a firm clasp. 'You're the third person who has said that to me today.' She was smiling, but her heart was thumping. She was with her mother's only brother. 'C'mon, we'll take the weight off our feet,' Eddie pointed to a table over at the far window, 'away from all the curious.'

When they sat down he looked at John Kenny. 'Fire away – ask me what you want.' But he was still examining Ciara, grinning and muttering, 'Jasus, 'tis amazing.'

John Kenny outlined the situation, telling Eddie that Ciara had asked him to take on the task of tracing his sister Aileen and possibly her father Stephen Rodgers. They would be grateful for any relevant information. Was there any word in the place that might suggest that Stephen was dead? Who had the farm now and who might have inherited the assets?

'All right, let me think, let me think. You know, when Stephen disappeared I knew there was something wrong. My father and my unfortunate mother, God be good to her, fobbed me off with stories about Aileen going to a finishing school in London. Wasn't I the innocent gobshite to believe them? I used to hear them talking and often my mother crying – you'd think the world had ended and what was it, but a girl having a baby for a fella that was cracked about her? God, when you think about it, weren't we very ignorant people? But things were like that then. 'Tis only in the last ten years this country has got off its arse – excuse the language, the wife is always on to me. By the way, Ciara, she'd love to see you, but my father isn't too good and we have four kids. If she's not wiping their noses she's cleaning their arses – there's not a minute.'

Ciara laughed, a warm genuine laugh.

'God, if I can't see a look of her in you now,' Eddie went on. 'The laugh and a look about your mouth. But you're the spit of him – he was as black as a bloody crow.' Eddie told them that his parents approved of the adoption, knowing that Peggy would eventually settle in Dungarvan; at that time they didn't want to see the child.

'I know it's hard to think that now, but times were different then. We wrote to Aileen for a while after she went to America, but then she moved away from Chicago and a few letters were returned and we never heard from her again. About the farm? Sure it was the talk of the place when a For Sale notice went up on it, and the whole thing was done by a Dublin auctioneer for some crowd in England. The place was run down, but poor Joe did his best, always hoping that Stephen would come back. It's well known that Joe Power and Máire Ryan were taken care of – in fact Joe only lives a few miles from here. He must be in his eighties now, but his mind is as sharp as a needle. I'm sorry, lads, but I can't throw more light on things.'

'Do you think, Eddie,' John wanted to know, 'that when he thought things over, realised that he was trapped in a way, that he might have gone under for a few years and then, when things had cooled, sold the farm and started a new life?'

'Never. I was with them the first day they were ever together and he was a goner then. He couldn't take his eyes off her. We went fishing to the river, and when my mother found out she went wild because he was supposed to be the son of a gypsy. Anyway, there was blue murder. Didn't put them off, though.' He stopped, looking at Ciara's dark, youthful loveliness, her deep interest at every word that dropped from his mouth. 'God, girl, but you're welcome into the family,' he said as he put his arm around her, giving her a resounding kiss on the cheek. 'Little did I know I had a niece like a film star. Wouldn't I like to walk you around the place and show you off to all the old biddies and all the gossiping hoors who remembered it all?'

'And I'd like to walk with you,' Ciara said huskily. Both men were aware that she was near tears. Eddie told them that Maeve was living in Dublin; she was married to a schoolteacher and had two children. He told them a little about his own children and his wife, Sheila: 'A townie from Waterford, I had some trouble breaking her in.' He wanted to know if Peggy and Bob Fitzpatrick minded that she was conducting her search.

'No, Eddie, I honestly don't think they do. Nothing will ever change the way I feel about them. Sometimes I wonder why I'm doing this to myself, but it's something inside me urging me on. It's hard to explain.'

When they were leaving to visit Joe Power, Eddie told her, 'When the father is better you must come and stay with us – and stay as long as you like, mind. And by the way, tell Joe I'll be over to see him soon. Don't forget now.'

The little thatched cottage was just in off the road, with a small garden in front. There was a light on in a front room and when they knocked at the door, there was a frenzied barking inside.

'Down, down,' a voice growled inside as someone slowly walked to the door. When the door opened a few inches and the old man peered out, the smell of heat, turf and confined dogs drifted towards them.

'Mister Power, I'm John Kenny and I wrote to you a while back about the possibility of seeing you. I wondered, if it was all right, could we have a few words now?'

The old man seemed to weigh up the situation, but when he focused on Ciara, his eyes narrowed and he looked intently for a bit. Then he shook his head as if dispelling some notion or another.

'Come in, come in. 'Tisn't like Buckingham Palace, but 'twill do, I suppose.'

They followed him in to a flagstoned kitchen with a big open fire. The sheepdog growled and wagged his tail simultaneously, as if unable to make up his mind whether they were enemies or friends.

'Will ye look at him, he's gone like meself, don't know if he's comin' or goin'. Will ye sit down? Would ye like a sup of tay?'

'No thanks,' Ciara told him, sitting down near the fire. There were a few old wooden kitchen chairs near the fire and Ciara got the impression that maybe Joe's house was a bit of a drop-in for elderly neighbours who might like a chat.

When all three were seated, Joe looked at Ciara with a puzzled look in his rheumy faded eyes.

'We came, Joe,' John Kenny started, 'because we're hoping you might be able to help us. We're wondering if you know anything about Stephen Rodgers who lived in this area. You see, this is his daughter, and she wants to try and find out what happened to him – that is, presuming he is still alive.'

If Joe Power was shocked, he hid it well. Instead, he fixed his eyes on the girl's face, taking in every single feature. His eyes slowly strayed to the black hair, the long slim lines of her body, as she sat upright on the wooden chair. After quite a silence, he calmly said, 'Aye – you could be, at that. I don't think he'd deny you. There's a look of Teresa – a right terror she was too.'

Slightly taken aback at Joe's calm acceptance of the situation, she blurted out, 'Joe, I only found out he was my father six weeks ago. I just want to try and find out what happened. I'd dearly like to know anything – anything that might help.'

Joe was silent for so long that she thought maybe it had been a mistake to visit the old man. Maybe his memory, like so many old people's, was faulty. Joe slowly stood up and, reaching up to the mantelpiece, got down his pipe and an old brown tobacco pouch. Wordlessly he started to shred his tobacco in his hand. Then he slowly and thoroughly packed it into his pipe and pressed it down. John Kenny leaned over with his lighter, but Joe refused. 'No, I prefer to get it goin' with a bit of paper – 'tis better for the baccy.'

'Can you tell us anything about him that we mightn't know?' There was almost a note of pleading in Ciara's voice.

'I can only tell ye that there was them that wiped their feet with him in this place. They secreted away his girl when she was goin' to have his child, keepin' him in the dark as to her whereabouts. And you wouldn't mind, but most of the craw-thumpin' wimmen were over the jumps themselves before they got married.' He looked again at Ciara, waving his hand and dispelling the smoke so that he could see her clearly. 'So you're the child. And a fine girl you are. A sight for sore eyes, you are.'

'Thanks, Joe,' Ciara said gently.

John Kenny could see that the long day had drained her and that tears weren't too far away. 'Joe, can you tell us anything bout his disappearance, anything that might have happened to him?'

'Maybe I could. Maybe I could. I saw no need to do it until now. 'Tisn't much, but 'tis somethin'.'

Ciara and John looked at each other with hope as he stiffly got out of his chair and walked slowly to his bedroom. They could hear him muttering to himself as he tried to open what was obviously a stuck drawer, unused to regular use. He came back into the kitchen with a tin box and, placing it on the table, started to search inside. Muttering to himself, he withdrew a letter and handed it to John Kenny.

It was from a firm of solicitors who were acting on behalf of their client, Stephen Rodgers. The letter told Mr Joe Power that the farm known as Tulla was to be sold; on the completion of the sale, he was to receive the sum of three thousand pounds for faithful services rendered. 'I got it after a long time, and I bought this place. Máire got her share too, but she's gone now, God be good to her. I wrote to them and asked could Mr Stephen Rodgers write to me, and I got another one of them dry letters telling me he wasn't in a position to correspond, or somethin' like that, and to send on some parcel.'

John Kenny saw that the letter was dated June 1964, nearly four years after Stephen Rodgers's disappearance. Ciara's eyes were blazing with hope. This letter was the most important breakthrough they had had.

Joe was talking again, every word directed at Ciara. 'Something must have happened. He wouldn't leave like that. You should see the care he took with old Tom after he got a stroke. And he ran the farm too. Sure the only time he left that man's side was to see Aileen. I'll never forget the Christmas she didn't come home from school up in Dublin. He was like a caged animal, so he was. Then he got a letter on Christmas Eve, and accordin' to poor Máire he was over the moon. They say he was the son of a gypsy, but there was nothin' in that lad only good breedin'. Anyone that knows anythin' about nature could see it. There was a bit of his mother in him too.'

'What was she like?' Ciara asked, as if she'd never tire of finding out things about the family she had never known. Her eyes, almost black now in the light, never left Joe's old, lined face.

'Aye, she was a right one. She had me in the palm of her hand. Ye'd cut yer right hand off if she asked you. She was the light of Tom's eyes. But she went in the end – ran off and left us all. It looks as if her son did the same, but old Joe here knows he wouldn't. 'Twasn't in him to do a thing like that.'

Later, Ciara and John gladly accepted his offer of a cup of tea. John Kenny asked him if he could have the letter from the solicitors concerning the sale of the farm, and old Joe readily gave it. 'Sure, Stephen's daughter can have anything she wants. 'Tis like a miracle to see her, so it 'tis.' He looked at Ciara again with a sort of wonder in his eyes. ''Tis like they were all jumbled inside you. I can see a bit of old Tom and even a bit of Ciss, his wife – your hair reminds me of young Teresa, and there's so much of the lad in you 'tis like a miracle.'

'Oh Joe, I could talk to you for ever,' she told him. 'Can I come back some day and do that?

He looked at Ciara again and for the first time he smiled, showing crooked teeth yellowed from a lifetime of the pipe. 'Ah, now that I know who you are, you're welcome to cross that threshold more than anyone I know. Why wouldn't you be? Wasn't your father all I had?'

Ciara flung her arms around him, hugging him close. 'I'll be back, Joe Power – and what's more I'll have news for you, so I will!'

Chapter Thirty-Three

'Tell me, have you uncovered any more relations, skeletons in the cupboard or whatever since the beginning of your search?'

Peter was smiling indulgently, a bit like you'd smile at a fractious child. He and Ciara were in their favourite pub, the Dungarvan Inn, sitting at the quiet end of the lounge. Ciara was sipping a glass of beer – she had refused all spirits and wine since the night of his mother's dinner party – and she grimaced as she took a mouthful. 'How do you fellows down pints of this stuff?'

'Practice, love, practice. You haven't answered my question?'

'No, we've uncovered nothing too skeletal – just some lovely people.'

'I note the royal plural.'

'John Kenny, you know, the investigator, came along with me. He thought it might be easier that way.'

Peter was silent, noting that Ciara's dark eyes had lost some of their haunted, shocked look. She wasn't like any girl he had known. Nature had been so kind to her that she made little effort with her looks. On the short journey from the car to the pub her hair had got quite wet in the rain. She had thrust the unruly black mop inside her jacket collar, as if out of sight was out of mind. Did she look a little more assured of late? A little more preoccupied, as if her foolish search with this so-called Dublin detective had become top priority? 'You really believe you'll find them? You know that the chances are very, very slim.'

'John tells me there's a success rate of nearly thirty per cent.'

'So he's John now, is he?'

'Yes, he's John and I'm Ciara, and it's just a friendly business. He's a casual, easy sort of person and one feels relaxed with him and yet confident somehow. It's hard to describe.'

'What about us? Remember, we were supposed to get engaged at Christmas and supposed to be planning a wedding for September?'

She looked at him now, noting for the first time how like his mother he was, the stylishly cut fair hair, the hazel eyes, slightly hooded, the well-cut suit that enchanced his tall physique, the glimpse of the gold cuff link as he lifted his drink. She didn't want to hurt him – yet she knew an engagement in a matter of a few weeks wasn't her top priority any more.

'Peter, I don't want to appear unenthusiastic about us. But I wonder would it be best if we left our engagement till Easter. Maybe we could still get married in September. You see, this business has sort of taken me over. When the time comes for us, I don't want anything to interfere – but now I just want to find what I'm looking for. Right now nothing else matters.'

'Not even me?'

'Look, Peter, I love you as much as ever – but I just want this out of the way. It has become an obsession with me. I didn't want it – you know that.'

'And if you find them, what then? Do you fall into each other's arms? Will you all live happily ever after, three total strangers? Listen, Ciara, you're carried away with all this foolishness. The blood tie is like anything else – it has to be worked at and nurtured like any other relationship. If they're out there, they're black strangers to you – to each other, by this time. I think you should stop now and settle for what you have – and you have a lot. Frankly I think that chap up in Dublin is in it for the money. These guys set themselves up as private investigators and they have little or no training. They're cowboys mostly.'

'You're wrong.' Her eyes flashed a dark, hurt look. 'He's not like that. He's as ex-guard, he's in his thirties, he has a successful business and a sizeable team working for him. He seems to care about people.'

'Don't expect me to be as carried away as you.'

She could see he was hurt and disappointed that their engagement, planned so happily on a carefree evening when everything was so bright and uncomplicated, was on hold. 'I'm sorry, Peter, but try not to be too annoyed. If I succeed or if I fail in my search, one way or another, we'll go back to square one. I promise.'

Her word did little to lift his gloom. Though he ordered another drink, they didn't seem to have that much to say to each other. At ten o'clock he glanced at his watch. 'Tomorrow I have an early start. I must go up to the Four Courts in Dublin. I'll be away for a few days.' He leaned over and dropped a light kiss on her mouth. 'When I come home maybe you won't be so obsessed.'

'Funny, I thought you of all people might understand.'

They were silent as they walked out into the night.

Christmas crept in and the lights on the big tree in the town square were switched on. The window displays were so attractive that people lingered to look at them. Fitzpatrick's shop was like a fairyland. In the window, Santa rode through the snow on his laden sleigh as the snow fell gently and persistently; the February before, at the London Toy Fair, Ciara had been so enraptured with a stand where the snow actually fell that she had ordered the electric device there and then. Now her investment paid off as hordes of small children crowded round to gaze.

Ciara seemed to put as much enthusiasm into the weeks before Christmas as she ever did. She talked, laughed and advised young mothers who weren't quite sure what Santa was to bring this year. The Chipmunks and the Cabbage Patch dolls were all the rage she had predicted. They had to be reordered again and again. As she went about her daily routine, no one knew about her obsession. Neither Peggy or Bob said much, but they both knew she wasn't quite with them. The odd questions she popped at all sorts of strange hours hinted at the fact that she was living in a sort of limbo – a twilight land dominated by Aileen MacMahon and Stephen Rodgers.

Ciara got through the festive season. She accepted the beautiful gold chain from Peter with much appreciation, and he seemed delighted with the unusual silver cigarette case she had picked up in an antique shop in Waterford. They were seen smiling and laughing at the dinner dance on Saint Stephen's night in Twomey's hotel, at the candlelight dinner in the golf club, at the Christmas dance in the tennis club. But the social-set watchers who had predicted that Peter Murray and Ciara Fitzpatrick would become engaged were disappointed. They seemed so much in love, and were the finest-looking young couple on the social circuit; there was no doubt – it hadn't been money that had stopped them. Everyone knew that the Murrays were loaded. Rumours had circulated that Ciara Fitzpatrick had discovered that she was adopted and had been very upset about it. In fact, the girl had been so distraught she had taken one too many at one of Beth Murray's dinner parties and had blurted it out, to the fury of her hostess. There was some question hanging over her real father's lineage. But, sure anyone looking at the girl could see that there was good breeding there. And wasn't it the late seventies? People didn't pay much heed to such gossip any more. Still, could that be the reason there wasn't a diamond flashing on her left hand?

John Kenny had explained to her how slow and tedious the business would be from now on, so she was surprised to get a call from him in the second week in January. When she heard his deep voice and the unmistakable Clare accent, her heart missed a beat. He had warned her of the possibility of an impasse, and she waited with palpitating heart and dry mouth.

'I'm phoning because I thought it would be better. Didn't want to send you a letter.'

'That's nice of you. Is there any news at all? Does phoning me mean you have bad news?'

'Please, Ciara, be patient. Don't ask me how, where or why. But I have definite leads on both – I'm not sure as yet what these leads may mean. But the signs are good. When I have more details about the situation I'll be on to you immediately. All right?'

'No, it's not all right. Tell me a little more. Are they alive? If so, where are they?'

'I'm sorry, Ciara. ' She heard the determination in his voice and knew she would have to be patient, even if it meant her nerves would be in shreds.

'Oh, all right – I'd better pray for your success. You'll let me know the minute, the second, you know more?'

'When you're praying, I think you'd better ask Saint Jude for patience.' He was rewarded with a laugh.

'As the song goes,' he could still hear the laughter in her voice, 'you're getting to know me.'

'Maybe I am. Then again, I know dozens of impatient types like you.'

'I suppose you do.' He didn't know if the forlorn tone was due to the fact that he didn't enlighten her further, or to the thought that she might be one of many.

'Ah sure, I'm joking, Ciara Fitzpatrick Rodgers – you're one of a rare breed, so you are.'

'I'm beginning to think I must be.'

He still thought she sounded a little lost. He also thought it a pity that her life had to be turned upside-down at this stage. Had she been told when she was a small child that she was adopted, the news would have run off her like water off a duck's back. But then again, if that had happened she wouldn't be on the other end of the phone with her hopeful questioning.

'All right, Ciara – I'll be in touch. I must warn you, even if I do find them, all the other negative things could still happen. Don't expect too much. Promise?'

'I promise.'

She waited two more nerve-wracking, disquieting weeks to hear from him again. Weeks during the cold bleak month of February when the east wind blew, when there was a flu epidemic, when Dungarvan Bay looked grey and bleak, when it seemed that the summer was a lifetime away, when Peter came and went to Dublin with more frequency than ever before. Sometimes, lying in bed unable to sleep, she told herself she was a bloody fool to have upset herself and everyone else in a quest that was bound to end in disaster. After all, her mother had made the choice to have her adopted. Aileen knew Ciara was with Peggy and Bob. She need only pick up the phone and make inquiries to discover her whereabouts. She hadn't because she hadn't wanted to – that was as plain as the nose on her face. And yet, Ciara recalled how Peggy had described the way Aileen had dressed her up the day she was saying goodbye. There was a poignancy about that.

Stephen Rodgers was a different kettle of fish. Even if he was alive, more than likely he would have married and have five or six kids by now. Maybe in the quiet hours he drew a breath of relief that he had got out of the trap of an early marriage.

The doubts crowded into her head at the strangest of times: when she was with Peter, when they were surrounded by young people, when she was sitting having dinner, even when

William or Paul were nagging her about something or another. The doubts came to her in the shop when she was smiling, listening to long stories from people who thought she had nothing better to do – but mostly they came in the small hours, when she tossed and turned, when half-broken dreams came and went and she fantasised that she found her parents and they didn't want her. At times like that she upbraided herself for upsetting everyone by her curious, thirsty desire for information.

Chapter Thirty-Four

Aileen MacMahon glanced at her mail. She supposed that amongst the pile was the usual hopeful, unsolicited features from freelance journalists, or a plethora of letters from readers over some feature or other that had appeared in last month's magazine. She decided she would deal with the pile later.

Today the magazine was going to print. Looking at the pasted pages of the fashion spread with the photo shoot in place, Aileen found herself sighing. She found herself sighing a lot of late. It was six years since she had been appointed fashion editor. She had been in on the success of *Woman Now* almost from the beginning. When Frank Dixon had approached about joining a new magazine, she had been happy to go along with him. She had been with the *Newark Evening News* for six years before that, doing a weekly column on fashion, pieces on the fashion designers, human-interest features, interviews with the famous and not-so-famous. When Frank had offered her a change she had been glad to move on.

Now she wondered had the time come to move on again. She was thirty-six, not getting any younger, although Frank told her she didn't look twenty-six. When she looked in the mirror she could see that she had worn well. The face staring out at her was unlined, the blonde hair still luxurious, but at times the hopeful blaze in her blue eyes surprised her, as if out there, somewhere, there was more on offer than was happening right now.

It was nineteen years since she had come to America. She had spent the first ten years living in Chicago working at all sorts of jobs. She had worked in stores or in restaurants while going to night school, where she had studied journalism for three years. After that followed a number of jobs, from copy-reading to doing small snippets for various evening papers. Her cool blonde looks and the intense blue of her eyes had made editors look at her speculatively and send her to the top fashion houses to cover the latest trends. She had eventually become assistant fashion editor on the *Newark Evening News*, and by the time she moved to *Woman Now* she brought considerable flair and talent for the job. She had made quite a number of friends over the years. The fact that she had never married, despite a number of proposals, surprised them all. The latest to ask was Frank Dixon, who had been widowed three years earlier when his wife Paula had died from cancer. It was over a year since he had asked her to marry him. She had put him off so often at first that he had impatiently wanted to know what was wrong with her. He told her she was the most mysterious Irishwoman he had ever met. The breed was usually talkative, extrovert, enthusiastic. He had even joked that she wasn't getting any younger – didn't she want a few kids to brighten up her old age? She had taken all he had to offer in her stride, smiling that enigmatic blue-eyed smile. He had exploded, telling her she was maddening.

Now she and Frank went out together a lot, sometimes dining alone, sometimes with others. They had gone on weekends to the country to married friends who invited them often. They had shared much, particularly in the past year, but when she refused to let him take her to bed, he had asked her gently if she had had a bad experience or a problem when it came to men.

She had told him she didn't think so, and that if her refusal to sleep with him was causing him embarrassment she was sorry. Their friends had accepted the situation, shrugging and telling each other that Aileen was Irish and Catholic and obviously had a strict moral code.

When the magazine was finally put to bed, Aileen still felt a peculiar restlessness, Normally at that stage she felt fulfilled and awash with a feeling of satisfaction at a job well done. Today she didn't feel like that at all. Maybe it was the spring, or maybe it was decision time in her life. She must seriously decide whether she wanted a future with Frank. She had never wanted to keep him on a string – it simply wasn't her way. So why was she holding back? She liked him so much, and maybe liking was more important than loving. But in a way she did love him – his caring ways, his wit, his generosity. She had been very friendly with his wife, Paula. They had enjoyed a closeness that was the nearest thing to sisterhood she had known since her friendship with Niamh. When Paula had died

Aileen had known a great loneliness – a void had come into her life that she had never filled.

Aileen wondered if Paula would mind her marrying Frank. She probably would have been glad.

Frank and Paula had had one son, Gary, who was seventeen now and who seemed to like Aileen a lot. So maybe the time had come. Maybe this week she should accept him. She was thirty-six, after all – not that young, but still young enough to have children, to find fulfilment, to know what family involvement would be after so many years wandering in the dry desert of her own making. Yes, maybe that time had come. Maybe this coming weekend she would give him the answer he so desperately wanted.

Aileen picked up the mail. At a glance she knew what most the larger envelopes contained. Endless publicity handouts from fashion shows she or her assistant were unable to attend; press news of yet another miracle cream that would reduce the ravages of age; a new revolutionary cream that would actually melt fat off thighs; and – and what was this? Her heart thumped and seemed to miss a beat as she saw the Irish stamp. She hadn't seen one for years. She looked at the typewritten envelope and the postmark – 26 February 1978. She looked at the stamp again. It was green and the design was that of winged oxen. Part of her wondered what winged oxen commemorated, and another part of her screamed 'Open it, for God's sake – you haven't had a letter from Ireland since you broke all links a thousand years ago.' Her hands were shaking as she tore open the envelope. It was from a firm of private investigators in Ireland, and was typewritten and brief.

Dear Miss MacMahon,
I am acting on behalf of my client Ciara Fitzpatrick, who approached my company in an effort to trace her natural parents. I have made it quite clear to her that there is no obligation on your part to acknowledge her existence, to write or to communicate with her in any circumstances. She fully accepts the situation. My client told me to inform you that she is very happy living with her adoptive parents and their two sons. The reason she contracted me to trace her natural parents was due to the fact that she heard only last October that she was, in fact, adopted. She wishes me

to inform you that if you do not want to write or communicate, she will understand.

John Kenny.

*

He had long since become accustomed to this vast country, accustomed to the heat, the arid land, the dust, the flies and the palpable loneliness. Though it was only twelve years since he had bought the sheep station in New South Wales, his success had brought grudging admiration from the stock men, the seasonal influx of workers, and the neighbours and acquaintances from as far away as Sydney. His working of the gargantuan hours necessary to return the run-down station to profitability had impressed not only the men who worked for him, but also the neighbours who had advised him. He was always more than willing to listen, to act on the advice of people who were familiar with conditions on this vast continent.

Sitting in the timber outhouse he used as an office, he glanced at the post which Andy had dumped on the desk. The usual assortment of brochures, miscellaneous bills, a letter from his solicitor who was in the process of finalising a deal to add three hundred more acres to the station. Suddenly he noticed the Irish stamp. Strange, he thought, one hand examining the unfamiliar stamp, the other fingering the gnarled scar that ran from his black hairline across his cheekbone to the top of his ear. Men had looked at it and wondered what brawl had caused it. Yet despite the disfigurement, he was considered a handsome man. They wondered why he hadn't married. So did the few women he had met. His black hair was slightly brushed with silver at the temples, and it was guessed that he might be on the wrong side of forty. On the few occasions he had stayed in Sydney on business, he had been seen in the company of women. But as the years went by and nothing became of the relationships, it was accepted that he was happy with his bachelor status.

Stephen Rodgers opened the letter from Ireland. He slowly read it. He read it again and again. He put it down, shaking his head in wonderment and disbelief. Christ in Heaven, he thought, this couldn't be happening now. He closed his eyes, wondering if it was the old trouble playing up again. But no – the letter was still there on top of the pile. A daughter. Her name was Ciara – a beautiful name – and she was alive and

410

well and living in Dungarvan in Ireland. She had heard only recently that she was adopted and now she wanted to find him, her natural father. She wanted to find him – to know him. Christ, he thought, the irony of it now.

He sat unmoving for so long that his dog Jacko sniffed and whimpered at his stillness. He didn't notice; neither did he hear the men laughing and joking in the stockyard. He didn't hear the troublesome dingo that never seemed to go away; he barely nodded to Helena when she brought his jug of coffee.

He could see her as if it was yesterday, standing there waving, her blonde hair darkened with rain, her coat belted over her thickening waistline, over the place where the child was growing – the child who was now a young woman who wanted to know him.

He remembered the yellow lights, the swirling mists, the strident repetitive sound of the ambulance siren, the terrible searing pain, the wetness and then the blankness. He didn't remember the agonising months of nothingness that somehow stretched into years.

Afterwards he had been told that his head injury had been so bad that it was a miracle that he had survived. Sometimes vague half-formed pictures flashed into his head and he could recall the patient probing of doctors as he was referred from one hospital to another. Then he had found himself in convalescent homes, one after another. Eventually he had been told that a new appointee, a bright young psychiatrist, had taken an interest in his case. Then there was an eventual breakthrough. Small scraps of memory came, and they widened and widened until he could hazily recall things. He told them his name was Stephen and he was from County Kilkenny. Before the fog closed in again, he had felt a terrible sense of grievous loss. Why, he didn't know – there were endless questions, probing voices, machines clipped on to his head, drugs administered to help what was diagnosed as deep-seated amnesia.

It had taken all of four years to pierce the fog, to lift him from his twilight zone. During that time he had had no contact from anyone who might be able to shed light on his whereabouts.

Now Stephen recalled his return to comparative normality. He went to the house in Islington, to hear that the Fitzpatricks had returned to Ireland. He went to Johnnie Davis's bedsit only to hear that Johnnie had moved to the north of England. He returned to Islington and visited Peggy's next-door neighbour, a helpful woman who told him that as far as she knew, the girl Aileen had gone to the States with another student she had met when she was doing a secretarial course. She had given him the name of the college. When he went there, he had been told that all that was known was that two of their students at that time, Aileen MacMahon and Sara Harris, had got employment in the States.

The young psychiatrist who had not only cured him, but also befriended him, advised Stephen to start a new life, to settle his affairs in Ireland and go elsewhere. Arrangements were made through a firm of solicitors to put the farm on the market. After it had been sold for a substantial sum, Máire and Joe were adequately compensated for their years of service. One request made to Mr Joe Power on behalf of the client by the firm of Eavens, Morgan and Sloane had been that a small parcel containing two diaries was to be sent, registered post, to the above address. Mr Joe Power had complied with the unusual request.

When Stephen had been about to embark on the frustrating search for a girl who had emigrated to America four years earlier, he had suffered a relapse. The fog had descended for another year before he had been cured.

It was now over a dozen years since he had come out to the continent that had beckoned since he was a boy. He had found fulfilment in the hard work, in the company of men who accepted one another on face value and on their ability to achieve and get along with other men. Stephen Rodgers was respected by the men who worked for him, but they never got close enough to him to know him, to know his past. There was something about the black, brooding look, combined with the terrible scar, that kept people at bay. Even when he relaxed and had a drinking session after the shearing was over, before the seasonal workers moved on, Stephen somehow kept his distance.

Now he read the letter for the fourth time, then he drank his coffee from the enamel mug. It was cold now, and the milk had congealed into little white rivulets which floated on the top. Helena came and told him that there was a man up in the house who wanted to see him. He looked at her with those

412

disturbing dark eyes, and she could plainly see that something had happened to shake him from his normal day. Was it excitement she saw in the black depths? Was it something she had never seen before – a blaze of hope, a look of promise, as if he had heard something wonderful? Maybe it was the letter in front of him that had caused it. Whatever it was, she was glad that something had happened to warm his heart.

'Tell him I'll be up in a while. Tell him I must reply to an important letter, and I want to catch today's post. Keep him happy, Helena, till I get there. Whatever his business, this is more important to me now.'

Towards the end of April Ciara received two letters. It seemed a lifetime since John Kenny had phoned, telling her that there was no longer any doubt – both her parents were alive. She had received the news with a mixture of euphoria, wonder, fear and mouth-drying excitement.

'I can't believe it,' she had yelled down the phone. 'How do you do it? It's a miracle! I love you.'

'I doubt that now. And it was no miracle – didn't I tell you we have ways and means?'

'Oh, I can't believe it, John – they're both really alive. I know I'll owe you a fortune – but I'll pay you if I have to slave for a lifetime. God almighty, I can't believe it! Do you think I should write to them?'

'Of course you write to them. And immediately, and by airmail. I want to tie up all the loose ends and see you happily married to your Peter. I want you to live happily ever after and let me get on with my life.' John's tone was dry but Ciara got the impression he was smiling.

Over the phone he gave her the two addresses. She couldn't believe that the two people who had inadvertently caused her so much trouble, who had dominated her dreams, who had obsessed her waking hours, who had caused so much upheaval in Peter's life, lived in the actual places she was writing down with a shaking hand on a torn slip of paper grabbed from the drawer.

Two weeks later, Peggy, looking at the letter with the American stamp, asked, 'Would you like to be on your own to read it?'

413

Ciara saw a look of fear, worry – maybe apprehension. 'No, Mum, stay. No matter what it contains, it makes no difference to you, Dad or me.' She opened the letter, her fingers stiff and clumsy. Had she seized up completely? She couldn't think now, and yet she had imagined getting that letter a thousand times.

The address was Teelin Publishing, Unit 621, Fairmont Tce, Newark, United States.

My dear Ciara,
I was indeed happy – very happy – to hear from Mr Kenny. I dearly wish I knew how to bridge a gap of nineteen years, but, sadly, I don't.

I would like to stress that this inadequate letter will in all probability be the most difficult I will ever write. I can only imagine your shock and astonishment when you heard that Peggy and Bob weren't your true father and mother. Dear Peggy and Bob – how good and kind they were to me during my stay with them.

After you were born, Peggy didn't have just the token interest or indeed the fondness most babies generate. She simply couldn't take her eyes – eyes that were filled with a naked love – off you. Ciara, it might be extremely difficult for you to accept my decision, but I thought at the time that the very best thing – the very best, I repeat – would be for Peggy and Bob to adopt you and for me to fade out of your life – indeed out of all your lives. I felt that their passage, and indeed yours, would have been easier. If I had stayed longer I simply would not – and I emphasise *would not* – have been able to part with you. I was only seventeen at the time, and I was advised by many to start a new life, to go abroad and to forget the past, Ireland and everything that had happened to me. I was young and fairly ignorant and very vulnerable, and did just that. Of course, what made it easy was the fact that I knew Peggy would take care of you far better than I ever could.

I have had an interesting life and I have learned much. I work on a magazine as a fashion editor. I have made good friends and up to now have not married. My boss is a man named Frank Dixon, and he is a widower and actually wants to marry me. After long hesitation I have made up

414

my mind and have decided that I will. I'm thirty-six now, and as they say at home, getting long in the tooth.

I know, Ciara, that you would like to know more about your father, Stephen. I can only tell you that during my young years I thought he was a very fine person. If he is alive, and I very much doubt it, I can only hope that he too, found some sort of fulfilment and happiness, two things which eluded him when he lived in Kilkenny.

Now that we've been in touch, I hope it will cause no pain or hurt to Peggy or Bob. I would love to meet you. The world gets smaller every day and money would be no object at this end.

All my love to you and to Peggy, Bob and the boys. I suppose they're men now.

Aileen.

Ciara read the letter twice before silently handing it to Peggy. The older woman's hands shook as she put on her glasses. Ciara watched her as she read the letter, then she heard her sniffling, and suddenly they both dissolved in tears. With their arms around each other they sobbed, though whether it was with joy that Aileen was alive and well, or with sadness that her young life had been torn asunder, they weren't sure. What was obvious was that the tears flowed readily.

'What's up? Have ye fallen asleep?' They heard Bob shout up the stairs. 'We have a business to run, Ciara – will you get off your backside and come down?'

The women smiled watery smiles through their tears. Ciara looked around and, finding an old kitchen towel, mopped up.

Peggy shouted down the stairs. 'Come up here, Bob Fitzpatrick – we've something to show you, so we have.'

They could hear him coming up the stairs, muttering and mumbling about gossiping women and how, when they got together, there wasn't a tap of work done. But when he opened the door and saw the tear-stained faces he got alarmed.

'It's all right, all right,' Peggy told him. 'Ciara here got a letter from America – she wants you to read it.'

It was Bob's turn to fix his glasses as he slowly sank into the chair. The only sound in the kitchen was the ticking of the clock and the drip from the tap he was always going to fix.

When he finished Bob cleared his throat noisily. 'Aye,' he

muttered, his eyes meeting Peggy's, 'she was a lovely girl and it's good to know that she is alive and well. That fellow in Dublin did a good day's work, and 'tis only right that you should meet her. Only right, girl – after all, she is your mother.'

The second letter came in that same week. Ciara was in the shop and the early-morning rush was on. Men going to work wanted their newspaper; young lads in secondary school surreptitiously bought their cigarettes, and children their sweets. Peter came in for his cigarettes also. He had come back from Dublin the night before, and when she handed him his favourite brand his smile was quizzical and a bit questioning. 'Tell me, how is the search going?'

'I have the most wonderful news! Wait for it – you won't believe it. I got a letter from my mother and am hoping for one from my father. I simply can't believe it.'

'So your John Kenny did a good job. He wasn't taking you for a ride after all.'

'Of course he wasn't.' Her exasperation showed. 'Your problem is that you don't trust people.'

'When do you reckon will all this be over?' he asked.

'Soon, soon. When it is, I'll be as content as a sandboy.'

'I doubt it,' he said, but he was smiling. He blew her a kiss and then he was gone.

When the postman walked in and thrust the letters into her hand, Ciara could see that top one had an Australian stamp. She felt the missing heartbeat that seemed to be part of her life now. I won't read it yet, she thought. I'll wait until my eleven o'clock break. The address on the back of the envelope read 'Tulla Station' with an indistinguishable name and, clearly, 'New South Wales, Australia'. It had to be him. It had to be the man who had walked away when the going got tough.

How she put in the next hour, Ciara was never to know. The shop was quite busy as Easter was coming, the Easter eggs had been delivered and had to be stacked on shelves. Young mothers came in and placed their orders for the eggs, saying they didn't dare bring them home or the young horrors would devour them. She nodded and agreed and talked Easter eggs, her heart racing but her face giving nothing away as she listened to the gossip and the hopes that it would be a good summer. There was always a few who glanced at the headlines in the newspapers and expected her to be an expert on world affairs, or at least to know how to comment on them. One man, looking at his paper, said, 'I see that the Arabs are shoving up the price of oil again. Can't see America taking that in their stride. They won't let those sheik fellas call the tune.' Ciara smiled and told him he was right, absolutely right, before she made her escape.

Peggy hadn't returned after ten o'clock Mass. Ciara plugged in the electric kettle and sat down to read the letter. She saw to her satisfaction that it was fairly long.

Dear Ciara,

I'm afraid I haven't words to describe the happiness your letter has brought me. I simply cannot believe that I have heard from you. When I got it I thought it might have been a trick of the sun, or that I was hallucinating, or some other such thing. Believe, me it would take me a whole lifetime to explain everything to you, but I'll try and give you a sketchy outline of what I believe happened before you were born.

When I heard that Aileen, your mother, was to have a child, I immediately went to London to be with her. I met her and we made plans to marry and have a future together. I left her and tried to make my way back to the place I was staying in London, before getting ready to return to Ireland to sell out and come back to her. Having little or no experience of traffic or movements in a big city, this redneck from Ireland walked out in front of a bus and was, according to all, in a critical condition for weeks afterwards. They say that life is stranger than fiction, and what followed proved it. I was in various hospitals and places for the next five years having completely lost my memory. Total amnesia was the diagnosis, and I have a grand scar to bear out my story. For an unknown Irishman with no identification on him I was treated very well. I did have some hundreds of pounds on me; maybe that helped. I had gone into the bank at home when I heard about Aileen and had withdrawn more than I needed.

When I made a reasonable recovery years later I tried to find her without success. Sometimes, out here in the

New World, as they call it, I often wondered did I try hard enough.

By the way, I'm a sheep farmer and I never did marry. I thought you might like to know. I reckon you must be nineteen now. God, I'd dearly love to see you. Are you blonde and blue-eyed like your mother, or are you black-haired and dark-eyed? Or do babies come out a mixture of both?

I promise if we could meet there will be no compulsion on you to keep up the relationship if you don't want to. But pity a lonely sheep farmer out in this arid land and say you will.

Love, Stephen.

Chapter Thirty-Five

'But you see, Peter, l must see them. I simply must. I didn't spend all these past months thinking, dreaming, doing something as positive as hiring a private detective, just forget all about it just when we succeeded. I simply cannot do that.'

'I don't see the point, and I never did in this business. You were perfectly happy with Peggy and Bob, and you're going to marry me – your life is going to follow a set plan so what's the use in wreaking havoc on so many people?'

Ciara looked at him with her dark, puzzled eyes. 'You don't understand at all, do you?'

'Maybe I understand more than you know.'

Their evening finished on a unsatisfactory note. They were having a drink after a film in their favourite corner of the pub. He's unimaginative, she thought, he only sees things in black and white. He has our lives planned on a set course and he doesn't want anything to upset his plan.

Her insistence or obsession with finding her parents – going as far as hiring a private investigator – he considered unwarranted, even dramatic. She had expected him to be more supportive and more caring, she had thought he would bring some measure of under standing to the situation than he did. They drove home and kissed goodnight, and she agreed to go to the dinner dance in the tennis club on Easter Monday night.

That night as she lay in bed, an idea was born. My God, she thought, maybe it would work, maybe it wouldn't. Maybe if she acted fast they would come.

They would come before her mother married that Frank person. Of course, Ciara thought, it was possible she was being a hopeless, stupid, emotional romantic. Everyone who had an iota of sense knew that love deepened when people shared things. The two people she had in mind hadn't shared anything for nearly twenty years. But it was peculiar, to say at least, that neither of them had married. Was that a sign? Or was she an imaginative fool thinking that youthful obsession could survive for decades? Still, what had Peggy said? *You could almost feel the love they had for one another.* Niamh and Richie Casey had given that impression also.

She'd phone John tomorrow and tell him the wonderful news about the letters. She'd outline her plan. She could already see his clear grey eyes, hear him teasing, telling her that life wasn't like that. Still, she'd phone him. No, better still, she'd take a run to Dublin to meet him. It might be better that way.

Two days later, she was sitting opposite him over lunch in the Clarence Hotel on the Quays in Dublin. He listened as she animatedly outlined her plan.

'And when I finish,' she told him, 'please don't tell me I'm an idiot, a hopeless romantic, a bit of a head-the-ball.'

'No, I won't tell you that.' He tried to look serious, but her youthful exuberance, the excited nuances in her voice, the way she moved her hands, the way those dark long-lashed eyes almost pleaded with him, made him think that Peter Murray was a very lucky fellow. Not for the first time, John wondered what it would be like to take her in his arms, and slowly kiss away all that restless energy, starting at that wonderful mouth, those eyes, then running his hand through that black mop of unmanageable hair – Christ, he told himself as he dragged his wandering thoughts back, it must be the spring or something like that, but thinking of taking Ciara Fitzpatrick in his arms made him decidedly uncomfortable.

'You're not even listening to me,' she almost wailed.

'Oh I am, Ciara Fitzpatrick or Ciara Rodgers or whoever you are. I am, I swear I am.'

She saw a peculiar expression in his eyes, but she hadn't time to think what it might mean. 'You know what it means to me to see them. But just forget about me – what might be more important still is that they meet each other. Don't you see, John? Neither of them knows I've been in touch with both of them. Say, if I telegram them and say I'd dearly love to see them. Maybe they'll come here or to London. Maybe I can surreptitiously arrange that they meet. Okay, it's twenty years, but wouldn't it be wonderful, really beautiful if it worked out?'

'I know you feel I'm a bit of a wet blanket,' he said

carefully. 'But I doubt it if would work out. I've helped people find each other, and always, after the initial excitement, they discover there is nothing left. Take a man who is released from jail after a long sentence. His wife thinks of nothing only the day he's released. But time proves they both have changed so much they can't pick up the pieces.'

'Forget all that. Will you help me if I go ahead with this, this –'

'Manipulation,' he prompted

'All right, call it what you like. Will you?'

'Sure, you have me hooked now, so I suppose I will. And by the way, you'd better start drilling for oil because that's what you'll need to settle my bill.'

'You're a Shylock at heart. I'll pay you over the years – will that do?'

'Yes, I might settle for that.'

Together they decided on a plan of campaign. John Kenny thought London would be the best place to meet. 'Just in case there's a reluctance on both their parts to come to Ireland.' He had a friend who was banqueting manager in the Grosvenor Hotel in London and who might facilitate them with satisfactory arrangements. She would send telegrams and ask both of them if Tuesday, 29 April, two weeks after Easter, would be suitable. She looked at him and he could see that the early excitement was dying out of her expressive eyes.

'God, now that it's all happening I'm terrified. You will be with me at least for a day or two, won't you?'

'Yes. But tell me, what has your fiancé to say about all this?'

'Nothing much. He thinks I'm mad.'

'Maybe you are.'

After lunch Ciara and John went for a stroll along the quays and up Grafton Street. The famous street was thronged with shoppers enjoying the spring sunshine. They wandered into Stephen's Green, John Kenny telling himself he was a fool, that he should be back in his office minding his business. But somehow he didn't want to leave Ciara with so much time on her hands before she caught her train. Her mood alternated between high excitement and troughs of worry, but mostly she was like a child whose birthdays were all coming together.

'Look at those tulips, aren't they divine?' She pointed to

the colourful flowerbeds. 'They're like colourful islands in a sea of green velvet.'

'Haven't you the great turn of phrase?' he joked. But he had to admit to himself that Stephen's Green had never looked lovelier. Young office workers, girls in bright dresses, sat on the seats, enjoying their lunch. He noticed a few courting couples over near the trees who seemed to be enjoying a lot more. Two elderly ladies were feeding the hungry, gobbling ducks, giving the impression that it was possibly the highlight of their day.

Ciara saw a seat being vacated as three girls stood up to go. She grabbed John's hand and ran with him over to it. She had never held his hand before, and he was aware that his flesh tingled with her touch. Sitting down, she continued to hold his hand as if it was the most natural thing in the world. She was like a capricious child who had no idea what she was doing to him. Reluctantly he removed her hand. 'I must think of getting back, young woman – I have so much work to do.'

She looked at him, her eyes roaming over his face as if she was seeing him for the very first time as a man, not a hired private investigator. Suddenly she leaned over and brushed her lips over his. 'John Kenny, I can never thank you enough for everything. You've been so good, so patient and helpful, and I've been demanding and unthinking. I must remember what you called my situation – a run-of-the-mill case. I really must remember that.'

'Do,' he told her. 'It might be better if you did.' He gently pulled her off the seat, giving her a small push. 'Come on, we must get going. We have things to do.'

There was only three days between the arrival of the telegrams. Surprisingly enough, the Australian one came first.

WILL TRAVEL TO LONDON ARRIVING ON THE 28TH APRIL STOP WILL MEET IN GROSVENOR HOTEL TUESDAY 29TH STOP. LOOKING FORWARD TO MEETING STOP.
LOVE STEPHEN

The mssage from Aileen was in a similar vein.

422

DEAR CIARA HAPPY TO FALL IN WITH YOUR PLAN
FOR MEETING STOP. WILL TRAVEL ON SUNDAY
26TH. APRIL ARRIVING AT GATWICK AT 1 O'CLOCK
ON TUESDAY. WILL MEET IN GROSVENOR LOUNGE
AT 12-30 PM STOP.

Aileen couldn't believe that things were working out so well.
'Mum, isn't it unbelievable? It's Saint Anthony. I nagged him
to death – I have him nearly burnt away with candles.'

'I prayed too,' Peggy told her. 'I prayed that if it was all for
the best, it would happen. You have no idea how much I'd
love to see Aileen again. Maybe she'll visit us some day.'

'Why don't you come over with me? I'd love that.'

No, I'll stay with your dad. It's better we don't intrude. Is
your Mr Kenny going with you?'

'Yes, I have him nagged too. He's coming over for a day or
two just to give me a bit of support. He's great like that, sort of
dependable. You know, Mum, I really like him.'

'I know, I got that impression.' Peggy's tone had a dry
edge to it.

The bright spring days were sunfilled as the summer stock
trickled into the shop. Every other day Ciara dealt with yet
another craft worker who was hoping to sell into the shop for
the coming tourist season. Bob called them the table-mat
brigade and left Ciara deal with that end of the business. With
her mind saturated with coming events, she tried to look interested in the crochet tops, Irish linen table cloths, hand-knitted
Aran sweaters, knitted hats, tweed hats and skirts. As she
handled the merchandise she often wondered if the day would
come when she might look back on this past year, and maybe
joke and laugh with Peter about her obsession with the past.
She tried to conjure up pictures of what the future might hold,
but they were hazy and ill defined.

As the time for meeting her parents inched nearer, she still
met Peter regularly and they still went to their favourite
haunts. Sometimes she thought he looked at her with a
mixture of puzzlement and uncertainty, tinged with a little
regret. Once she asked him, with a decided impatience, 'Are
you afraid that the man who is supposed to be my father will
come here, a mixture of stockman, sheep farmer and gypsy,

423

and kick up a shindy and make a show of us? Is that's what's wrong with you?'

'No, Ciara, I'm not as imaginative as you. Neither am I as dramatic.'

Sometimes when they were parting for the night, his kisses were as passionate as ever. Sometimes she felt sorry for him, for Bob, Peggy, for herself. She wished she had never heard the conversation that had send her down the road on a search that was going to end soon.

As the week slipped by she wondered what she would wear. 'I don't want them to think I'm an old-fashioned *cailín*,' she told Peggy. She finally settled on a light tweed suit with heathery colours of green and pale purple and a velvet collar, and a pale linen green blouse. 'I can take my new light trench-coat with it and I'll look like a world-weary traveller. What do you think, Mum?'

'If you went in sackcloth and ashes you'd look all right,' Bob growled, looking at her dark anxious eyes through his pipe smoke.

*

MUST POSTPONE VISIT FOR ONE WEEK STOP. WILL MEET ON 5TH MAY INSTEAD STOP. HAVE DECIDED TO MARRY FRANK DIXON AND WE WILL HONEYMOON IN EUROPE STOP. HOPE THIS IS ALL RIGHT STOP. BOTH SEND OUR LOVE AND I CAN'T WAIT TO SEE YOU STOP.
LOVE AILEEN.

'Jesus Almighty,' Ciara wailed, as she flung the telegram on the table.

'What is it?' Peggy asked, looking at her distraught face. 'What's wrong?'

'She's postponing her visit for a week. Getting married, mind you. Imagine, getting married now of all times, just when she's on the brink of meeting Stephen. Oh God, I'll have to stop it, so I will.'

'Shut up, Ciara. Stop ranting and raving, will you?'

Ciara, taken aback at the sharp tone, handed Peggy the telegram.

'It makes sense,' Peggy said when she had read it. 'Why not combine her trip with her honeymoon? And maybe she

424

feels you should meet the man she is marrying. Put your fairytale ending out of your head, love. Your mother is in her middle thirties, Stephen Rodgers must be over forty. Their feelings have to have changed in twenty years. Anyway, as I said, it makes sense that your mother brings her new husband with her.'

'It doesn't, not a bit. It's terrible. I'll have to send a telegram to Stephen and put him off for a week. And there she'll be all aglow with her new husband and it'll be terrible, hopeless, sick,' she wailed.

'No, love, don't put Stephen off. Take a holiday. It will be interesting for you to meet new people, to take a break.'

'No, Mum, it wouldn't. I wanted them to meet more than anything else. I thought it a miracle that neither of them had married, and now this Frank guy comes out of the woodwork. Why the bloody hell couldn't he have stayed there for another while?'

'Mind your language now. Peter wouldn't like to hear you going on like that.'

'Shag Peter. Oh Mum, I'm sorry. I didn't mean that, and Peter is grand. But honestly this is too much. I'll phone John later, he'll advise me. I'd better go down and let ⌐ ↲ up for his lunch.'

Peggy watched her go. She's so preoccupied, she thought, that she's lost interest in everything. Even at weekends she no longer jokes or laughs with William or Paul. She no longer even fights them. It's as if she's moved away into a dream world of the past. The only time she's comes alive is when she's on the phone with John Kenny making plans. 'Tis almost as if she's afflicted with a sort of madness, she thought sadly.

As soon as Ciara got a quiet moment, she contacted John Kenny to tell him of the change in plan. 'I'm in bits, so I am. I had great hopes for them. Should I telegram her and tell her Stephen Rodgers is alive? Maybe she'd change her mind if she knew. God, John, tell me what to do? Maybe I could phone her – she isn't on the moon, she's only in America. Please tell me what to do.'

'First, calm yourself. You're losing your sense of propor-tion about this whole business. If your mother is getting married, she's certainly not doing it without great thought.

She's a mature woman and knows exactly what she wants. Phoning now and saying stop would be ridiculous. How often have we to tell you not to plan other people's lives? You can't do it.'

'You can,' she said stubbornly. 'Look at all the matchmaking that went on in this country – didn't that take all sorts of planning? All I was trying to do was to bring together two people who were cheated out of a lifetime of love. That's all I was trying to do,' she ended on a sob.

'I know, Ciara, I know. But I'm an old hand at the game of life. Things don't work out like that. My advice is to do as Peggy suggests. Go to London and stay the week, and meet your father first. Get to know him, and then stay on and meet your mother and her new husband. It's the sane thing to do.'

'I know I should listen. My head tells me you're right, my heart tells me you're wrong.'

'You asked for advice and I gave it to you.'

'Will you come with me?' she surprised herself by asking.

'I can't go to London for a week, Ciara. I couldn't leave the job as long as that. It wouldn't be fair to Peter Murray, either. Remember? The guy you're supposed to be marrying?'

'I know, I'm only a run-of-the-mill case.'

'That's true, in a way. But I'll tell you what I will do. I'll go with you until you're safely in the arms of your father and then I'll come back. How's that?'

'It's okay, I suppose,' she said, disappointed. 'So I won't phone or stop her. Maybe I'll pray to Saint Jude that the Frank chap will break his leg or have a heart attack or something.'

'You know what?' John told her

'What?'

'I think you are mad. Maybe there was somebody as mad as you in the family tree.'

'I'll find out soon, won't I?'

Chapter Thirty-Six

On the 28th of April Ciara and John flew to London. Ciara had travelled up to Dublin on an early train, and had met John Kenny at the airport an hour before the flight. When she came into the airport lounge she saw him sitting at a table in the bar drinking a cup of coffee and reading a paper. He looked up as she approached him, his grey eyes taking in her pale face, her eyes darker and more shadowed than he remembered. He noticed that her hair had been trimmed and was now shoulder length and under control. Her slim waist and full breasts were highlighted by the perfectly cut, soft wool tweed suit. She carried a suitcase and what looked like a light raincoat.

'Do I look a frump?' she wanted to know.

'No, I wouldn't say you look a frump.'

'Do I look all right?'

'Yeah – I'd say you look all right.'

'Gee, thanks. God, I do hate men,' she muttered under her breath.

John laughed so loudly that the middle-aged couple at the next table glanced over. They were going to see their first grandchild. The new grandmother, in her new blue coat, whispered to her husband, 'Do you think they're newly-weds? She's lovely, isn't she? Did you ever see the like of her? Would they be newly-weds?'

'Don't think so. Newly-weds would come in together.'

'Maybe they're running away,' she whispered.

'Doubt it,' her husband told her. They haven't that look about them, and he is a bit old for her, I'd say.'

'Would you say they're in love?' his wife asked, getting quite carried away with the couple at the next table.

'He is anyway. I could see it in his eyes when she walked in.'

John glanced up. 'The couple at the next table have us under surveillance,' he told Ciara, 'their ears are sticking out like antennae.'

Ciara flashed a half-smile at the pair and then returned to her problem. 'Say if he doesn't turn up? Say if he gets sick or something? Say if I have absolutely nothing to say to him? Say if I clam up?'

'Ciara, will you relax and have a drink? I'm getting myself a good stiff one. With you I feel I need it.' He was smiling.

'Thanks, I could do with one.' She watched him as he walked up to the bar. He wore a brownish suit she hadn't seen before. His hair – she was never sure her whether it was brown or auburn – had been cut, and she could see that he had shaved off his side locks, the fashion foible of the seventies, sported by every male in the country. 'So you got rid of some hair,' she joked, nodding at his clean-shaven face when he rejoined her with her drink.

'Yes, and so did you.' His glance swept over her new haircut. 'We're all cleaned up to meet your dad.'

'Don't say that. You're making me nervous all over again.'

It was late when they got to the Grosvenor Hotel. A small dapper man approached, hand outstretched, his face wreathed in smiles.

'Ah, dear Mr Kenny, how good to see you looking so well.' Then he dropped his voice and whispered, 'Jasus, John, sure you haven't changed a bit since we played for Saint Joseph's in Kilrush. And who is this gorgeous girl?'

John introduced Ciara to Michael Griffin, his old school friend from Clare. 'She's a client of mine – so take your lewd eyes off her now,' he laughed.

Michael stuck out his hand, and pummelled Ciara in a warm handshake, 'So you're only here on business and no hanky-panky. Still, girl, get this fella to show you the sights of London – he still has his Communion money.'

'I will,' she laughed, 'I really will.'

They had two single rooms beside each other. Ciara thought hers was very luxurious, and was quite intrigued by the little inbuilt area where she could have tea or coffee when she needed it, and the glass-fronted minibar where she could slot in her money to buy all sorts of drinks.

As she undressed to shower before dinner she was swamped with a mixture of nervousness and fear, and yet a strange excitement dried her mouth and made her heart pound. The warm water flowed over her body and she thought, Tomorrow, in this very place, my father will shower, eat, sleep.

Her nervousness didn't evaporate when she dressed for dinner. She first put on her red dress and then decided it was a bit much; after all, she was only here on business, a run-of-the-mill case with her hired private investigator. About to take it off, she recalled Peggy advising her to look on the extra days she had to spend in London as a well-deserved holiday. She decided to leave it on. Before going down to meet John, she looked at herself in the mirror, her eyes apprehensively examining her face and figure. She could see a hint of cleavage and she tugged and pulled at her dress, reminding herself once again that it was a sort of business dinner and not a romantic date.

Maybe I should wear my grey dress with the white collar and cuffs, she thought. Peter had told her she looked like a postulant in it, and she had flicked her finger in a glass of wine and spattered it on his nose; he told her he'd take her out in the rain and spank her bare bottom. 'Just try,' she had warned him. It had been funny then, but now it seemed another time, almost another life.

Her thoughts were scattered by a knock at her door. John Kenny was standing there in a dark, well-cut suit she had not seen before.

'Wow,' she grinned, 'you look great.'

His grey eyes roamed over the slim figure in the red dress, briefly straying to the cleavage she had tried so hard to hide, the long slim legs encased in nylons and the black fashionable low-cut shoes. 'Wow ditto,' he said, trying to hide the admiration in his eyes.

They walked to the lift and not a few eyes strayed to the handsome couple as they entered the dining room. Michael Griffin had obviously tipped off the waiter, because they got an excellent table, secluded, and yet allowing them to watch all the comings and goings to their hearts' content. The meal was excellent and as they lingered over the courses, Ciara was quieter than usual.

As she played with the main course John asked, 'What has become of my ebullient run-of-the-mill-case? You have to do better then that.'

'I'm terrified,' she told him.

'Don't be. Remember, you have me with you.'

'Isn't that what keeps me going?'

She slept badly that night, turning and twisting for hours on end. At one stage she glanced at her watch and saw that it was only two-thirty. She was tempted to get up and go in to see John, but she changed her mind, more than likely he would have shushed her out, telling her to pull herself together. She idly wondered if he was in any way attracted. Sheer nonsense, she told herself. She was just a client he was helping. Did he do as much for other clients? Probably – he was that sort of guy. Peter came into her mind and she dismissed him – thinking of him right now would only complicate things. Peter belonged to the future – a future where she would feel secure, where the ghosts of her real mother and father would no longer torture her. A future where her father would be happily working on his sheep station and her mother happily married to her Frank. A future where she would bring her children to visit them. A future where they might even visit her. She finally fell into a disturbed sleep where half-formed dreams touching on nightmares came and went.

The next morning, over breakfast, she told John Kenny that she was a new woman. 'I won't be a quivering wreck any more. After all, I'm sure this happens every other day – a girl meets her father for the very first time.' Her eyes had a dark pleading look as she waited for his answer.

'I wouldn't say every other day – but it happens more than people realise.'

After breakfast John suggested a walk. He felt it would be a distraction, and would help take Ciara's mind off what lay ahead. He knew that the idea of hanging around the foyer would be abhorrent to her, and that by the time anyone remotely resembling her father came through the swinging doors she would be in shreds.

It was cool for April, although the day was sunny and the pavements filled with people, all walking briskly as if on important business.

'Should we walk like they do, as if we're hell-bent on getting somewhere?' Ciara asked, trying her best to smile.

'Maybe we should. At least it'll get the circulation going.'

They stepped out and, unthinkingly, she clasped his hand. He didn't object, and the warm touch of his hand calmed her.

'Would you like to walk to Westminster Cathedral? It's very near,' he asked. 'A spot of sight-seeing, you might say.'

She nodded in agreement and as they walked up the steps of the vast red-bricked church her heart started to thump nervously again. All the old doubts crowded back in. Maybe she should have left well enough alone; maybe she was opening up old wounds that might never heal. At the door she withdrew her hand from John's and dipped it into the holy-water font. She sprinkled them both – 'For good luck.'

They went in and knelt down. Way up at the altar the tabernacle glinted dull gold. She saw the red glow of the timeless lamp and, closing her eyes, she prayed as she had never prayed before. *Dear Jesus, let it all turn out well. Maybe I shouldn't have interfered with people's lives, but now that I have, let me not be disappointed.* Then she realised that her prayer was selfish, so she changed it. *Let the two who are my parents not be disappointed in me. Let Peggy and Bob not be too hurt over all this, and please, Jesus, let them turn up – let them get here safely and I'll be a better person for the rest of my life – that I promise.*

It was a long time since she had prayed with such intensity. When she opened her eyes she realised that there were very few people kneeling. Most seemed to be tourists walking round slowly, gazing at the wonders of the great cathedral, making notes, talking in quite loud voices, pointing to the stations, the soaring stained-glass windows, which had miraculously survived the Blitz. It was different from the church in Dungarvan or indeed any other church in Ireland; still, she supposed, it was the same God, and she dearly hoped He had been listening.

She must have combed her hair a dozen times and gone to the bathroom almost as often. Stephen Rodgers had told the hotel he would be there at eleven-thirty. At eleven forty-five her mouth was dry, her heart hammering off her rib cage so loudly she was sure that all the impassive-looking people who strode purposefully through the lounge could hear it. 'He's not coming. He's not coming at all.'

'Will you have a grain of sense? Even in Dublin you allow

a hour for traffic. The fellow is coming from Australia, for God's sake.'

'If you weren't with me. I'd be dead. You know that.'

They fell into silence.

Five minutes later a tall blonde woman walked through the door and went smartly up to reception where they were sitting.

'The name is MacMahon,' she said. 'I've made a booking for one week. It was a late booking and I was fortunate there was a cancellation.'

Ciara jerked up at the sound of the name. She looked at John, her dark eyes opening in amazed consternation, and mouthed, 'Could it be? Could it?' With her wretched heart pounding so much, she felt dizzy and sick. Yet she stared in total fascination as the blonde woman reached out, got her key, smiled at the receptionist, and walked past them to the nearest lift.

Ciara watched her every move. She was slim and looked quite young. Her thick blonde hair was in a French pleat behind her neck. She wore a pale grey trouser suit and flat-heeled shoes, and carried a cherry-coloured coat over her arm. She was smiling at the porter who followed her with the rest of her luggage.

Ciara herself was the first to break the silence. 'Jesus in Heaven above,' she croaked, 'did you hear? She called herself MacMahon. Am I going utterly cracked, finally flipping the lid? Did you hear her?'

'I heard her,' John said, 'so you're not entirely flipping the lid. I can check with the porter. By her luggage she looks as if she's staying for a bit.'

'What about the telegram? What about the Frank fellow? What about her marriage?'

John was smiling at her now, but she was too agitated to see that his smile was tender and loving. 'You'll have to ask her – won't you? After all, she is your mother.' He looked up towards the heavy swing doors. 'And if I'm not mistaken, your father is coming in now too.'

Chapter Thirty-Seven

'Oh my God,' Ciara muttered as she followed John's gaze towards the tall, dark, rugged man who had come through the doors and who was looking around with an air of uncertainty. He wore a light grey coat and carried a simple zipped hold-all. She could see that his black hair was streaked with grey. His eyes, dark and deep-set, glanced around and finally rested on her. Her legs were shaking so much she found it difficult to stand up. As she took a few uncertain steps towards him she knew that as sure as God made little green apples, that this man was her father. Despite the tan, the lines of weariness around his mouth, despite the jagged scar, he looked so like herself that all remnants of doubt evaporated.

She held out her trembling hand. 'Hi,' she whispered. 'I don't know what to call you.'

'Call me Stephen,' he told her.

'Okay, Stephen, I'm Ciara, your daughter.' Suddenly she was in his arms as he hugged her to his broad chest, his movements a bit clumsy, a bit awkward, as if he was unused to hugging people. Finally, he let her go and, holding her at arm's length his black eyes slowly strayed all over her. 'You're a sight for sore eyes so you are.' He closed his eyes briefly and repeated, 'A sight for sore eyes.' Then, looking at her again, drinking in every facet, every line, every feature, 'You know what? You're not a bit like your mother.'

'I know, Peggy tells me that too.' Then the tears came and she sobbed, 'I don't know why I'm crying, because I'm happy. I am, honestly.' She tried to brush the stupid tears away. He reached out and she could feel his rough and callused hand lifting her chin looking at her.

'Don't cry. Sure you're the best thing that has happened me in years.'

She glanced around and saw John standing apart from them, obviously not wanting to intrude. 'I want you to meet

John Kenny. He's the man who made all this possible.'

Stephen took the younger man's hand in a firm grasp. 'It can't have been easy,' he said.

John smiled. 'I keep telling her that – she doesn't appreciate me at all.'

Stephen, glancing around, excused himself, telling them he'd freshen up and be back in minutes so they could celebrate and eat and go places. He hadn't seen civilisation for so long.

When he was gone Ciara turned to John. 'Will we tell him my mother is here? Will I try and see her? Will I go to her now? Tell me, what'll I do?'

'First of all,' John said, 'you'll try and calm yourself. Now that you've achieved your goal, there's not much point having a heart attack.' He was smiling and his tone was gentle.

Despite pressure from both of them, John Kenny insisted on not joining Ciara and Stephen for lunch. Over simple chicken and what Stephen thought might be a decent bottle of wine, they talked. Though his eyes never strayed from Ciara's face, now and then he seemed to shake his head in sheer wonder as she told him all about herself, all about her life in Dungarvan with Peggy, Bob and their two sons. 'I thought they were my brothers until eight months ago, but in a way, they'll always be my brothers.' She told him about Peter Murray and how they intended to become engaged and how she had put it off when she had discovered she was adopted. She told him about her obsession with trying to trace her parents. 'It became such a driving force that nothing else mattered. I feel drained, but whole, somehow, now,' she ended simply.

'About Aileen. You haven't heard anything?' Stephen's question was easy and his eyes expressionless, and yet she knew, somehow she knew, that for him right then time stood still as he waited for her answer.

'She's here. Right here in this place.'

He didn't reply but she had never seen such an expression in any human eyes before. She saw wild hope, confusion, disorientation and something that looked like sheer wonder. 'She can't be, can she?'

'She can and she is.'

Could they all have been wrong, Ciara wondered. Could Stephen's love for the young Aileen have survived a lifetime?

She reached out and took her father's hands in hers. He was still tightly clenching the silverplated fork, and she gently removed it. 'She doesn't know I'm here – she most certainly doesn't know you're here.'

Then Ciara explained everything, telling him all about the letters and her childish dream that she might bring them together despite the fact everyone told her she was mad. 'Then I got this telegram telling me she would meet me one week later than we originally arranged. She said that she was going to marry her boss, a guy named Frank, and that she would combine her honeymoon with our proposed meeting.' Still holding Stephen's hands, Ciara went on, 'But when we were there, John and I, waiting for you, a woman came into the lobby and she went up to reception, and as clear as day I heard her give her name – MacMahon. I couldn't believe it – I just stared, my mouth hanging open, and then you walked in and here we are.'

Stephen let the news slowly sink in.

'I could get her room number and see her. It would be all right, because she's probably here to see me. Will I go and make myself known to her and then maybe tell her about you?' Aileen could see how strained her father had become. A nerve at the side of his face was throbbing, and the terrible scar seemed much more pronounced than before. She felt a surge of love and a feeling of protection for this man whom she had met only a few brief hours before, and who had obviously suffered terribly.

'Look, Stephen, this is a shock for you. Let's go for a walk – Westminster Cathedral is only a short distance from here. Maybe we'll go and pray, and gather ourselves. What about it?'

For the second time that day Ciara walked to Westminster Cathedral. She hadn't realised how tall her father was. He was so handsome that he got more than his share of admiring glances from passing females.

'You know, I haven't been to a Catholic church in twenty years,' he told her. 'When I was a young fellow I used to wait to get a glimpse of your mother outside the church at home.'

'I know. Eddie told me.'

He shook his head in astonishment. 'You met Eddie?'

'I did. You see, I had to get all the information I could before John started tracing you. I even met old Joe.'

'Good God, don't tell me he's still alive?'

'Alive and kicking. I can see, Stephen Rodgers, you have a bit of catching up to do.'

It was the first time Stephen had seen his daughter smile. 'You're not all me, you know,' he said. 'You smile like your mother – did anyone ever tell you that?'

Inside the cathedral she knelt beside him and tried to pray again. But he was such a distraction to her that she failed. She noted that he had his hands over his face, and she didn't know if he was praying or remembering. After a while, she nudged him, whispering, 'We must go, we have things to do.' He removed his hands and looked at her and she could see he had some difficulty focusing. Was he remembering the pain and hurt he had suffered as a boy, or was he remembering a time when he loved and possessed a fair-haired schoolgirl who broke all the rules of the time to be with him?

As they walked the dusty London pavements, she outlined her plans. 'When we get back I'll get her room number and I'll go up and make myself known. In her letter she said she wants to meet me, so that part should be okay. Give us an hour or thereabouts, and then come along. It's the only way, isn't it?'

'Yes, Ciara, it seems the only way.'

She washed her face, brushed her mob of black hair and put on a little fresh lipstick. She recalled that her mother was wearing a trouser suit, so she decided on her black trousers, thinking they were all right with her pale green blouse. The assurance and calmness she had felt outlining what now seemed such a stupid plan, deserted her as she buzzed the bell of Room 200. She heard footsteps coming to the door and then it opened.

The woman standing there didn't look as if she had been sleeping away the hours of jet lag. She had changed into a grey, light wool dress with a V neck and a wide belt, emphasising her slim waist. Her blonde hair was brushed and secured at the nape of her neck. Her face was unlined except for a faint tracery around the eyes and mouth. By far her most startling features were the almost electric-blue eyes which had a hint of a question as they looked at the black-haired girl standing uncertainly at the door. 'Yes? May I help you?' There was definite hint of an American accent there.

'Maybe you can. You see, I'm Ciara. Your daughter.'

The woman looked startled. Then, as her blue eyes slowly took in the face and figure of the girl before her, she whispered, 'Oh my God,' as all her composure left her. She reached out and drew the girl into the room, 'Oh my God, Ciara,' Aileen whispered again. 'I just can't believe it.'

Suddenly they were in each other's arms, Aileen MacMahon forgetting she was a career woman, and Ciara Fitzpatrick forgetting that this woman had given her up for adoption twenty years before.

At last Aileen held her daughter at arm's length. 'You're beautiful,' she said softly, as once again she raked every single feature of the girl she had last seen as a baby. 'You're so like your father it's uncanny. Has anyone ever told you that?'

'Well, not many. Very few ever saw him, with the exception of Peggy.'

'Of course they didn't. Please sit down –' Aileen waved to a small sofa near the window. 'Shall I order coffee or tea, or a drink perhaps?'

She looked vulnerable and a little lost, as if she didn't know what to do to please.

'No, I don't want a single thing – I only want to talk to you. What will I call you?' She repeated the question she had asked her father only a few hours before.

'Aileen, if that's all right with you. I suppose you want to keep Mam or Mum or Mother for Peggy, am I right?'

'Yes, you're right. As they say in Dungarvan, old habits die hard.'

'Ciara, I just can't believe it – I can't believe this is happening. I'm afraid I'll wake up and find myself back in my apartment in Newark.'

'Aileen,' Ciara said, the words tumbling out of her, 'there is so much I want to know. In fact I want to know desperately. Please tell me things. You know, things about my father.' She surreptitiously glanced at her watch and saw that they had less than an hour before he came. She wondered could they cover two decades in such a short space of time. She hadn't the slightest inkling of what her mother's feelings might be for the man who was now under the same roof as she, the man who had walked away from her on a London street, declaring his everlasting love. Would all the years have wiped the memory away?

Ciara already knew that the memory of Aileen meant something to Stephen, but how much she wasn't sure. But the throbbing facial nerve and the way he had nearly broken his fork at lunch were some sort of giveaway.

'First let me explain why I'm here a week earlier, particularly when I told you I had other plans,' said Aileen. 'We had to postpone our wedding because Frank's son had a bad motor-car accident and we thought we should wait. The news is good now; he's no longer critical. So I came here to do a bit of business and take in a few winter fashion shoots for the magazine.'

Ciara wanted to say, 'Enough, enough. These things are nothing in comparison to the plans I have for you. You must remember Stephen Rodgers, my father – you must. God knows, you suffered enough because of your love for him and I'm proof that it happened.' But she didn't; instead she listened intently to her mother's softly spoken words. After all, hadn't she prayed for this minute? She had turned so many lives upside down because she wanted this minute for so long. Hadn't she dreamed and fantasised about it for months? Well, it was here now and she must listen and not let her fanciful hopes make her miss a single thing this elegant woman was saying. Then again, maybe Aileen didn't want to talk about Stephen. Maybe she'd find it difficult to remember. After all, she had lived in the States for years and she was a fashion editor. No doubt that carried much weight in America.

'I accept, Ciara, that you would want to know about things that happened so long ago.'

I'm right, Ciara thought helplessly. She looks on it as something that happened long, long ago. Something in the remote ice age. Or maybe she can hardly remember Stephen, who would be here in a little more than a half an hour now.

'I'll order tea – it'll be a bit cosier,' Aileen said as she walked to the phone. When she came back she sat on a small chair, facing her daughter. 'I knew your father since I was a very young child. We went to the same national school, but he left a year or so after I started. He was brought up by his grandfather and had a very lonely life. Where we lived, there were all sorts of stories about his mother and even more about his father.'

'I know,' Ciara prompted gently.

'You do?' Aileen's blue eyes showed surprise. 'Peggy?'

'Yes, poor Peggy,' Ciara told her. 'You see, I nagged her to absolute death when I found out I wasn't her daughter. I know all about Teresa Rodgers running away with a gypsy, I know about her death and how her son was cold-shouldered, I know how you were banished because of the baby – me. Oh, Aileen, I know so much. Please tell me – in all the years did you ever think of him, my father? Did you wonder what happened him or what? You must have!' There was a look of pleading in Ciara's dark eyes.

'For the first ten years there wasn't a day went by when I didn't think of him, didn't wonder. You see, he was strong, reliable – a stupid word but I can't think of anything else to describe him. It was so strange that he vanished into thin air – it was so out of character really.' Aileen paused, maybe remembering, maybe wondering if she should go on. 'There is something you should know. Stephen's father wasn't what they all thought. His father was a writer, of English and Spanish blood, who lived with the gypsies and travelled with them. Seemingly he was writing a book about the Irish travellers. I think you should know this, though maybe you don't consider it important. His Spanish blood accounts for your colouring; your father was as dark as you could imagine.'

'Of course it's important. I have a positive hunger to know who I am, where I came from, who my grandparents were – everything. I'm like that, Aileen, a curious sort of bee.'

'Tell me more about yourself – it's only right that I should know all about my daughter.' Aileen's smile transformed her face and made her look like the girl in the faded photos that Niamh Casey had shown Ciara.

'I'm sort of engaged,' Ciara told her. 'I'm going out with a fellow named Peter Murray. He's a solicitor and his mother is a bit of a snob – in fact, quite grand. You know, dinner parties, golf, flower societies and stuff. In fact they are high society in Dungarvan.' Suddenly Ciara started to laugh. 'At one of his mother's dinner parties I drank too much wine. I had just heard that I was adopted – I'm not making excuses now, but anyway, I got tipsy and blurted out that my grandfather was a gypsy, and you wouldn't believe the absolute consternation.'

Aileen's laughter was warm and genuine. 'I think you must be like Teresa, your grandmother. Stephen got her diaries

439

from an old gypsy who knew her. He was so excited; somehow getting them made all the difference to him. They told him all about his mother, his father, their last year together. They described how his father had died. After reading them he felt different – he felt better. Up to then there had been so much rumour and innuendo about who he really was.'

There was a shrill ring at the door.

Ciara's heart froze. She didn't want him to come in yet. She felt it was only right to prepare this woman who was her mother, who had been treated so badly in the past. She already felt the stirrings of affection, friendship, even love for her.

Aileen walked towards the door and Ciara closed her eyes. She didn't want to see the first reaction when they met.

But it was only the teaboy.

Ciara's hands were shaking so much when she took the cup of tea she thought that Aileen would notice. *Tell her now*, a small inner voice prompted. *Don't keep her dangling like that. After all, she's a woman of the world, things like that won't take a feather out of her.*

'Aileen.' Ciara put her cup down. She noted, as if from a distance, that it rattled noisily against the saucer. 'There is something I – I feel you should know. When I hired John Kenny, the investigator I wanted to find both of you. I wanted to find Stephen too.' As she spoke she watched Aileen. She saw her stillness, her blue eyes filled with naked questioning, as if she was waiting for – had waited forever for – something.

There was another ring at the door.

Aileen seemed unable to move.

Ciara jumped up, her thoughts confused and terrified. Maybe Peter was right. You shouldn't interfere with people's lives. What had he said? *Sometimes it's better to let sleeping dogs lie.* John had called what she was doing manipulation.

She hardly remembered opening the door. She hardly remembered him coming in. But until the day she'd die, she'd remember the way he stood there with the door open behind him. She'd remember the way Aileen stood, the blood slowly leaving her lovely face, making her eyes stand out like sapphires.

For a while they stood there, just looking. Then in one stride he was beside her, and she was in his arms, and it seemed that time stood still, that the child of their young love

440

had never existed, because they were kissing – kisses so desperate so hungry, so tearing that Ciara thought it wrong, intrusive to witness them. It would be far better to steal quietly away.

At the door something made her look back.

He had removed the slide from her mother's hair, releasing a pale blonde curtain that fell to her shoulders. She thought she heard Aileen sob as she reached up and touched the ugly scar that marred Stephen's face so badly.

Walking down the long carpeted corridor, something came stark and clear to Ciara. She wouldn't think of it now. She would sort it out when she got home. Neither would she interrupt them any more today. They had a lot of making-up to do. They had a lifetime of making-up to do.

Ciara recalled her prayers in Westminster Cathedral. She knew, as certainly as night follows day, that they had been answered.

John Kenny was sitting in the lounge. Was it hours or years since she had left him? There was something rock-like and strong about him. He exuded a sort of inner peace, alien to her restless impulsive nature.

'Well, how did it go?' His grey eyes sought hers.

'It went well,' she told him, licking her dry lips to moisten them. 'It was the most beautiful end to an ordinary run-of-the-mill case I ever saw.'

Epilogue

She had never felt as exhausted, as drained or as happy and whole. It hadn't been the easiest of times. She hadn't seen Aileen or Stephen until the next morning. She hadn't expected to see them even then; she could only imagine how it went, how much loving they had to make up, how much had to be said.

John suggested dinner and a show, and the two of them went to see *Jesus Christ Superstar*. Sitting beside him in the darkened theatre, Ciara was filled with a strange unfamiliar contentment. When the evening ended she had kissed him goodnight before parting. He had pushed her away gently. She had apologised, telling him that the events of the day had gone to her head.

'Sure, haven't I seen the way you get carried away?' he smiled at her.

Before she fell asleep, the small hurt had evaporated.

The next morning Aileen and Stephen joined them for breakfast. Aileen looked radiant, dressed in a pale green linen suit. Stephen was casual in sweater and slacks. Their contentment and fulfilment were so apparent that Ciara finally understood what Peggy meant when she said, 'You could almost feel their love for each other.' Feasting her dark eyes on her parents, it was hard to believe she had been unaware of their very existence until just a few months before.

Aileen was the first to speak. 'Ciara, we're hoping that in the next week we can do a lot of things together – have a good time, get to know each other, make up for so much lost years.'

John Kenny stood up. 'I'm a bit superfluous now. I'll go out for a bit –'

'No, John,' Aileen told him. 'Without your help this would never have happened.'

'True, John,' Stephen said. 'You can take a walkabout some other time – we'll sit and let these women prattle.'

Aileen looked at Stephen with naked love blazing in her eyes. 'Now you sound just like an Australian,' she smiled.

'Why wouldn't I, woman?' Stephen met her gaze with equal love. 'Haven't I lived a lonely life there for twelve years or more?'

'Will you all stop and listen to me?' Ciara told them, her dark eyes smiling. 'John and I are going home tomorrow. His work is done and I've left poor Dad in the lurch at a very busy time. Anyway, look at you – it's a disgrace having parents so young. We've a lifetime to get to know each other. A whole lifetime.'

They spent the day sight-seeing like four happy tourists, and had dinner that evening in a restaurant in Soho where Stephen and Aileen quietly outlined their plans. They would get married as soon as possible. She would wind up her business in the States. They would honeymoon in Europe and return to Ireland for a spell before going to Australia. Aileen admitted that she was concerned about how her decision would effect Frank Dixon, but she hoped he would understand.

She asked Ciara about her family in Ireland; Ciara filled her in about meeting Eddie, how Maeve was married and living in Dublin, how her father, Denis, had a slight stroke, and how her mother had died long before. There was a stillness about Aileen as she listened to the news. Only once did she flinch, and that was when she heard that her mother was dead.

Ciara wondered if there was any bitterness left in Aileen over the way she had been banished because of her love for the man who now sat so protectively beside her. If there was, it didn't show.

Stephen said he hoped old Joe would hang on until he got home. Ciara told him laughingly that Joe would see them all down. Neither Aileen nor Stephen could wait to see Richie and Niamh.

At the airport, Stephen handed Ciara a small brown parcel.

'These are my mother's diaries, and as you're my only daughter, and a fierce curious one at that, I want you to have them. I know you'll read them.' She was enveloped in his strong arms; he kissed her, holding her close, telling her he'd meet her soon. There were more hugs, kisses and tears as Aileen said goodbye.

Ciara got a window seat, and as the plane rolled down the tarmac she got a glimpse of her parents standing close together in the viewing area. She watched them as they waved and waved, and then her eyes misted with tears and she could see them no more.

Peggy couldn't hear enough. She was never tired of listening. Bob wasn't much better. Ciara even got an attentive ear from William and Paul.

Breaking it off with Peter Murray hadn't been easy. They had gone to the Salmon Leap, and even before the evening had ended, Ciara had known what she had to do. She had seen real enduring love at close quarters and now she knew what she felt for him wasn't enough.

He looked more surprised than hurt. 'You can't be serious.' His tone was incredulous.

'Peter, I am. I'm very serious. In fact, I've never been as sure of anything. We're different really. You're ambitious and hard-working, and you'll be very successful. You'll live in Dungarvan, keeping the Murray flag flying. You'll want a wife who will be a social asset, a member of the best clubs, who will give superb dinner parties and who will say and do the right things always.'

'All that nonsense about finding your parents has upset you. You'll feel normal in a few weeks, you'll see.' He still sounded surprised and uncertain.

'I never felt more normal in my whole life. Peter, I'm sorry, I really am. I really like you, I probably even love you in a way. But it's not enough. I know what the real thing is now, and we don't have it – we really haven't. Anyway, you will be snatched up in days. Aren't you the biggest catch in town?'

'Is there someone else? Is it this Kenny chap?'

'Right now there isn't anyone else. John Kenny has kept our association strictly on a business level. He kept telling me I was a simple run-of-the-mill case.'

'But you feel something?'

'Peter,' she implored, 'believe me when I tell you I don't know what I feel. But I do feel I'm right about us.' Ciara tapped her breast. 'I feel it here.'

He was silent as he drew the silver cigarette case she had given him for Christmas out of his pocket. He slowly removed

444

a cigarette and as he lit it she noticed that his hands were trembling slightly.

'I'm sorry.' Her tone was gentle.

He looked at her, taking in the black glossy hair, the dark eyes, the wide mouth, the firm chin and the thought came again that she was unlike any other girl he had ever known.

'I thought we could make it,' he said quietly.

'I thought so too. But you'll find someone far better than me. A girl who's in tune with you. Someone not indifferent about the things you want. As for me – I don't know what I want. I might never find it.'

'Knowing you, I believe you will,' he answered, leaning over and kissing her on the mouth.

Ciara looked so drained when she came in that Peggy suggested an early night. 'Why don't you take a hot-water bottle to bed and make a nice cup of cocoa and read? That's a nice way of ending the day. And by the way, John Kenny phoned.'

'Do you know what he wanted?'

'He just said if you weren't too late in to give him a buzz.'

'Hi, how are you?'

'I'm fine.' She wasn't fine. Her hand was trembling and her wretched heart thumping.

'I was wondering would you have dinner with me on Saturday evening?' He cleared his throat and she wondered if he could be nervous too. 'It's May Day, the first day of summer. I would enjoy the drive down. That is, if you're free.'

'Yes, I'm free.'

'Do you know that in my part of the country they light bonfires on May Day? Something about burning away the cares and troubles of winter. Maybe my little run-of-the-mill case might like to celebrate the occasion.'

'She might,' said Ciara. 'She might indeed.'

Lying in bed, Ciara felt a strange contentment suffusing every fibre of her being. She couldn't fathom why. After all, she had just ended her relationship with Peter, Peter who was rich, acceptable and considered a good catch. In all probability, Peggy would be disappointed.

445

Ciara's eyes fell on the two black diaries she had removed from the parcel Stephen had given her. They looked old and yellow – even the edges had a scorched, burnt, look. She knew Stephen had wanted her to read them. She plumped up her pillows and opened the first one. The name was still legible: *Teresa Rodgers, Tulla, Co. Kilkenny*. The date was 1940.

Before she settled down, Ciara flicked through the pages, and odd sentences in the faded slanting writing jumped right out at her.

Here I am, only seventeen years of age, with a good life. – only daughter of a wealthy farmer and Denis MacMahon in the palm of my hand. Another girl would give her eye teeth to be in my position. But I'm not content. If I was, why would I be here sitting on a rock waiting for someone I can never have or even be seen going out with, because in a way he really is one of them – one of the tinkers?

Much further on another little entry intrigued.

I held out my hand at Margaret's bidding and she held it in her gnarled, nutty brown hand. She bent down, her long grey locks hiding her face. She seemed to have trouble seeing, because she peered closer and brought me nearer the leaping flames.

'I see great happiness for you and Hugh when you become man and wife. You'll know the kind of joy only few know. I see you will have a boy child. I see – I see –' Suddenly she stopped and gently put my hand from her. She looked up and I don't know if it was the shadows cast by the fire, but right then she looked as old as time. Her lips were in a tight grim line and her eyes were expression-less. 'I'm too old to see things now, son. Maybe I've seen too much in the past. Things do be clouded now.'

And a few pages further on, another entry caught Ciara's attention.

I had foolishly and childishly told Denis MacMahon that I wanted to be fascinated. I wanted to sky to explode, the very earth to move. And it did. After Hugh and I made

446

love, I knew that all the tears I would shed in a future that stretched so unknowingly ahead wouldn't be for Laddie, for my father, for Joe, for my old way of life – they would be for me, if anything ever happened to separate us. Dear diary, I love him. I love him so much it frightens me.

Ciara turned to the first entry – January 1st, 1940. Already she felt an affinity and closeness to this girl, who had, maybe on a whim, chronicled the events of her time.

Ciara snuggled down in the warmth. She knew she was in for a very long night.

THE END